PRIMORDIAL THREAT

M.A. ROTHMAN

ISBN-13: 978-0-9976793-1-1

Technothrillers:
- Primordial Threat
- Darwin's Cipher
- New Arcadia (coming in 2020)

Levi Yoder Series:
- Perimeter
- The Inside Man
- Never Again

Epic Fantasy / Dystopian:
- Dispocalypse
- Seer of Prophecy (Coming mid-2020)
- Heirs of Prophecy (Coming mid-2020)
- Tools of Prophecy (Coming mid-2020)
- Lords of Prophecy (Coming mid-2020)

CONTENTS

Chapter 1	1
Chapter 2	13
Chapter 3	25
Chapter 4	37
Chapter 5	50
Chapter 6	55
Chapter 7	60
Chapter 8	72
Chapter 9	79
Chapter 10	83
Chapter 11	93
Chapter 12	100
Chapter 13	108
Chapter 14	124
Chapter 15	137
Chapter 16	147
Chapter 17	152
Chapter 18	162
Chapter 19	179
Chapter 20	186
Chapter 21	211
Chapter 22	223
Chapter 23	233
Chapter 24	241
Chapter 25	251
Chapter 26	261
Chapter 27	271
Chapter 28	275
Chapter 29	287
Chapter 30	301
Chapter 31	309
Chapter 32	318
Chapter 33	332

Chapter 34   339
Chapter 35   343
Chapter 36   346
Chapter 37   350
Chapter 38   361
Chapter 39   374
Epilogue   383
Author's Note   387
Preview of Darwin's Cipher   390

Addendum   401
About the Author   411

For those who boldly go where nobody has gone before....

Special thanks go to:

Dr. Charles Liu, Professor of Astrophysics – I wanted to especially thank you for keeping me relatively honest from a physics point of view and also for giving this book its title.

Lieutenant John Grimpel, NYPD – thank you for your patient responses to my seemingly never-ending questions on all things police and NYPD procedures.

I also want to thank Dr. Harold "Sonny" White, working out of the NASA Johnson Space Center, as well as Dr. Miguel Alcubierre for both inspiring key scientific elements in this novel.

CHAPTER ONE

"Doctor Radcliffe, I was wondering if you could take a look at the data I just got from my latest survey. Something's not right." Carl, one of the new hires for 2066, loomed over Burt's desk, sounding puzzled. Not unexpected, since he'd been on the job for less than a week.

"Did you talk to Jake Parish?" Burt didn't even look up. "He's maintaining the database for all the Near-Earth objects."

"He's on sabbatical."

"Oh." Burt looked up from his own stack of astronomical survey data and took in Carl's six-and-a-half-foot form. He noticed the man's concerned expression and sighed. Even though Burt was only fifty, he'd found himself getting more and more cranky when people wasted his time. Trying to keep the annoyance from his voice, he carefully measured his words. "What exactly do you mean, something's not right? Can you be a bit more specific?"

Carl hesitated for a moment, then placed two printouts on Burt's desk. He pointed at an image from one of the observatories and explained, "Well, as you can see, this was the survey image I took yesterday."

Burt leaned closer, scanned the text describing a surveyed comet, its location, and its approximate size. Below the text was a dark image showing nothing but empty space.

"I was surveying the area where comet Kowalski C/2011 S2 was supposed to be, but there's nothing in the imaging system's field of view." Carl tapped the other image. "Here you can see the same region but this time I used the Hubble2 satellite, and I got nothing there as well."

Burt felt anger building within him as he turned his attention to the terminal on his right. There was no way an object multiple miles across had simply disappeared. He typed the name of the comet and yesterday's date. The data, projected at eye level, showed the space object's uneven shape, chemical composition, trajectory and estimated location. He glanced at the printout and compared the coordinates. They matched. With a huff of frustration, he handed the papers back to the confused researcher. "This doesn't make any sense. Take this to Doctor Patel and have her double-check your information."

The young researcher's eyes widened when Burt mentioned Neeta's name.

With some effort, Burt suppressed a smile. Neeta Patel was one of the other department heads at NASA's Jet Propulsion Labs, and she was known for having much less patience for wasting time than he did. He waved Carl away. "Tell Doctor Patel that I asked you to go to her with this."

The hulking researcher turned and trudged out of the office.

People learned the most by making mistakes, Burt thought, and Neeta would be a great teacher. She'd tell the newbie exactly what he did wrong and be pretty blunt about it. A lesson Carl wouldn't forget.

Burt chuckled lightly, but his amusement faded as he turned to the large stack of papers on his desk.

"I hate sabbatical coverage."

"You what?" Burt stared open-mouthed at Neeta, who sat on the far side of his desk. She was in her mid-thirties, had long black hair, and dressed in jeans and a black-and-orange CalTech hoodie. He'd only worked with Neeta for a few years, but she'd already proven herself to be one of the most brilliant people he'd ever met.

Neeta leaned back against her chair and rubbed her eyes with the heels of her hands. "I agree with him. That guy you sent to me with the 'missing' comet, he wasn't being a total muppet." Her British accent rang pleasantly on Burt's ears. "I was actually tracking an anomaly with another comet when he found me. Burt, something is up, and I don't necessarily understand what's going on yet. All I can tell you is that I expanded the survey areas for both of the near-Earth objects and managed to find them in totally different spots than they should have been."

"You found them..." Burt trailed off, frowning at the improbability of what Neeta was describing. "That doesn't make sense. It's almost infinitesimal odds that something could have hit one of the comets and knocked it from its trajectory, though I suppose it *could* happen. But two knocked from their trajectory? Could they have somehow collided?"

Neeta's hair swayed back and forth as she shook her head. "No chance. They haven't crossed orbital planes since the last time we verified their positions."

"I don't need to tell you that we've got to figure out what's going on. That's kind of our job."

"Of course." Neeta waved dismissively. "I already put a few people on surveying that area to see if we have any more unexpected path deviations. It might take a while because we don't have twenty-four-hour telescope or satellite access. Besides, those comets are way out past the planets, near the Oort cloud."

Burt placed his elbows on the desk just as his phone rang. He tapped the wireless receiver in his ear and a woman's voice suddenly broadcast loudly in his head.

"Doctor Radcliffe?"

"Yes, this is Burt Radcliffe."

"This is Anita Wexler, Doctor Phillip Johnson's admin. He asked me to make arrangements for you to have a face-to-face meeting with

him here in Washington DC at your earliest possible convenience. When's the earliest I can send a car to pick you up?"

Burt tapped on his ear, muting the call. He leaned further over his desk and whispered, "Why the hell does the new head of NASA want a one-on-one with me?"

Neeta shrugged. "Why the bloody hell are you asking me? Maybe *you* should ask him."

Burt tapped again on his ear. "Anita, is tomorrow morning early enough?"

"I'm sure that will work. I see a flight leaving LAX at 8:00 a.m., I'll arrange for a car to pick you up at your house no later than 5:00. Is that okay?"

"That's fine."

"Okay, Doctor Radcliffe. I'll book your flight, and you'll have a driver waiting for you upon your arrival."

The phone disconnected, and Burt glanced down at the jeans and t-shirt he was wearing. "I guess I need to get home and make sure I have something decent to wear."

Jon Stryker slipped into his windbreaker, peeked at himself in the bedroom mirror, and ran his fingers through his dark-brown hair.

Not bad for a thirty-four-year old cop with two kids living with his sister.

"Shit, who am I kidding?"

It was only 6:00 a.m., and as he walked across the hallway into his kids' room, he heard the light sound of Emma, the six-year-old, snoring in bed.

He smiled. His youngest had lived up to her household nickname, "Blanket Thief." Sometime during the night, she'd managed to steal the blankets off her brother's bed, and was now lying underneath them and a heavy comforter, happily snoring away.

Turning his gaze toward Isaac's bed, he spied the eight-year-old dressed in his flannel pajamas. His arms were wrapped tightly around his ragged teddy bear, yet the lack of blankets had left him unfazed. He'd be howling about the blanket thief as soon as he woke up and noticed his sister's burglary.

Blowing a kiss at them both, Stryker closed their bedroom door and noticed the aroma of freshly-brewed coffee.

He followed his nose downstairs to the kitchen and was greeted by the sight of his sister and ex-wife drinking from steaming mugs at the small breakfast table.

Seeing his ex was always a jolt. Every time he saw Lainie's pixie-like face framed by her blonde tresses, his mind flashed back to the moment when he'd received the divorce papers while deployed overseas.

Though that had been four years ago, the hurt hadn't dulled. It didn't help that she still looked as stunning as ever.

Stryker leaned over, gave his sister a peck on the cheek, and did the same to Lainie. "I guess it's Saturday, eh?"

Lainie raised an eyebrow and gave him a crooked grin. "Why else would I be here? I'm taking the kids to my parents for the weekend." She hitched her thumb toward Stryker's sister. "Jessica was filling me in on how they're doing in school."

Stryker's sister taught at an elite prep school in Midtown, not far from his regular patrol of Times Square. The kids were lucky enough to both go there tuition-free because of his sister's job, a fact that Stryker was ever-grateful for.

Jessica motioned toward the half-full coffee pot. "Today's batch is pretty strong, if you want some."

He glanced at his watch and shook his head. "Thanks, but I can't. I have a rookie assigned to walk the beat with me today, so I need to get to the precinct early."

"You'll be back by four, right? You promised to help me hang stuff up in my classroom."

"I'll be there." Stryker grabbed his keys off the kitchen counter and turned to Lainie. "Expect Isaac to start yelling when he wakes up. Emma stole his covers again."

She smiled, and for a moment, Stryker saw the woman he'd married fourteen years ago.

He steeled himself against her brilliant smile and reminded himself how much resentment they held for each other. She'd hated that he risked his life to make a living, and he'd hated that she couldn't respect his choice of career.

But they had kids together. They both still had responsibilities ... if not to each other anymore, to the kids.

With a final wave, Stryker turned and headed for what he figured would be yet another uneventful day with the NYPD.

~

It was a crisp spring morning as Stryker walked the streets of Midtown Manhattan.

He'd lived his entire life in the same neighborhood and so many things had changed since he was a kid. It had always been a tourist Mecca, especially with Times Square, the Empire State Building and Grand Central all within walking distance.

Stryker missed the gritty atmosphere, the sound of honking cars and revving engines, but those noises were long gone, especially since the city mandated the Automated Vehicle Routing systems for all cars within the city limits. Nowadays, cars were almost all electric, and built with an AVR system. The system saved untold lives by taking commuters safely from point A to B, and traffic flowed flawlessly through the boroughs, but oddly enough, Stryker still thought New York was strange without its snarled streets, sirens, and people yelling about the traffic.

"Hey, Jonny," a woman's husky voice called from across the street. "You up for a good time?"

He glanced across the street and saw a young woman in her late teens. Stryker walked across the street and shook his head as he approached the stunning brunette. She was wearing a skin-tight red dress that highlighted her substantial curves.

He'd seen her hundreds of times near Times Square, but here on

Madison Avenue, she was a bit astray from her normal place of business.

As he approached Sheila, he caught a whiff of her jasmine perfume and her sly smile grew.

Stryker glanced at his watch. "Listen, Sheila, it's not even 7:00 on a weekend. People are still asleep. Do me a favor, if you're going to hawk your wares, do it in Times Square, or do it quietly when you're around here."

Sheila put her hands on her hips and took a gliding step closer. "That wasn't a no," she purred.

He showed her the time on his watch and winked. "My shift starts in thirty minutes. Sorry, honey."

He turned away and shook his head at how things had changed. Sheila was one of the neighborhood kids he'd watched grow up. Even though prostitution was legal nowadays in the city limits, the street cops tried to keep things civilized. After all, this was still his home, and his kids played here.

He turned right on East 35th and strode purposefully past the Empire State Building, the edge of Koreatown, and eventually into the Garment District where the Midtown South Precinct was located.

Stryker walked into the locker room, where a dozen other officers were getting ready for the day. He opened his locker and began changing into his uniform.

"Hey, Stryker, did you hear about last night?"

He glanced at Brian Decker, who was staring at himself in a mirror. "No, what'd I miss?"

"Jenkins and McCullough had to use OC on a bunch of whackos demonstrating in the lobby of the Grand Hyatt."

"Ouch," said Stryker. "How many people were demonstrating?"

"I think they brought in almost a dozen."

Stryker shrugged the Kevlar vest around his trim six-foot frame and shook his head. OC stood for oleoresin capsicum: pepper spray. It was something he'd rarely had to use in his four years on the street.

"Any idea what they were belly-aching about?"

Still staring at himself in the mirror, Decker lightly slapped his own

7

cheeks and let out a loud yawn. "Nah, I just heard the basics from Sharon at the booking desk."

Doing a final check to ensure his firearm was securely holstered, Stryker followed the rest of the officers out of the locker room, grabbed a cup of coffee and prepared himself for roll call.

Burt had never had a reason to meet the previous head of NASA, but now he found himself standing in front of Phillip Johnson's desk. The man had recently been placed in charge of nearly 20,000 civilian employees, and Burt couldn't fathom why he'd been asked to talk face-to-face with what was likely his boss's boss ... or maybe it was his boss's boss's boss. He couldn't quite be sure, especially the way upper management played fifty-two-card pickup with NASA's org charts.

Johnson stood, and Burt felt a bit startled. The administrator was nearly a half-foot taller than Burt's own six-foot frame and looked like at least 250 pounds of solid muscle.

"Damn, Radcliffe, you look wound up tighter than a banjo string. Have a seat."

The Administrator's strong southern accent caught Burt by surprise. He sat on one of the two padded leather chairs in front of the desk and focused on keeping the nervousness from his voice. "Doctor Johnson, I flew over as soon as your admin called, but I'm not really sure why I'm here."

Johnson leaned forward over his desk and smiled, his teeth a brilliantly white contrast to his otherwise dark complexion. "Burt, I'll cut to the chase. I just signed off on you becoming the new Director of the Near-Earth Object program. You'll be reporting to the Director of JPL, but I want all of your future status reports coming to me as well."

The blood drained from Burt's face. He blinked, uncertain if he'd heard the man correctly. "But, sir, why me? I think—"

Johnson laughed. "Do you remember working on that Bayesian learning computer system? It was being pitched by some generals as a new way of getting soldiers out of the business of war. Saving lives and all that."

For a moment, Burt stared at the man, trying to remember what he was talking about, and then it hit him. "Sir, that was over twenty years ago. December 18th, 2045 was when I scrapped that part of my life and started over. I remember it well. I couldn't be a part of deploying a Turing-capable computer system. But what does that have to do with you wanting me to be the new Director?"

Johnson drummed his fingers on his desk and nodded solemnly. "I was a colonel in the Army doing research at the US Army War College at the time, and I'd been charged to evaluate some of what you'd created. It was brilliant, if you don't mind my saying so. Frankly, it scared the *bejeezus* out of many of us. I read one of your academic papers on what might happen if computers were empowered to handle life-and-death choices. I vividly remember the warning you gave in your paper, 'What if the machines figured they were less expendable than we were?'" Johnson leaned back in his chair and ran his hands over his clean-shaven scalp. "Anyway, I talked to the head of JPL and he gave me a list of likely candidates for the Directorship. When I saw your name on that list, that was good enough for me."

Burt's mouth gaped a bit, and suddenly he realized he was looking like an idiot in front of his boss. "Thank you, sir. I'll do my best."

"Hold on, I've got a special task for you." Johnson slid a small storage card across his desk. "It's encrypted, so you'll only be able to read that in a secure location, but it has all the known notes on DefenseNet. The President asked NASA to pick up that ball, and we've received extra funding to deploy that project. Burt, that's now your baby, you got me?"

"DefenseNet? Wasn't that supposed to be a bunch of geosynchronous satellites to help detect and destroy incoming asteroids?"

Johnson stood and walked around the table, as Burt also got to his feet. The man placed his thick arm over Burt's shoulders and escorted him toward the office door. "That's exactly why I agreed to take it on; because I knew that it was a project that NEO should be all over. And as head of NEO, that means I need *you* to be all over it."

9

As they approached the door, it slid open automatically, and the head of NASA patted Burt on his shoulder. They shook hands.

Johnson pointed across the hall at a set of double doors. "That area is a SCIF. You have at least five hours before your flight, so you might want to take advantage of that place."

"Skiff?"

"Sensitive Compartmented Information Facility." The Administrator pointed at the storage card in Burt's hand. "You'll find a secure reader in there so you can start noodling on what I've just gotten you into. There's also a SCIF at the JPL facility, you've probably just never used it."

He gave Burt a final pat on the shoulder and turned back to his office, the door sliding closed behind him.

Burt stared at the palm-sized plastic card with the red "Top Secret" hologram.

How'd I end up signing up for this?

~

A few hours after having flown back, Burt poked his head into Neeta's office and asked, "Have you looked over the DefenseNet plans I shared with you?"

Neeta swiped the air with her right hand, and her desktop computer projected the Earth's image with two-dozen interconnected satellites slowly orbiting around it. She stared at him through the semi-transparent globe hovering between them and snidely remarked, "Nah, I just figured I'd get around to it when I had nothing better to do." Shaking her head, she motioned at the Earth before her and barked, "Of course I've been poring over the plans. What do you think I've been doing?" She flicked at the glowing red power button projected at the bottom-left corner of the hologram, and the image vanished.

Burt glanced at the computer. "Well, I see you've at least begun modeling the network. That's great. However, I couldn't understand the point behind having the satellites interconnected. Did you figure out why they're linked?"

"Unfortunately, no. I didn't have much to do with this when I was at the International Science Foundation, so I'm going by the data you gave me. If we really wanted to know why, we'd have to ask Dave Holmes, the former head of the ISF, and as far as I know, he's dead—or hiding in some hole so deep that nobody's going to find him."

Burt sighed as he pondered the problem. "These plans aren't complete, or at least parts of them make no sense. I was reading through some of the notes that mentioned space elevator anchors, but nowhere do I see any mention of tethers or what they'd be needed for. Besides, there's no need for a hard connection to the satellites. Hell, all we need is to equip each of the satellites with a bank of solar panels, and that'll charge the onboard batteries for the lasers. Any other communications can happen wirelessly."

Shaking her head, Neeta frowned. "Dave was no fool. He wouldn't have designed something without a purpose."

Leaning against the doorway to the office, Burt frowned as he folded his arms across his chest. "Frankly, that's what makes me nervous about this whole project. I think we can build it and make it work, but are we even building the right thing? What did he really have in mind?"

Suddenly the lights in the room flickered red and they both glanced at the Potentially Hazardous Asteroid warning scrolling across the desktop computer's monitor.

"Bloody hell," Neeta exclaimed. "I don't have time for a PHA alert."

Burt stared at the alert text and shook his head. "A .00 Minimum Orbit Intersection Distance? That's going to ruin someone's day."

"I'll say." Neeta swiped the text from the monitor so that it projected in the air, then began typing on the keyboard. "Whatever it is, it's 200 meters across, and the computers are giving it a ten percent chance of hitting us."

Burt ran the figures in his head as Neeta continued typing. "If we're talking about a dense rock, traveling at about fifteen kilometers per second, with an insertion angle of roughly forty-five degrees, I'm guessing we'll have a 400-megaton disaster if it hits. Definitely a city if not a small state killer."

"I've got it at 430 megatons, but don't forget, seventy-one percent of the Earth's surface is water. If it hits in the middle of the ocean, well ... the resulting tsunami will likely not be as devastating."

Glancing up at the clock, Burt barely suppressed a yawn. "You're on call tonight, so before you leave, can—"

"Burt, I know what I need to do."

"I know you do," Burt shrugged. "I just don't like to assume anything."

Neeta glared at him for an instant and harrumphed. "As soon as we stop talking to each other, I'll round up the team and have them track this PHA down and figure out why it isn't on our list. The computers say it's going to take nearly a year for it to cross our orbit, well ahead of our current schedule for DefenseNet's power on. That being said, I'll have the team start tracking this. Hopefully it'll be a false alarm."

"Thanks, Neeta." Burt finally allowed the yawn he'd been suppressing to escape. "Call me if there's anything that needs my attention."

He turned away as Neeta spoke into the intercom system, "Jenkins, Hsiu, Smith, and Pederson, come to my office. We've got an unidentified PHA that needs our attention."

CHAPTER TWO

A chill raced through Burt as he stared at his bedside speakerphone. Its dial tone filled his bedroom, but as he hung up, the room was cloaked with eerie silence.

"I can't believe I just finished talking with the Secretary of Defense," he muttered. His heart thudded loudly in his chest as adrenaline coursed through his system.

The tablet PC, which Burt had accidentally knocked to the floor, flashed red with another alert from the Jet Propulsion Lab.

He leaned over, grabbed the tablet and scrolled through the long list of incoming alerts.

The phone rang again, and he nearly jumped out of his skin.

The answering machine picked up immediately, and Burt heard the frantic sound of Neeta's voice yelling, her British accent thicker than ever. "Damn it, pick up! You're the bloody head of NEO and this place has gone bonkers. Hanford just sent—"

He smashed the "pickup" button with one finger. "Neeta, get ready. I'm picking you up in ten minutes."

~

Burt buckled himself into the airplane seat opposite Neeta. Wearing a smoky-grey skirt and matching blouse that complemented her dark complexion, she appeared composed and professional, even though they'd argued all the way from Pasadena to Edwards Air Force Base.

"Neeta, the thing that bothers me the most isn't the number of alerts we've received; it's why we're suddenly getting them. I'll be frank—when I got that first report coming out of Hanford, it seemed ridiculous. Did all of our systems somehow get some kind of virus? It seems unlikely, so what does it all mean?"

The way Neeta tugged nervously at her long, black hair, which she'd gathered into a thick braid, revealed her state of mind. "It seems like the universe has gone mental, hasn't it?" Her proper enunciation couldn't hide the nervous tremor in her voice.

Burt nodded, staring at his second-in-command. "Didn't you Brits invent the concept of keeping a stiff upper lip? You and I need to not get ahead of ourselves, and if we stay calm, the others won't make mistakes, and nor will we. We can't afford mistakes, agreed?"

Neeta took a deep breath and nodded.

The lights dimmed in the cabin as the small passenger jet began taxiing. It took only seconds before Burt felt himself pressed against his seat as they took off from Edwards Air Force Base. As the jet banked north, Burt glanced out the window and saw the unending line of headlights below. Having just struggled with the early morning Los Angeles traffic, he grumbled, "It's 2066, we have colonies on the Moon, we cured Multiple Sclerosis, and yet the L.A. city planners can't solve the 5:00 a.m. traffic snarls—unbelievable."

A 3D image of their flight plan appeared at eye level as the pilot's voice broadcast through the cabin, *"Doctors Radcliffe and Patel, the Hanford site does not have a runway, so we will be landing at Joint Base Lewis-McChord. It is currently oh-five-thirty hours and we should be touching down in approximately two hours.*

"From there, you will be transported by helicopter to the Hanford site.

"The weather is clear along the West Coast and we should have a smooth flight."

The glowing animation of their anticipated route to Washington State vanished and with a white-knuckled grip on her armrests, Neeta's voice took on a frustrated tone. "It's hard to believe what the Hanford people are reporting. It all seems dodgy, but with all the data they've transmitted to us, it can't be a mistake, can it? The whole situation is…" Her voice trailed off, and she took a deep breath.

Burt's ears popped as the plane banked slightly, and he swallowed hard as he felt the plane begin to level off.

"Let's think this through," said Burt. "How is it possible that we suddenly have not one, not two, but *hundreds* of space rocks hurtling toward us from the edge of the solar system? Do you have any idea how we didn't see this coming?"

"I should have seen it." Neeta shook her head and began speaking in a rapid-fire manner. "Most of those objects are traveling at tremendous speeds, and we could easily have missed some of the smaller ones, but bloody hell, one of those alerts is for something nearly one-hundred miles across."

"Neeta, we're both only as good as the data we're given. I'm not blaming you, nor should you take any blame on yourself. I just can't fathom how something like this could happen all of a sudden."

With a deep shuddering sigh, Neeta rested her head against the back of her seat. "At the pace some of that stuff is traveling at, we've only got three-hundred days or so before some of that rubbish reaches us. I hate to say it, but it's probably even worse than we think, because at the current distance, we can't yet know how many smaller objects we'll be facing. Even if we get DefenseNet up six months ahead of schedule, it might not be enough."

Burt stared at Neeta's worried brown eyes and sighed. "Well, we've already gotten funding approval from the Secretary of Defense to accelerate DefenseNet's deployment. You talked to our crew at JPL already, right?"

"I've got them sorted out," Neeta agreed. "They'll start testing the DefenseNet lasers right away. But I'm worried about what we'll find out at Hanford. It can't be a coincidence that just as we detected all of these incoming objects, the fellows at Hanford start bleating about a gravitational wave disturbance in the same area of space." She drew a shuddering breath. "There's something out there—I'm worried that I somehow—"

"Neeta, stop blaming yourself." Burt shook his head. "At this stage, there's no use second-guessing, let's deal with the facts at hand. After all, that's why we're heading to this place in the middle of nowhere. There's got to be a logical reason that we've got a cloud of debris heading our way." Burt leaned back in his seat and closed his eyes. "Get some rest. We're going to have a very long day."

It was almost noon when Burt stepped off the helicopter and took in the empty, brown surroundings. As the downdraft of the chopper kicked up clouds of the loose bronze-colored dirt that dominated the landscape, he glanced in Neeta's direction and jutted his chin toward the low building in the distance. The electric whir of the helicopter's engine quieted as Neeta hopped out. She nodded at him, ducked and began jogging toward the main building of the Laser Interferometry Gravitational wave Observatory, otherwise known as LIGO.

While Neeta went inside to get things ready, Burt puffed on a cigarette and stared across the thirty square miles of brown emptiness surrounding the Hanford, Washington location, wishing he didn't have what felt like the weight of the world on his shoulders. In the distance, Jeeps carrying Military Police patrolled the edges of the newly-sealed site, while MPs guarded each of the building's entrances. As of four hours ago, by order of the Secretary of Defense, the site had been closed and troops from Joint Base Lewis-McChord had converged onto the observatory grounds, putting it into lockdown.

Burt took one last drag, dropped his cigarette, and ground it into the gravel with the heel of his cowboy boot. "Damn you," he said to the smoking butt, cursing his nicotine demon for breaking loose amid this tension.

With a dissatisfied grunt, Burt strode to the cinder-block building and displayed his badge to the heavily-armed soldier wearing the camouflage fatigues that were the standard issue Army Combat Uniform.

The steely-eyed MP held Burt's ID up at arm's length, comparing the picture with his haggard face. Then he unclipped a portable retinal scanner from his belt and placed it in front of Burt's right eye. "Doctor Radcliffe, please stand still."

A moment later, a green LED lit on the scanner and the soldier nodded. He returned Burt's ID, then stepped aside. Burt walked past, into the silent halls of the building that housed the LIGO control room. After his conversation with the Secretary of Defense, only a dozen people were authorized to enter the building, all of them senior scientists with Top Secret clearances. No other countries had broken their silence yet, though Burt knew that observatories in Germany and Australia had detected the same event. They all would come to the same conclusions once they'd analyzed the data. If the public found out, there would be chaos in the streets.

He walked through the musty, beige-colored halls of the Hanford facility and turned into the control room. Burt felt like a bear jarred from hibernation, and his mood soured further when he inhaled the control room's acrid odor of burnt popcorn. He shook his head as he spied a half-opened bag lying next to an ancient microwave on the back counter, blackened kernels spilling from it.

The forty-by-twenty-foot room seemed eerily like the one in which he'd spent the last ten years in at the Jet Propulsion Labs in Pasadena. However, instead of the quiet nervous energy he'd expected to encounter, he found Neeta and another engineer arguing loudly about the observatory's readings.

"What the hell do you mean you saw a blip in that sector three months ago and didn't notify anyone?" Neeta looked like a thunderhead ready to explode as she confronted the LIGO engineer who was easily a foot taller and well over twice her weight.

"Doctor Patel, I don't think you understand." The red-cheeked scientist turned from Neeta's ominous stare and pressed his lips together as he tapped heavily on the terminal in front of him. After a few seconds, he pointed at the main screen on the wall, which showed a signal graph dated nearly three months earlier. "We detected a gravitational anomaly in the same general direction eighty-nine days ago, but per our protocol, we didn't alert anyone because we couldn't get a solid confirmation in the readings from the other sites—"

"Well, your protocol is shit, Steve. I should have been told. You *do* realize what we're facing, right?"

Glancing at the badge clipped on Steve's broad chest, Burt recognized his name and knew that he was the lead engineer at the Hanford site. Clearing his throat, Burt turned to the harried scientist. "Neeta's right, we should have been notified. Why weren't you able to confirm the readings?"

Steve turned in his seat and stared at Burt as he settled into one of the swivel chairs, regarding him with a worried expression. "Director Radcliffe, we couldn't confirm the location with only our readings. It was a weak signal blip, so we didn't have high confidence. The LIGO site in Australia was offline for repair at the time, and our location in Livingstone only got a flicker whose strength was insufficient to confirm a hit. We didn't get any solid new readings from that sector until about 3:00 a.m. this morning."

Neeta's eyebrows knit together as her scowl deepened. Just as she opened her mouth, Burt held up his hand to forestall what he feared would end up being an unproductive fight with the local staff. Neeta snapped her mouth shut and continued fuming as Burt grabbed a rubber band that happened to be lying on the nearby tabletop. He gathered his shoulder-length hair into a ponytail, fully aware of how atypical it was for a man in his position to wear a ponytail, button-down shirt, cowboy boots, and blue jeans. But even though he was fifty, he still thought of himself as one of the engineers.

"Listen, Steve, what's done is done." Even though Burt felt frustrated with the LIGO staff, he needed to keep the peace. "I received your e-mail notification this morning and that's why Neeta and I are here. What do you have for us?"

The engineer anxiously tapped a few keys on the terminal and one of the monitors on the wall displayed a series of recent "hits" that the observatory had detected. "Director Radcliffe—"

"Call me Burt."

"Burt, LIGO has registered thousands of sources for gravity waves over the years. We only see these unusual gravitational waves when large masses accelerate rapidly, causing a disturbance in space-time. Almost like a pebble dropped into a calm lake, we're able to detect the slightest ripples of the event—"

"Steve, I've been doing this kind of crap long before you'd ever taken your first math class. Just give me the technical details."

The engineer blinked. "Sorry, sir. Uh, as you probably know, the gravitational waves we receive are usually produced by the merging of binary systems, such as two neutron stars colliding. Or if there's outflow from a star rotating around a black hole, we might see hints of that as well. However, we don't often receive bursts of gravitational waves. In fact, we've only encountered a dozen or so in the last decade, and we've never determined what caused them. Yet as of 2:53 a.m. this morning, we've registered over a dozen bursts of gravitational waves—"

"And you've checked with the other LIGO sites and confirmed the origin of these bursts?" Burt leaned forward, studying the pale face of the scientist.

"Yes, sir. We've triangulated with the other two sites, zeroing in on the same quadrant in space, and...." He tilted his head toward Neeta. "Per Doctor Patel's suggestion, I contacted NASA. They've routed a secure channel to us for the use of the IXO 2 satellites. We have full access to the satellite web. Only five minutes ago, I had the satellites aim their x-ray detectors at the source of the gravitational waves."

Steve punched a few keys on the terminal. The main screen on the wall displayed a running time counter, but was otherwise black, like a perfectly clean old-style chalkboard.

Burt leaned back and stared at the empty image on the one-hundred-inch screen, as Neeta asked in a much calmer tone than she'd used before, "Steve, when's the last gravity burst you detected?"

"About fift—" Steve glanced at a wall monitor and pointed at the flickering light coming from a live video feed monitoring one of the detectors within the site. "Wait, the laser has gone out of phase!" He looked around the room as the burst of activity registered on all of the control room's screens. "We're getting a new set of signals!"

Burt stood, walked past the engineers gathered around the computer terminal, and stared at the main screen. He glanced at the video feed showing the laser interferometer image on the leftmost wall monitor. He knew that the flickering light in the video feed was a sign that the facility had been hit by a gravitational disturbance, temporarily knocking one of the arms of the laser interferometer out of phase.

Everyone breathlessly watched the various screens flicker and update. Some monitors showed the intensity of the gravity waves, while others displayed the received data from the other LIGO sites.

Burt focused on the main screen; the empty blackness of the monitor drew all his attention, while all else faded into the background.

Suddenly, a white dot appeared.

Amid what had been blackness, a small, bright spot came to life, sending Burt's heart racing.

He pointed up at the monitor and turned toward the scientists huddled around terminals fifteen-feet away. "There! Is that a hit from the x-ray detectors?"

Steve dove at his keyboard and pounded a series of commands into the terminal. "Sir, I'm verifying..."

Burt strode to the gathered scientists, as raw data scrolled on the screen and Neeta pointed at one column. "There it is," she yelled. "We got a positive hit from the x-ray satellite."

Burt stared at the lone dot on the black monitor and knew what he was seeing. But they needed more data. More time.

An engineer raced to a garbage can and the sound of painful heaving echoed through the control room as he emptied his stomach. Everyone in the room was a highly qualified scientist, an expert in their field. They all knew what they'd just detected within the boundaries of their own solar system.

Wiping nervous sweat from his forehead, Burt announced, "All we can do is wait for more signals. We need to know how big it is—its trajectory. How much time we have."

"Sir?" A trembling engineer looked up at him. "What can we do?"

The chill that Burt felt wasn't from the air-conditioned room. It felt as if the grim hand of the Reaper were reaching for a victim. He knew what the consequence of their discovery was. X-rays were typically only produced by very high-temperature events. Material being heated by unimaginably strong gravitational fields was the primary cause of such emissions.

"Let's focus on getting more data. We don't even know which direction it's going yet." Burt sighed, plopped himself on the nearest chair, and waited. It was the only thing any of them could do.

Burt prayed that the cause of the x-rays wasn't heading their way. It was one thing for DefenseNet to deal with asteroids. There were ways to handle them, given enough time. Even with Moon-sized objects, something could conceivably be done. He looked up at that glaring spot, contrasted against the blackness of the screen, and his chest tightened with worry.

As Burt waited, his gut told him that what he was staring at would be the end of them all. They'd be consumed by the insatiable hunger coming from an interstellar whirlpool of death.

A black hole.

A handful of hours had passed, and Burt paced along one of the musty hallways in the LIGO facility, trying to clear his head. Having verified the existence of a black hole within the boundaries of the solar system explained many things. Black holes typically spun at a ferocious rate, and even though people thought of them as voracious space-based vacuum cleaners that ate everything in sight, most didn't understand that black holes were very messy eaters.

Sometimes, the twisting of gravity around the black hole would fling things away, like an infant with his or her undesired pea soup.

Burt's stomach churned as he considered the options.

"Let's just pray this thing is just skirting past," he muttered to himself. "Then maybe we have a chance."

Then he froze, as he heard Neeta's voice coming from one of the nearby offices. "Mum, I'm okay. I just wanted to hear your voice. Give Daddy a hug for me."

"Princess?" A man's voice came across the office's speakerphone. *"It's been ages since we've seen you. Are you okay? Has some boy broken your heart?"* The man chuckled lightly.

"Dad, I'm thirty-seven. Nobody's gotten my heart to break it. I'm kind of married to my work, and you know that."

Burt felt a surge of guilt as he found himself listening to Neeta's private conversation. She never spoke about anything but work, so it seemed strange for him to think of her actually having a family.

"Pumpkin, then maybe it's about time you let me help find you a proper husband—"

"Rajesh Patel!" A woman's voice yelled in the background. *"You stop harassing our daughter. She'll find someone and give us grand-kids when she's good and ready."*

"Daddy, I love you, but I have to go. Hug each other, and if you don't hear from me for a while, just know I'm pretty busy at work. I love you both."

"We love you too, Poppet." Her mom's voice echoed warmly from thousands of miles away.

The buzz from the connection became silent, and almost immediately Neeta walked out of the office and gasped with surprise as she saw Burt standing in the hallway.

She quickly wiped the tears from her face. Burt stared at her, not sure he'd ever seen this side to the woman.

Ignoring the tears, he asked, "Do you want to grab some coffee with me?"

Neeta nodded as Burt turned and headed toward the break room.

~

Burt stared at the large center screen of the control room and sighed. Nearly one-hundred dots were lit, all of them appearing along the edge of a dark circle. Each spot represented an object's last gasp as the massive forces of the black hole heated and ripped it into subatomic particles before swallowing it.

He aimed a red laser pointer at the edges of the circle and glanced at the pale-faced engineer, who'd taken over at the terminal. "Give me a width. What are we dealing with?"

Closing his eyes, Burt listened to the tapping of keys and the engineer's trembling voice as he announced, "Sir, the diameter of the event horizon seems to be approximately three kilometers."

Burt was surprised by the reported size. Over one-hundred years ago, three famous physicists had established the Tolman-Oppenheimer-Volkoff limit, which dictated the upper limit for the mass of a neutron star. Doing the math in his head, he knew exactly what they were dealing with. "Well, isn't that interesting. We're dealing with a two-mile-wide rip in the fabric of space."

One scientist, a middle-aged man with a brilliant shock of red hair, asked, "But, sir, how's that possible? That's below the TOV limit, isn't it?"

Burt nodded. "About one-half of a solar mass, if my mental calculations are right."

He glanced at Neeta, and she nodded grimly. "Confirmed."

Suddenly, his old-style phone vibrated in his pocket. He retrieved it and glanced at the name: his brother. "Now is definitely not the time," he muttered, as he shoved the phone back in his pocket.

Then he looked up and addressed the room. "Half a solar mass, eh? Folks, that would explain why nobody had detected it until now. Its minimal gravitational lensing wouldn't have given us a visual clue, allowing it to sort of 'sneak up' on us. We're clearly dealing with a primordial black hole. Something birthed while the universe was in its infancy and during a time when temperatures and pressures still allowed for such things to be created. It's no different, nor any less dangerous, than the black holes we've all learned about in school. I suppose that's something ... we've detected the first of its kind. Or more to the point, it's discovered us."

Glancing at the dots on the screen, Burt knew that as each dot appeared, the satellites would register its location. "Have the computers plotted a confirmed trajectory yet? Do we have a speed?"

The engineer at the terminal stared open-mouthed as data scrolled across the screen. He seemed frozen in place, so Neeta shoved him aside and took over.

"We have a confirmed trajectory," she said. "It's heading toward the center of the galaxy." Neeta rapidly typed a new set of commands and her frown deepened. "I'm afraid that we're directly in its path."

With that statement, Burt knew that the world's fate was sealed.

A deathly calm settled over him. It was as if a shroud had dampened any emotion he should be feeling. Quietly, he asked, "How long do we have?"

"Director Radcliffe, we have 345 days at the current speed and trajectory before the black hole crosses our orbit."

"Start a countdown. E-minus 345 days." His pronouncement was effectively a countdown to the end of humanity. With a grim sense of obligation, Burt rose to his feet and motioned to Neeta. "I'll need you. This is something we'll have to tell the current administration in DC, face-to-face. They'll be asking about contingencies." He pointed at the other engineers and snapped his fingers. "Nobody is allowed to say a word about this outside of this room. The rest of you, keep monitoring, and let me know if anything changes."

Neeta walked toward him, a confused expression on her face. "Contingencies?" She whispered, "I don't understand, what contingencies?"

The concept was almost laughable. Even if life on Earth managed to survive the onslaught from dozens of killer asteroids, nothing could survive when the black hole raced across Earth's orbit.

"Don't worry," said Burt, "I'll be doing most of the talking." Opening the control room's door, he glanced over his shoulder at Neeta. "We're about to inform the President of the United States that we all have less than a year to live."

CHAPTER THREE

Chuck Rehnquist leaned over his desk and stared through the portal at the mining team as they drove stabilizing pylons into the rocky surface of the asteroid. The pylons were what the team used in low-gravity environments to help keep downward pressure on the exploratory drills. Knowing that this was one of the most dangerous parts of the asteroid-mining operation, and despite all their scans and safety protocols, they couldn't be completely certain that nothing would go wrong. Only a few weeks ago, everything had looked fine when one of the pylons had been driven into a weak spot on a rather large asteroid. At that moment, the giant rock split cleanly in half, almost like a gem cutter splitting a diamond. No matter how many of these multi-kilometer-wide mountains floating in space they drilled on, Chuck always worried about surprises. In space, surprises were often deadly.

Slapping the button on the communication console, he yelled at his men, "Peters! Kennedy! Cross! Make sure you don't repeat what happened on 1-Hutchinson. Use the ground sonar before cracking the surface."

"No worries, boss, I don't want to repeat that either. One moment I'm

standing on solid ground, and the next I'm floating in space as the damn asteroid splits in half underneath me. No thanks."

A red light flashed on Chuck's desk, notifying him that the mining station had just received a transmission from home.

He tapped on the touch-sensitive tabletop, and immediately an alert was projected in mid-air. The shimmering red text declared that the message was critical in nature.

*** NASA EMERGENCY ALERT ***

All space exploration stations and personnel are recalled.
Immediately return to Earth orbit under Emergency Protocol X-55. All other priorities are vacated.
Confirm receipt.

"What the hell?" Chuck tapped on the intercom symbol on his desk, and the science officer responded.

"What's up, chief?"

"Jennifer, go look up what Emergency Protocol X-55 is. We just got a recall notice from NASA."

"Roger that, give me a second."

Chuck pressed the button on the communications console and yelled into the microphone, "Boys, drop what you're doing and shuttle back up here. We've got something going on."

"But we've already got two of the pylons in—"

"Get your asses up here now, and that's an order. I don't care if there's a pile of gold turds lying ten feet away, get your butts back on the ship, and I mean immediately!"

"Understood."

"Sir?" The science officer's voice broadcast through the speaker

hidden in the table. *"Protocol X-55 signifies a critical issue of an unspecified nature and requires the ship and its contingent to return to Earth orbit within 270 days."*

Through clenched teeth, he hissed, "Just fucking lovely, isn't it?" It dawned on him that with their current load, there'd be no way the crew would get any bonus pay for this trip.

"Sir, you don't understand. The Earth is on the other side of the sun from us, and we got this message through a relay. We can't comply with the timeline. The best I can figure is that we'll take just about double that time to get back into Earth's orbit."

With a sigh of frustration, Chuck pressed the palms of his hands against his temples. "Jennifer, how long does it take for our transmission to get back to Earth and for us to receive a response from NASA?"

"About thirty minutes or so each way, so figure at least an hour for any responses."

"Fine," he replied. "Just make sure the miners get their shit squared away and go talk to engineering. Even though we're not about to do anything until I get confirmation from NASA, let's batten down the hatches and prep for departure."

"Will do."

Chuck leaned forward in his chair and began typing a response to NASA.

"They want us to do *what?*" Chuck couldn't believe what he'd just heard.

With the entire twenty-two-person crew gathered in the room that served as both their dining room and planning area, Jennifer, the forty-three-year-old dark-haired science officer read once again from NASA's most recent response.

"Immediately jettison all mining payload, equipment, and processing wings.

"Unfurl the primary and backup solar cells to increase thruster output to 95% critical.

"We have provided a new path to shave roughly twenty-five million miles off the return route—"

"Jesus H. Christ!" Chuck exclaimed. "Dump all our payload? We've got 1.5 million metric tons of high-quality ore, and that's hundreds of millions of dollars of equipment we're just leaving behind!"

"Don't forget that they want us to jettison entire sections of this vessel," blurted one of the miners.

Chuck focused on Jennifer and asked, "Did those engineers you talked to give any rationale behind why we're being recalled? There's got to be some big reason why they're doing this."

Jennifer shook her head. "I asked three different times, and they never answered."

Chuck asked, "And is that going to get us there in time?"

"No. Best they can figure is that we'll still be about ninety days over their deadline. NASA said they're working with their engineers to come up with more adjustments to speed up our trip. They seem real stuck on the 270 days."

With a deep sigh of frustration, Chuck pushed back from the table and announced, "Well, you guys heard the lady. Let's get all this shit straightened out." He pointed at one of the cargo engineers. "Put a beacon on the ore carrier. When we come back out here, I want to be able to find the damned thing again."

Peering out the portal into the darkness of space, Chuck silently wondered what in the world was going on.

Turning right on East 42nd Street, Stryker breathed in the aroma of grilled meat coming from one of the halal stands on the corner. He motioned toward the people coming and going from a nondescript building's entrance, fifty-feet ahead.

"That's Grand Central," he said to his partner, Kevin. "You've been there before, right?"

Kevin Taylor, a twenty-five-year-old rookie, shook his head. "Nah, I've heard of it, but I'm from Washington State. All our trains are pretty much aboveground."

Stryker turned into the large entryway of the railroad terminal, and as he led his partner deeper into the cavernous building, he panned his arm across the giant expanse. "Well, this is part of my regular patrol."

Without missing a beat, he began giving the rookie a tour. "The main concourse building that you see now was built in the early 1900s. It's roughly three hundred by one-hundred feet long, and as you can see, the ceiling, is over twelve stories high." Looking up at the ceiling, Stryker pointed at the astronomical mural above. "My granddad used to tell me that back in the 80s, the ceiling was practically all black from people smoking in here. When they restored the ceiling back in '96, they left a small black patch up there that you can see if you look carefully. Pretty much gives you a feel for how bad the smoke must have been. Just imagine, people were breathing that stuff in all the time."

Stryker walked past the crowd at the ticket booths and led Taylor toward the subway platforms.

As they pushed through the slow-moving sea of humanity heading toward the main concourse, Stryker glanced at the rookie and smiled. "Luckily, it's only 11:00 a.m., so it's pretty empty in here."

"Woah, *this* is empty?" The rookie's eyes darted back and forth, taking in the crowds of commuters walking past them.

"This is nothing," Stryker chuckled. "Mornings and evenings are killers around here. That's when all the travelers are doing their thing, and it's also when we get the most problems called in."

"What kind of problems do we get here?"

"Nothing too bad. It's usually some kids looking to pick a pocket or two. Or if a panhandler is getting too aggressive, someone will call in a complaint. But usually, it's nothing too serious."

The rookie wore a nervous expression; his hand drifted to his service belt. "What's the worst that you've run into down here? Anything that needed serious intervention?"

The newly installed ventilation systems hummed loudly as a train approached. Stryker breathed in the cool, crisp air and shrugged.

"Well, I think I've used pepper spray or my Taser only a handful of times in my five years on the street. Never needed it down here."

"You've never had to shoot anyone?"

Stryker turned to the rookie and studied the man's wary expression. "No, I've never shot anyone as a police officer." A dusty memory flashed into his mind from ten years ago. He had killed someone in the past, but that was a different time. A different place. And certainly a different uniform. "Kevin, just remember this: in almost all cases, the presence of any uniformed officer will stop most things that might otherwise escalate. That's why we do our patrols and make ourselves seen. It stops more trouble than you can imagine."

The rookie nodded, yet he held a haunted expression, almost as if he expected someone to pop out of thin air and attack.

Stryker motioned to one of the side passages. "Come on, let's finish the morning rounds and grab a bite."

～

"All units, be advised, there's a 10-50 at the corner of 47th and 7th."

Stryker lowered the volume on his radio and took a seat opposite the rookie. They sat in a local diner: Stryker's favorite.

With a look of uncertainty, Taylor lowered the volume on his radio as well. "Isn't that something we should take a look at?"

"Nah, it's just a non-criminal disturbance. Some tourist probably got the vapors from being in the middle of a large crowd." The aroma of freshly-brewed coffee wafted through the air of the local diner, and Stryker nodded toward a waitress. "Besides, we've called in our lunch break already. If you let it, street patrol will keep you away from bathroom breaks or eating from now until the day you retire.

"If it turns into one of the 10-30 codes, *that's* when we get our asses in gear."

Stryker's regular waitress arrived at their table and smiled. He hadn't seen her in a few days, and the previously wrinkled skin on her face was stretched taut, giving it an unnatural plastic sheen. Probably from one of the new over-the-counter skin tightening products that were all the rage.

"Honey, you want your usual?"

"Hey, Janice. Coffee black and a cheese Danish would be great."

She turned to his partner and peered at the name under the badge. "What'll it be, Officer Taylor?"

Taylor's eyes seemed unfocused, and he held a faraway expression.

Stryker snapped his fingers in front of the rookie's face. "Hey, you in there?"

"I'm not hungry," he responded with a distracted, almost annoyed tone.

"Suit yourself." Janice turned away from the table, and in almost no time set a mug of steaming black coffee and a pastry in front of Stryker.

Taylor pulled a small paper packet out of his shirt pocket and placed it next to Stryker's coffee. "This is an all-natural sweetener. You should try it." He tilted his head toward the glass canister of sugar and other packets of artificial sweetener. "It's way better than that junk. That stuff will kill you."

"I appreciate the offer." Stryker pushed the packet back toward his partner, lifted the mug to his lips, and took a sip. "But I prefer it unsweetened anyway." He hitched his thumb toward the window facing the street and asked, "So, how're you liking your first day so far?"

"I suppose it seems pretty calm. I kind of expected a more action-packed day, is this pretty normal?"

"Ha, someone fed you a line at the academy if they told you to expect non-stop chases. This is pretty typical. Like I told you before, most of the incidents we get around here can be prevented just by one of us being around."

Stryker took a big bite out of his Danish, got up, and pointed at the menu still laying on the table. "You might want to get something quick to tide you over, since we probably won't get another break until shift change. I'll be right back, the restroom's calling."

～

When Stryker sat back down at the table, the rookie was staring through the window, focusing on the bustling pedestrian traffic on Seventh Avenue.

"You order anything?"

Taylor shook his head as he continued staring through the window.

Just as he was about to grab the last of his cheese Danish, the radio crackled with noise.

"All available units in the vicinity of Broadway and Seventh, 10-34 in progress, officer needs assist. Crowd of ten or more demonstrators. Repeat, 10-34 in progress, officer needs assist at Broadway and Seventh."

"Shit!" Stryker launched himself from his chair as he pressed a button on his radio. "201, I'm two blocks away, en route."

He caught the waitress's gaze.

She nodded and motioned toward the door, knowing he'd settle up after the call.

"Come on, Taylor, let's hoof it!"

The rookie, for all his talk about the lack of action, seemed unfazed by the call. He motioned toward Stryker's unfinished meal. "Aren't you going to finish?"

A surge of anger flushed through Stryker as he growled, "Move it."

Stryker raced out of the diner with the rookie scrambling to catch up. He turned left on Seventh and raced north as the sound of sirens and people yelling grew louder.

"Out of the way," he yelled, as he pushed through the throng of humanity crowding the streets.

Just as he ran past West 44th, he spied a large ring of people surrounding what looked like a disabled vehicle.

The noxious fumes of burning rubber were nearly overwhelming.

Stryker grabbed his radio. "201, I'm 10-84, at the scene. Twenty protestors. Street blocked. Car disabled and smoldering, need fire response and additional units."

"10-4, 201. Additional units en route, dispatching fire and rescue."

Taylor stood next to Stryker and smiled. "What should we do?"

"Just wait and watch, for now. Backup's incoming."

The tires had been slashed and the rubber was burning as one of the protestors, who wore what looked like blood-stained white robes, climbed up onto the roof of the smoldering sedan.

The protestors surrounding the car began a low monastic chant as the man on the roof raised a bullhorn.

"The End Times are approaching! Do you all understand what that means?

"A great darkness is falling over the land and only the faithful will survive."

Taylor took a step toward the speaker and glanced over his left shoulder.

"Jon, are you a believer?"

"Am I a what?"

The man preaching from the top of the smoldering vehicle pointed toward the edge of the crowd.

"Those who are faithless and wish to prevent the End Times are heathens. For only through the darkness will we see the light of our Lord. Those who'd stop the darkness must be eliminated!"

Stryker panned his gaze toward where the man had pointed, and his blood ran cold.

Through the crowd of people, he spied someone in a blood-stained police uniform lying on the ground.

His pulse racing, Stryker pressed the button on his radio and yelled into the transceiver, "201, 10-85! 10-85! Officer down, we need backup units here now!"

From a few blocks away, sirens blared as the speaker standing on top of the car used his bullhorn to break through the din.

"Even though I walk through the valley of death, I shall have no fear, because you are with me."

At that moment, a police car arrived with lights flashing. The men who'd surrounded the burning car immediately raced toward it.

Feeling the adrenaline pour into his bloodstream, Stryker's pulse quickened.

A brick flew from the crowd and smashed into the cruiser's windshield.

People screamed and began running away as Stryker unclipped the pepper spray canister from his belt, praying that more backup was incoming.

Suddenly, he felt a sharp prick in the back of his arm and whirled to his left.

His Taser drawn, the rookie held a feral expression as he pressed the button on the weapon he'd just fired into Stryker's back.

Stryker flinched as he heard the clicking sound; 50,000 volts passed through the two thin wires connecting him to the Taser.

He didn't feel his muscles convulse. A surge of rage flooded through Stryker as he brought the pepper spray to bear. Sending a squirt of the OC into the rookie's face, he immediately aimed a kick at the man's knees, knocking Taylor from his feet.

"No," the rookie screamed as he fought the effects of the pepper spray. "You can't stop what's coming!"

Through burning eyes, Taylor's face contorted as he aimed a kick toward Stryker, who just managed to step out of range.

The rookie grasped at his belt, and the world seemed to slow.

His heartbeat thundering in his ears, Stryker watched Taylor flip open the retaining strap to his service weapon.

"Don't," he yelled, just as the rookie pulled the semi-automatic from its holster.

Taylor's shooting arm began to pan toward Stryker just as his own weapon fired.

For the first time since leaving the Army, Jon Stryker had shot someone.

Another shot rang out, this time from Taylor's weapon, as the rookie's head rocked backward with the force of Stryker's bullet.

Stryker felt the thud as Taylor's head and weapon hit the asphalt simultaneously.

∼

Everything after the shooting seemed to happen at once.

Other officers from his precinct swarmed the area, some interviewing eyewitnesses, others helping cordon off the scene. The forensics team began inventorying the evidence.

"Stryker, how are you doing?"

Stryker looked up at Lieutenant Malacaria and shrugged. "I don't know what happened to him. It's like he was all mellow and normal the whole day, and suddenly he went psycho."

"Listen, Jon, we saw what went down from the precinct as it was happening. The body camera images were crystal clear. It's just lucky the rookie wasn't thinking when he Taser'd you. One of the leads obviously didn't connect—"

"The vest stopped it. I felt something hit, but I don't get it. Why'd he go psycho on me? I thought the academy weeded out any borderline folks during training."

Malacaria shrugged. "I don't know what to tell you about that. Our guys will look into it and see what happened. Luckily, he's the only fatality. It turns out Eric Johnson, the first guy on the scene, got beaned by a rock and stabbed, but he'll make it." He patted Stryker on the shoulder and said, "Listen, I'm here to tell you that you're off the street for now while they finish the investigation—"

"But—"

"It's just a formality. Believe me, nobody's going to give you shit over this. Just take a few days off, play with your kids, and come back on Monday. If you need counseling or anything—"

"Lieutenant, I don't need counseling. I'm fine."

"Good, then just get some rest and the Captain will probably be calling you tonight to check up. You want a ride home?"

"No, I'm good. I have to settle up my lunch bill at the diner anyway."

Stryker shook hands with the Lieutenant and a couple of other officers, then crossed the yellow tape and headed back toward the diner.

~

He entered the quiet restaurant, and Janice waved and shot him a smile. "Hi, honey, everything's still where you left it. Do you want some fresh coffee?"

Stryker glanced at the table where he'd sat and walked toward it, contemplating whether he should have any more caffeine. He was pretty wound up as it was.

Something prickled at the back of his neck as he stared at the table.

He was on edge. The adrenaline hadn't completely flushed out of his system. His senses tingled, and Stryker suddenly felt uneasy as he panned his gaze across the restaurant. He hadn't felt this way since the last MP patrol he'd pulled, the one that led to half of his squad coming home in body bags.

Nothing seemed out of place. The mug with the half-drunk coffee was still there. Same with his half-eaten pastry.

Stryker's eyes widened as he gritted his teeth.

He looked up at Janice and asked, "Has anyone been at this table?"

She shook her head. "Nope. Nobody else came into my section, and it's been pretty quiet since you raced out."

Stryker pressed the button on his radio and said, "201 to dispatch, I need an evidence team at 43rd and Broadway."

"Roger that, 201. Units are in the vicinity."

With a puzzled expression, Janice asked, "What's wrong?"

"Probably nothing." Stryker shook his head as he stared at his half-eaten meal. "But either way, let's just leave this table as is."

"Okay," she said, shrugging and greeting a customer as he walked in.

Stryker fumed as he clenched his fists and stared at the spoon, which lay next to the now-cold mug of coffee.

It had freshly-dried coffee stains on it.

His mind raced as he replayed the brief lunch.

He'd never touched the spoon. He felt sure of it.

"What the hell did Taylor put in my coffee?"

CHAPTER FOUR

When Burt and Neeta landed at Andrews Field, a member of the Secret Service assigned them a staff car, briefed them on security procedures, and gave Burt explicit instructions on how to activate the navigation system's programming so that it would take them to the White House's private entrance. The SUV smelled of new leather, and as he glanced at the battery gauge, he noticed that the car barely had any charge left. As the sun peeked through the clouds, he hoped that the solar paint would absorb enough energy to keep the battery charged so they could make it to their destination.

Following the preprogrammed directions in the navigation system, Burt stared at the backed-up traffic on I-395, and huffed with impatience. The car was no longer making any forward progress, and what should have been a twenty-minute drive was taking much longer.

He glanced at Neeta, who sat in the front passenger seat, a tiny figure engulfed in the massive leather seat. "Do they have traffic like this in London?"

Shaking her head, she waved dismissively at the brake lights directly ahead. "By the time I was old enough to get my driver's license, Parliament had already mandated that every car have an AVR system without the paranoid settings the U.S. uses. We actually trust our computer systems back home."

"Automated Vehicle Routing," Burt's lip curled with disdain. "It's more a pain in the ass than it's worth, the way we've done it."

Neeta tilted her head and stared at Burt. "Don't get me started. Bloody hell, AVR was invented in the U.S. and deployed throughout the British Isles almost thirty years ago. You'd think it would be more of a thing here."

Burt shrugged. "I'm old school and haven't seen it do anything all that useful yet. Besides, they promised that it would fix our traffic problems, and after five years of being active, look at this." He waved at the barely-creeping cars ahead.

"That's because it was deployed with a paranoid set of rules that force unreasonable traffic length requirements. I mean, let's be serious —the computers have much better reaction times than we do. Your system here is totally bonkers."

Staring ahead, he silently acknowledged that Neeta might have a point. All of the cars on the street had a mandated two-and-a-half car lengths between each other. Burt figured that somewhere, someone figured it would make a nice aerial photo op to have all the cars lined up looking very neat and tidy. But that kind of fastidiousness created its own set of issues, and traffic flow was one of them.

The phone in Burt's pocket vibrated, and a speaker in the car broadcast, *"Incoming Call. Carl Radcliffe. Answer, yes or no."*

Burt sighed and glanced at Neeta. "If you don't mind. He tried calling earlier and I blew him off."

"Better now than when we're talking to the president." Neeta held an amused expression.

"Yes." Burt spoke emphatically to the car's phone system and the sound of kids laughing in the background filled the SUV.

"Burt, are you there?"

"Hi, Carl, what's up?"

"Um, it's the twins' birthday, and they keep asking when Uncle Burt is showing up."

Burt winced and felt a pang of regret deep within his gut as Neeta stared at him, her expression suddenly inscrutable. This was the first birthday that he'd missed since those boys were born six years ago. "Damn, Carl, I'm so sorry. I'm actually out of town right now. I should have—"

"Oh, that sucks, but I understand. Listen, Jenny and I have a house full of six and seven-year-olds running around wreaking havoc."

"Shit, Carl, I'm sorry—"

"No, it's cool, get what you have to do done and don't worry about it. I'll tell the boys you'll make it up to them. Oh, damn, someone just spilled punch everywhere, I've got to run."

"Best of—"

The call disconnected, and suddenly the image of his nephews' disappointed faces popped into his mind's eye. Burt swallowed hard against the lump that had formed in his throat.

"You'd make a really good dad," Neeta remarked, as she stared intensely at Burt.

Burt shook his head slowly and sighed. "Those boys are the closest to kids of my own that I can imagine."

"This might be inappropriate, but why didn't you get married and have kids?"

The car inched forward as the traffic ahead progressed at a snail's pace.

Taking a deep breath, Burt dredged up painful memories that he'd not talked about in over twenty years. "I did get married, but she died from an aggressive form of breast cancer. She was diagnosed two months after we got married and died six months later."

Neeta gasped, covering her mouth with the palm of her hand. "Oh, Burt, I'm so sorry."

Burt shook his head. "It was a long time ago, and ever since then, I've sort of poured myself into my work. As to the kids thing, I kind of regret not having a legacy to leave behind when I'm gone. After all, isn't that what kids are all about? A way of leaving a little fragment of yourself to carry on?" His mind wandered to his nephews, and then he glanced at Neeta and smiled. "Since we're on the verge of the end of everything, I suppose I could ask the same of you. Why didn't you get married and make your own little legacies?"

Neeta snorted. "Are you kidding? Even I know what kind of a bitch I can be. Who'd want to put up with that?"

"Hah!" Burt laughed. "You're not nearly as bitchy as you make yourself out to be." He turned his attention to the traffic ahead and grumbled. "Anyway, sitting in this backup isn't getting us anywhere."

He pressed and held the emergency manual-override button, and Neeta raised her voice. "What the hell are you doing?"

With a crooked smile, Burt veered off I-395, taking the Maine Avenue exit, and hit the accelerator. "Showing you how it was done in the old days. Besides—we need to get there in our lifetimes."

Neeta shrieked, pressed her feet against the dash, and buried her head between her knees.

Burt laughed. "Neeta, I swear you'll be fine. And besides, how can this upset you when the London traffic patterns don't? I swear, when I saw *all* the green lights turn on at once and hundreds of cars flew through the intersections at nearly sixty-miles-per-hour, I nearly crapped myself."

"Yes, but the computers are all handling things. I trust them to weave the cars around without hitting each other. I can't say that that level of trust extends to your driving." Neeta kept her head down and refused to look up as she gave her muffled response.

Seeing her genuinely frightened stirred something in Burt, and he reached out and patted her shoulder. "It'll be okay—"

"Keep your hands on that bloody wheel!"

He smiled and focused on the road. "Remember, the AVR system is still tracking our car. Even if I screw up, the other cars will swerve out of the way. We'll be fine."

Later, as they followed Driscoll Matthews, the National Security Advisor, down the well-lit hall toward the Situation Room located under the West Wing of the White House, Burt watched Neeta nervously knead her hands together. He couldn't exactly blame her. If Burt had any sense whatsoever, he'd also be nervous. Leaning over, he whispered to Neeta and reminded her, "If you're called on, just stick to hard data, and don't give opinion unless asked for it. You don't want to say anything you can't defend."

Neeta glanced at him with a sour expression. "Well, duh."

Her dark complexion had taken on a greenish hue that Burt hoped was just a trick of the light.

Driscoll paused, and Burt's gaze was drawn to the man's red power tie, which contrasted with the black pinstriped suit and highly-polished dress shoes.

Burt suddenly felt conscious of how under-dressed he was. He'd forgotten his suit coat at home yesterday, and hadn't had a chance to pack anything whatsoever before taking the cross-country flight to DC. He'd only just managed to borrow an ugly paisley tie from one of the White House staffers, and was consciously trying to ignore that he was still wearing jeans and cowboy boots.

The National Security Advisor motioned toward a basket lying conspicuously on the credenza, which ran along the length of the hall-way. "Please put your cell phones or any other electronics in the basket. They're not allowed in the Situation Room."

Burt dug into his pocket for his old-style touch-based phone as Neeta carefully extracted her phone bud from her ear and placed it in the basket.

Just as Burt deposited his handheld phone into the basket, Driscoll asked, "You guys ready?"

Burt glanced at Neeta, and even though she still appeared nauseous, he gave Driscoll a curt nod.

The National Security Advisor took a few steps forward and opened a wood-paneled door at the end of the hallway, revealing the large room that lay immediately ahead. "Director Radcliffe, Doctor Patel, welcome to the White House Situation Room. Have a seat at the table. The president should be here any moment."

The room smelled faintly of wood polish and leather. Burt immedi-ately noticed a handful of people sitting at the long wooden conference table that dominated the center of the room. Television monitors lined the walls, along with random photos of historic events. Burt noticed that there was a black placemat located on the table in front of each of a dozen black leather chairs. On each mat lay a pre-printed cardstock folded lengthwise, with a person's name and title on both sides. He didn't recognize any of the people sitting at the conference table, but thankfully, the pre-printed names helped prevent some awkwardness. Leading Neeta toward their assigned locations, Burt pulled out one of the chairs for her and took his place next to her as others filed into the room.

Someone behind him sniffed loudly, and as Burt turned, he saw Greg Hildebrand walk stiffly by; the strong smell of cologne tickled the hairs in Burt's nose. Greg stopped, placed his hand on Neeta's shoulder, and said, in a nasally voice that reminded Burt of Templeton the rat from the old Charlotte's Web cartoon: "Patel, I'm hearing that the shit has hit the fan, and we've got you to thank for it all."

Neeta rolled her eyes and shook her head. "Greg, you've always had such a lovely command of the English language. Clearly some things have gone nonlinear, so they had to call in the experts. Certainly, that's not what *you're* here for."

Greg sniffed disdainfully as he walked to the far end of the table, just to the right of where the president was expected to sit.

Neeta glanced at Burt and whispered, "What's he doing here?"

Burt leaned closer, partially covered his mouth, and whispered, "He's the president's Chief Science Advisor and heads up the Science Advisory Council. I'd expect the president will lean on him for second opinions, and aside from him, most of the rest of the people look like military folks from the Joint Chiefs of Staff, Secretary of Defense, and some look like they're from the National Security Council."

"I thought more of the president before you said that," Neeta harrumphed.

"Behave," Burt warned. Neeta might be small, but she was a bulldog with a very low tolerance for stupidity in others. He glanced at the photograph of the president hanging at the far end of the room, and even though he personally didn't share her politics, he couldn't help but admire what she'd accomplished at the relatively young age of fifty-three. Being the first woman to ever lead a Special Forces assault team was Margaret Hager's first claim to fame. After retiring from the Army, she'd become a star of the political scene, and now, as president, she was the head of the most powerful nation on the planet.

A planet on the brink of extinction.

Suddenly, a door opened on the far side of the room as a deep voice announced, "Please rise. Margaret Hager, President of the United States—"

"Let's dispense with the formalities," Hager's assertive yet feminine voice interrupted the Sergeant at Arms. "From what I understand, we don't have time for any of that crap."

A smile grew on Burt's face as the nearly six-foot-tall, blonde woman motioned impatiently for everyone to take a seat.

"All right, someone give me the unvarnished truth. What are we dealing with?"

Burt cleared his throat and stood. "Madam President, I'll try to be brief...."

Beside the dark-stained walnut of the conference room table, the president's hazel eyes took on a darker, almost brown hue. It was easy for Burt to imagine President Hager barking orders to a squad of soldiers. This wasn't a woman anyone trifled with. With a grim expression, she summarized what Burt had spent the last five minutes explaining. "So you're saying that if we, by some miracle, manage to dodge or blast the asteroids that are heading towards us, we're still screwed because there's a tiny black hole heading straight for us."

"The black hole may be small, but it has nearly half the mass of our sun," Burt clarified. "The gravitational distortion will almost certainly tear us apart, but if it doesn't, it will toss the entire solar system into chaos as it plows through the sun. The resulting impact and explosion would effectively wipe us all out."

"Fine, we're doubly screwed." The president glanced to her right. "Okay Hildebrand, you have anything to say?"

Greg Hildebrand had a sour expression as he adjusted his tie. He'd been flipping through the pages of Burt and Neeta's report and turned to his boss. "I ... I'm afraid, based on Doctor Radcliffe and Patel's report, along with the independent confirmations I received just in the last hour before this meeting, that there's little that can be done. The object heading toward us can't be shifted, moved, or destroyed. It's beyond anything any of us dreamt could happen—"

"That's bullshit and you know it, Greg," Neeta growled. Her nostrils flared as she stared daggers at him.

Burt hissed, "Neeta!"

Greg glared right back at Neeta, and before anything could escalate, the president aimed the palm of her hand at her Science Advisor, silencing him. Her gaze shifted to Neeta. "Explain."

Staring wide-eyed at Neeta, Burt watched her stand and clear her throat. He had no clue what she was about to say, and that terrified him.

"Madam President," she began, "I happen to know that there was someone who had known something about this impending disaster for almost a decade, and your Science Advisor was instrumental in getting him silenced and removed from the ISF."

"Neeta, that's a total misrepresentation of what happened!" Greg stood and leaned over the table. "Holmes was making shit up and admitted he was exchanging information with the North Korean Supreme Leader. He spent trillions of the ISF's funding on a bunch of delusions."

Putting her hands on her hips, Neeta shook her head with an expression of disgust etched on her face. "It's unbelievable. Millions and millions of sperm and *you* are the best your father could produce? Pathetic."

"Okay, enough." The president pointed at Greg and Neeta. "Do you two know each other? If so, get over this personal bullshit and tell me what you're talking about."

Neeta tore her glare from Greg and focused on the president. "I'm sorry, President Hager. Yes, we know each other. We were both at Caltech. I graduated number two in my class. I remember Greg quite vividly. He drove me crazy asking for help with his classes. Let's just say that he never quite got over me doing much better than he did, and he especially hated Dave Holmes, the guy who graduated at the top of our class."

"Hold on." A look of comprehension washed over the president's face. "Holmes? The same boy genius who won the Nobel Prize in Physics when he was sixteen or something? That's who you two are talking about?"

"Nineteen, but yes, ma'am. I'm only giving Greg a hard time because he was the guy who started the ball rolling to kick Dave out of the ISF." Neeta glanced at Greg and wrinkled her nose. "I have no idea how Dave knew it, but he told me ten years ago that something bad was going to happen this year—"

"Last I checked, the North Koreans are our enemies," Greg blurted, his face red with fury.

"Damn it, Hildebrand!" The president yelled, as she slapped her open palm on the table. The report of the president's hand smashing against the wooden surface coupled with the tone of her voice instantly shocked everyone into silence. "I don't care if Satan himself gave us the information. Clearly Holmes was right, or we wouldn't be *here* talking about the end of humanity. Let's all be adults, put aside the bullshit from the past, and talk about the present." She looked toward the far end of the table. "Director Radcliffe, Doctor Patel, where is our boy genius now? Seems like he should be in this meeting, unless one of *you* has some bright ideas on how to save our collective asses?"

A wave of nausea washed over Burt, and he frowned. "I'm afraid I don't have any good news on alternative solutions, and as far as I know, Doctor Holmes went missing soon after the whole ISF financial crisis hit the news." He turned to Neeta and cocked an eyebrow, unsure if she had any more hidden nuggets of information.

Neeta sighed. "Where's Dave? Truthfully, I don't know. It all went to hell a little over four years ago, while I was still the assistant program director at the ISF—"

"Exactly what happened," interrupted the president. "I wasn't ever briefed on it, since no ISF issues have come up since I've been in office."

Neeta leaned forward in her chair. "Dave was in charge of everything, but especially the project he called Changing Venue. Even though I was his second, I only knew about small pieces of it. He called me just after he'd pitched the rationale for the expenses to Greg." She pointed toward him, and he blinked rapidly in response. "Greg had wiggled into a politically appointed role as a civilian Science Advisor to the Department of Defense. At the time, they oversaw a large part of the funding of the ISF. Anyway, Dave called me and said that it had gone terribly and that he wouldn't be surprised if he got fired. I personally thought he was being paranoid, but it turned out to be the last time I heard from him. That was over four years ago."

Burt's eyes narrowed as he watched everyone's reaction to what Neeta had said. The military advisors looked perplexed, the president had a worried frown, and the Science Advisor's pallid complexion showed a sneer of disgust.

The president glanced at Greg and he held his hands up and shook his head. "I vividly remember that interview. He was jabbering on like a crazy man. Talking about conspiracies, North Korean scientists, and all sorts of nutty predictions that demanded his attention. And this was the man the world had entrusted with the future of our science research! It was ridiculous. All I know is that he was put into Walter Reed's psych department for observation and he escaped soon after. I have no idea where he might be."

The president glared across the table. "Anyone else know where our wayward scientist is?"

Burt shook his head, and noticed the rest of the room was also denying any knowledge of the man's whereabouts.

With a brusque exhalation, the president frowned. "Well, I'll tell you what I'm *not* going to do. I'm *not* going to panic the American people, and with them the rest of the world, until I have no other choice." She turned to Greg. "I want you to gather the best minds we have. Have them read-in on Indigo and I want to hear about contingencies. I don't care about the costs and the risks, I'm willing to entertain any kind of skunkworks that can save our bacon. We just need to know what our options are right away. You got that?"

Greg nodded. "Understood. I'll collect the resources and do everything I can to get you an answer."

President Hager turned to the rest of the room with a grim expression. "You've all been read-in on Indigo. Mum's the word, and I want each and every one of you hunting for this David Holmes." She wagged her finger at the different heads of government agencies sitting around the table. "I don't care if he's in a brothel in Thailand or in some friend's attic. I want him found and brought back so we can talk about possibilities, because right now, the options are grim. Do we all understand each other?"

A chorus of "yes, ma'am" or "yes, Madam President" echoed across the Situation Room.

She stood, and with a grim expression, announced, "It's not over until it's over, folks. Just remember that." Then she turned on her heel and immediately exited the room.

Burt whispered to Neeta, "Let's talk on the plane."

The small twelve-passenger jet accelerated as it launched into the air, banking smoothly to the right as they returned to their first stop: Los Angeles.

"So what's this crap about North Korea and Holmes knowing about a pending disaster?" Burt strapped himself into the seat next to Neeta. "I can tell you know more than you let on back there."

Neeta had a white-knuckled grip on the arms of her seat and looked nauseous. "I'm not sure if Dave ever said this to anyone else, but when he said it, even I thought he'd gone mental. He claimed that the North Koreans had seen a glimpse of the future."

"He what?" Burt's eyebrows knitted together.

"I know, I know, it sounds crazy, but he said something that makes much more sense now, years later. Supposedly, in an effort to survey the outer edges of the Oort Cloud, North Korea had launched a series of space probes nearly thirty years ago, kind of like our Voyager probes from the twentieth century. Dave said that one of the satellites saw our future."

"Is there a record of any launches by North Korea during that time?"

Neeta nodded and closed her eyes as the jet banked. "After Dave disappeared and everything went to hell, I did look into it. There were a handful of liftoffs from North Korea in that timeframe, but the payloads were all registered as broadcast satellites for television—"

"Which almost certainly is a lie," Burt harrumphed. "The only people over there who actually have Internet access or can watch TV are the generals and the Supreme Leader."

"Nonetheless, I don't know what kind of information Dave and the North Koreans ended up sharing. I just remember that eerie comment about having glimpsed the future. Maybe one of those probes ended up getting sucked up by the black hole when it was further out, and that's what set Dave off?"

The plane hit a patch of turbulence, and Neeta began breathing heavily, maintaining a death grip on the arms of her seat. There was something about her irrational fear of flying that endeared her to Burt. It was a vulnerability that he'd otherwise never seen before. He patted the top of her left hand.

"Burt, are you sure this plane is safe?"

He smiled. "I swear to you, it's fine. It's a C-37A, fitted with high-capacity power cells. It can go over 6,000 miles at a clip without a charge. We're certainly okay for a hop from Andrews to the West Coast, so don't worry. So, about this North Korea thing ... how in the world did Dave form a relationship with them? They're still a pariah state, backwards technologically, and from all indications, not particularly friendly with our government."

The plane hit another small patch of turbulence, and Neeta grabbed Burt's larger hand and squeezed as she took in a deep breath. "Mind you," she finally said, "I'm only guessing, but Dave used to hang out with a Korean student he knew as Frank. I also knew him, and he was utterly brilliant. He and Dave used to talk about concepts in theoretical physics that were just beyond me at the time. It was years after we'd all graduated that I saw someone who looked exactly like the Frank I'd known on the news. Evidently his father had just died and Frank, the guy who I'd taken classes with at Caltech, was suddenly the leader of North Korea."

"Are you serious?"

"As a heart attack."

Burt pressed the button on his seat and reclined a bit. "So do you have any idea what Dave was working on that might help us out? I can't imagine what we could possibly do. There's nothing I know of, or have ever read about in research, that could affect a black hole, other than something nearly as massive. I don't know about you, but I don't have another black hole to throw at this one to nudge it off course."

Neeta reclined as well and closed her eyes. "I only know pieces of what he was working on, but none of it made any sense to me. At least none of it seemed related to our current problem. But if anyone could figure a way out of this, Dave could. Burt, you don't understand. Dave was beyond anything you and I can even comprehend. If there's such a thing as a savant, he was definitely one. He was usually pretty good at explaining things, but when he got into his own zone, even when he tried to explain what he was talking about, it was like nothing I'd ever experienced with another person. I sometimes felt like a total idiot when I was around him."

"Well, any ideas where he might be?"

Unclasping her grip on Burt's hand, Neeta laid her arm across her eyes. "I have a few ideas where we could look, but they're wild guesses at best."

"Guesses are better than what I've got, which is nothing."

CHAPTER FIVE

The engines of the lunar shuttle hummed, thrusting Dave heavily against his take-off seat as the ship rocketed from the surface of the Moon. Glancing across the cargo bay, his gaze settled on the lunar rover parked only ten feet away. When he noticed that two of the horizontal thrusters had been damaged on the vehicle and they'd have to be fixed, he let out a silent groan. If they *weren't* fixed, the entire launch mission would be a waste of time.

Unbuckling his harness, Dave took a step and immediately slammed hard against the deck of the cargo hold—the full effect of the shuttle's g-forces pushed him to the floor. With a grunt of exertion, he righted himself and crawled toward the heavily-modified rover parked next to a tremendous spool of graphene, the carbon-nanotube ribbon he'd soon be deploying.

For years, graphene had been a darling substance of research scientists. Being two hundred times stronger than steel by weight, as well as an extremely efficient conductor of both heat and electricity, it was a fundamental component to many basic advances in scientific research. But Dave was long past the research phase. For him and everyone else on the Moon colonies, graphene would ultimately be a key ingredient in saving their lives.

Wearing the required spacesuit, Dave struggled against the ever-present forces as he peered under the front edge of the rover. "We've got damage to the aft thrusters, but I think I can fix it."

"Mister Carter," the disembodied voice of the shuttle captain echoed loudly in his helmet, calling him by the assumed name Dave had been using since his arrival on the Moon four years earlier. *"Are you certain you're qualified to make such repairs?"*

Dave rolled his eyes as he opened one of the cargo bay's tool chests, retrieved a pry bar, and wedged it into the valve's opening. "Don't you worry your pretty head," he grunted as he strained against the bar, trying to pry open the valve as the metal groaned in protest.

As Dave strained every muscle he had, trying to open one of the thrust valves on the rover, he admonished himself for his carelessness under his breath. "I must have landed the damned thing too hard on a rocky outcropping and bent the hell out of this."

In his helmet, he heard the pilot sniff with disdain. He knew the woman who was piloting the ship, and she'd always been a prissy, self-important bitch who looked down on all the miners. She never said anything rude, but her condescending tone nearly drove him crazy.

Slowly, the valve began to give way, its yawning mouth finally showing the opening to the thrust jet. Setting aside the pry bar, Dave peered inside the thruster and groaned. Wedged deep inside was a lunar rock that he'd need to retrieve, and to do that, he'd have to take the entire jet assembly apart.

Grabbing a screwdriver, he lay under the rover and began to work on the assembly. With the thrusters still pressing him against the floor, just lifting his arms was a struggle. As he tried to manipulate the screwdriver, Dave grew ever more frustrated. The thick fingers of his gloves made fine motor movement nearly impossible.

"This crap would be a lot easier if I didn't have to wear this monkey suit, you know."

"Mister Carter, you do realize that it's for your own safety, don't you?"

Dave tried to wipe his forehead, and immediately realized the stupidity of that move as beads of sweat dripped into his eyes. He let loose on the voice projecting fake concern from within her cockpit. "Oh, fuck off, you glorified tour guide. I'm not the one sitting pretty pressing a button every once in a while. Some people are actually working here, you know?"

"Chief Hostetler warned me that you get grumpy, so I'll ignore your rudeness and do my job. Why don't you just do yours?" A rash of static echoed through the speaker in Dave's helmet and the voice of the pilot muttered, *"Typical miner trash. Not sure why I bother talking to them. They're all uneducated vulgarians of the first order."*

Dave's mood lifted as he realized that the pilot must have accidentally left her transmitter on.

Having posed as one of the Moon Colony's miners for nearly four years, he'd admittedly gained some rough edges and had managed to fit right in with the rest of the workers. Fitting in was the only way Dave could have made any progress on his plans and be assured that he wouldn't be found out. Only the mining company's Chief of Operations knew who he really was: the same Chief Hostetler who had actually quit a rather high-level position at the ISF under protest when Dave's troubles were made public.

Blinking sweat from his eyes, Dave continued his work, knowing that he'd likely be at it for hours.

Dave grabbed a metal file and scraped at one of the freshly reassembled thruster valves on the side of the rover. It had been his idea to use the rover to help deploy the space elevators, and so far, it had worked perfectly.

The shuttle's vertical thrusters had ceased their acceleration a long time ago, and the shuttle was currently spinning like a top. In so doing, it artificially simulated the gravity on the Moon, and Dave had been easily moving about the cargo bay.

After inspecting the rest of the rover and giving it a clean bill of health, he began to meticulously file the scorch marks off the thrusters.

Soon, he felt the g-forces lessen as the pilot slowed the spin of the shuttle.

"Mister Carter, we're approaching the requested 55,000-mile altitude from the lunar surface. I'll be opening the cargo bay doors in approximately five minutes."

"Roger that," Dave replied, easing himself to his feet and latching his safety harness to one of the metal loops on the cargo hold's floor.

As the shuttle's thrusters halted the spin and leveled the ship, Dave felt the familiar nauseous discomfort as the spin-induced gravity disappeared and he experienced the weightlessness of space. With the magnetic soles of his spacesuit now activated, he plodded very much like Frankenstein's monster, struggling to lift his foot and place it ahead of him as he marched toward the giant spool of graphene ribbon. This ten-foot spool was three-feet wide and would easily weigh a few tons on Earth, but thanks to the lack of gravity, Dave was able to easily turn the spool on its spindle and grab the metal rod that had been melded to the end of the ribbon.

He slowly pulled on the rod, and watched as the dull semi-transparent ribbon unfurled behind it. Dragging the end of the ribbon toward the rover, he fed the metal rod and about two feet of the attached ribbon into a slit on the top of the rover and slammed his gloved fist onto a button next to the opening. The opening immediately clamped shut, securing the end of the sheet of graphene to the rover.

Running his fingers along the seemingly fragile ribbon, it was hard to imagine that even though the ribbon was less than the thickness of a hair, it could easily hold many tons scrambling up and down it. After all, that was the purpose of a space elevator.

As far as the mining company was concerned, the network of space elevators would be used to help lift cargo to and from the lunar surface, so the orbiting shuttles never had to actually land. This made for a plausible explanation, but it wasn't the truth. Nobody would ever believe the truth if they heard it.

The bored voice of the pilot announced, *"Evacuating the air from the cargo bay in three ... two ... one...."*

Suddenly, a horn blared in Dave's helmet. As the air escaped from the cargo hold, the ribbon fluttered. He leaned over the rover and checked its settings. "Hey, Pilot, have you detected the infrared designator on the surface for the rover to home in on?"

"Of course. It's broadcasting at the designated 1,033 nanometers."

Dave grabbed the rover by one of its handholds and wheeled the weightless vehicle over the still-closed lower hatch of the cargo hold.

Staring at the wide ribbon of graphene attached to the rover, his gaze followed the transparent film up to the giant spool and nodded with approval. "The rover is aligned with the spool. I'm ready here." He took a few steps back, away from the cargo doors, as the yellow warning lights flashed through the cargo bay.

"Roger that. Opening the lower cargo hatch in three..."

Through the soles of his boots, Dave felt the vibration of the heavy latches unlocking, then he watched as the cargo bay doors yawned open. The rover floated above the opened doors, its programming automatically activated. With its vertical thrusters, the rover slowly lowered itself below the deck, following the infrared beacon that had been planted on the surface of the Moon.

The ribbon unspooled faster and faster while the rover thrust itself toward the Moon's surface.

Just as he began to wonder about his transport, Dave felt another vibration in the shuttle and smiled.

"Mister Carter, your transport down to the surface has docked."

Walking to the airlock, Dave imagined the rover in a controlled descent, speeding ever faster with the long ribbon that would form the basis of the space elevator's scaffolding trailing behind it. He knew how much was at stake for everyone in the Moon colonies. These things he was putting in place would be so much more than a simple way of transporting stuff off the surface; they'd eventually save all of their lives.

CHAPTER SIX

As he lurched into a sitting position, Yoshi's heart thudded heavily in his chest. He blinked the sleep out of his eyes and felt the ship shake as the navigation thrusters engaged, placing them behind the orbit of Titan, Saturn's largest moon. The unusual maneuvers had become a frequent event as sporadic asteroid showers flew past, devastating Titan's surface and causing flashes of brilliant light when they struck Saturn's surface.

However, the ship's vibrations hadn't been what woke him. Yoshi cringed as the hidden implant in his head sent uncomfortable jolts through his nervous system, alerting him that he was about to receive a message from the Brotherhood.

Yoshi stared out the viewport just above his bunk, and despite having been stationed in the Matsushita Science Station for nearly six months, he was in awe every time he saw Saturn, the yellow-orange gas giant with its telltale ring looming large in the background.

Since having left Earth, Yoshi had not received a single communiqué from the Brotherhood, nor had he expected any. There'd be no reason to send a signal hundreds of millions of miles out in space just so he could hear it. But that tingling was a sign that he was mistaken.

Swinging his legs off the side of the bed, Yoshi silently prayed for no more than half a minute when a voice only he could hear echoed loudly in his head.

"Brother Watanabe, the time has come.

"The End Times are here, but remember, in the wake of the darkness comes a great light. There will be those who are scared of what's to come, but the faithful will see the glory of the Lord as the darkness approaches.

"Brother, you have been blessed beyond comprehension. We have signs showing that our faith is being tested. By allowing God's test to proceed unhindered, by exhibiting the faith that we know you possess, the Almighty will make his presence known to you.

"His test comes in the form of the void. An utter blackness that, for those without faith, spells their doom. Yet for the faithful, it is a time of awakening. An opportunity for the unworthy to be saved, and for the faithful to become a First Witnesses to God's glorious presence amongst us."

Yoshi's heart raced; the thrill of what was to come felt almost overwhelming. To be a Witness was what all of the Brotherhood had been promised since time immemorial.

"Brother Watanabe, be warned. If you don't show faith in our Lord, if you shy away from His test, then He will know that you've forsaken His trust. And in so doing, the darkness of the void will leach through your soul and forever remove it from the Tree of Life. God will turn his back on you if you don't show faith. Don't allow others to doom your immortal soul. If there are believers with you, you may share the joyous news, but for the heathens, there can only be one fate.

"Earn the title of First Witness, and let your soul sing forevermore.

"You know what to do."

The tingling of the implant faded, but the words of the Brotherhood had not. With a surge of righteous energy flowing through him, Yoshi retrieved the knife he kept hidden in his dresser drawer.

He gently kissed the blade and smiled as he stared at the Japanese symbols his father had carved into it. It was a single word: Righteous.

With a practiced flip of the knife, Yoshi clenched it in his fist.

Having spent six months with these people, he knew none of them were believers. They wouldn't be able to stomach being a Witness. They'd try to save themselves from the darkness, and in so doing, risk God's wrath.

He knew what he had to do.

～

Staring in awe through the portal above the administrator's workstation, Yoshi felt an exhilarating tingle as the wake of some unseen power gripped the space station tightly.

It had been two days since he'd received the Brotherhood's message. Dozens of audio messages had been broadcasting through the space station from JAXA, the Japanese Aerospace Exploration Agency. And when no responses were received, they kept trying to remotely recall the ship, which Yoshi repeatedly overrode.

Suddenly, the administrator's computer console let out an alarm. Yoshi glanced at the screen and scraped away the dried splatters of blood that blocked his view of the incoming message.

*** NASA EMERGENCY ALERT ***

All space exploration stations and personnel are recalled. Immediately return to Earth orbit under Emergency Protocol X-55. All other priorities are vacated. Confirm receipt.

With a feeling of disgust, Yoshi shook his head at the message and lectured the unhearing computer. "I'll never forsake my Lord. It's only through our faith that he will walk amongst us again. Anything else is utter damnation."

Glancing over his shoulder, Yoshi spotted the crumpled body of one of the space engineers.

"Blasphemy against our Lord cannot be tolerated."

Having strapped himself into the administrator's chair, Yoshi held strong in his faith, even though the space station seemed to be shaking to pieces. Sparks flew throughout the cabin, and the near-deafening sound of metal shrieking was nothing compared to what Yoshi saw through the portal.

Titan, the moon that the space station had been orbiting, had for some reason separated from Saturn's orbit. The moon, with the space station in tow, was now racing into the emptiness of space.

Yoshi stared in awe. "It's as if the finger of God is nudging me along a preordained path. I go where You lead."

No more than several hundred miles away, Saturn's former moon was being ripped apart.

The mountain-sized pieces of Titan swirled around a void in space. There were no stars, just blackness. Yet the space station rushed ever faster around this void, almost like water swirling around a bathtub's drain.

Praying for a sign, Yoshi watched as Titan ripped into ever-smaller chunks.

The space station approached ever closer. The groaning deepened as one of its arms sheared off with an explosive force, and all the lights blinked off.

The shuddering vibration became stronger as Yoshi experienced a sensation that was almost like going down a steep rollercoaster, while the station became part of the swirling vortex.

Just as another arm of the space station ripped from the main body, Yoshi gasped, and a sense of euphoria flushed through him.

As the station swirled rapidly around the mysterious void, the darkness began to shine.

Flares of scintillating light formed a coruscating shimmer across the center of the swirling maelstrom.

The g-forces were too great for Yoshi to pull in a breath, but inside him, his mind sang loudly as he watched the darkness bloom into a beautiful rainbow of colors.

Over the deafening sound of the chaos all around him, Yoshi yelled with his last breath, "I believe!"

Just then, the station ruptured and fell into the gaping maw of the black hole.

CHAPTER SEVEN

Dave hopped over a small crevice on the lunar surface as other workers laid out the last of the solar panels for the Alpine Valley solar farm. It was the largest solar grid they'd ever installed on the Moon and it promised to yield tens of gigawatts of power.

"Carter," the Mining Director's voice echoed loudly in Dave's space helmet. *"Schedule says we're due to connect Alpine Valley to the dielectric heaters tomorrow. How's it looking?"*

He panned his gaze across the field of panels, and they all looked uniformly seated. Not more than fifty feet from the solar farm was a foot-thick power cable that hadn't yet been connected to the panels.

"It looks like we'll be done today. Just a few dozen more panels to install and then we'll connect the power cable—"

Suddenly, a flash of brilliant white light erupted on the lunar surface several hundred yards away, followed almost immediately by a half-dozen more near-blinding flares. Dave nearly lost his balance as the ground vibrated heavily and the speaker in his helmet crackled to life. *"What the hell? A moonquake?"*

With Dave's heart racing, he motioned to the other workers to stay behind as he hopped toward the nearest impact site. "We just received a series of meteor strikes!"

Racing toward the impact site, Dave slowed as ejecta ranging from fist-sized rocks to pebbles began to fall all around him.

"Shit, is everyone okay? Any damage?"

He switched his comms unit to the engineering team on the lunar surface and asked, "You guys okay?"

"Roger, no injuries. But Carter, if you're talking to the Director, tell him we've got a butt-load of work to do. We've got debris all over the solar farm and need to clean it off. Also, it looks like we might have some damaged panels, and we need to run diagnostics on them. This'll push our schedule out at least twelve hours."

"Understood," Dave switched his comms unit back to the Moon base frequency as he stared at a forty-foot-wide depression in the lunar surface. Tiny rocks dribbled down the sides of the impact crater. "Everyone's fine," Dave announced, trying to keep the worry from his voice. "There was only minor damage, and it shouldn't impact our overall schedule by more than a single work shift."

Drenched with nervous sweat, he backed away from the crater and turned his gaze toward space. The impacts were almost certainly not a coincidence. It was the first in what he knew would likely be a hailstorm of impacts in the coming months.

Images of a catastrophic explosion sent Dave lurching up into a sitting position, and he barely suppressed a terrified yell as the dream left his heart racing. Blinking sleep from his eyes, Dave mentally grasped for the details of his nightmare, but the memories vanished like a wisp of smoke from a candle's extinguished flame. As his heart thudded heavily, Dave suddenly remembered that he'd forgotten to get himself assigned to tonight's drilling crew. He knew himself well enough to know that he was too much of a control freak to let them connect the thermal transfer pipes to the Alpine Valley solar farm without him.

Leaning back on his elbows, Dave yawned and glanced at the clock on his nightstand. From his bed, he stared out the six-inch-thick window and saw the familiar image of Earth sitting just above the horizon, a blue gem in the dark backdrop of space. As he stared at his birthplace, breathless anxiety washed over him. Dave's chest tightened, and he suddenly felt like a drowning victim, desperately searching for that last breath that would never come. Gripping the bed sheets, he began struggling to breathe and began feeling light-headed. Dave closed his eyes and willed himself to relax, knowing that there was only so much he could do. Feeling the muscles around his chest slowly loosen, he sucked in a breath of sweet, sterile air and wished it could all somehow be different.

Dave had known about the pending disaster for almost a decade. What had transpired since then had aged him more than he'd have liked to admit. He ran his hand through his tightly cropped Afro, knowing there weren't any grays up there yet; but he felt every one of his twenty-nine years. Deep down, Dave wasn't sure if he'd live long enough for his first gray hair. He'd done everything he could, but he wasn't sure that it would be enough.

Back when he'd lived on Earth, he'd become the youngest head of the International Science Foundation. It was the same year he'd been awarded the Nobel Prize for Physics at the "ripe old age" of nineteen, and that was only one year after having earned his second PhD from Caltech. Back then, the science journals had predicted he'd surpass the accomplishments of Einstein.

Nobody thought that anymore. He'd been disgraced and shut out of the ISF, likely forgotten by the vast majority of people who'd ever heard of him, and that was actually okay with him. He'd never sought fame—quite the opposite. Dave had tried saving the world and failed miserably.

It was now April 5th, 2066, the fourth-year anniversary of his arrival at Moon Base Crockett and the restart of his life.

The recurring nightmares about explosions reinforced Dave's nagging worry that the roughnecks might screw something up when attaching the dielectric heaters to the solar panels. He sighed and swung his legs out of bed.

With fatigue wearing on him, he knew he needed sleep, but he couldn't risk having his last chance for survival being messed up by other people's carelessness. None of the miners in the space colony knew about the approaching danger.

His thoughts drifted to the mining operation as he dressed, and Dave's mind raced through all of the possible ways the miners could screw something up catastrophically.

He shuddered as he whispered to himself, "The thermal energy couplers—if they don't connect them properly ..."

Walking underneath a newly-constructed, fifteen-hundred-foot-wide geodesic dome, Dave squinted through the clouds of dust floating in the low-gravity environment and heard the grunting of the roughnecks before he actually saw them.

As he approached the far end of the enclosure, some of the dust thinned, and he saw two teams working at once. One was busy drilling a new hole into the lunar surface, while the other team was in the process of slowly lowering an ever-lengthening metal pipe into a pre-drilled hole. The pipe was a dielectric heater whose sole purpose was to generate heat from electricity.

The foreman, one of the most senior members of the roughneck crew, glanced in his direction, wiped his sweaty, dirt-streaked face with his arm, and yelled, "Carter, what the hell you doing here? Your shift ain't starting for another three or four hours, so unless you're going to get your ass to work, get the hell out of our work space!"

Dave held his hands up and took a step forward. "I'll help out, where do you want me?"

With an amused shrug, the foreman pointed at a large pile of pipes and yelled, "Relieve Doran and help with the pipes."

Grabbing a six-foot-long section of twelve-inch metal pipe from the pile, Dave grunted as he lifted it up and threaded the end onto the portion of pipe sticking out of the hole. With a large metal wrench, another burly worker twisted clockwise on the upper-half of the pipe, connecting the two pieces and yelled, "Goop it!"

One of the crew slathered the pipe with a thick gray paste that was used as a thermal conductor, while another grunted as he pulled a three-foot-wide transparent sheet of graphene from a giant spool and wrapped it around the pipe.

The foreman yelled, "Make sure you get a good even seal with that graphene or I'll pound you something awful. That shit's supposed to help heat the underground rock to well over 1,000 degrees, and I don't want to see what'll happen if the boss man says the thermal transfer isn't working right."

As the pipe slowly turned and was lowered deeper into the hole by a hydraulic winch, one of the men slathered more goop on the pipe as the graphene rolled off the spool. Dave grabbed another pipe, heaved it up onto the top of the protruding pipe and the process repeated itself.

After only a few minutes, he was soaked with sweat from the back-breaking work, but he found peace in the monotonous but satisfying progress. He'd been doing this type of thing, side-by-side with many of these men for nearly four years. Little did the rest of the workers know that he, in fact, had invented the process for trapping excess solar energy and storing it as heat, deep within the Moon.

To them, he was just an anonymous mineral miner who mostly kept to himself, but on occasion got assigned to work as a roughneck by the Mining Director. As far as Dave knew, none of them realized or cared that he'd always managed to get himself assigned to the roughneck crew just as they were about to connect one of the thermal pipes to one of the multi-acre-sized solar panel farms splayed on the lunar surface.

The pile of pipes eventually dwindled, and just as the last one was lowered into the hole, the foreman waved his right arm and yelled, "Clamp her shut! We're at the bottom. Get the power cable ready, and the rest of you, stand back."

Dave, along with two others, began heaving on a thick power cable that was attached to the nearby acres of solar panels laid on the lunar surface. Even though the gravity was only one-sixth that of Earth, the cable was over a thousand pounds. He'd lost count of how many muscles he'd strained in the past, dragging a similarly cumbersome bundles of wires across the lunar surface.

Having placed himself at the front of the cable, Dave and the others worked smoothly as a team. They began lifting the end of the foot-thick power cable, and Dave steered their movement carefully as the cable reached a level height with the top of the dielectric heating pipe.

The foreman yelled out a warning: "Make sure you align that cable properly, or I'll fire each and every one of your asses that isn't burnt to a crisp."

With a grim smile, Dave grunted, "Okay, guys, just a little closer..."

Suddenly, the cable slammed into the heating pipe with a loud metallic *thunk* as the electromagnetic field around the end of the cable automatically sealed the connection.

Dave heard the familiar humming sound as tens of gigawatts of power began flowing into the eight-mile-long pipe. He breathed a sigh of relief.

The foreman yelled, "Jenkins and Stevens, you two seal the top of the hole. The rest of you clean up, and job well done. That'll be it for this shift, but we've got lots more drilling to do before this contract's over. Carter, you've still got a shift to pull in a couple hours, and I'm expecting you to be there."

Wiping the sweat off his face with his sleeve, Dave waved at the foreman and nodded.

"Sir," one of the men who'd been wrapping the graphene around the heater glanced worriedly at the near-empty spool. "We just received a huge shipment of the heater pipe, but we're running low on this graphene."

"I noticed that yesterday," Dave yelled. "I'll be talking to Hostetler later about that."

The foreman pointed at Dave with a serious expression. "Carter, you better make sure the Director understands, or I'll take it out of your hide. The last thing we need is a delay that screws up our drilling schedule."

Dave's fatigue overwhelmed any anxiety he'd been feeling. As he waved to the crew, he let out a yawn. He turned to grab a quick shower and go back to his warm bed, knowing that he'd have to have a long talk with his friend about heading back to Earth.

As Dave snuck back into bed, Bella squirmed, wrapping the sheets around her and snuggling next to him for warmth. Looking down at her pale face, full lips and vivid red hair, she was the answer to any man's dreams—but she was fragile, and some had called her mentally unstable. He knew her for what she was: a genius with intelligence that in some ways went beyond his comprehension. The irony of it all was that he'd met her in the Walter Reed Inpatient Psychiatry Ward. It had been a rough time for them both.

With the tips of his fingers, Dave gently stroked Bella's cheek as she slept. Even though he'd first met her just over four years ago, it seemed like only yesterday.

Everyone believed that, as the head of the ISF, he'd managed to squander trillions of dollars, but Dave had known what he was doing. He'd kept his projects under wraps until he had no other choice but to reveal them. Dave hadn't believed that anyone would be able to comprehend the gravity of the situation the world faced, yet their only chance would be if he acted preemptively. He couldn't prove what he'd known, at least not then.

When he was finally forced to tell the stuffed shirts in Washington what he was doing and why, they'd freaked out. He couldn't be sure whether they didn't believe him or didn't *want* to believe him. Either way, they weren't going to let him continue, regardless of the stakes. Dave had decided to stop repeating himself at some point during the day and night interrogations; it was as if they were deaf to anything he told them, so he purposefully went mute. He was done with them, and for a few weeks, he didn't really care what happened to him or the rest of the world. When they'd pressed him harder about the details of what he'd done, and why he'd been in communication with North Korea, all they got out of him was silence. After all, none of them believed him, nor understood, even when he told them the truth about absolutely everything. It was pointless talking to any of the government imbeciles anymore, and based on some of their questions—asking if he'd somehow faked all of his prior accomplishments—it was obvious to him that some of them even harbored racist beliefs.

What? A black kid who grew up in foster care couldn't possibly be smarter than they were? Despite his humanist upbringing, Dave had moments when he truly wanted some of these people to suffer an agonizing fate.

After weeks of interrogations, in which Dave had failed to utter a single word, they decided to commit him to a government-controlled psychiatric facility. That was how he ended up at Walter Reed, a place normally reserved for active-duty military or members of their families.

There he'd first spied Bella, sitting in the corner of the activity center. It was a thirty-by-fifty-foot room, painted a sickly yellow with a variety of chairs, activity tables for playing games, and a lot of open floor space. It had a single door that was monitored by a bored-looking guard, but people were free to wander in and out during the day.

Bella kept to herself, a beautiful woman in her early twenties, yet nobody gave her a second glance. Most of the patients in the ward were silent and kept to themselves, but some wandered into the room to play cards or talk to each other.

But Dave wasn't interested in socializing. He ignored everyone as he sat in the corner and tried to lose himself in his nightmarish thoughts of what was coming. However, something about the woman on the other side of the room intrigued him.

At first, he'd occasionally glance at her, but eventually, he found himself staring, drinking in her every detail. Gone were his nagging worries of the impending apocalypse. His mind was lost in her bright-green eyes, red hair, and pale porcelain-like complexion—she was breathtaking. However, Dave noticed one strange thing: she held tightly to a dog-eared book that never seemed to leave her side.

Day after day, she'd carry the same book. Even though he'd never seen her open it, she clutched it tightly.

On the third day of his hospitalization, a nurse walked into the activity room to deliver some medication to one of the patients. As she handed the patient his medicine, Dave heard the clear, almost bell-like sound of the red-head's voice.

"Thirty-three thirty."

The nurse looked to her right, met the redhead's gaze, who was motioning at her mouth, and smiled. "Yes, Jane, it's almost time for food."

Dave blinked in astonishment. One patient sitting near him made a dismissive noise and chuckled under his breath. "Pfft. That crazy girl speaks in numbers? I wonder what sixty-nine means in her language." Some of the people within earshot laughed.

Dave stood, not wanting to be anywhere near the others but also not wanting to return to his room, which held only a hospital bed and a chair. He scanned the room, looking for a place to be alone. Finding none, he glanced at the redheaded woman, and before he even realized what he was doing, he found himself strolling toward her.

As he approached, she frowned and glared at him. He sat next to her. She said, "Nine two-hundred-fifteen four eight."

Dave stared at her, uncertain what in the world that could mean. He glanced at the book she was holding, but she clutched it tighter to her chest, stood, and left the room with a huff.

It took him a few days to solve the puzzle, but the key ended up being her book. She was carrying a dog-eared copy of *The Hobbit*, which he'd also managed to acquire a copy of from the hospital's sparse library.

Dave read it cover-to-cover and realized that the code he was trying to crack was deviously simple, yet profoundly difficult. It required memorization of every word of the book, along with each word's position on the page.

Luckily, Dave had an eidetic, near-perfect memory, so when he recalled what the red-haired girl had said to the nurse, "thirty-three thirty," his mind alighted on the word "food," the thirtieth word on page thirty-three.

When she'd said, "Nine two-hundred-fifteen four eight" as he sat down next to her, she was clearly telling him, *"Stay away."*

A smile crossed his lips as he left his room, armed with the key to the girl's speech. The nurse manning the nurse's station glanced in his direction, but didn't stop him or bother to ask him anything. After all, he was the "genius who'd lost his mind and gone mute."

He studied the patients' names written on the whiteboards at the entrance to each room, and finally found "Jane Doe" scribbled on one of the rooms.

Dave lightly knocked on the door, even though it was ajar. He wasn't certain if she was in the room. He heard a flush, and moments later, the red-haired beauty stepped from her bathroom wearing a white, shapeless cotton sleeping gown. Her bright-green eyes flashed a warning as she growled, "Twelve one-hundred-sixty-nine!"

Leave!

He shook his head and tried to give her his most endearing smile. "Two one-hundred-ninety-four four one-hundred-ninety-eight eighteen one-hundred-fifty-one?"

Can we talk?

She blinked at him, her mouth hanging open.

Dave continued speaking haltingly in the numbered phrases, as he searched for the appropriate words and their locations. "I think you're special."

Her stunned expression melted away as the first hint of a smile crossed her lips. She motioned for Dave to sit.

For the first time since Dave had been in middle school, warmth crept up his neck, and he fought against the shyness that had plagued him as a child. She hopped up onto her bed, sat cross-legged and happily began spewing what seemed like an endless stream of numbers.

Now, Dave pulled his gaze away from Bella and surveyed their simple lodging. The relatively comfortable quarters were fifteen-by-ten-feet long and consisted of a bed, a small desk, and a set of drawers for their clothes. Everything else at the Moon colony was communal. It was a simple life, but one he hoped to perpetuate for as long as he could.

He shivered as the air vent in the ceiling clicked, sending a breath of the temperature-controlled air stirring through the room. They kept the air in Moon Base Crockett a few degrees lower than Dave would have liked, but he understood the rationale, and in fact it was on Bella's suggestion that he'd convinced the facility's managers to lower the temperature to sixty-five throughout the colony. The less energy it took to maintain life support, the more energy they could store in the core of the previously lifeless Moon.

With Bella's left leg flung across his waist, Dave settled back into the comfort of his bed and sighed contentedly. The warmth of her body against his was something he'd never imagined for himself when he was younger. He'd always imagined himself alone, with others intimidated by him. But Bella was anything but scared of him. She didn't see him as a freak, or some unfathomable intellectual deity. In fact, Dave felt awed by Bella in almost every way. Sure, she was unusual, but he'd grown up being told how unusual he was, too, so to him, Bella was a beautiful enigma. An enigma that he simply accepted without feeling compelled to unravel.

Bella's entire life was cloaked in mystery. She had no memories before the hospital's psych ward, and even her identity and language had become lost in some dark recess of her mind. Not having an identity, she'd assigned herself a new one. The only named female in the book she'd been carrying as a lifeline to her lost humanity was Belladonna Took, so that was the name she'd assigned herself. Dave smiled and kissed Bella's forehead as she slept. "I'm glad you didn't name yourself Gloin."

Dave glanced at the digital clock on the nightstand and closed his eyes. He had another two hours before he needed to get back to work.

He'd made a network of allies within Moon Base Crockett, people he'd trusted from the ISF and a few others. There was so much to do and so little time to do it.

Lying in bed, the dread fingers of guilt clamped around Dave's chest, making breathing difficult. He knew there was no choice if he wanted to save the lives on the Moon base. Years ago, when he thought he'd still be able to save the planet, Dave had spent a huge fortune stashing away the supplies he knew they'd need back on Earth. However, now that saving Earth wasn't possible anymore, Dave needed those supplies if he was going to do anything about saving the Moon.

As Dave closed his eyes, he silently prayed for the billions who would be torn apart, and wished that things could somehow have been different.

CHAPTER EIGHT

Having already dressed, Bella glanced at the mirror and nodded approvingly. Always dressing for comfort, she'd worn the baggy grey-pants-and-shirt combination that attracted the least attention from others. She hated it when people stared at her; it made her feel less like a real person and more like a freak.

She turned her attention to Dave as he dressed for work, and even though the room was dimly lit, she noticed his muscles flexing beneath his chocolate-colored skin. He'd had a medium-sized build when she first met him, but unlike most people who waste away in low gravity, Dave had grown larger from all the manual labor.

The thought of touching people, or worse yet, being touched by others, made Bella's skin crawl with revulsion. She knew it wasn't normal, but try as she might, Bella had never grown comfortable in the presence of others until she met Dave.

Having been with him for so long had awakened a comfort she couldn't have imagined with another human being. With a smile, she walked toward him and trailed her fingertips across his naked back. Even though Bella felt like a bit of a freak, she could touch Dave and feel what it was like to be normal.

Most of her past life was shrouded in the unknown; she couldn't remember anything before waking up at the hospital over four years ago. When she'd met Dave, everything changed; it wasn't just having to relearn how to speak so that others could understand her. Through him, regaining a glimmer of her lost humanity seemed possible. Yet Bella still knew that there was something inherently different about her.

Touching Dave made something inside her feel good. It felt right. And yet making physical contact with other people was a nausea-inducing struggle for her. Bella felt guilty at times. She knew that people looked at her with concern when she backed away from them. Even the idea of brushing past people made her shiver with disgust, but touching Dave sent a tingle of emotions through her that she couldn't properly explain. It was like how she reacted when she heard beautiful music. It excited her.

Being with Dave helped her relate to the world around her, and she couldn't bear to let that connection go. She'd tried to distance herself from him in the past, but she couldn't do it. Even though Bella knew that she was very different from everyone else, it didn't matter as long as Dave was around. She needed him, and sometimes, she could help him do things that he couldn't figure out on his own. It was a good match.

Dave turned to her as he buttoned his shirt and smiled. "Are you ready?"

Bella reached toward him, ran her fingers along the backs of his arms, and felt a pang of apprehension as she asked, "Is today the day?"

With a wink, he wrapped his arm around her waist and kissed her on the cheek. "It'll be okay, trust me."

As Dave escorted her from their room, she tightened her grip on his large, calloused hand. Bella had always trusted him, and over time, she'd learned the words that she knew had a magical effect on him. Those words that set him at ease and made him feel better. She leaned her head against his shoulder and whispered, "I love you."

The cacophony coming from the cafeteria made it hard for Bella to concentrate. She sat next to Dave on one of the empty bench seats, and across from them was Jeff Hostetler, the gray-haired chief of operations for the Moon colonies. Dave leaned forward and whispered to his former ISF employee.

"Jeff, I know we're behind schedule on the drilling, but it won't do us any good unless we retrieve more spools of graphene. They're not just for the elevators. Without more graphene for the thermal conductors, we'll be digging for no reason whatsoever."

Jeff, a fifty-something-year-old former Section Chief of the ISF, had a worried expression etched on his weathered face. "I just don't understand why you have to be the one that goes. All the government folks are excited about the minerals we're uncovering here, and I can explain away the space elevators that you've installed. But some of the rest ... I'm really on a limb here. I can't explain half of what we're doing here with the thermal storage, and I know that I'm totally over my head. I trust you, but I have people I need to answer to. I really need you here to help me guide that part of the operations, because if something goes nuts, I won't have a fucking clue what to do. Why can't someone else go?"

Bella studied the older man, who looked somewhat panicked, and wondered what it would be like to be so afraid. Watching Dave's facial expression, she sensed his growing sympathy for Hostetler. For a long time, she'd tried to understand some of the different emotions that Dave felt, but it just seemed as if she wasn't made to feel the same things. For her, people either excited her, like Dave did, or they felt somewhat like an anchor, almost as if they drained energy from her. She'd tried to understand others, but that wasn't something she'd yet mastered.

"Jeff, I have to be the one going because the place where I've stashed this stuff has a biometric lock keyed to me and me alone." Dave smiled and motioned Jeff closer, so their faces were less than a foot apart. "Listen, this whole operation is really simple. We've got hundreds of square miles of photovoltaic film, spread across this side of the Moon, gathering energy for us. As you know, it's hundreds of times what the base needs for operations, and the excess is being stored as thermal energy within the core of the Moon."

"Dave, I'm not an idiot, I understand all that. Heck, I even understand that we've already got hundreds of banks of batteries with enough energy stored for years of operations. We've even placed them evenly along the circumference of the Moon, like you'd asked. What I really don't understand is what you're planning on doing with even more of that graphene ribbon. Why do we need so much energy? From what I can figure, we've dumped the equivalent of nearly a thousand years' worth of the Moon base's energy requirements into the center of this big rock. I don't understand why we need to continue doing that, and even if we *do* need it, how in the world are we going to be able to use it, and for what? Is this some plan you've got buried in your head for somehow terraforming the Moon? Eventually, I'll need to give answers that make sense to the bean counters when they ask."

"Trust me, there's a big plan for it all, but I can't share it quite yet." Dave pointed at Jeff's mug of lukewarm coffee. He tilted his head toward the box-like thermal tuner, located at the end of their table. "Jeff, humor me and warm your coffee to 180 degrees."

Remembering one of Dave's lessons from when they'd first arrived on the Moon colony, Bella smiled. She knew what Dave was about to show Jeff.

Without any memories prior to waking up in the hospital, Bella couldn't recall ever having gone to school, but that hadn't stopped her from learning. Dave had taken the time to explain basic things to her, which had at first baffled her. But he only ever had to explain it once. She vividly remembered sitting at this table nearly four years earlier when Dave explained the internal workings of a magnetron, microwaves, ambient energy motors, and their purpose on the Moon.

Bella had assumed that everyone learned things the way she did. She remembered every second since the moment she woke in the hospital. Every word she'd ever heard spoken, Bella could repeat verbatim. It had been a shock to her when she realized that most people couldn't.

Dave motioned once again toward the metal device sitting on the end of the table.

Jeff placed his mug in the thermal tuner, adjusted the knob to 180 degrees and tapped "start" on the tuner's control panel. The light within the box immediately turned on as the mug slowly rotated.

"As you know, thermal tuners have been around for a while now. Raising the temperature is simply a matter of exciting the molecules of your coffee. Thus, they're gaining heat. Infrared temperature sensors tell the machine when to stop—"

"Dave," Jeff interrupted, giving him a lopsided grin. "I'm a good bit older than you, and remember how a microwave works."

The tuner beeped, and Bella noticed the steam rising from the now-heated coffee.

"All right Jeff, now let's lower the temperature of your coffee to forty degrees."

Jeff's eyebrows furrowed in confusion, but he did as he was asked. The moment the elder scientist hit "start," Bella heard a gush of air within the tuner.

"Back when we were both at the ISF, I was staring at a thermal tuner not much different from this one. As you know, the concept of heating things in such a device had been around for almost eighty years before someone decided to be clever. Previously the concept of laser cooling had only been used for quantum physics research, and all it took was for a scientist who'd just burnt their tongue drinking coffee to ask themselves, 'If I can lower the temperature of a single atom to near-zero, why couldn't I do something similar to reduce the average temperature of my coffee?'"

The thermal tuner beeped. Dave retrieved Jeff's mug, stuck his finger in the coffee, and smiled. "It's ice cold."

"Yes," Jeff frowned at his coffee, setting it aside as Dave wiped his finger on a napkin. "But what's your point?"

"Well, it was almost ten years ago when I was sitting in my office at the ISF, after having also burnt my tongue on some too-hot coffee, when I began to wonder, 'We use lots of energy to cool something, but couldn't we instead harness all the latent kinetic energy?' That's when I began to think about Nikola Tesla's ambient energy motor. At the time he'd proposed it, the material sciences weren't capable of doing what needed to be done. But with the advances of the last 150 years, I decided to give it a shot. With the thermal conductivity of graphene and high efficiency engines, I was able to get something working."

Jeff's eyes widened, and a look of understanding washed over him. "Oh, so you're going to use the Moon's core as a big battery?"

Bella didn't need to see Dave nod to know that Jeff was right.

Jeff leaned closer. "But what in the world are we going to need so much power for?"

Dave pursed his lips and Bella knew that he wasn't ready to share their secret.

"Jeff, just believe me. We'll need every drop of that power, and more." Dave glanced at Bella. "Right?"

She knew exactly how much energy had been stored, how much of it would seep up to the surface and be lost into space. As her mind stirred, she calculated the time left between now and the planned departure date. "By the time we begin, we'll have accumulated ten months of thermal reserves before the bubble collapses," she said. "We'll need no less than nine months."

Dave hitched his thumb toward Bella. "You hear that, Jeff? As it is, we're cutting it way too close."

Jeff leaned back, a puzzled expression on his face. "Bubble?"

Shaking his head, Dave plopped his hand onto Jeff's in reassurance. "Trust me. We need to keep going as planned, and I need a crew to help me retrieve the rest of the supplies. We've only got eight months before things start going to hell."

With a sigh, Jeff roughly clasped Dave's hand. "Fine. You've got it. I know there's a lot you're holding back, and I'm sure it's for a good reason. Just promise me that this'll all be for the best."

With their hands clasped, Dave pulled Jeff up as he stood and patted Jeff's shoulder with his free hand. "I promise you that anyone who stays up here will be infinitely better off than the poor saps down there on Earth."

A twinge of guilt washed through Bella as she thought of the

Earth's fate. She replayed in her mind's eye what Dave had described to her, and the image of the Earth being ripped asunder sent a shiver racing through her.

Everyone down there would die, and even though the people she'd dealt with on Earth had all made her miserable, Bella didn't like the idea of them dying. Secretly, she wished there was another way.

CHAPTER NINE

Sitting on a hard-backed chair in the center of the Oval Office, Margaret Hager stared at Greg Hildebrand expectantly as he took his seat on one of the sofas facing her. "Okay, Greg, out with it. What do the country's finest minds have to say about conjuring up a solution to the Indigo problem?"

A flash of discomfort showed on Greg's face as he withdrew a sheet of paper from within his suit jacket and cleared his throat. "Madam President, I gathered two dozen of our top research scientists, and we've spent the last five days almost nonstop trying to lay plans for a reasonable skunkworks solution, given the limited time we have left. We came up with a few scenarios, but ... none of them are ideal."

Margaret motioned impatiently. "I don't need you politicking the answer. Just spit it out."

"Well, the first solution involves our fleet of shuttles. We have thirty in-service shuttles, each with a cargo bay large enough to sustain forty people for about six months. It was thought that as the danger approached, we could launch the roughly one-thousand people out of the danger zone—"

"And then what?" Margaret asked skeptically.

"Well, that's just it. I suppose it depends on what's left after the passage of the black hole. But given the likelihood of total annihilation, I'm afraid there'd be nowhere to go for those in the shuttle."

"That's absolutely ridiculous!" Margaret snarled, feeling a sense of revulsion. "They'd get the pleasure of watching everyone die, and then they'd slowly starve to death. I hope you have something better than that."

"We have another possibility," Greg nodded. "Again, only nominally better." He took a deep breath and consulted the sheet of paper gripped tightly in his hand. "Some of the scientists speculated that it might be possible to spread a large series of rocket-like engines on the surface of the Moon and break it from Earth's orbit. With the help of the existing Moon base's growth labs, it could be self-sustaining for upwards of one-thousand people, given the current Moon base facilities."

Margaret pursed her lips. "Okay, but what are the risks? Also you said it *might* be possible. Well, is it? Can it or can't it be done?"

"Well, there was a lot of arguing back and forth about whether or not we even have sufficiently powerful engines that can do the job. The scientists gave it a ten-percent chance of even being possible, if we had the necessary engines. We don't, and it's uncertain if we could make enough in the time we'd need them. However, even if we could get it all put together, the downside is that if the black hole ends up destroying the sun or there's some other type of explosive reaction to the sun's interaction with the black hole, there's almost nothing we could do."

With a shake of her head, Margaret sat back and frowned. "Is that it? Are those my choices?"

"Well, the only other choice isn't one I even wanted to mention. But there's enough underground tunnels strewn throughout the country that we could bring millions of people underground. It would probably save them from the barrage of impacts that we'd likely receive. But in the end, we'll either get swallowed up by the black hole, or get thrown out of orbit and eventually freeze to death."

"That's a ridiculous choice," Margaret waved dismissively. "So you're telling me that there's really no viable choices other than finding Doctor Holmes, our boy genius, and hoping to God that Doctor Patel was right and he had some kind of plan?"

With a sneer, Greg exclaimed, "There's no way that Holmes could have an answer to the Indigo situation—"

"Damn it, Greg!" Margaret snapped. "It's as if you don't *want* there to be a solution." She leaned forward in her chair and jabbed her index finger in his direction. "I don't care what personal shit you're going through, I want you to get over it and help find this Doctor Holmes. Do you understand me?"

With a grim expression, Greg nodded. "Understood."

"Dismissed." Margaret waved him away, trying to keep her nausea under control.

As Greg walked out of the Oval Office, Margaret turned to the old man who'd been sitting silently in the corner of the room, watching. "Doug, I want you to organize a status briefing for Indigo right away. I also want profiles on all of the players involved. I need psych screens and background data. I need to know what type of folks these scientists are that I'm dealing with."

Hopping up from his chair, the spry seventy-something-year-old man nodded and announced in a loud gravelly voice, "I'll make all the arrangements."

Doug strode purposefully out of the room as Margaret looked up at the ceiling and silently prayed for a miracle.

"Madam President, we already deployed the National Guard, but as I was saying, I wouldn't ask on behalf of my state if I didn't think it were necessary. These protests are draining our resources, and I'm afraid we might have real panic on our hands if it gets out of control."

The speakerphone fell silent in the Oval Office, and Margaret weighed the tone of the New York Governor's voice.

He was worried.

She glanced across her desk at her Chief of Staff, and he stared back at her with an inscrutable expression.

Leaning back in the leather armchair, she closed her eyes. "Listen Bill, I'll talk to the Secretary about getting some folks out there to help. I'll have someone call your office with next steps, but we need to keep the peace, no matter what."

"I heard something about protests in North Carolina that sounded a lot like what we're experiencing. Is there something going on that I need to know about?"

"Nothing's going on, but we'll help. Listen, let me get off the phone and I'll get things mobilized. Is there anything else?"

"No, ma'am, and thank you."

The phone line disconnected, and Margaret frowned at the wrinkled man sitting across from her.

"Doug, this is getting out of hand."

"Well," Doug responded in almost a whisper, "this is probably going to spread. Did you want me to arrange conversations with the other governors?"

"Yes, and soon. Let's keep this quiet, but I want to meet with them all at the same time and disclose what we're facing. Some drastic things will need to be done."

"I'll find a secure location for the disclosure," he said. "Anything else you need me to arrange?"

"Get Walt on the line. We'll need help trying to bottle this up, you got me?"

The gray-haired man stood, nodded, and left without a word.

Margaret frowned and muttered, "Indigo must have been leaked."

CHAPTER TEN

Stryker stared across the table at Emma, his six-year-old, as she practiced her poker face over a handful of Uno cards. "So, what's your move?"

She stuck the tip of her tongue out of the side of her mouth, concentrating on the cards in her hand, and then with a devious grin she placed a "Draw Four" onto the discard pile. "Sorry, Daddy. I can't let you win. "

Groaning dramatically, Stryker drew four cards as Isaac, the eight-year-old, pointed at his sister and asked, "What color?"

"Blue."

Isaac huffed with disappointment as he drew a card, and then another, and then another. "Darn," he exclaimed, as he drew yet another card.

"Isaac, language…."

"But Dad, it's not even a bad word." Isaac finally stopped drawing and placed a blue "two" on the discard pile.

"It's close enough, and I don't like it."

"Uno!" Emma declared, as she placed a "wild" card on the discard pile.

Hearing the front door open, Stryker turned to see Lainie come in the house, right on time.

"Mommy!" Emma's high-pitched voice rang across the townhome. "I'm about to win at Uno!" She turned to Stryker and pointed at her wild card. "I pick blue again."

"You're not winning," Isaac retorted. "I've got something up my sleeve."

Stryker discarded a blue "skip" card and Isaac moaned, "Dad!"

With a brilliant smile of triumph, Emma placed another "Draw Four" card on the discard pile and yelled, "I win!"

"Congratulations to the winners and losers," Lainie declared as she walked into the living room. "Now go upstairs and bring down your overnight bags. Nana and Poppa said that they got snow last night, so if we get there in time, maybe you guys can play in it."

Stryker smiled as the kids raced upstairs, excited about a weekend with their grandparents.

Lainie plopped herself onto the chair Isaac had been sitting on and smiled. "How are you doing?"

He shrugged, and breathed in the lilac scent of her body wash. "Things are fine. How about you? Is the accounting gig keeping you busy?"

She laughed. "You know better. It's the beginning of April, I'm swamped."

Hearing her laugh stirred warm memories that he tried to forget.

"So, Poconos this weekend?"

"Yup, my parents rented a cabin. Dad was going to do some kind of cookout and roast marshmallows and stuff with the kids." With a slight hint of a frown, she asked, "Do you know anything about those protests from last week? I heard a cop got shot or stabbed or something."

"It was overblown by the media. It was nothing," Stryker lied. He didn't like lying to her, but the fact was, she wouldn't understand. Hell, *he* barely understood what had happened. All he knew was some kind of chemical had been put into his coffee. He tested clean, so it was probably put in the mug while he'd gone to the bathroom.

The doorbell rang, and Stryker hopped up from his chair.

He opened the door and a mail courier greeted him with, "I've got a registered letter for a Lieutenant Jonathan Stryker."

Stryker stared at the unmarked envelope and signed for it.

Walking back into the living room, he pulled open the sealed flap and extracted the typewritten pages. "Oh, shit."

"What is it?" Lainie asked.

He scanned the papers and frowned. "I'm being reactivated."

Lainie stood with a concerned expression. "What does that mean?"

"Well, it looks like I've got to report in, but that's weird. They're not assigning me to my regular reserve unit. I'm being assigned to the 504th out of Lewis-McChord." Stryker felt an electric thrill rush through him. What in the world could be happening that needed him to report to the MP battalion in Washington State? "Lainie, this has me reporting there in two days. It must be some kind of crisis or something. Can I ask a favor?"

With a stone-faced expression, she took in a deep breath. "What?"

"I don't know how long I'll be gone, but would you mind staying here with the kids? And besides, Jessica and you get along well, right?"

Lainie stared daggers at him. "You've asked me before, and I told you. It's stuff like this that separated us." She glanced up at the stairs, where the kids were yelling at each other about some nonsense. "I have to help get the kids ready."

Giving Stryker a hard poke to his chest, Lainie spoke through gritted teeth. "You tell the kids that you aren't going to be around. I'm not doing it."

"I will, but can you—"

"Yes, I'll bring some of my stuff over after this weekend." She glared at him and pointed upstairs. "Go tell them. And after they're done crying, I'll somehow manage to pick up the pieces ... again."

With his stomach in knots and Lainie still glaring at him, Stryker turned to the stairs and felt like a complete shit.

Dave held tightly to Bella's hand as the shuttle jolted, due to turbulence, while descending through the clouds. His heart thudded heavily in his chest, even though the other sixty miners in the passenger compartment seemed unfazed. Sitting directly opposite of him were the four men Jeff Hostetler had assigned to him. He wasn't sure exactly what the Director of the mining operations had told them, but their job was simple: help drag supplies back up to the Moon base.

Knowing that the government probably still wanted him, it was dangerous for Dave to be back on Earth. But he had no choice in the matter. If they were going to stand a chance at avoiding impending doom, Dave needed the spools of graphene that were hidden in a nearby ISF-owned warehouse.

The lights blinked in the shuttle passenger bay as the speaker on the wall announced, *"Final approach into Cape Canaveral, landing on runway 33 in two minutes."*

The shuttle tilted as they glided into position, and Dave glanced at the men who Jeff had assigned to him. They were large-muscled brutes who served as members of the colony's security force. He wondered whether they were chosen for their ability to haul cargo or to keep him safe; either way, they were a welcome sight.

He replayed the plan in his head and knew that time was of the essence. They needed to take advantage of the night, load the cargo, and head back up to the Moon before anyone even knew what had happened. That gave him only twelve hours.

Pursing his lips, Dave focused on the task and whispered, "It's going to be a tight schedule."

As Dave peered out the passenger window of the Moon shuttle, the sun hung low in the west above Cape Canaveral. The shuttle had just landed, and it took only minutes before they coasted to a stop and everyone began to queue at the exit. As the door opened and Dave stepped onto the escalator leading to the tarmac below, he savored the warm, salty breeze coming off the coast. Unlike the odorless and highly-filtered air circulating throughout the Moon colonies, this air smelled of the ocean. Even the pungent smell of the ozone that accompanied the shuttle reminded him of the chlorine from the NYC public pool when he was a kid. He whispered to nobody in particular, "I miss these smells."

"I wish I could remember smelling this before," Bella said, and then sighed.

Dave wrapped his arm around her waist as they left the shadow of the large Moon transport. It had been nearly four years since he'd been to Earth, and even though he worked out regularly on the Moon, he acutely felt his weight as they walked the quarter mile between the shuttle and the Arrivals Gate. "Bella, are you okay with the weight change?"

She nodded as she flicked away a strand of her red hair that had blown into her face. "I'm not feeling too fat, if that's what you're asking."

Just as Dave was about to protest, she nudged him and smiled. "I'm teasing you. I feel fine. It's a little weird going from twenty-five pounds on the Moon to almost one hundred and fifty here, but that's why you've had me wear weight belts up there, right?"

"Well, it's so we can keep up our bone density and not waste away while we're on the moon."

As they approached the Arrivals Gate, a man jogged toward the line of recently disembarked passengers. Wearing an ISF badge, the man approached Dave and motioned for him to halt. "Joshua Carter, can I please see your identification?"

Dave nodded and handed the pudgy, red-faced man his falsified passport.

The ISF normally didn't involve themselves with immigration activities, but when the Moon base had been established almost twenty years earlier, transport to and from the Moon became their domain. As the ISF officer studied his passport, he noted, "Mister Carter, you must have friends in high places, because I was asked to find you and imme-diately escort you and your guests through customs." He glanced at

Bella and the other members of their party. "Can I see the rest of your party's paperwork as well?"

Bella and the four rather beefy members of the security crew handed the man their passports, as the other passengers from the shuttle walked past them toward the Arrivals Gate.

The ISF officer waved a handheld scanner over the passports. Seconds passed, and a green light flashed on the scanner. The officer nodded, but just as he returned the passport to Dave, he paused. His eyes met Dave's, and his mouth hung open with a stunned expression. "Holy shit, it's you!"

A chill ran up Dave's spine. Suddenly, the man blurted, "I always believed in you even when they said ... never mind. Sir, it's an honor."

Before Dave could respond, the officer cleared his throat, returned the rest of the passports, and asked, "Did any of you have baggage you needed to retrieve from Baggage Claim?"

"No," Dave shook his head. "Officer Kirkpatrick, we're all traveling light today."

At first the ISF official appeared surprised, and then he glanced at his own badge with his name printed on it and smiled. He nodded and motioned for them to follow. "I'll take you through the diplomatic wing. Nobody will see you, and I'll get you where you need to go."

"Officer Kirkpatrick, it would be much better if you kept what you knew to yourself, the—"

The officer turned abruptly with a look of determination. "I swear on my children that your presence here will go to my grave. I simply feel better knowing that you're still around, and I have all the faith in the world that you'll do what's best for us all. Sir, if I might add, you still have a lot of support in the ISF, despite all that's been said."

Dave placed his hand on the man's shoulder and gave him a light squeeze. "I appreciate that. The quicker we finish some things here, the better."

Officer Kirkpatrick nodded curtly, turned, and set a vigorous pace toward a lonely-looking door that led into the Arrivals building.

Holding Bella's hand as they raced after the officer, the burden of guilt weighed heavily on Dave. He knew what fate had in store for

Officer Kirkpatrick and everyone else on Earth. That nagging seed of shame grew within him, reminding him that he was letting the world down.

Unfortunately, there was nothing he could do about it. Earth was doomed.

Scanning the desolate beaches of Rum Cay, a remote island in the Bahamas, Dave searched the darkness as the rest of the crew disembarked from the motorboat. The tropical breeze was like a warm breath carrying the scent of the ocean, while the sound of waves crashing on the beach competed with the squawking of a flock of seagulls overhead. The birds seemed quite agitated, clearly unused to nighttime invaders disturbing their nesting site.

Glancing up at the annoyed birds, Dave whispered, "I'm sorry to wake you guys, but it can't be avoided."

It was almost midnight and the crescent Moon hovering above the horizon gave just enough light for Dave to spot a darkened building in the distance.

With Bella lightly holding onto his arm, Dave motioned silently for the men to follow as he stepped off the lonely wooden pier and began trudging up the sand embankment.

After a few minutes of climbing, a square-shaped warehouse emerged from the shadows near the top of the hill. It was larger than Dave remembered; the nearest wall was almost one-hundred-feet long. Spotting a side entrance, Dave led his entourage to a metal door that seemed small for the fifteen-foot-tall building. The stone-like stucco that covered the exterior acted as camouflage during the day, but underneath the thin veneer, he knew that the warehouse was constructed like a fortress.

The ISF's warehouses were often located in remote places, and when Dave had commissioned their construction, he'd focused on preventing unauthorized access. Composed largely of steel-reinforced concrete, these buildings contained millions upon millions of dollars worth of supplies, but it wasn't the cost of the materials that worried him. Most people had no idea that the fate of the world rested on having available the material that was stored in the ISF warehouses scattered throughout the world. Now, much of that material would be used solely for saving the Moon.

Flipping open a rectangular weatherproof box attached to the metal door's frame, Dave revealed a keypad onto which he typed a long sequence of numbers. Just as he pressed the last digit, a green LED lit, followed immediately by the sound of a heavy lock disengaging. The well-oiled hinges swung inward as old-style fluorescent lights flickered to life along the ceiling.

Glancing over his shoulder, Dave motioned everyone to come closer. "Let's get this over with quickly."

The shadows lurking throughout the warehouse vanished as the lights grew brighter. Long rows of cryptically labeled wooden crates were arranged throughout the building. There were hundreds of crates with labels such as "ISF-BT10000," which Dave knew were 10,000 amp-hour batteries. These industrial high-capacity batteries had been designed to be used as part of DefenseNet.

Dave smirked as he thought about DefenseNet. The whole concept behind it had been a ruse that he'd used with the governmental types. Everyone could understand the concept of needing to destroy or nudge a wayward asteroid that threatened Earth. Even though many of the components he needed to deal with the impending danger were the same, he would never have been able to gain approval for what he'd been planning. The ultimate solution was beyond most people's ability to accept.

Dave strode quickly to the far end of the warehouse. He felt barely aware of the footsteps of his companions as they rushed to keep up with him. At the far end of the warehouse, a brushed steel wall greeted him. Scanning the expanse of the blank metal wall, he nodded, knowing what was hidden behind it. He'd built the vault to house some key components that had proven oh-so-difficult to produce in mass quantity.

Dave looked up at the corner of the warehouse ceiling, then panned his gaze across thirteen of the soundproof ceiling tiles. From that position, he trailed his focus down the brushed-steel wall until he locked onto a blank space directly in front of him. Placing his hand on the cold metal, Dave felt a tingle of electricity, just as a beam of green light shot out from the wall. Squinting through the uncomfortable brightness of the scanner, he remained still until he felt a click under his hand.

With a sigh of relief, Dave gave the metal wall a slight push. Slowly, the half-ton door noiselessly swiveled, revealing another room, and what he'd ultimately come for.

Stacked from floor to ceiling were giant spools of graphene ribbon. Previously, graphene had only been manufactured in small quantities. Only through sheer luck had Dave finally stumbled onto a practical means to mass-produce it.

He glanced over his shoulder, past Bella and the burly men, to the assortment of advanced batteries, generators, and engines strewn throughout the warehouse. Unlike the graphene, which represented years' worth of manufacturing time, the rest of the warehouse's contents were known technology that could be replaced without much worry. Knowing that practical quantities of graphene were still extremely hard to create, Dave couldn't afford to lose what little he'd managed to make. He motioned toward the large spools. "Guys, be careful with this stuff. Treat this like your life depended on it."

"Your lives *do* depend on this," Bella abruptly added matter-of-factly.

The squawking of gulls in the pre-dawn seemed to come from all over the island as Dave nervously watched spool after spool of the precious graphene exit the warehouse. Even though the ribbon was stronger than steel, Dave couldn't risk damaging it by rolling the spools over the rough terrain of the island. The men staggered under the weight of each spool as they slowly trudged toward the boat.

The eastern horizon was just beginning to lighten. Morning wasn't far away, and they needed to get going.

Dave reentered the warehouse, brushing past Bella, and walked into the inner storeroom. He frowned as he settled his gaze on the remaining stacks of graphene spools laying floor to ceiling. "It looks like we have about half of them still in here." He glanced at Bella, who stood in the doorway; her tousled red hair framed her green eyes. "Is that enough for what we need?"

With only a moment's hesitation, she nodded. "It should be—"

The lights suddenly flicked off, plunging the warehouse into darkness.

"What the hell!" Dave yelled, figuring someone had accidentally turned off the lights. He immediately reached for and found Bella's hand, then felt his way toward the warehouse's exit. As he trailed his hand along the wooden crates lining one of the aisles, Dave could barely make out the slight variation in the shades of darkness.

"Damn it, I guess either the solar chargers on the roof aren't working or the batteries that are supposed to be powering this place aren't any—"

Without warning, Bella screamed. Her hand ripped away from Dave's grasp, and he was suddenly struck by something hard on the back of his head.

As his knees buckled, Dave felt hands grab him by his arms just as he lost consciousness.

CHAPTER ELEVEN

Margaret sat on the sofa, where despite her exhaustion, she bore a bittersweet smile as she watched her three-year-old son George run around the desk in the Oval Office, screaming with a three-year-old's exuberance. In the week since the scientists had informed her of the danger facing the world, she'd been plagued by disturbing dreams of disembodied voices and images of chaos in the streets. They kept her up at night. Little George had just had a birthday party, and she couldn't help but worry that her son would never get to have another.

George hopped up onto the sofa and sat next to her, his favorite book about animals in his hand. Margaret swelled with emotion as he carefully flipped the pages and pointed at pictures, naming everything with complete confidence. Having gone through infertility treatment for years without success, she'd scrubbed having children from her life's plan. And then George happened.

Now, she couldn't imagine what life would be like without him. She only wished that her grandfather, who she'd named George after, were still alive to see him. She could almost sense her pappy's presence in the room, watching over them.

As she ruffled George's dark-brown hair, Margaret's attention veered to the Secret Service agent standing at the entrance to the Oval

Office. He briefly pressed his hand to his ear, nodded, and peered in her direction. "Madam President, Doug Fisher and the members of the senior staff you asked for are in the building."

She nodded. "Tell Brenda to let them in when they arrive." Margaret held up a finger, holding the agent in place, as she kissed the top of George's head and whispered, "Go with Agent King. He'll take you to Daddy. I'll be upstairs to play later."

Without another word, George gave her a sloppy kiss on her nose. Then he obediently walked to Agent King and grabbed his hand as they exited the room.

Almost as soon as the door closed, it opened again, and Doug Fisher, her Chief of Staff, entered with a couple of grim-looking people following in his wake. "Good afternoon, Madam President—"

"Nothing good about it, Doug." Margaret groused. "Last I heard, we're all still screwed." She motioned toward the other sofas in the room. "Let's dispense with the niceties and get down to business."

As the cabinet heads sat down, Margaret's focus settled on Doug. He was a short, wrinkled man in his early seventies, but despite his age and size, he still had the spring of youth and the booming voice of someone ten times his size. He was deeply connected into the heartbeat of the capitol, seemed to know everyone in D.C., and made a point of keeping her apprised of the comings and goings of people outside her inner circle. He was also especially good at running these types of meetings and unobtrusively keeping everyone on point.

Just as her eyes connected with Doug's, he gave a quick nod and glanced at his notepad through glasses that sat low on the bridge of his nose. "Jim, what were the results of the discussion with the other countries regarding Indigo?"

Margaret's attention focused on James Arroyo, her mustachioed Secretary of State, as he flipped through his notes on Indigo, the codename linked to the upcoming disaster.

"Madam President, I've talked with representatives from Germany, the United Kingdom, Australia, and the People's Republic of China. They're all briefed on Indigo and what looms ahead. For now, they've each bottled up any possible leaks from their respective countries, hoping that someone out of the ISF will have some insight on what the next steps should be."

Margaret glanced at the disarmingly handsome man sitting on an old Victorian chair opposite her. Kevin Baker was the Director of the CIA, one of the few in that position who'd actually spent time as an operations officer. In fact, he'd spent his entire thirty-year service at the Agency. Unlike Arroyo, who was charged with diplomatic relations, Kevin was tasked with international intelligence gathering.

"Kevin, the ISF has remained silent, I presume? Also, any other chatter about Indigo elsewhere?"

"All our monitored resources have been silent on Indigo," Kevin immediately responded, without looking at any notes. "The scientists that know are mum, and I cross-checked with the NSA's Utah Datacenter—neither of us have caught whiff of unusual communications anywhere else."

"Good," Margaret leaned back on the sofa with a sigh. "I don't need to tell you guys what would happen if the public knew about Indigo. I already received a briefing from Carol Chance—"

"Secretary of Agriculture," Doug interjected.

"She's using a significant portion of her allocated budget to incentivize farmers to produce excess supplies, and with that, we'll almost certainly have granaries and other storage facilities at near capacity by the end of the next growing season. Obviously, whatever additional prep we do needs to be masked under other projects or initiatives."

"Excuse me, Madam President." Walter Keane, the Secretary of Defense interjected. "But do you know when we'll learn more about possible contingencies? We have the greatest military force known to man, but with Indigo, it's a difficult task to plan for without more data—"

"Walt, trust me." The president held up her hand, interrupting the former General's comment. "I know where you're going with this, and for the fiftieth time, I don't yet have what you need. We don't yet have an enemy that you can fight."

Just as Walt opened his mouth, Doug's booming voice cut him off.

"Excuse me, but it might make sense to hear what in-country intel we have."

Margaret glanced at the reed-thin woman to her left, who was charged with all in-country intelligence. "Karen, what does the FBI have to say about Indigo's main actors?"

Karen Fultondale, the Director of the FBI, opened a large three-ring-binder sitting on her lap and trailed her finger across her notes. "Madam President, I pulled the records you'd previously requested and I'll start with Greg Hildebrand. We have a surprisingly thick file on him, since he'd previously applied for several government positions over the years. We have a detailed psychological profile on him. Mister Hildebrand is a borderline narcissist with a strong sense of self-importance; he's preoccupied with advancement and also has a strong sense of entitlement. These, along with violent domestic disagreements, were the contributing factors for his three failed marriages. Coincident with his failed marriages, he's had to declare personal bankruptcy, and is currently at a high risk of having his clearances pulled."

Margaret sighed and made a rolling motion with her hand for Karen to move on. Greg had been a friend of the family, and she hated hearing about how he was failing at life.

The FBI Director flipped to the next tab in her binder and paused as her eyes darted across the data. "It is true that David Wendell Holmes was placed in protective custody under Mister Hildebrand's direction. However, that only lasted a few weeks before Doctor Holmes managed to escape with the help of another patient."

"Who was the other patient?" Margaret asked, her interest piqued.

With a frown, the FBI director sighed, "We know almost nothing about her. She's the daughter of General Albert McMillan, former head of the clandestine research wing of the Defense Intelligence Agency. Approximately half a year before her escape with Doctor Holmes, General McMillan, along with his wife and a twenty-two-year-old daughter, were in a tragic car accident that killed both the General and his wife, leaving the daughter in a coma for nearly six months. The medical records indicate that when she woke from the coma, the accident had left her unable to communicate and emotionally unstable. We've not had any hint of either of their locations since their escape."

The president cocked an eyebrow. "Well, the good doctor clearly figured out how to communicate with the young woman. Tell me about our illustrious head of NEO and the man charged with doing something with DefenseNet. He was kind of quiet at our first meeting. What's *his* background?"

"Madam President, I'm surprised you've not heard of him," the Secretary of Defense chimed in. "He nearly caused L.A. to go dark due to his runaway invention. Radcliffe was the man who invented the first Turing-capable computer."

"Turing-capable?" Something about that term rang a bell in Margaret's head.

Walt leaned forward, his elbows pressing down on his knees, and nodded. "The machine could actually think for itself. The story is that someone broke into the lab during the middle of the night to try and steal something. The computer detected the break-in and managed to lock everyone out of the building while it alerted the police."

"That doesn't sound unreasonable—"

"You'd think so," he broke in, with a lop-sided smile, "but something in its protocol went haywire. When the police arrived to collect the criminal, the damned machine wouldn't unlock the lab. As soon as they tried to force their way in, the thing pulled power from the rest of the building, overloading the circuits and shocking the hell out of everyone in the building. It wasn't until the city administrator cut off the power to the entire twelve-square-block grid of downtown L.A. that the computer was disabled and the mess could get cleaned up."

"Okay, so he's a computer nerd." Margaret barely suppressed a smile as she imagined the chaos of the situation. She turned her gaze back to the FBI Director. "Karen, what do you have on him?"

"Madam President, we don't have much in the way of a psychological screen on Doctor Radcliffe, but he's been under observation ever since he became the head of NASA's Near Earth Object program. He has a double PhD in Computer Science and Astrophysics; there's no doubt he's well-disciplined and methodical. From the interviews we conducted with his current and past associates, he seems to be level-headed, and has the respect of his coworkers. Evidently, he has pacifistic leanings. He's written many papers on the peacetime usage of artificial intelligence ever since the L.A. incident, and he's also done his best to destroy the computer technology he invented, fearing its further use and declaring it the biggest mistake of his life. The Defense Department has approached him in the past, trying to recruit him to further develop aspects of his intelligent computing, but he refused to even take a meeting with anyone who might want to leverage it."

Margaret held up a finger, and Karen paused. The president pursed her lips as she gave thought to what she'd just heard, and the room grew silent, waiting for her to do something.

"What about the scientist who'd accompanied him? Isn't she his second in command at the NEO program?"

"Yes, Madam President, Doctor Neeta Patel is most assuredly one of the top scientists in the nation. She was also a former department head at the ISF, reporting to David Holmes—"

"The same Holmes who's missing?" Margaret interjected.

Karen nodded. "Doctor Patel likely didn't get the notice that she might otherwise have gotten because she'd been in the shadow of Doctor Holmes, who by all accounts is a freak of nature—"

"Woah," interrupted Walt, the Secretary of Defense, with his gravelly voice. "But he's *our* freak of nature—and we need to understand that!"

Margaret sighed. "Let's just hope that we find—"

A loud knock echoed through the Oval Office. Just as one of the interior doors flung open, a Secret Service member rushed in. "I'm sorry to interrupt, Madam President, but you asked for instant notification on this ... we just received a call from a field office in Florida. Doctor Holmes has been found by Mister Hildebrand and is being transported to D.C. as we speak. We expect him to touch down at Joint Base Andrews in four hours."

Margaret hopped to her feet. A surge of energy flushed through her as her heart raced with hope. She turned to her Chief of Staff and aimed her pointer finger at him while barking orders. "Round up everyone. I want the full contingent of the national security advisors in the Situation Room before that plane's wheels are back on the ground. Make sure our representatives from NEO are here as well."

"B-but, Madam President," Doug stammered. "I know Doctor Radcliffe is on the west coast—"

"Listen to me," Margaret set her jaw. "I don't care what it takes." She glanced at Walt. "Even if you have to put our good Doctor on a fast mover with in-air refuel, get them here, now! Are we all on the same page?"

As Margaret listened to the resounding chorus of assurances, she waved everyone off, dismissing them to their tasks. A chill ran through her as she stared grim-faced out the windows of the Oval Office.

What if Doctor Holmes doesn't have any good answers?

CHAPTER TWELVE

As Neeta arrived at the Cape Canaveral spaceport, she vaguely remembered a conversation she'd had with Dave years before when he'd let something slip about the Moon being part of a plan. *"Neeta, it's more complicated than you think. With Changing Venue, there's also a big rocky satellite I have to contend with..."* She'd never learned what that was about, and he'd never mentioned it again. If Dave was still around, he'd have long ago adopted a pseudonym, so it would be pointless to try and remotely search through the Moon shuttle logs for his name. He wasn't stupid enough to make himself that easy to track. She was convinced that if Dave hadn't been found by the government, he'd either be dead or hiding in a place so remote, that very few would think to look for him. It didn't get much more remote than the Moon, and besides, that place was largely a mineral mining operation dominated by a bunch of roughnecks. Who'd expect Dave to be there?

Breathing in the warm, salty air of the Florida coast, she sat in the outer lounge with a few dozen people, all of whom were waiting to cycle back up to the Moon. Most of them were rough-looking miners, returning to their jobs after having come back to Earth to visit with family or friends.

Neeta focused her attention on the shuttle, only a few hundred yards away, and watched as nearly a dozen maintenance personnel scurried all over it, each executing their preflight safety checks.

Over the din of the random conversations coming from the miners, the sound of heavy vehicles approaching from the nearby coastline drew Neeta's attention. A convoy of military transport vehicles was rushing away from the beach. She watched them aim for a large military aircraft that had turned itself onto the runway, getting ready for takeoff.

The convoy stopped fifty yards short of the airplane as the whine from the jet's engines blocked out any other sounds. Soldiers piled out of the vehicles, yet there was one person in civilian clothing, directing the men to board the plane.

Leaning forward, Neeta witnessed another man in civilian clothes being dragged out of one of the vehicles. She instantly shot out of her chair. The man was obviously unconscious, but that wasn't what had gotten Neeta up onto her feet, sprinting toward the distant convoy.

There was something about the black man that instantly reminded her of her old boss. As Neeta raced closer, a squirming woman with a shock of red hair was also ripped from one of the covered vehicles and dragged toward the plane.

As Neeta approached, her confidence grew. As the large black man was pulled up the portable stairs leading into the military aircraft, despite the screaming whine of the jet engines and the distracting smell that reminded her of ozone, her senses screamed: Dave!

Just as she got within fifty feet of the first of the convoy's vehicles, a soldier grabbed her arm and yelled, "Ma'am, you're not allowed to be here. Please return to—"

"You don't understand—" Neeta screamed, as she pulled toward the receding figure of her friend. "Dave!"

"Neeta Patel," a familiar, nasally voice caught her attention. "What in the world are *you* doing here?"

Neeta glanced to her left, into the sneering face of Greg Hildebrand. "Greg, you found Dave! Is he okay?"

Greg waved away the question and turned to the soldier. "Gutierrez, make sure you keep that crazy red-headed bitch separated from Holmes. I'll be right up."

"Greg, you have to let me go with you! We were both asked to find him, but I just want to talk to him, see if he's okay."

Greg frowned. "As long as there's no confusion about who managed to find him, I suppose it's okay if you hitch a ride. I know you're a fan of his, but I just hope there's a point to all this. I can't imagine that there's a way out of this situation, and maybe in the end, I'll finally have an opportunity to tell the illustrious David Holmes, 'I told you so.'" He glanced at her, and then back to the waiting area she'd raced from. "If you need to grab anything you left behind, we're taking off in two minutes, so hurry."

The last soldier from the convoy scrambled up the steps leading into the large cargo jet, while a spaceport worker manning the controls of the portable stairs motioned toward his wristwatch to indicate that he was about to pull away from the plane. Neeta held up a finger toward the man as she put one foot on the base of the metal stairs. She yelled, hoping that her phone would pick up her voice over the noise of the airplane's engines.

"Burt! Hildebrand managed to find Dave! We're at Cape Canaveral and I'm about to go back to DC with him. Can you hear me?"

Neeta covered her ears, and across the crackling connection, she could barely hear Burt's voice.

"Neeta, I just received an alert about that from the White House and they're having me meet you guys. I'll be arriving in Andrews in about two hours."

"How's that possible? Aren't you in L.A.? That's over 2,000 miles."

The man at the controls of the stairs frowned at Neeta, motioning for her to continue up into the plane or get off.

Slowly, she inched up the stairs as she struggled to hear what Burt said through the static.

"When the president wants you somewhere badly enough, evidently she has her ways. I'm being stuffed in a flight suit as we speak...."

The static got worse as the electric fuel-cell-powered engines of the jet whined even louder and the man at the base of the stairs yelled something unintelligible. For a few seconds, Burt's voice dropped in and out, so she only heard pieces of what he said.

"... fighter jet at ... on supercruise ... with mid-air refueling."

"Refueling! They're actually using gasoline and refueling in midair? Isn't that insane?" The whine of the engines lessened for a moment and the connection suddenly became static-free.

"Neeta, they used to do that kind of stuff all the time fifty years ago. None of the fuel cells of the local jets can go full speed the entire way, so they've dug up something that can handle the trip. Anyway, they're rushing me off to the tarmac, I'll—"

The phone connection cut off with a surge of static, and Neeta raced up the stairs, all the while thinking, *God, I hope Dave's got some answers for us.*

Neeta held tightly to the armrests of her seat as she was pressed against her chair by the plane's sudden acceleration. The uncomfortable feeling of the pressurized cabin and the sudden skyward launch sent a shudder through her. She tried to control her sense of panic. Before last week, she didn't remember having a fear of flight, but out of nowhere, Neeta couldn't help but feel a nervous energy any time she was in the air.

The interior of the cargo jet was sparsely furnished, very much like she'd have imagined a military transport would be. She sat in the back of the plane with Dave, on an isolated bank of seats that seemed to have been bolted to the floor at the last minute. Only twenty feet toward the front of the plane were approximately a dozen soldiers, sitting on chairs that reminded Neeta of the type that flight attendants used on civilian aircraft. Their seats pulled down from the wall, and a long bank of them lined the sides of the jet.

Beyond the soldiers was a closed compartment, where Neeta presumed the pilots were located. Greg wasn't anywhere in sight, and she wondered if he didn't want to be amongst the common soldiers.

"Greg, you were always an ass, even in college." Neeta shook her head and gripped the armrests even tighter as her stomach lurched with the plane's sudden change of course.

Coming from one of the few windows in the cabin, a beam of sunlight moved across the plane's interior as the jet banked to the left. The plane tilted at an extreme angle for a moment, away from what had been a southbound direction, and eventually leveled off again, presumably aiming north for the country's capitol.

Tearing her mind away from her nervous stomach, Neeta focused on the man sitting across from her. Dave's arms and legs were strapped to the chair, effectively tying him to the flight seat. When one soldier had led her to her seat, she was given firm instructions that she wasn't supposed to touch any of Dave's restraints, on Mister Hildebrand's orders.

Neeta thought the order was strange, considering Dave was the man the world was depending on to save them, but Greg and Dave had never gotten along—so why should that have changed over the years?

Dave was still unconscious, and Neeta worried about what might have caused the need for the thick, bloodstained gauze taped across the side of his head.

He looked different than she remembered. Even though Dave had never had a frail build, working out had never been his focus. Yet he now looked strong enough to tear someone in half. Even though his head lolled to the side, unconscious, his neck was thick, more muscular than she remembered it being, as was the breadth of his chest and arms. He looked like he'd been working as a day laborer, and not as the preeminent scientist of this world and a Nobel Prize winner.

As Neeta pondered the rough life Dave must have been living, a strong feeling of sadness washed over her. She leaned forward in her seat and tried hard to swallow the lump that had formed in her throat.

"Dave, I'm so sorry you've been put through this." She breathed the words across the few feet that separated them. "Your days of hiding are over; I swear—"

Dave groaned as his eyes fluttered.

"Dave!" Neeta's heart raced. She reached forward and patted him on the knee, as he blinked his eyes open and stared with a confused expression at his surroundings. "Dave, its Neeta, Neeta Patel. Remember me?"

The confused expression vanished as he sat up straight and craned his neck to look behind him. He yelled, "Bella! Bella, where are you?"

Neeta leaned closer to Dave and asked, "Is Bella the red-headed woman—"

Dave wheeled his gaze toward Neeta and spat out the angry words, "Where is she? She needs to be with me."

Neeta leaned back with concern as his gaze turned toward his restraints and he pulled against them. The blood vessels in his neck and forearms bulged. All the while, he yelled for Bella.

Neeta unbuckled her seatbelt and stood not more than a foot from him. "I'm going to see if I can help," she whispered. "I'll be right back."

~

"Greg, why don't you let Dave see this Bella person?" Neeta confronted Hildebrand near the entrance to the front compartment. She figured that someone had probably alerted Greg that Dave was awake, because he came barreling from the front section, slamming the door behind him.

Dave continued to yell for the mysterious Bella, and Greg sneered. "And this is who we're depending on? What a joke."

Neeta glared at Greg and blocked his view of Dave. "Greg, I'm talking to you! What's the story? Dave's freaking out about that red-headed woman." Pointing at the door, she asked, "Is she in there?"

Greg nodded, and tilted his head toward the door. "Yes, but she's clearly got issues. I think it's the same chick he escaped the mental hospital with." He turned toward the door and waved for Neeta to follow. "Take a look for yourself."

He opened the door and waved away the soldier guarding the entrance to the forward compartment.

Neeta walked in, and the soldier yanked the door closed behind her. The plane was even bigger than she'd imagined. There were many more of the pull-down seats lining the walls of the front compartment, yet Neeta's attention was drawn to the woman who knelt in the middle of the compartment, bobbing back and forth. Her shock of long hair was like an angry, red cloud masking her features and Neeta wondered what was wrong with her.

As Neeta took a step closer, Greg warned, "She's a nutcase. Don't get close. She punches and kicks with the best of them."

Neeta hesitantly cupped her hands to her mouth and yelled, "Bella? Is that your name?"

For a moment, the bobbing stopped. The woman glanced in Neeta's direction, spat out a long stream of gibberish, and resumed her rapid rocking motion.

Blinking, Neeta realized it hadn't been gibberish. That woman had just yelled a bunch of numbers at her.

"What in the world," Neeta whispered, more to herself than anyone else.

"I told you, she's crazy."

Ripping her gaze from the woman, Neeta turned to Greg. "I'm guessing you found Dave with her, so why not see if bringing her to him will calm them both down?"

Greg shook his head vehemently. "Not a chance in hell. I'm charged with bringing Holmes back." He hitched his thumb toward the red-headed woman. "The crazy chick isn't part of the equation."

Taking a deep breath, Neeta tried to keep the anger from her voice. "Greg, I know you're trying to do what's right, but think about it. You've got Dave trussed up like a Thanksgiving turkey. He's not going anywhere. What harm is it just getting a couple of the soldiers to bring this woman within sight of Dave and see if anything changes? I've never seen Dave so angry. He's freaking out."

"All the more reason I'm not doing anything."

The soldier unlocked the door to the rear compartment, and Neeta knew that was her cue to leave. She wasn't going to get anywhere with Greg Hildebrand.

~

Sitting across from Dave, Neeta tapped the cell phone bud in her ear and whispered, "Phone ... signal."

"There is currently no available signal," her cell phone said in her ear.

She knew that the likelihood of getting a signal was almost zero at their cruising altitude, but she had to try.

"Phone, call Burt Radcliffe."

"There is currently no available signal. Do you want me to continue trying, and if so, how frequently?"

"Yes ... frequency ... one minute."

"Confirmed."

Neeta stared at Dave, struck by the angry scowl on his face. His eyes were closed, but she knew he was awake. She'd managed to get a few affirmative grunts confirming that the redheaded woman was, in fact, the Bella he'd been yelling about. However, he refused to answer any questions or say a word to Neeta. She'd seen Dave frustrated, but never angry—she wouldn't have believed it was within him to get so angry. Clearly she was wrong.

"Dave, as I told you, I already tried to help and Hildebrand wouldn't listen. I promise you that I'll twist every arm I need to so I can get someone's attention who can help you."

Dave blinked open his eyes and turned his gaze toward her. A hint of a smile creased his lips. "You were always a bully, Neeta. I'm glad you haven't changed."

CHAPTER THIRTEEN

Burt watched as the man who'd piloted him across the continent hopped out of the cockpit and scrambled down the ladder to the asphalt, as quickly as a spider monkey. In contrast, Burt felt every one of his fifty years as he unplugged his G-suit, unwedged himself from his seat, and somehow managed to climb down the ladder without killing himself.

Just as Burt took his first steps, the pilot came to him, clapped his hand on Burt's shoulder, and smiled. "Feeling a bit sore?"

Glancing at the young pilot, who'd already taken off his helmet, Burt stared at him through his open visor. "Sore? Are you freaking kidding me? I feel bruised from my hips to the tips of my toes. I don't ever want to wear another of these glorified torture devices again."

"You'll be fine soon enough. Trust me, that squeezing you were feeling helped keep the blood in your head so you didn't pass out. In truth, we didn't ever really pull many G's, so the G-suit shouldn't have squeezed you too bad."

As Burt tried to figure out how to undo his helmet's chinstrap, he shook his head and frowned at the young pilot. "All I know is that when you kept dropping us out of the sky like a rock for refueling runs and then launching us back up into the stratosphere, it messed with this old civilian. I'm not used to this stuff."

"Well, I was told we needed to get you here ASAP, so I did what I was told." The pilot chuckled and motioned toward the distant concrete building as Burt finally managed to slip off his helmet. "Doctor Radcliffe, it looks like your welcoming committee has arrived."

Burt glanced to the east and noticed a black SUV speeding toward them. A flashing blue light on the dashboard indicated some type of police, or possibly Secret Service.

Within moments, the SUV came to an abrupt halt, and a man wearing the basic dark suit and tie that most Secret Service agents wore hopped out of the passenger seat and motioned to Burt. "Doctor Radcliffe, the president has asked me to bring you directly to the White House."

Burt tossed his helmet to the pilot, who deftly caught it. "Major Sanchez, I don't think I'll be needing that anymore. Thanks for bringing my sorry ass here in one piece."

The pilot waved good-naturedly as Burt was escorted to the back of the SUV. "Anytime, sir."

The agent opened the door, and Burt climbed into the vehicle. The smell of new leather greeted him. The agent shut the door and hopped back into the front passenger seat. Burt leaned forward and asked the driver, "How long of a drive will it be?"

"Sir, I'd say at this time of the day, it would normally be about an hour and a half, but buckle up. We've got a Priority-One override on the AVR system, so I plan on getting you to your meeting in about thirty minutes."

Burt pressed the seatbelt button, and the safety belt immediately snaked itself across his chest until he heard the familiar click. The SUV lurched, and within minutes, they were racing through traffic at break-neck speed. Burt silently groaned as he tensed for a heart-thumping ride.

They were five minutes from the White House, and Burt watched as the SUV's priority emergency signal overrode all of the traffic lights and forced the nearest vehicles to give them a wide berth. The SUV was racing through yet another intersection when Burt's phone began vibrating. He fumbled with the flight suit he was still wearing, trying to extract his phone from its hidden pocket. When he managed to touch the screen to answer it and put it against his ear, all he heard was static.

He glanced at the readout and recognized Neeta's number.

"Are you there? Neeta, aren't you still in the air?"

A rash of static erupted from his phone's speaker, and suddenly the line went silent. "Neeta? Neeta, you still there?"

"Burt, can you hear me?"

"I can hear you, but you're fading in and out—"

"Status report. I'm in the plane, but I think we're beginning to descend. Dave's here and he needs help. He's frantic about the welfare of a woman who accompanied him onto the jet, and Hildebrand is keeping them separated. I've no clue why, other than it seems he wants to be a total ass. Dave was also unconscious when they brought him in and he's got a big gash on his head. Dave's really pissed about how he's being treated, and I told him I'd contact someone who might be able to help."

"Neeta, I'm about to meet with the president. I swear that I'll talk to her about—"

The phone howled with a rash of static and suddenly lost connection.

Burt leaned over, peered through the windshield, and saw the White House looming ahead as the SUV raced through the traffic.

Lieutenant Jon Stryker watched as shoppers in the parking lot of the South Hill Mall walked by and stared at the unusual sight.

After all, it wasn't every day that forty members of the 66th Military Police Company gathered in a public space, dressed in their ACUs and loaded for combat.

Hearing the traffic from South Meridian, the main artery of the small town, Stryker pulled in a deep breath and addressed the four squads lined up in front of him.

"The Company Commander has assigned us to augment the local police. You've all been briefed, but let's not forget why we're here.

"Yesterday, the Washington State Governor went public with a warning about some of the violent protests that we've all been briefed on. The governor doesn't want what's happened in other states to happen here.

"We've been assigned to Puyallup and the nearby towns because the local police force has noted some unusual protests in the area. We're here to support the local law enforcement in their effort to keep the peace and prevent things from getting out of hand, nothing more. We all understand that?"

"Hooah!" All forty soldiers responded loudly in unison.

Turning his attention to the three sergeants standing at attention in front of their respective squads, Stryker barked, "Lopez, Carlson, and Johnson. Your squads focus on the South Hill and Graham area. Work out between the three of you how you maximize your coverage." Stryker jabbed a finger in their direction to emphasize the point. "Be smart, nothing less than two-man patrols. You'll probably want to focus on high traffic areas, like this mall and all the plazas along Meridian. You got me?"

"Yes, sir," was the immediate response from all three. Stryker turned his gaze toward the sergeant leading the squad primarily composed of 31Ds, the criminal-investigations part of the company.

"Cohen, I need your CID team to work with the investigators at the Pierce County Sheriff's Office. They've got leads on who some of these characters might be and will need help following up on them. If people are trying to organize terrorists in our midst, it's on you to track them down.

"I got a call this morning about some activity over on the edge of our patrol range, so I'm off to visit with the Chief of the Orting PD to see what's up.

"Everyone, watch each other's sixes, keep your eyes peeled and your radios on. Are there any questions?"

The simultaneous report of "No, sir!" rang across the mall parking lot, and Stryker yelled, "Dismissed!"

～

Standing in the office of the Orting Chief of Police, Stryker watched as Chief Mia Sterud scanned the paperwork he'd handed her.

She had dark skin, dark hair, and almond-shaped eyes set above high cheekbones. Her features all hinted heavily at her Native American heritage. The Chief had an ageless look to her, but he'd wager she was somewhere in her thirties. She'd have been attractive if it weren't for her stern expression.

With a loud sniff, Mia handed back a copy of the orders he'd received. "Lieutenant Stryker, you'll have to excuse me, but I don't see that there's much good you can do for us here. It's not like you know the area or the people."

"Chief, I've been assigned to patrol the Puyallup, Graham, Orting, and South Hill region with the MPs under my command. We're not here to do anything else but provide assistance to your officers. However, I'd received a report that there was an incident two days ago in this town about someone rabble-rousing. Can you tell me what happened? I have people I need to report to."

The Chief leaned back in her chair and pursed her lips.

As she did so, Stryker couldn't help but notice that despite the obvious bulk of the bulletproof vest under her police uniform, she had a slim figure.

"Lieutenant, I don't know how this got back to you, since it wasn't that big of a deal. Nonetheless, we did have a disturbance near the high school."

"What kind of disturbance?"

"Just an old hobo ranting about religious stuff. He was preaching all sorts of dark messages, you know, material out of Revelation, but he was harmless. He just spooked some of the regulars and they called us in to see if we could calm him down."

Stryker felt a tingle at the base of his neck as he heard her describe the religious preaching. That religious undertones were a common factor in almost all of the protests had purposefully been kept out of the news. "And did you?"

"Did I what?"

"Calm him down? What'd you do with this hobo?"

"Nothing." She shook her head. "He wasn't there when one of my officers arrived at the scene, but before you even ask, no, I didn't particularly plan on following up. He wasn't exactly doing anything other than maybe disturbing the peace, at worst." Mia paused and stared up at him. "Lieutenant, we're a small town of roughly 8,500 people. I have only a handful of officers total, and that pretty much means that there's usually only two to three people on shift at any given time. Believe it or not, chasing an old vet back into the woods where he's hidden himself away for the better part of a few decades isn't high on my list of things to do."

"Listen, I completely understand. Can you show me where you think this guy is? I'd like to follow up with him."

Levering herself up out of her chair, Mia walked over to the wall, where a large poster depicted an aerial view of the Orting area, and placed her finger on an image of a building. "Look here, this is the high school, and just one-hundred yards northeast is the Puyallup River. Across from that is some really dense woods. He lives up there, kind of off the grid. We don't really pay him much attention, since other than that one incident, he's never been an issue."

"So, if you point me to the rough location, I'll hunt around for him. Frankly, I just have some questions for him. Nothing more."

Mia tilted her head and stared at Stryker with a furrowed brow. "You're serious, aren't you?"

"Of course I am."

"So what did ... no, never mind." She glanced over her shoulder, grabbed a windbreaker with *Orting PD* stenciled on the back from a coat rack, and said, "Let's go."

"I thought—"

"You'll never find him on your own, and if it's so important that the Army is sending someone to my town, I'll do what I can to help."

The Chief patted at her sidearm, grabbed keys out of her desk drawer, and pointed at her open office door.

"Let's go."

~

The air was heavy with the scent of pine as Stryker ducked under a branch and pushed through the dense evergreen forest. Mia led him up a steep trail through the woods. He glanced at his digital mapping device, and noted that they'd climbed roughly three-hundred feet since crossing the river.

He breathed heavily as he worked at keeping up with the nimble chief of police, who seemed able to effortlessly flit through and around the obstacles that lay before them. "You mentioned that this guy's a vet. Do you know who he is?"

Mia glanced up at where the sun streamed through the canopy and shifted the angle of her ascent. "I don't know his real name, but everyone in town is pretty familiar with Old Rick. Rumor has it, he fought in the Iraq war back in the early 2000s, but he's lived off the grid pretty much since I've known of him."

"How long have you lived in the area?"

"All my life. My family has been in these lands for pretty much forever."

"You're part of the Pew-all-up tribe?"

The Chief turned to him and smiled. "I'm impressed. Most folks butcher the pronunciation of Puyallup unless they're from here."

"I practiced," Stryker admitted. "So is there anything else to know about Rick? Sounds like he's at least in his late seventies or early eighties, if he goes back to the Iraq campaign."

She shook her head and stepped over a fallen log. "Not really. He kind of wanders into town every couple weeks, visits the bank, buys some supplies, and takes off."

"I'm guessing that he's probably pulling a pension or disability. That would explain how he paid for anything."

Mia pointed toward the steep rise ahead and said, "His cabin, if you want to call it that, is up ahead at the top of that hill."

Stryker pulled alongside Mia and stared at the shaded spot she'd indicated. To him, it looked like a mottled upwelling of brush and sticks. "I'm not really sure I see anything from here."

"The only reason I even know it's up there is because my brother and I used to hunt for deer and we'd stumbled into it ages ago. The old guy must have heard us coming back then, because he shooed us away as soon as we got within sight." Without warning, Mia cupped her hands to her mouth and yelled, "Rick, you up there?"

As her voice echoed loudly through the trees, Stryker cringed and wished she hadn't done that.

He'd rather have had a chance to approach without warning the old guy.

"He's old, he might not hear that well anymore." Mia began climbing up the slope, and Stryker followed closely.

As they drew near, he saw that the cabin was draped in the living foliage of the surrounding forest. Wood-sorrel covered the walls and entrance of the building, making it look like a natural extension of the forest floor.

A breeze filtered through the canopy, sending beams of light coruscating across the forest floor, illuminating the entrance to the cabin.

Mia took a step closer.

Stryker launched.

He hit her in the gut, lifting her off the ground.

They tumbled back downhill, toward a nearby tree, as the bomb exploded.

The blast slammed into Stryker's back, knocking the wind out of him as he covered Mia with his body and ducked his head.

He felt a sharp sting in his shoulder and grimaced.

Something had gotten a piece of him.

A large plank of wood slammed only six inches from Stryker's head, and with his heart racing, he grabbed Mia by the arm, cringing with pain, as he lifted her over his shoulder and ran from the cabin.

He set the police chief down behind a tree and knelt in the dirt, while debris continued raining all around them.

"How did you know?" Mia gasped as she sat up.

"I saw a light glint off the tripwire just as you were about to step on it."

Stryker leaned back and probed his right shoulder.

"You're bleeding!"

He nodded as he examined the wound. "It's superficial. Whatever hit me just took a bite, nothing more."

"Oh, damn, you really got hit." She reached toward him, grabbed at his body armor and plucked something out.

A ball bearing.

Feeling a hot surge of frustration, Stryker shook his head. "I should have seen it earlier."

Staring at the steel ball in her hand, Mia gasped, "You saved my life!" She leaned over and gazed at the cabin with a wide-eyed expression. "Why the hell would—"

"He clearly didn't want visitors." Stryker pressed a button on his radio, and nothing happened. "Shit, radio's dead."

"My ears are ringing."

"Yeah, I've got an orchestra full of bells ringing in my head too." He noticed the chief rubbing at her neck. "Hey, Chief, are you okay?"

"I'm fine." She barked out a nervous laugh, brushed the leaves out of her shoulder-length hair, and hopped up to her feet. "Thanks to you. Holy shit...." She stared at the half-demolished cabin for a few seconds and shivered.

Stryker's senses were on edge, as the scent of dirt and char momentarily sent him back to another time and place.

He'd seen what improvised explosive devices could do. "We were lucky."

Mia pointed to some debris next to the remains of the cabin. "Some of the wood over there is smoldering. We better put it out."

Glancing over his shoulder, he motioned for Mia to stand back. "Let me clear the area first. "

"But what if there's another—"

"Listen, if I'm paying attention and still set something off, I deserve what I get."

As Stryker carefully approached the smoldering remains, he heard Mia's voice as she spoke on her radio.

"Meredith? Reach out to the Pierce County PD, I need their bomb techs out at my location ASAP. We've got a situation."

The Pierce County PD ended up calling in the Army's Explosive Ordinance Disposal team, and those guys began actively scouring the area, searching for bombs and collecting evidence.

As the EOD team processed the scene outside the cabin, Stryker hovered over the body of an elderly man lying inside it. The man was dressed in a heavily-stained sleeveless t-shirt, threadbare camo pants, and a pair of well-used hiking boots.

The sour smell of death hung in the air as Stryker scanned the sparse remains of what had been the man's living quarters.

"Did he die in the blast?" Mia asked, standing at the entrance to the partially-destroyed cabin.

Wearing latex gloves, Stryker pushed aside the scraggly gray beard, noticed an odd hourglass-shaped tattoo on the side of the man's neck, and felt for a pulse. "No chance, he's cold. He's been dead for at least a day and a half or more."

"How do you know that?" Mia approached and sat on the back of her heels with a grim expression. "He was in town two days ago."

Stryker squeezed the man's thigh and nodded. "His muscles are flaccid. In a dead body, the muscles begin to stiffen up after a few hours, and usually thirty-six to forty-eight hours after death, the body loses rigor. Since this body is cold, he's been dead more than a few hours, but since his muscles are no longer locked, that means he's been dead not much less than a day and a half. So I'd set the time of death to be somewhere between thirty-six and forty-eight hours ago."

Not seeing any obvious marks on his face or clothes, he lifted the old man's bare right arm and nodded. Purple stains ran underneath it. "Notice the bruises all along where his arm rested against the ground. That tells me he hasn't been moved since he died."

He leaned forward, lifted one of the man's eyelids, and noticed red dots on the whites of his eyes. "Huh, interesting."

"What's so interesting?"

Scanning the dark recesses of the cabin, he noticed a discarded plastic bag and frowned. He took the latex gloves off, he pulled a phone out of his pocket, and began rapidly dialing.

With the phone on speaker, the ring reverberated through the cabin and almost immediately someone picked up. *"What's up, Stryker?"*

"Sir, I need a full forensics team here. I've got a dead guy with signs of petechial hemorrhaging. I see a plastic bag nearby, and this all looks wrong to me."

"Shit. Roger that, I've got your GPS coordinates and I'll arrange for some folks to meet you up there with a full forensics kit. Oh, and Stryker, I just got word from on high. I don't know what's going on, but the flag officers are buzzing like their hornet's nest just got kicked. Anything we find is off to USACIL, no exceptions. Keep your eyes peeled and keep me posted on what your team finds."

"Will do, Captain." Stryker ended the call and glanced at Mia, who stared at him with her dark-brown eyes. "What?"

"I didn't understand half of that. Plastic bag? USACIL?"

Not wanting to disturb the scene any further, Stryker motioned for her to follow him out of the cabin. "It's actually pretty basic forensics. Our dead guy back there had some bleeding in the eyes. That's what those red splotches in the whites of his eyes were. That typically is a sign of some kind of stress. It can come from heavy coughing, vomiting, or asphyxia ... strangulation. That plastic bag looks totally out of place. You put these things together and it sets off a whole bunch of alarms in my head."

"So you think he was killed?"

He shrugged. "I can't really tell. We need him to get a thorough exam, so the forensics team is probably going to cart him and half of these woods off to USACIL to get to the bottom of it all."

"USACIL?"

"Sorry, that's ... how do you say it? It's kind of like the Army's version of Quantico. It's where the Army sends stuff to be analyzed in a lab environment."

"Sir?"

Stryker glanced over his shoulder as one of the EOD guys approached, holding a plastic baggie full of what looked like bomb fragments. "What's up, Sergeant?"

"We found another explosive on the far end of the hill. It was a basic setup with C4, blasting cap, ball bearings, and a tripwire to set it off. We've disarmed it. From the fragments found so far, it looks like it's a twin of what you guys stumbled into."

"Are you done with the perimeter sweep?"

"We did a laser and a GPR sweep. GPR didn't find any under-ground booby-traps, but we're doing a laser sweep one-hundred yards further out to make sure whoever did this didn't have anything else in the area."

"GPR? A laser sweep?" The sheriff asked.

"Yes, ma'am," the sergeant responded. "We use ground-penetrating radar to sweep for mines. Didn't find anything, but that's not a surprise, since this entire area is nothing but glacial till. It's a real pain to dig in. As for the aboveground stuff, we use green lasers to light up the area we're scanning. Any tripwires across any of the open spaces will be pretty easy to see with the green light flaring off it."

Stryker nodded at the soldier. "Great job, and make sure you don't handle anything directly. Everything's going back to USACIL for analysis. Let your team know."

"Yes, sir. Will do."

"Dismissed, sergeant."

Stryker glared at the remains of the cabin. "How the hell did that old guy get access to C4?"

Burt couldn't believe how his life had changed in just the last few weeks. Normally, his day would be fairly mundane, split between teaching a couple of classes at Caltech and running the Near Earth Object program out of the Jet Propulsion Laboratory for NASA. And now the fate of the world was on a precipice, and he of all people was sitting on a sofa in the Oval Office, six feet from the President of the United States.

She leaned forward, her gaze locked on his. "Doctor Holmes has been injured? Is that what Doctor Patel said?"

"All I know is what I got from a thirty-second conversation with her while she was still in the air, but she did say that he'd received a gash on his head and was initially unconscious. Neeta was specifically requesting help." Burt hated to give reports secondhand, but in such a critical situation, he had no choice.

The president pursed her lips, her jaw muscles clenching.

"Umm, Madam President, can you make sure Neeta, I mean Doctor Patel, accompanies Doctor Holmes when they get here? She's the only one of any of us who knows him other than Hildebrand, and frankly, I don't think him and Hildebrand get along."

"They're not scheduled to land for another half hour," she muttered to nobody in particular. The president turned to her right and looked at the gray-haired old man sitting in one of the gathered chairs. "Doug, get in touch with the pilot for Doctor Holmes' transport and make sure the Hildebrand situation is addressed. And when they land, please make sure Doctor Patel is brought to the Situation Room, along with Doctor Holmes."

"Understood, Madam President," Doug responded, and despite his aged appearance, he hopped out of his chair and jogged energetically to the nearest exit.

Margaret turned her attention back to Burt. "Doctor Radcliffe, I've asked to meet with you for a very specific reason. But before we get into that, I need you to understand some of what we're dealing with.

"Unfortunately, we think that aspects of Indigo have leaked to some rather unsavory individuals. I can't be certain to what extent others know, but our intelligence services have intercepted broadcasts coming from a subversive religious sect calling themselves the Brotherhood of the Righteous. They've historically caused the world untold grief, but most of the countries have managed to keep them under control." Margaret craned her neck and spoke loudly, "Records keeper, display file BR13."

"Voice match confirmed," a disembodied voice proclaimed through a speaker in the ceiling. *"Displaying video clip BR13."*

A holographic image appeared in the middle of the room, displaying a dozen cloaked figures that looked surprisingly like medieval monks.

One of the figures stepped forward and pulled his hood back.

Burt's eyes widened at the shocking image: a good-looking man, with white hair and alabaster skin, a startling contrast to his coarse-weaved brown monk's garb. The man's vivid pink eyes stared at him with the spark of a fanatic's zeal. The monk smiled, approached the camera, and began speaking with a heavy Eastern-European accent.

"Glory to you, my brothers. The time is upon us. God, in his infinite wisdom, has willed that the time of reckoning come in our lifetimes— that time is now."

The man's tone was ominous, yet compelling. Burt easily understood how others might fall sway to him. There was something about the tone of his voice that was hard to ignore.

"Those who are within reach of my voice, don't allow the lies of false leaders to sway what you know to be the true words of God. For they will try.

It is said in the Bible that,

'I will show wonders in the heavens above

and signs on the Earth below,

blood and fire and billows of smoke.

The sun will be turned to darkness and the Moon to blood before the coming of the great and glorious day of the Lord.

And everyone who calls on the name of the Lord will be saved.'

Even the American President, a heathen, has foreseen the coming of our Lord. The prophecies in the Bible are coming to pass, and we must fight against those who would interfere with our Lord's plan.

Go, my brothers! Fight against the tyranny of the heathens. We must stop them, or may God have mercy on your souls."

Margaret looked at Burt and sighed. "That message is now broadcasting over and over. From what we can tell, these zealots come from all walks of life. They're represented by all racial, cultural and ethnic identities and so far, they've been very hard to root out. We've blocked and destroyed thousands of transmitters worldwide, but we know that the message is getting through to some of the Brotherhood's followers out there. You can't imagine how many bombs have been defused, or how many attacks have been thwarted. They literally believe that somehow, all will be fine if we allow the heavens to fall down to Earth. They see it as God's plan. I don't know about you, but I'm not about to let that happen if we can avoid it."

Burt grimaced at the spot where the hologram had displayed and shook his head. "They're crazy. It's one thing to have your beliefs, but to commit suicide and drag all of humanity with you?"

Margaret sniffed disdainfully. "I'm afraid that the trouble this so-called Brotherhood represents will only be getting worse."

Feeling uneasy, Burt asked, "You didn't show me that because you want me to figure out what to do about it, did you? That's not exactly what I do."

With a slight grin, the president shook her head. "No, that's more in my department. I wanted you to be aware of what we're dealing with behind the scenes." She pressed her lips together and gazed at Burt for a few seconds.

Burt felt a chill as the president stared silently at him. It was as if she was deciding whether or not to make his day or ruin it.

"Doctor Radcliffe," she finally said, "I've read your file and I'd like to ask you to take on a responsibility that is likely going to be rather distasteful for you. But I don't have a better alternative...."

CHAPTER FOURTEEN

Neeta watched, slack-jawed, as Greg Hildebrand yelled, "This has to be a mistake!" All the while, two soldiers half-escorted, half-dragged him into the forward compartment, while a third soldier approached and said, "Doctor Patel, I'm Platoon Sergeant Williams, and I've been asked to inform you that Mister Hildebrand has been relieved of command for this mission and will be detained until I hand him off to the security detail that will await us when we land at Andrews. I've also been asked to inform you that until the wheels hit the ground, you've got command." He hitched his thumb back toward the other soldiers, who were sitting on the seats that lined the walls of the plane. "The boys and I will help with anything within reason, if you need it."

Blinking with shock, she glanced at Dave, who gaped at both her and Sergeant Williams with a confused expression.

The meaning of the sergeant's words suddenly sunk in, and she sat up, resolve flushing through her system. She pointed at Dave's restraints. "Sergeant Williams, can you remove Doctor Holmes' restraints?"

The sergeant glanced behind him. He quickly pointed at his own eyes and then to Dave, and three soldiers hopped off their chairs, the seats producing a loud metallic clang as they slammed back up onto the wall. Sergeant Williams retrieved a key-like metal object from one of his pockets.

The soldiers gathered behind Dave, and before anything else happened, Neeta raised her hand and leaned toward her friend. "Dave, I don't know what Greg told anybody about you, but I think these guys are nervous about you doing something crazy if they unlock your restraints." She reached forward and put her hand on his knee. "You're fine, right?"

Dave glanced behind him and saw the wall of soldiers, then turned back and gave Neeta a wink. "I'm still the same self-absorbed nerd I've always been. Hildebrand is the only one that needs to worry about me."

He made two fists, and the veins and muscles in his forearms bulged.

The sergeant knelt to unlock the first of the straps that held Dave's legs to the seat, paused, and then glanced sideways at Dave, giving him a lop-sided smile. "Sir, despite my own personal feelings on the matter, I can't allow you to harm Mister Hildebrand."

"Understood, Sergeant. I'll behave."

Dave sniffed loudly as the soldier began unlocking his restraints. He turned his gaze to Neeta and asked, "What about Bella?"

Neeta stood as the last of Dave's restraints fell away. She curled her finger at Dave, inviting him to follow, and smiled. "I was hoping you'd be able to introduce me."

Neeta watched Dave and Bella ever so gently hold hands, remaining silent as if some kind of unspoken communication flowed between them. She'd never seen Dave like this. Neeta wasn't sure she'd seen anyone exude such a single-minded care for another.

A flush of warmth spread through her chest and infused her with something that seemed completely foreign. Watching the two stirred an unfamiliar emotion in Neeta, and inexplicably, the image of Burt popped up in her mind's eye.

Clearly Hildebrand's loss of his command could only have been made possible by Burt talking to the president. Nothing else made sense.

Stunned by these strange thoughts, she whispered silently to Burt, even though he wasn't there: "Thank you."

Dave turned to her and flashed a brilliant-white smile, which contrasted against his nearly black skin. He walked to Neeta with Bella following, and all the while she held onto his arm. "Neeta, I'd like to introduce you to my better half."

Bella's face lit up with a smile. She was pretty, likely in her mid-twenties, and there was something hypnotic about her green eyes. They seemed to sparkle with an almost incandescent fire.

"Neeta, this is Bella. Bella, this is Neeta Patel. She's a brilliant researcher with a real gift for complex math."

Neeta extended her hand, and Bella took a step backwards, an expression of pain or perhaps discomfort crossing her face.

Dave turned to Bella and spoke reassuringly. "It's okay. She's a good friend. You can trust her."

With a determined expression, Bella seemed to screw up her courage and slowly extended her hand.

Neeta moved cautiously, recalling Bella's rocking back and forth and shouting gibberish. She was obviously not one-hundred-percent there, and Neeta tentatively touched her hand, not sure what the girl's reaction would be.

Bella's eyes widened as her gaze locked onto Neeta's and she shared a shy smile. "I think you're a beautiful person, Neeta Patel."

Neeta blinked and wondered where the crazy girl who'd yelled numbers at her had gone.

The pilot's voice sounded through the cabin. *"Please take your seats, we're on final approach and should be on the ground in ten minutes."*

Dave motioned to the seats in the back of the plane and led Bella toward them while Neeta followed, almost in a daze.

In her mind raced all manner of thoughts and worries, but she couldn't help but wonder why in the world she was suddenly haunted by Burt's image.

~

"Neeta, you just don't understand," Dave noted emphatically. "It can't be done. At this stage, Earth is done for, and unless we can get ourselves and the graphene I've collected up to the Moon, we're screwed."

The plane began its descent as Neeta's frustration rose. Dave had that stubborn expression that told her he'd settled something in his mind, but this time, she wasn't about to accept it. "Damn it, Dave! Why are you saying that? I can guarantee you that the president will write any check and do anything to save everyone. She just needs your help, can't you understand that?"

Dave shook his head and sighed. "I understand just fine, it's *you* that don't understand—"

"Explain it to me!" Neeta yelled, her nostrils flaring as she barely suppressed an urge to smack him. "You bloody need to get your head out of your ass and start thinking about saving the Earth, because I'm pretty sure nobody is going to be allowed to return to the Moon."

Dave leaned back in his chair and pressed his lips together, as Bella glanced back and forth between him and Neeta.

Suddenly Dave's words echoed in her head, *"Unless we can get ourselves and the graphene up to the Moon,"* and she leaned forward and asked, "Why is the graphene so important?"

"It's key to everything, and it's not something that the president can just snap her fingers and make enough of. It's a royal pain in the ass to produce in quantity."

Hope bloomed within Neeta as a smile erupted on her face. "Dave, I remember what you told me about the graphene production way back when we were at the ISF, and I knew it was key to whatever you had been doing. What if I told you that before I left the ISF, I managed to convince the new Director to continue manufacturing that stuff in quantity? I talked to him six months ago and he was asking me what in the world we're going to do with hundreds of thousands of miles of graphene ribbon."

Bella nudged Dave and whispered, "If it's possible, you have to try and save them."

Dave's expression went from frustration to surprise. He glanced at Bella, and his expression seemed to soften. Turning his attention back to Neeta, he met her gaze and whispered, "Maybe it's possible...."

Stryker braced himself as the sergeant driving the Humvee stepped on the accelerator.

The large, lightly-armored vehicle bounced along the unnamed road at breakneck speed, leading a convoy of four other Humvees, each filled with heavily-armed soldiers.

He could barely see the flashing blue lights of the police SUV they were following, due to the clouds of dust it kicked up as they all sped southeast, paralleling the Puyallup River.

As the white peak of Mount Rainier loomed to the east, only nine miles away, Stryker adjusted the mic on his headset. "Listen, guys, we're almost on top of it. The road should be petering out in another half mile, and that's where things can get dicey. Remember, the police chief is handling the initial engagement, we're there to make sure the shit doesn't hit the fan."

Adjusting his headset to the police channel, Stryker asked, "Chief, anything else before we meet these folks?"

"Just remain chill, and we should be fine." Mia's voice carried a self-assured tone. After all, the militia encampment was located in a former Puyallup Reservation, and half of these people were likely in some way her distant cousins.

"Roger that, just remember that there's a reason we're hunting for these people—"

"Lieutenant, I got the message. There's possible terrorists in our midst, and I don't want them roaming free any more than you do. I'm just reminding you that these guys are better armed than most civilians

and they're the nervous types. I don't need anyone getting shot or anything blowing up around me. My ears are still ringing from that damned hill."

"Trust me, none of us want that. Just be careful."

He switched channels as the lead police vehicle slowed and the convoy followed suit. "Okay, we're nearing the border of the militia's encampment. Units Alpha, Bravo, and Charlie—you'll get out with me, I'm on point. Delta, I want you out here watching for anything. Sergeant Cohen, have one of your men manning the .50, just in case. You all got that?"

A chorus of affirmation returned in Stryker's headset as the Humvee slowed to a stop.

Hopping out of the car, Stryker rested his hand over the assault rifle hanging in front of him and jogged toward the forward position, meeting with Mia at the end of the dirt road.

Scanning ahead, he watched two men in camo step out of the edge of the forest. Both had AR-style rifles slung over their shoulders and a bandolier with a dozen magazines draped diagonally across their chests.

"Mia, what in the world is going on?" One of the men pointed in Stryker's direction as soldiers arrayed behind him.

Mia glanced at Stryker and motioned toward the man who'd spoken. "Lieutenant Stryker, let me introduce you to Billy Sterud."

"Sterud? Any relation?"

Billy stepped forward and extended his hand. "Older brother."

Stryker shook hands with Billy and nodded as the man frowned. "I can tell. You two have the same grimace."

With that, Billy snorted and flashed a brief smile. He glanced back and forth between his sister and the dozen soldiers and asked, "So, what's going on?"

Pulling a photo from her pocket, Mia showed it to her brother. "I've seen this guy hanging out with your buddies before. The lieutenant has some questions for him."

Billy glanced at the photo, and Stryker could tell by his reaction that he knew him.

"Never seen the guy."

"Billy..." Mia growled.

Billy sighed and took a closer look at the photo. The frown appeared once again. "That's Raven Miller. Do you have some kind of warrant?"

Stryker pulled a copy of the federal warrant out from under his battle vest and handed it over to him. "Mister Sterud, I'm here only to ask some questions. Nobody's in trouble, but we've had some incidents that we need to follow up on."

Handing the paper back, Billy shrugged. "Listen, lieutenant, Raven was here, but he's not anymore. You can look around, but there's nothing to find."

Stryker's earpiece suddenly crackled with activity. *"Lieutenant, we've got a man at nine o'clock, about fifty yards away, hiding in the brush. There's also one at three o'clock, same distance. They've both got rifles trained in your direction. We have both men in our sights and on a hair-trigger, just give us the word."*

Glancing to his left and right, Stryker caught a glimpse of the militia's men and pressed the talk switch dangling from his headset. "Roger that, hold steady."

"Billy, do you know where he might be?" Mia asked.

"No, and frankly, I'm not exactly inclined to tell you much more than that." Billy glanced at Mia. "You should have called. I could have saved you a trip." He turned back to Stryker and said, "Sorry, lieutenant, but I'm not about to help the military out when you guys have screwed my people over and over again. Even if you've somehow talked my sister into trying to help you, I'm not her."

Stryker pulled in a deep breath and stared into the man's eyes.

"Mister Sterud, I'm not going to pussyfoot around here. I'll lay it out for you as straight as I can, but either way, I have questions that I need to get answers to.

"I'm here to follow up on a rash of terrorist acts that have occurred across the country. Maybe you've heard about them in the news?"

Billy's eyes narrowed. "I might have. What's that got to do with us or Raven?"

"I don't know yet. I'm just following up on some leads. I have lots of questions and not enough answers. These scumbags aren't stopping at just cops, they've set bombs off that have killed kids as well. I figured since your sister is a cop, maybe you might want to help."

Mia interjected, "One of the people we were looking for just a day and a half ago set a bomb, and Lieutenant Stryker saved my life."

Billy's eyes widened as he stared at Mia. "What? There's no way Raven—"

"Not Raven, but someone else."

Billy shook his head and turned to Stryker. "Listen, I don't know what you want from us. None of us have any interest in killing cops or kids, we just want to be left alone."

Stryker pulled out a notebook. "This Raven guy is a suspect, that's all. Can you or any of the other folks here maybe answer questions about him? Who is he, where has he been, where do you think he's off to, does he have any tattoos, habits, unusual behaviors recently? I've got a long list of things I'd like to know about."

Billy stared at the ground for a full five seconds before raising his head and nodding. "Fine, I didn't really know him, but there's some around here who did." He turned, raised his arm and made an exaggerated circular motion.

"Sir, men are in motion in the woods. Our targets went back into the tree line."

Billy glanced over his shoulder and met Stryker's gaze. "Follow me, I'll take you guys in."

Stryker glanced at Mia and she nodded reassuringly. Pressing his coms button, he adjusted the mic and said, "Delta, keep watch out here. We're going in to gather some intel. It's 1100 hours. If we aren't back or communicating by 1300, you know what to do."

"Roger that. 1300 hours."

Mia walked after her brother, and Stryker followed with the rest of his team as the darkness of the woods enveloped them.

◦

With a campfire blazing in the center of a forest clearing, Stryker sat on a tree stump and focused on one of the older militiamen who'd evidently known the suspect, Raven.

The man was easily in his fifties, had an overgrown salt-and-pepper beard that covered most of his face, and spoke in a calm manner, despite a dozen army soldiers sitting in the midst of their encampment. "I don't know where Raven went, but I can tell you he'd been acting weird for the last two weeks."

"Weird in what way?" Stryker asked.

"Well, he'd been gone for about a month, which really isn't that unusual for some of us. Heck, I've got family in Idaho that I sometimes visit with for months at a time. But Raven, he wasn't the family type. He'd just up and vanished one day and when he came back, he'd gotten all weird. Said he'd seen the light and was talking all religious and shit."

The twenty militiamen who'd gathered around the campfire nodded, as if they'd experienced the same from the enigmatic protester.

Billy, who seemed to be one of the leaders of the militia, cleared his throat and asked, "Jeb, you talked to him more than anyone. What'd he say?"

The old man shrugged. "I wasn't brought up with much religion, and the only time Jesus Christ was ever mentioned was when my paps would yell at me from the front porch. But Raven was talking about God and shit. He was coming, and we needed to believe and have faith." Jeb drew a large Bowie knife from a sheathe hanging from his belt and smiled. "He didn't like it none when I told him the only faith I had was in this here knife."

Stryker leaned forward and scratched at his chin. "Raven got on our radar because he was reported to be talking about the end of the world and trying to get people to rise up against unbelievers. Did he ask any of you to do anything?"

"Yeah," one of the men chimed in. "Raven was talking about how the government was trying to keep the believers holed up and afraid.

He wanted us to fight, but I never really got an idea of who in the hell he wanted to fight with."

Another said, "He asked me if I'd join him in a war against the heathens. I'm not into that kind of mumbo-jumbo, so I told him he was barking up the wrong tree."

Others began affirming the same general message, and Stryker scribbled notes as they talked.

Finally, he flipped through some of his notes and asked, "So, Raven was gone for a while and came back talking religion. Did he mention at all where he'd gone? Anything else unusual?"

"I noticed he had a new tattoo," a teenaged militiaman spoke up. "And when I pointed it out, he didn't seem too eager to talk about it."

"What'd it look like?"

"It was two triangles laying on top of each other. Kind of weird. I only noticed it because one day when he took his shirt off, I saw the fresh red marks from the tattoo on his chest."

Remembering the tattoo he'd spied on the dead old man, Stryker grabbed a nearby branch and scratched a symbol of an hourglass in the dirt. "Something like this?"

"Yeah, that's what I saw."

A chill washed over Stryker. "Did any of you catch where he was heading?"

Most of the men shook their heads, and old Jeb hitched his thumb toward the east. "He just up and vanished a couple days ago. He might be back, since he left his footlocker locked up."

"He left stuff behind?"

Billy interjected, "We don't generally pry into other people's foot-lockers."

Stryker rose from the stump and asked, "Can you show me the locker?"

Billy pressed his lips together into a thin line, took a deep breath, and stood. "Follow me."

Stryker stared, eyes wide, as he and the group walked toward a large cave built into the side of a hill.

Mia, walking next to him, pointed at it. "You know what that is?"

"A cave?" He responded flatly.

"Well, duh." She chuckled and shook her head. "No, smartass, that's actually an old lava tube. Nobody thinks about Rainier being a volcano and spewing lava, but this is just one of the many tubes that lava flowed through ages ago."

They walked into the cave and lights flickered on, illuminating the fifteen-foot-tall cavern. Several dozen bunks were set throughout the natural shelter.

Old Jeb motioned as he walked toward one of the metal-framed beds and pointed at the locked metal box at its base. "This is where Raven bunked."

Stryker knelt in front of the three-foot-wide metal box and studied its padlock. It had a dial on the front and a keyhole in the back. He glanced over his shoulder and asked, "Anyone have the combination?"

"No idea what he set it to, but I've got this," Billy handed Stryker a bronze master key. "It'll open it."

With a quick twist of the key, the lock popped open, and as Stryker removed it, he broke out in a cold sweat.

Along the top lip of the metal case, Stryker noticed a copper sheen. A barely visible frayed wire was wedged between the upper lid and the lower portion of the footlocker.

Slowly backing away, Stryker glanced over his shoulder at the soldiers who'd followed him into the cavern. "Are any of you by chance EOD trained?"

"I am," Jeb replied. "Sergeant Jeb Macintyre. MOS 89D, retired 2045. Why? You think Raven booby-trapped his own footlocker?"

The rest of his team shook their heads, and with a feeling of resignation, he focused on Jeb. "Actually, yes."

"Shit," Jeb growled as he stared at the footlocker. "I don't have a drill and scope to look inside, do you?"

"No, we didn't bring anything like that." Stryker stared at the box and worried that he was just being paranoid.

Jeb turned and yelled at one of the militia members standing near the entrance to the cave. "Tyler, go get Betsy out of the armory. Jeff, get her parts bag."

"Betsy?" Stryker asked.

"You'll see."

Moments later, Stryker heard tank treads grinding on gravel as an old-style bomb-disposal robot entered the cavern. Both men followed Betsy; one held a remote control, while another hefted a large backpack over his shoulder.

"Where the hell did you get that thing?"

Jeb smiled sheepishly and shrugged as he grabbed the heavy backpack from one of the men and withdrew a long, metallic arm.

As Stryker watched, the former EOD member confidently replaced one of the parts on the robot with the mechanical arm from the backpack. Stryker figured Jeb had probably stolen the thing from inventory before retiring.

Grabbing the remote, Jeb fiddled with the controls, and the robot moved smoothly back and forth, extending and contracting the newly-attached gripping arm. "Okay, everyone, let's back out of the cavern."

Everyone filed out of the converted lava tube and didn't stop until they were deep in the woods.

Stryker hovered over Jeb's left shoulder as the man peered at the video panel attached to Betsy's remote control.

Jeb furrowed his gray brows as he adjusted a control on the remote.

"Okay," he said, "Betsy's got ahold of the right handle of Raven's footlocker."

"Are you dragging it out of the cave?" Billy asked.

"You bet your ass that's what I'm doing. Don't know about you, but if this thing's rigged to blow when you open it, I'd rather have a bed to sleep in than not."

Billy nodded as Jeb slowly pulled back on one of the sticks on the remote.

The speaker on the remote broadcast a loud scraping noise as Betsy pulled backwards, dragging the footlocker.

Jeb let out a big breath. "Well, if it's rigged to blow, it isn't motion sensitive." He pulled further back on the stick, dragging the box toward the cave's entrance.

Stryker watched through the small screen as the man expertly maneuvered the robot, and dragged the locker across the gravel outside of the cave.

"Okay, now to see what we've got in the box."

Jeb manipulated a different control stick on the remote, and in the monitor, the gripping hand came back into view.

Jeb blew on his fingertips and rubbed them together. "Here goes nothing."

Slowly, Betsy's metal gripper clamped down on the footlocker's latch and flipped it open.

"Latch is clear."

The gripper grabbed the edge of the lid, and just as Jeb pressed on the control stick, the monitor turned white.

The ground shook just before the sound of a massive explosion ripped through the forest.

Even though they were easily one-hundred yards from the cave entrance, Stryker felt the pressure wave hit as smoke billowed toward them.

"That motherfucker!" Billy yelled an extended string of profanities as gravel began falling from the sky.

Mia glanced at Stryker with a haunted expression. "That blast could have killed everyone in the cave."

Stryker blinked the dust out of his eyes as he stared toward the cave. "What kind of homicidal assholes are we dealing with?"

CHAPTER FIFTEEN

From that moment when Bella had first awakened in the hospital and the nurses had told her she'd been in a car accident, life hadn't made sense. She knew there was something wrong with her; something was missing. It was almost as if she'd stopped believing that she was human. Everyone else seemed to possess an innate humanity, a feeling that had eluded her until she met Dave.

It was with him that Bella had begun to feel something that resembled normalcy. Yet on the plane, when she'd been taken from Dave, it was as if something inside her shut down. The world stopped existing in a way that made sense, and everything around her became a jumbled mess, just like it had been before she'd met him.

She glanced at Dave, and even though he remained silent about the gash on the side of his head, she could tell that it still bothered him. Over the years, Bella had managed to learn Dave's physical cues and could almost tell what he was thinking. Yet the rest of the world still baffled her.

Bella held onto Dave's arm as they walked down the well-lit, cinder-block hallway, and sensed the nervous energy coursing through him. A small group of suit-wearing Secret Service agents escorted them through the long hallway underneath the West Wing of the White

House, and as they approached a wood-paneled door, one agent turned and pointed to a basket with a series of discarded electronic items. "We've arrived at the Situation Room. Please deposit any electronic equipment before entering."

Bella watched as Neeta extracted an implant from within her ear, placed it in a small paper envelope, and scribbled her name. As one agent's gaze turned to Dave and Bella, Dave shook his head and muttered, "I've not had a cell phone in years. I may not be an expert in cell phone tech, but even I know that today's anti-theft sensors are coded against the owner's DNA. I have enough of a clue how to avoid being tracked." He sniffed and glanced at Neeta. "Or at least I thought I did."

As the agent opened the door to the Situation Room, Neeta glanced backward, "Dave, I'm thinking you'll have to become a bit easier to get in touch with."

With a wry grin, Dave muttered, "Yup, I'd rather not repeat what happened today. I'm done with this cloak-and-dagger crap."

Walking into what turned out to be a large, wood-paneled conference room, Bella felt a wave of discomfort as she felt dozens of eyes peering in her direction.

A voice at the distant end of the room rose in volume above the others. "Neeta, please bring Doctor Holmes and ..."

"Bella Holmes," Dave said, loudly enough to be heard across the room, and Bella shrunk inwardly as she followed him. Everyone was staring at her.

As Neeta escorted them along the edge of the conference room, she pointed toward a man, glanced backward, and whispered, "That's Burt Radcliffe, the guy I was telling you about."

Dave eagerly approached him and smiled as he clasped hands with the tall man, his long, gray-streaked dark hair pulled back into a pony-tail. "Doctor Radcliffe, I can't thank you enough for pulling whatever strings you did—"

"Nonsense, and call me Burt." Burt's face took on a grim expression. "What that asshole did to you is beyond the pale." He pointed at the gauze on the side of Dave's head. "Are you okay?"

"I'm fine." Dave waved away the question and turned to Bella.

She knew what he was going to say just before he said it, and suspecting how unpleasant this would be for her, she cringed.

"Burt, let me introduce you to my better half, Bella." Dave wrapped his arm around her shoulder, knowing that she always hesitated when meeting people.

Burt extended his hand, and for a moment she stared at it and the man attached to it. She couldn't read anything from his expression, and something inside her quavered at the thought of touching him. She glanced at Neeta, who smiled encouragingly.

Holding her breath and expecting the worst, Bella braced herself as she touched his hand.

A strange warmth spread through her as she made skin-to-skin contact. Suddenly, she felt as if she could read Burt's expressions. He seemed sad. No, not sad, but there was a pain—a deep loneliness that she immediately related to.

Bella stared at the man's craggy face. He was unshaven and dirty, and she'd wager that most women wouldn't have thought him anything but plain. However, none of that even registered with her. Her heart thumped loudly, and something warmed inside her chest. She smiled up at him. "You're a beautiful person, Burt Radcliffe. I'm glad to know you."

Burt blinked as if stunned, glancing at his hand, and Dave laughed. "Burt, you don't know how much of a compliment that is, coming from her. Bella sometimes has trouble relating to people, but I'll tell you what," he leaned down and gave Bella's cheek a kiss. "In some ways, she's more brilliant than all of us put together."

Suddenly, the loud clack of a gavel repeatedly banging on wood drew everyone's attention.

One side door to the Situation Room opened, and a deep voice announced, "Please rise for the President of the United States, Margaret Hager."

~

Bella smiled as she watched Dave handle the niceties of introduction amongst the more than two dozen people in the room. He was in his element, and his apprehension had vanished after the president announced that Burt Radcliffe would be replacing Greg Hildebrand as the Chief Science Advisor to the President and that Burt would end up representing the federal government on the public stage in all matters of science. While the introductions were ongoing, several people handed out thick copies of a freshly-printed report to all in attendance. Bella's eyes were drawn to the glaring red text printed boldly both at the top and bottom of the page.

"TOP SECRET–INDIGO"

While Dave continued to talk, she reached forward and retrieved the bound stack of papers from the tabletop. She'd always had a love for the written word. Words often spoke to her in ways that held a deep meaning. It was as if each word had its own purpose, and it was Bella's joy to unravel the patterns that they formed, searching for hidden messages that most might not entirely see.

As she riffled through the pages, she saw the same red text scrawled as a warning on each and every page. There were many charts of statistics associated with the predicted Earth-orbit crossings. Many of the pages were also dedicated to mapping out the known debris fields between Earth and the incoming black hole. Pages and pages of raw numbers were associated with each map, each line in the report documenting an object's ICRS coordinate, its trajectory, estimated mass, and its current velocity.

In her mind, she saw the maps not as the flat images in the print-outs. Using the raw data, her mind's eye plotted the three-dimensional array of inbound objects as they traveled through space.

She'd watched Dave play pool in one of the Moon base's rec rooms once, and he'd always explained that the lower gravity made the game even tougher. It amplified errors, required an even more careful touch than the game did on Earth. To Bella, the dark spinning hole that was causing the threat was no different than a cue ball smashing through many targets of varying sizes. However, in this case there was no table holding everything on a flat plane. Instead, everything was located in a three-dimensional mesh.

Bella easily recalled all that Dave had taught her about how mass correlated to gravity, and how each object influenced the others near them. Over the years, she'd learned about the complexities of angular momentum and the modeling of chaos, which seemed to apply especially to the strong gravitational and magnetic fields that surrounded the black hole.

She was very good at focusing on something, such as the report in front of her, but a portion of her still paid attention to her surroundings. When the conversation veered from platitudes to something more serious, she put some of her musings over the report in the back of her mind.

"Excuse me, Doctor Holmes." Walter Keane, the Secretary of Defense, waved the thick packet in front of him. "It was very kind of Doctors Radcliffe and Patel to provide us with this, but I'd wager that I'm speaking for most of us in this room when I say that we're not well-versed in astrophysics, or the nature of what's heading toward us. Heck, I'm just an old military man who's trying to understand what we're dealing with and what our troops can do to help. Can you please explain exactly what the hell is going on in a way we'll all understand, and tell us what plans you may have to get us out of this damned pickle?"

Before Dave could respond, the president shifted her gaze to him. "Also, as far as I understand from Doctors Patel and Radcliffe, you were able to predict the presence of the thing that's approaching us more than nine years before the rest of the world even had a clue. That's a question that has been haunting me for quite a while. I hate to mention it, but what, if anything, does North Korea have to do with it?"

With a wry smile, Dave remarked, "No disrespect intended, Madam President, but I sense a bit of Hildebrand's prejudice and paranoia in that question. However, in your position, I can understand the concern."

Just as Margaret Hager was about to retort, Dave held up his hand. "Let me explain. The question deserves a response. I'm a scientist, we all know that—but we scientists still get inspiration at times from unconventional places. Newton had his proverbial apple, a myriad of scientists have in the past been inspired by the work of science fiction authors, and me—I was spurred into action by a dream. Actually a series of dreams. Imagine you're haunted by images that wake you in the middle of the night. The image of the Earth being torn to pieces as it's sucked into a two-mile-wide hole in space. Everyone you know, your parents, your children, your friends and neighbors—everything you ever loved—wiped from existence."

Bella panned her gaze across the room. Everyone's face held the same fearful expression. The image that Dave was painting had become all too real for everyone in the room.

Dave wagged his pointer finger at them. "I'll tell you what: you have that dream for weeks on end, and you'll suddenly become motivated to start studying the problem. Don't they say that necessity is the mother of invention? Well, I absolutely needed to focus on the problem that was haunting me; it's just the way I'm built. And it was during the time I was being haunted by these images that an old college friend called me with some startling news. When I was in college, there was a South Korean student I knew only as 'Frank.' He was brilliant, a savant really. Others are only now researching some of the things that we'd talked about ten years ago. However, it was only after we'd both graduated and gone our separate ways that I learned that 'Frank' was in fact the son of the North Korean people's Supreme Leader, and is, to the best of my understanding, currently ruling that country.

"Frank and I talked occasionally, but it was nearly a decade ago that he told me about the space probe that his father had launched."

"Space probe?" The president asked.

"Yes. From what Frank said, his father was obsessed with space exploration. Thirty years ago, he'd sent probes to the outer reaches of the solar system, beyond the planets we're all familiar with and deep into the cloud of debris that surrounds our solar system. I have no idea what his father was hoping to find, but one of the probes had sent back a disturbing set of signals. Frank shared it with me only after I'd sworn to keep the data secret. He needed help interpreting the information, and it only took me a few weeks until I was convinced I knew what it meant.

"The stream of data I was analyzing was the dying gasp of a space probe as it fell into a black hole. It was then that we knew there was a horrifying danger lurking unbelievably close. I couldn't be sure about the exact speed and trajectory, but we had some estimates. There was a very strong likelihood that we had not much more than a decade before that black hole drifted across our orbit. I knew that some of the things Frank and I had talked about in college were suddenly going to have to shift rapidly from theory into prototype. That was when my quest began, a quest to somehow evade the fate that the most powerful object in the universe had in store for my world."

Dave stood, and as Bella sensed that he was struggling to organize his thoughts, her own mind sorted through the raw data she'd been given. She was running through a complicated game of 3-D pool.

"That's really all there is about the North Korea thing. I have no other explanations that are worth talking about for now, but let's focus on the General's question. Almost ten years ago, I began to think about the problem we've been given. Some of the ideas that Frank and I had discussed helped me stumble onto a seventy-year-old paper by Miguel Alcubierre talking about gravity bubbles, and that got me thinking. It really comes down to the warping of the spacetime fabric that ..." Dave paused, and Bella sensed that he was concerned about how technical his description was about to become. "Make it simple," she overheard him admonish himself.

With a grim expression, Dave began to pace back and forth. "Actually, before I go into the solution, let me briefly talk about space and the danger that we're facing. We've all seen the pictures of planets and asteroids. We know that in space, there is great beauty; however, there are dangers almost beyond imagining. Would you believe that there are objects in space that are no bigger than ten miles across, yet if you were anywhere within several hundred miles, its magnetic pull would be so great that it could pull all of the iron out of your blood cells?

Well, such things exist, and they're called magnetars. They're what can happen to a giant star, much bigger than our own, near the end of its life when it collapses on itself. Yet when such a star collapses, its gravity is so strong that it crushes all the mass of the star together. Even the atoms themselves are crushed, leaving only neutrons behind."

Dave glanced at a nearby table that had been set up with coffee. He retrieved a teaspoon and showed it to the room. "Just a teaspoonful of one of those things would weigh billions of tons." He tossed the teaspoon onto the middle of the conference room table, and it clanked loudly as it bounced halfway along the table's length, grabbing everyone's attention. With an ominous tension in his voice, Dave said, "But that's nothing compared to a black hole. Imagine that there is gravity so strong, that it crushes even the neutrons into nothingness, falling into an infinitesimal dot called a singularity. At the center of the rapidly-spinning black hole is just such a point of unbelievable gravitational forces. Anything grabbed by the gravity well of this celestial monster will either be flung into the far reaches of the galaxy or gobbled up and added to its mass. That's the fate that awaits us. Our planet will either be swallowed whole or be flung in the cold reaches of interstellar space. I suppose the good news would be that we'll almost certainly never experience either fate, because before that, we'll be bombarded by asteroid impacts that will devastate the surface of our planet a thousand times over."

Dave turned to Bella and pointed to the stack of papers in front of her. "How long before the first objects cross Earth's orbit?"

"About 276 days," Bella replied confidently.

While Dave explained the dangers of space, Bella had finished playing her mental game of 3-D pool, the black hole being the spinning cue ball and the 114,483 objects in the report being the wide variety of objects in its way. Some would certainly be swallowed by the black hole, but many would be flung in all variety of directions. Many of *those* would be launched ahead of the black hole, while some would collide with others. But a good percentage flew unimpeded toward Earth. Those that would arrive first had spawned the answer she gave.

Many others would follow, but it would be 276 days before the first ones hit.

Neeta gasped and turned to Bella. "How could you come up with that number?" She rapidly flipped through the first couple of summary pages of the report. "I was told not to include that number. It was to be reported only verbally. And besides, it took our computers three days to model all the possible interactions between everything listed in our astral-body census."

Dave asked, "Was Bella right?"

Neeta stared wide-eyed at Dave. "Exactly right, but I don't—"

"Remember when I told you that Bella is smarter than all of us put together?" Dave winked in Bella's direction. "I wasn't kidding."

With a feeling of satisfaction, Bella leaned back in the comfortable leather chair and tried to keep an uninterested expression on her face. Once people realized what she was capable of, they shied away from her, which didn't bother her in the least. Dave had once explained that most folks were intimidated by people they didn't understand. He'd lived through that himself. Bella had watched as Dave coped with it, but she wasn't sure how to react to the praise he tended to heap on her. After all, she was simply doing what he'd learned to do—but just a bit faster.

Dave bent over the back of Burt's chair and asked softly, "Do you think we can get a more detailed survey of all the objects between the black hole and us, no matter how small? That'll help us get a more accurate picture of our timeline."

Burt nodded. "We've got a dozen of the most capable observatories working full time on that already, but we've had to limit it due to security issues."

The president, overhearing the exchange explained, "Doctor Holmes, we can't risk word of Indigo spreading further than it has. There would be panic in the streets."

Dave nodded. "I understand."

He stood up straight and addressed the others in the conference room. "I know I've been nonchalantly describing our impending extinction, but there's hope. I learned during the flight over here that some of the key preparations that I'd begun while at the ISF were actually continued. That was something I'd really worried about since I'd ... since I'd gone incognito for a few years." Dave tilted his head toward Neeta. "We can all be grateful to Doctor Patel that she'd managed to convince some of those people that I wasn't completely nuts, and some key things that we'll all need are still being manufactured and stockpiled."

Bella smiled as she noticed the flicker of wry amusement on Dave's face.

"I suppose I should explain what all of those trillions of dollars that I supposedly wasted at the ISF were for, and how they relate to saving all of our bacon."

Dave's expression became serious as he placed his hands on Burt and Neeta's shoulders, briefly making eye contact with everyone in the room, and then finally settling his gaze on the president. "What does any reasonable person do when their neighborhood suddenly becomes hostile and you have some awful neighbors moving in?"

With a confused expression, the president replied, "I suppose you could move."

Dave smiled brilliantly. "Exactly right." He turned to everyone and explained, "This solar system isn't going to be very pretty once that black hole is done with it, so that's exactly what we'll be doing before the riffraff comes too close.

"You, me, and the entire planet, we're all moving out."

CHAPTER SIXTEEN

Nearly everyone's jaws dropped at what Dave had said. He patted the air, trying to calm the silent shock of everyone in the room. After all, it's not every day that someone tells you that you'll be leaving your solar system. "I know it sounds crazy," he said, "but I'll explain.

"I knew there was nothing anyone had conceived of that would let us nudge a black hole from its current trajectory. Given that we can't move it, deflect it, or blow it up, what could we do? The only answer that made any sense was to get out of its way."

A man on the far side of the room exclaimed, "But there aren't enough rockets or fuel to get us anywhere. We don't have—"

"I know we don't have a way to transport everyone off the planet," Dave said, waving the comment aside. "Remember when I said I was haunted by the images of our destruction? I began to look into that seventy-year-old paper about ... let's just call it a gravity bubble. It took me weeks of pondering the problem before my eureka moment. That paper wasn't the answer, but it set me on the path."

Dave walked to the table along one of the walls, picked up a straw-berry from one of the platters, and held it up for everyone to see. "Imagine if I plowed a tremendous amount of power into a ring-shaped disc around an object ... let's say, this strawberry. Mind you, that the amount of power we're talking about is tremendous, much more than you're likely thinking. But if we did this, I could envelop this strawberry in a bubble that literally allows me to warp the fabric of space. Imagine you could contract space ahead of this bubble and expand space behind it—and from that, inch this strawberry forward across space itself." He paused for a moment, seeing everyone focused intently on him, many with confused expressions.

Pursing his lips, Dave struggled to come up with an analogy to help explain an immensely complex topic to his audience. "Forget about space for a moment. Just imagine that this strawberry was in a bubble, kind of like when you're underwater in a submarine. If I tweak how some of the power is used to create the bubble, it will begin to move in the direction I choose, as if I have an engine. But instead of a physical engine, it's one constructed out of the gravitational forces surrounding us."

Dave held the strawberry in mid-air and walked with it.

"However, if you moved in a submarine like this strawberry is moving, you'd feel the change in momentum. You'd feel yourself accelerate and decelerate. That's because your submarine is affected by the surrounding gravity, and you can feel yourself moving against it. Yet imagine if this strawberry were within a gravity bubble. Other than watching things move around, it wouldn't be able to feel its own motion because it's isolated from the Earth's gravity. If your submarine was in such a bubble, I'd be able to launch you across the room, and you would see the motions all around you, but you wouldn't *feel* a thing. You wouldn't have felt yourself being launched, nor would you have felt yourself suddenly stop, either."

With his right hand, Dave dangled the strawberry, then let it drop into his other hand. "I'll have you know, that I was able to model this exact experiment in my lab at the ISF nearly nine years ago." Dave looked at the strawberry in his left hand and gave his audience a lopsided smile. "However, when I dropped the strawberry, it never fell. Imagine a strawberry very much like this one hovering in mid-air."

"For you, my dear." Dave tossed the strawberry to Bella. Surprised, she cupped her hands and just managed to catch the fruit.

"I proceeded to do more experiments. Accelerometers trapped within the bubble didn't register any changes, no matter how quickly I moved the bubble around."

Dave walked toward one of the doors and knocked on its wooden frame. "Knock on wood, that's how I plan on moving us out of the way. We'll need an unimaginable amount of energy. From my calculations, it would require nearly seventy-five percent of the world's total energy output. Using the same mechanisms, we'll be able to envelope the Earth in the same type of bubble I put around my strawberry."

Half the room immediately began talking, all at once.

"Quiet down," shouted a loud voice from the corner of the room, and everyone immediately quieted. The old man with the booming voice nodded in the direction of the president and smiled. "Madam President."

Dave felt surprisingly calm, despite having just told a roomful of people what he'd been keeping secret for nearly a decade. He looked at the President of the United States, and surprisingly, she held a determined expression.

With a firm voice, she said, "It's going to take a lot of arm-twisting to get everyone to consume only twenty-five percent of the power that they do today."

Burt, who sat just to the right of the president, leaned closer. "Madam President, I'm thinking that when faced with the choice of human extinction or making sacrifices for a chance at life, the answer is going to be predictable."

The president raised her eyebrows. "Remember what you and I talked about. You'll be the one explaining all this crap to everyone."

Burt rolled his eyes and gave Dave a look as if to say, *"Look what you've done to me."*

Glancing at the president, Dave asked, "Madam President, do you think I'll be able to get access to a lab facility, preferably my old lab? I need to test a few things before we deploy the scaffolding for the warp bubble."

She turned her attention toward Burt. "Can you make that happen?"

Burt nodded as Dave patted his shoulder. "Just remember, this has to begin almost right away. I know Bella said we have about nine months before the first possible impacts. That means we need to be on our way two months before that, so we can get out of the way."

"Everyone," the president announced loudly. "I should have said this at the beginning, but obviously this is a special access intelligence briefing, so I shouldn't have to remind everyone. But I will. None of you are allowed to say anything to anyone unless they're on the read-in list, and you're in a secure location. Each of you will be briefed sepa-rately on the things that need to be done. Clearly there are some things that are already underway, such as the stockpiling of emergency rations, but there are a variety of things that will need quick action."

"Madam President," Walker Keane, the Secretary of Defense said with a frown. "It strikes me that the welfare of Doctor Holmes is a matter of national security. Heck, international security. At some point, this all will become public, and we'll need to make sure the crazies don't get access to someone so critical to our welfare. Should I make arrangements for his security?"

Dave sat down in his seat and pondered what had just been said. Despite being on the run for years, it hadn't dawned on him that anyone would truly want to harm him. He'd always assumed it had been Hildebrand who'd been the idiot in charge of his career's demise, but he'd never believed that he'd be anyone else's target. It dawned on him that, no matter how ridiculous and counterproductive it would seem, he might actually become a target for someone's anger.

"Thank you, Walter, for the reminder." The president nodded. "Please have some troops available in case they're needed, but I've already talked to the Secret Service, and there'll be a detail waiting for Doctors Holmes, Patel, and Radcliffe." She smiled at Bella and added, "And I'll make sure that the agents assigned to Doctor Holmes also include Mrs. Holmes in their assignments."

Dave leaned forward in his seat and gazed across the table at the president. "Madam President, there's really a lot that needs to be done, and I'm afraid some of it will require me to get started right away. Do you think—"

"I understand perfectly." Everyone in the room immediately rose as

PRIMORDIAL THREAT

the president stood. "Doctor Radcliffe, whatever Doctor Holmes needs, make sure he gets it. You have my full authority." She pointed at everyone collected around the long conference room table. "I'm sure that each of you have a bunch of questions for Doctor Holmes. Let me be clear, none of you are to disturb the scientists in their work. Doctor Radcliffe has thankfully agreed to become my Chief Science Advisor, but he's much more than that. Most of you will arrange time with Doctor Radcliffe to best figure out what, if anything, you and yours can do." Her gaze focused on a man with a large mustache. "Jim, I need my Secretary of State to reach out to ... well, to everyone. There's a lot of convincing we're going to have to do."

Burt leaned closer to Dave, the haggard expression etched deeply on his face. "Dave, you and I will need to talk about all sorts of things if I'm going to be able to fend off all the crazy questions I'm about to get asked."

Dave nodded and leaned back in his chair, his mind racing ahead, planning.

Burt glanced at Neeta. "Please make sure that Dave gets a cell phone. That'll make my life infinitely easier."

Thinking about all of the things he had left to do, the item that rose to the top was the need to actually launch a network of space elevators, thus building the scaffolding for the giant gravity bubble. Creating the space elevators had been a success on the Moon, with its lighter gravity. However, he'd only had a chance for a single practice run on Earth before he'd gone into hiding. He had no time left for practice; he had to get it right. With a nervous energy building within him, he worried, recalling the results of that first practice run.

"I just hope the graphene-based tether doesn't snap this time."

151

CHAPTER SEVENTEEN

Along with the rest of the Security Council, Margaret stared breathlessly at the video image projected above the Situation Room's conference table. Jupiter loomed large, like a striped marble, against the pitch-black background of space. Every minute or so, a bright white flare erupted from its surface, giving the upper atmosphere of the solar system's largest planet what looked like yet another in a series of dark, circular scars. To Margaret, it looked like Jupiter had a bad case of the measles.

Walter Keane pointed at the image and spoke with an ominous tone. "That's all heading our way."

Through the video feed, a scientist, whose name Margaret had already forgotten, began narrating the scene being received through a secure channel from the Mount Palomar observatory. *"President Hager, what you're seeing is a portion of the first large wave of debris as it crosses Jupiter's orbit. Each of those flares we're seeing is the equivalent of about 150,000 megatons of TNT."*

"Good God," Walter exclaimed. "Just one of those would wipe us all out."

Suddenly, a flare of white light brightened the right-hand side of the video screen, and the disembodied voice of the scientist proclaimed, *"Ganymede, one of Jupiter's moons, has just been struck...."*

As the light dimmed, Margaret noticed a cluster of glowing rocks slowly tumbling away from what had been the point of impact.

"Spectrographic readings show what look to be elements of Ganymede's exposed core. We'll need to do further analysis to determine the size of the object that impacted Jupiter's largest satellite, but it looks like Ganymede has been destroyed."

A chill raced through Margaret as she watched the devastation unfold in front of her eyes. "Palomar, how far out is the first wave?"

"At its current rate, the leading edge of the first wave of debris will cross our orbit in approximately 245 days."

Margaret turned in her chair and curled her finger at the head of her security detail.

The dark-haired member of the Secret Service approached, and as he leaned down, Margaret whispered, "Where is Holmes now?"

Without hesitation, the agent responded, "He's at the ISF headquarters in Ithaca, NY. I believe they're running some kind of tests."

"Let them know I'll be there tomorrow. I want to see what they're doing firsthand."

"Yes, ma'am. I'll make the arrangements."

Every muscle in Margaret's body ached with tension as she walked through the halls of the ISF's headquarters in Ithaca. The thought of hanging the fate of the world on a solution she'd never seen and had trouble understanding was beyond stressful. She was willing to accept certain things on faith, but *this* she needed to see for herself.

Just as she approached the end of the dimly lit concrete hallway, the double-doors swung outward, and Margaret spied the tall figure of Burt Radcliffe riffling through the pockets of his lab coat.

Burt glanced up and his eyes widened. "President Hager! I didn't realize you'd arrived already." He glanced at the pack of cigarettes in his hand, and with a regretful expression placed them back into his pocket. "Welcome to the ISF's Environmental Test Laboratory."

"Burt!" A woman's voice called from beyond the doorway. Neeta suddenly raced into the hallway and nearly slammed face-first into Burt's back. Several lab coats were draped over her right arm. "I was supposed to tell you that the Secret Service called and—"

"Let me guess ... the president has arrived." Burt chuckled, grabbed the lab coats from Neeta and began handing them out to Margaret and her Secret Service escorts.

Margaret donned her lab coat and followed the two scientists as they turned and walked through the doorway into an enormous room. Margaret panned her gaze around, taking in the immensity of the chamber. The lights from the ceiling were well over thirty feet above, yet they illuminated every inch of the lab. The room itself was easily three-hundred-feet long and just as wide.

Burt pointed toward the far wall, and Margaret spied a tall, circular metal door. "That's the actual environmental chamber where the ISF does its space simulations. They can emulate the conditions in space by pumping out the air and either raising or lowering the temperatures, depending on what that day's test requires."

He motioned for Margaret to follow him and said, "You're just in time to watch the graphene tension test that Doctor Holmes is conducting."

Margaret walked across the room, her medium-heeled shoes clacking loudly on the poured concrete floor as she spied the lower half of someone working under something that looked like a large hydraulic press. Between her and the machinery was a series of large see-through barriers on wheels that she guessed were meant for protection of some sort. With a loud grunt, the man scooted out from underneath the equipment, and she immediately recognized Doctor Holmes. Sweat dripped down the sides of his face, and he held a two-foot-long metal wrench in his right hand.

He cast a brilliant smile at Margaret, shoved one of the transparent barriers aside, and approached. "I'm glad you're here. We're about to see whether or not some of the new rolls of graphene are going to work out for the scaffolding we need."

She extended her hand and said, "You look like you're getting a workout."

Dave hesitated, wiped his palm on his lab coat, and shook Margaret's hand. "Sorry about the sweat. I didn't want to take any chances, especially when I'm about to have the equipment begin tension testing in excess of 100,000 pounds. Any mistakes and it could get ugly pretty quick." He glanced at Neeta. "Can you check on how Bella's doing on the recharging of the capacitors? Now that the president is here, we'll need that sooner versus later."

Neeta nodded and walked quickly toward one of the chamber's half-dozen exits.

Margaret motioned toward the test equipment that Dave had been adjusting. It looked a bit like a long steel table with large metal clamps on either side; attached to each clamp was a long piston. "So tell me what you've got set up here."

Dave rolled another one of the shields out of the way and strolled over to the right-hand side of the table.

Margaret noticed for the first time that attached to the clamp was a clear film stretching over the length of the table. The film was kept taut by the other clamp on the far side.

Dave tapped on the clear film and it made an odd wooden sound, almost as if he'd knocked on a door. "This is graphene. It's one of the lightest and strongest substances we know of, and it has a variety of amazing attributes. However, the only thing we'll be focused on for this sample is its tensile strength."

Margaret ran her fingers over the nearly transparent film and tapped her nails on it. She'd never imagined such an odd stiffness to something that looked no different from the cling wrap she used to wrap sandwiches with. "It's so thin. How strong is it?"

"Well, that's what we're about to find out." Dave motioned for Margaret to take a few steps back.

Margaret stepped behind the clear shields, where a group of nearly a dozen others had collected to watch the experiment.

As Dave pushed the shields back into place, he explained, "Graphene has historically been very tough to manufacture in massive quantities while maintaining a good quality. It's just like the old saying, 'You're only as strong as your weakest link.' The same can be said for the graphene we're using. The strength of the material comes from the quality of manufacture, and what we're testing is a sample of many layers of graphene sandwiched together into a matrix. So even though we're tolerant of some imperfections in the manufacturing process, I can't exactly know if what we've got is good enough without stress testing it. After all, the last time I did this kind of test was a little over four years ago, and the test failed. Well ... it didn't completely fail, it was good enough for the lower gravity demands of the Moon, but it wasn't good enough for what we need here on Earth."

Burt leaned closer to Margaret and noted, "Neeta said that they've improved things since then." He handed her a pair of safety glasses and earmuffs, the same kind of hearing protection she'd often used at the shooting range.

"Everyone," Dave announced loudly. "Eyes and ears on. We're about to start."

Margaret donned her safety equipment and turned on the hearing protection. The speaker inside the headphone clicked, and she distinctly heard the rustling of people around her. For a brief moment, wearing the ear protection reminded her of the communication head-sets she'd used on combat missions. The headphones were specifically made to allow the wearer to hear perfectly—in fact, often better than they normally did—but when a loud sound occurred, the speaker would immediately muffle it.

Dave turned to her. "When that film snaps, and trust me, it's going to snap, it'll be as loud as a bullet." Retrieving a remote from his lab coat, he yelled out a countdown. "Three ... two ... one ... go!"

As soon as Dave pressed a button on his remote, Margaret heard the sound of the hydraulic pumps being activated. Staring at the table, she didn't really see anything happening other than the clamps pulling away from each other ever-so-slightly.

Margaret glanced at the device in Dave's hand and noticed that it had a readout, with numbers that were rapidly increasing.

Dave yelled, "20,000 pounds … 50,000 pounds … 85,000 pounds … 135,000 pounds of pulling strength."

Margaret noticed a strange keening sound coming from the table, and just as Dave yelled, "175,000 pounds," the sound of a bang blasted through the chamber.

A puff of smoke appeared over the middle of the table, and Margaret immediately noticed remnants of the transparent film hanging from both of the clamps. She turned to Dave and asked, "So was that a pass or a fail?"

Dave smiled and tossed her a thumbs up sign. "We needed 50,000 pounds of tensile strength at a bare minimum, but it looks like this stuff will do just fine. I'll need to check our stocks, but this graphene will work for addressing Indigo's needs."

Reflecting the relief that Doctor Holmes was demonstrating, Margaret felt a bit more at ease. However, she still had the same nagging questions she'd entered the facility with. Those had not yet been satisfied. She'd not even thought to worry about the strength of the graphene or the making of these so-called space elevators; it was what they were going to be used for that terrified her. "Doctor Holmes, can you show me this gravity bubble thing that you talked about? I know you described it, but it's still hard for me to imagine what that's even like. And since much of our future hinges on this thing working on a huge scale, I'd really like to see it in action."

With a pensive expression, Dave removed his safety glasses and nodded. "President Hager, I think I can arrange a demo that should impress you."

～

"The capacitors are fully charged and we're ready when you are." Neeta's voice crackled through the handheld speakerphone that Burt was carrying.

The light dimmed, and Margaret suddenly heard a loud hum echo through the giant laboratory.

Burt brought the phone closer to his mouth and said, "I read you loud and clear, Neeta. Dave just routed the power to the electromagnets, so we're good to go here. Bring it in."

"Be right there."

Burt walked toward the end of a long yellow strip of paint that ran down the middle of the three-hundred-foot length of the laboratory floor and said, "President Hager, let me explain what you're about to experience—it's rather fantastic."

He motioned at the painted strip. "Underneath the painted line is an unbelievably strong electromagnet. The ISF uses it to test a variety of things, but in this case, you'll see it being used to help kick start this experiment."

One of the doors suddenly opened on the right side of the chamber, and Margaret stared at the odd sight of a large, upholstered armchair being wheeled toward her by Bella and Neeta. The chair had a large horizontal wooden hoop attached to it, and just as Margaret was going to ask what it was, Dave's voice chimed in from her left.

"Excellent, looks like we're ready." He held a tablet PC with a long antenna extending from it. He motioned toward the beginning of the yellow line and said, "Let's set it up at the starting position."

Margaret noticed that the wooden hoop surrounding the chair was attached with a set of three wooden spokes, leaving the front of the chair unobstructed so that someone could sit on it.

Dave turned to her and extended his left arm toward the chair. "Madam President, if you can duck under the outer ring and take a seat in the chair, I'll explain what we're about to do."

The Secret Service agent broke in, "Madam President—"

But Margaret waved dismissively at him. "I don't care to be lectured about your safety protocols, I'm doing this." She turned to Dave and asked, "You're sure this is safe?"

"Yes ma'am," Dave grinned and nodded. "I've run this type of test countless times, and it's perfectly safe. In fact, at this scale, it's actually rather fun."

Margaret's curiosity was piqued. She ducked under the wooden ring in front of the chair and sat in the rather comfortable chair.

Dave motioned toward her feet. "If you don't mind, I'd rather not have your feet hanging over. Can you sit cross-legged or—"

"How about this?" Margaret tucked her feet underneath her and sat back. She felt odd, sitting in such a relaxed position in public.

"Perfect." Dave knelt in front of the chair and pointed at the wooden hoop. "As you can see, this isn't exactly a normal chair. Imagine that this chair represents Earth and you represent humanity. The spokes that are holding this hoop where it is represent the space elevators we're going to be installing, and the hoop is the circle that represents the circumference of the gravity bubble we'll be creating. Notice that I have both the spokes and the circle itself wrapped in a thin film of the same graphene that we'd tested earlier. The spokes themselves aren't what's going to move you. They're simply holding the ring in place, which will create the gravity bubble, and it's the bubble that will move you around."

Margaret leaned forward, touched the smooth surface of the wood, and nodded.

"We'll demonstrate this in three steps. First, I'm going to activate an electromagnet buried underneath the concrete. This will lift the chair up enough so that when the gravity bubble forms around the chair, nothing untoward will happen to the floor itself. Second, there are some very high-capacity batteries built underneath that chair you're sitting in. These are things I've home-brewed, and they have the special property of being able to store tremendous amounts of energy, and on-demand, they can also discharge very quickly. We'll need it, because even at full charge, this demonstration will last no more than forty-five seconds. I'll activate the bubble remotely, and even though you'll remain seated, you might feel an odd sensation of weightless-ness. Just, whatever you do, don't attempt to get up. And finally, I'll show you what it's like to travel inside this bubble."

"And you're sure it's safe?" Margaret's stomach churned. "If I'm going to become weightless, does that mean we'll be weightless as well when you activate the bubble around the Earth?"

"Dave gave me a ride earlier this morning," Burt interjected from somewhere behind her. "It's safe, but memorable. And no, we won't become weightless when we do it for real. The Earth's gravity will still be there, holding us down like it does today."

Dave nodded. "Correct. And in this experiment, since you'll be isolated from any gravity effects coming from outside the bubble, you'll become weightless while the bubble is active."

Leaning against the back of the chair, Margaret gripped the armrests and breathed deeply. "I'm ready. Just talk me through this while you're doing it."

Dave took a few steps back, retrieved his tablet PC, and swiped his finger on its surface. "Activating the electromagnet...."

Margaret suddenly felt the chair rise from the floor.

"Everything okay?" Dave asked.

"Just go ahead," Margaret groused, feeling a touch impatient. "I'll yell if I have an issue."

"Okay, activating the bubble, you might hear a bit of a hum as the spokes carrying the energy to the ring create the bubble effect."

A vibration started under the chair, and Margaret suddenly felt herself rise slightly on the cushion. She felt as if she were on the apex of a rollercoaster.

"I've turned off the electromagnet and you are currently floating in the air, isolated from the effect of Earth's gravity. When I move the bubble, you won't feel any sensation of motion whatsoever. I'm actually manipulating something called spacetime. Imagine, if you will, that you're on a rubber sheet. Instead of you moving, I'm going to shrink the space ahead of you and expand the space behind at the same time. This will end up moving you forward.

"I also know that our eyes can fool us sometimes, so to help you appreciate this experiment, close your eyes for a second."

Margaret glanced back at Dave, and he nodded reassuringly. She closed her eyes and said, "Okay, they're closed."

"Open your eyes." Dave yelled almost immediately, but his voice seemed oddly distant.

When Margaret opened her eyes, she gasped. During the mere

second that she'd closed them, she hadn't felt a thing, but suddenly Doctor Holmes was yelling at her from over two-hundred-feet away. Margaret's pulse began to race, and she smiled.

"President Hager, are you ready for your return trip?"

"Yes!" She yelled, and without warning the world rushed past her, as if she were watching a race on TV. Without any sense of acceleration, two-hundred feet flashed past her in less than half a second, and she suddenly felt a bout of dizziness. Her heart thudded heavily as Doctor Holmes continued talking, and the chair lowered to the floor.

As Burt helped her out of the seat, her legs felt unsteady. But Margaret's mind was racing. "I can't believe … no, I *do* believe, and I suppose that's exactly the point." She shifted her gaze toward Dave and the other scientists gathered around her. "You're sure you can scale this up to what we'll need?"

Dave glanced at Neeta, and she nodded. "Madam President, we'll do everything we possibly can. As long as we have the materials and the power to feed the ring, we'll be fine."

Margaret smiled and clapped her hand on Dave's shoulder. "I believe you. It's now my job to make arrangements with all of the other countries. You'll have what you need. When this is over, the world's going to owe you, big time."

Dave shook his head. "This is a team effort, like most things are. Speaking of which," he turned to Neeta and asked, "do you think you can help me take inventory of the raw materials required for the network of space elevators? I'm worried about whether we have enough of this new batch of graphene."

Neeta glanced at Burt. He nodded and said, "Neeta, go do what you need to. I'll juggle DC and the NEO program until you're free."

"Okay, we've all just confirmed that we should be busy doing other things," Margaret stated emphatically. "And with that, I'll bid all of you adieu."

CHAPTER EIGHTEEN

As Burt strode deeper into the underground concrete tunnel, the door he'd passed through automatically closed behind him. The sound of metal sliding against metal echoed ominously through the tunnel as the lock engaged, sealing him in.

Meeting him at the end of the tunnel were two men dressed in black suits. They looked almost identical to the two who'd brought him here in a blacked-out cargo van. The only thing he'd been told was that he was being brought to an old nuclear bomb shelter somewhere underneath Manhattan. At first, he'd thought they were part of the president's Secret Service, but now Burt suspected these guys were from some other branch of government that nobody talked about. Most of the Secret Service agents he'd met were reasonably friendly, but these folks were ... different. More serious than anything else.

One of the men approached with a long scanning wand, the same kind used at the airports. "Arms up and to your sides, Doctor Radcliffe."

Standing near the end of the concrete tunnel, Burt stared ahead at the brushed steel of a metal wall while the agent slowly swept the scanner down the side of his chest.

Not seeing any obvious door, button, or other means to get past the wall, Burt asked, "Are we meeting people in this tunnel?"

The agent continued his agonizingly slow sweep of every inch of his body, without a word in response.

Burt had been told that he'd be briefing some people in a confidential setting, but he'd never realized to what extent the word "confidential" could actually be stretched.

The stone-faced agent who'd been scanning him for what seemed an excessive amount of time finally nodded to his partner. "He's clear."

The agent next to the wall pressed his hand against the metal barrier. A green glow leaked from under his splayed hand, followed by a loud metallic click.

He pulled his hand away as the sound of metal smoothly sliding against metal whispered from the wall. The agent turned to Burt, and in a firm voice, said, "This location doesn't exist, nor did this meeting ever happen. The people you are about to brief weren't here, and even if you know who they are, you don't. Is this understood?"

"Sure, no problem." Burt smiled, thinking that this was all a bit extreme. After all, whoever it was past these doors, they couldn't be a bigger deal than the President of the United States.

Expecting a metal door to yawn open, Burt's eyes widened in surprise as he watched the foot-thick wall slide into the ground, only stopping its descent when its top was level with the floor.

The agents motioned for him to enter, and as he stepped over the "wall" an unseen motor reengaged, lifting the barrier once again and sealing him in the entrance to a large, round chamber.

The fifty-foot-wide domed chamber had been carved from the surrounding bedrock. Dominating the room was a large U-shaped black table, along which were seated approximately thirty men and women, all in business attire.

At the far end of the chamber, in the middle of the U, was a distinguished, elderly man, who stood as Burt entered.

"Welcome, Doctor Radcliffe." The man's British accent echoed loudly in the amphitheater-like chamber.

He extended his hand toward the lone chair that sat in the open space at the center of the room. "Please, have a seat. I'm sure you're wondering what exactly you are doing here, and why the secrecy. We too have many questions about what your government likes to call 'Indigo.'"

How the man said "your government" made Burt's heart skip a beat. He scanned the faces and clothing of the people arrayed along the table. They looked foreign, all of them. Their dress, their style of hair, most certainly the speaker's accent. What was going on?

How do they know about Indigo?

Burt had been told that he would be briefing a group of politicians. He wondered if he'd made a huge mistake. *Who are these people?*

"Doctor Radcliffe, let me assuage any worries you might have, said the British-accented man. "Your President knows you're here, and she'd be here herself were it not for the briefings she's already had the privilege of having."

Burt wasn't sure what to believe, but he slowly walked to the leather-upholstered swivel chair at the center of the room and asked, "What is this place? Is that why I'm here? To give you folks a briefing? Before I do that, I'd really like to know...." Burt panned his arm across the chamber. "What is all of this, and who are all of—" Suddenly, he stopped mid-sentence and recognized the man with the British accent. "Um, sir ... aren't you the Prime Minister of Britain?"

A smile slowly crept across the older gentleman's face, and Burt knew he was right.

"Doctor Radcliffe, this gathering doesn't have a name per se. We all meet at times of importance, and do so in a somewhat clandestine manner, both for political and security reasons."

Just as Burt opened his mouth to ask a question, the Prime Minister held up his hand. "Please, Doctor Radcliffe, before we start, let me tell you a brief tale which I hope will help you understand what we're looking for from you. Clearly, anything said within this chamber remains confidential."

With the man's smooth voice and accent, Burt experienced a surreal moment, almost as if he were playing a part in an old-style James Bond movie.

"Doctor Radcliffe, there was a time not so long ago that the world's nations found themselves at the brink of a disaster. Many of the world's citizens have religious beliefs, and that's all well and good. Hell, even though I'm loathe to admit it, I too believe in a higher power. Some might argue that religion has caused more harm than good, but that's a debate for another time."

Putting his hands on the table before him, the Prime Minster leaned forward and spoke with an ominous tone. "Even though the public never knew, there was a time not so long ago that three nuclear-weapon states lost control of their arsenals to in-country religious zealots. In all three incidents, these maniacs had a common link. They were all spurred by a desire to bring about the end of the world, and in so doing, they believed that God's hand would intervene. For some, this might mean the coming of the Messiah, or the second coming or whatever your religious faith would have you believe about the end times. I'd wager that you're most familiar with what Christian chronicles in Revelation. Nonetheless, the in-country security forces barely managed to quell the pending disasters and regain control of their respective domestic situations."

Burt's first thought was about what the president had shown him: the Brotherhood of the Righteous. Were these the same lunatics the Prime Minister was referring to? His mind raced as he tried to recall anything in the news about religious riots, and suddenly, something clicked. "Wait a minute, I remember there were a bunch of religious leaders' funerals that happened at the same time, like ten years ago. There was a huge thing made of it, but I thought they'd all died of heart attacks or—"

"Yes," the old man cut him off. "We need not talk more of the who and the what. Suffice it to say that the problem was taken care of, and taken care of quietly—without suspicion. It was only after that incident that the heads of the nuclear-capable states realized that we all had the same latent risk of security breaches. Cloaked under the shawl of a religious following, these suicide cults are still alive and well throughout the world, and with millions of followers or sympathizers. We, as a civilized set of nations, could not abide their ever gaining control or inciting global unrest."

Burt recalled the image of the albino monk, and shuddered at the thought that there might be millions of those zealots throughout the world.

The Prime Minister motioned toward his peers arrayed on either side of him. "In each of our respective countries, we cull those who would be the most problematic amongst the cult members. We ensure that procedural votes do not give them sway in our respective governments. We also limit their access and success in business."

Pausing for a moment, a wry grin bloomed on his face. "I suppose we as a group aren't very much unlike the boogiemen of many a cheap dime-store novel, those who control things in less-than-honorable manners. But we do it to keep the rest of humanity safe."

Burt nodded ever-so-slowly.

Oddly enough, none of this bothered him. He wasn't particularly religious, and he certainly didn't want to accelerate that hand of God in any way, shape, or form. Burt may not have been perfectly content with some of the turns his life had taken, but he certainly wanted to continue living. "Prime Minister, if you know about Indigo, then why did you all need me here? Why tell me these things?"

"Actually, the answer is quite simple." The Prime Minster leaned back in his chair and motioned toward the others in the room. "We all wanted you to understand why this group exists. You needed to know that we're fighting against a significant portion of our society, a portion that's ready to believe almost anything, given certain circumstances. With the possibility of what Indigo presents, it seems clear to us all that if the truth were known by the public, we'd have a global disaster. Hell, even if our interstellar friend decided to forego visiting us, and this was all some kind of mistake, the public knowing of this threat would be a calamity of epic proportions. These suicide cults need only an excuse, or what they might deem as a sign from above, to wreak havoc on the civilization that we hold so dear." The Prime Minster glanced at the others, and with a grim tone, explained, "There are activities already underway in each of our nations to stifle the reactions of those with whom we are concerned. From you, we want to fully understand the nature of what we're facing and the preparations that will need to be done. This group might also have some suggestions on what to expose to the public and what not to expose, but first, let's hear what you have to say."

Sitting comfortably on the plush leather chair, Burt slowly wheeled it closer to where he'd walked into the room, so that he could see everyone at once.

With a brief cough to clear his throat, he projected across the room, "As you all I'm sure realize, a black hole is one of the most dangerous..."

Burt felt supremely relieved that he'd spent nearly two days straight talking with Dave about all of the science regarding his solution, and considering the issues that might arise. After the nearly two hours of rather detailed discussions with the thirty-four heads of various countries, he felt drained. Almost as if he'd been on trial, suffering through a prosecutor's interrogation. However, instead of one prosecutor, he'd needed to face down thirty-four of them, all asking pointed questions and probing every conceivable angle. In some cases, the dynamic debate resulted in heated arguments amongst the world leaders, and it was only after the British Prime Minister produced a gavel from somewhere and began banging loudly on the table that he managed to bring the room back to order.

The only definitive conclusions that Burt could discern were that more discussions needed to occur, and each of the countries would be sending a representative from their scientific community with instructions from their government.

As the group stood and began to migrate toward a table heavily laden with food and refreshments, the Prime Minister approached and patted Burt on the shoulder with a sympathetic smile. "Doctor Radcliffe, I apologize for some of what you just experienced. I know it must have been a bit trying, dealing with us politicians, many of whom who can barely *spell* physics, much less debate it in a cogent manner. Most of us are fairly level-headed, but we have our moments."

Burt shook his head and smiled. "No worries. I've seen worse. There's an old saying in academia, 'Academic politics are so vicious because the stakes are so small.' That being said, I've waged these kind of verbal battles before."

The elderly gentleman nodded, but sighed heavily with an expression of regret. "Yes, I suppose you're likely right about that. Just don't be surprised if things for all of us get quite ugly before everyone falls into lockstep. People aren't going to want to hear what needs to be said, but I'm sure you'll do fine." The Prime Minister pasted on a smile that almost certainly was intended to be reassuring, but nonetheless left Burt feeling even more worried. "You handled yourself very well, and I'll be telling Margaret exactly that." Glancing at a table with a large, silver tea set, the Prime Minister patted Burt's shoulder once more. "I don't know about you, but I need a spot of tea to soothe my frayed nerves."

Just as the gray-haired man turned, Burt felt a tap on the middle of his back, and he turned to see a short Asian man not more than a foot away, staring intensely at him.

"Oh, hello." Burt immediately recognized the middle-aged and slightly overweight man as the one who'd sat at one of the ends of the U-shaped table. He'd never said a word, even when the others were yelling at each other. "Did you have a question?"

"Radcliffe, arrange a time for me to meet privately with Dave Holmes. Dave and I are old friends."

Blinking, Burt was taken aback. "Uh, I don't really have the authority to arrange meetings with Doctor Holmes for anyone. I'm afraid you'll need to reach out to the president or maybe you ... I'm sorry, I don't mean to be rude, but who are you?"

The man tilted his head at an angle and smiled. "Talking to your President may be difficult. There are many in my administration who aren't particularly friendly with those in hers. When you talk to Dave, tell him Frank wants to talk about the power converter."

Burt took a step back, at first not sure if the man he was talking to was sane. But suddenly, the name Frank popped into his mind. "Frank? As in, North Korea Frank—the same one who went to school with Doctor Holmes?"

With an unexpected burst of enthusiasm, Frank clapped his hands together gleefully. "So he talked about me? He needs to know that I've made progress on the project he and I had talked about."

Suddenly, he grabbed Burt by his upper arm and pressed his face closer. "I *need* to talk to him."

Shrugging his arms out of the man's grip, Burt stepped back, and Frank's eyes widened. Being the supreme leader of his country, he probably wasn't used to dealing with people who weren't cowed into total subservience when in his presence.

Frank leaned forward and whispered in a hoarse, somewhat desperate tone. "There's more, but I can't really talk about it here." The short man glanced nervously over his shoulder. "And the information I have ... I just can't be sure. It seems crazy, half-baked, but that's why I need to talk with him. Dave had always been good at unscrambling things, finding the worth in the half-baked and ill-formed ideas that sometimes inspired me." A sad expression bloomed onto his chubby face, as if remembering a time from long ago. "Even though he's American, he's really..." Frank paused, seeming to weigh his next words carefully. "He's really smarter than any of us, no offense intended."

"Trust me, I understand." Burt nodded. "Dave is beyond brilliant. I'll talk with the president on your behalf and see what I can do, but I can't promise anything more."

The pariah state's Supreme Leader sighed. "It's important. You can tell your Margaret Hager that I'm doing what I can to keep my generals in line, but only so much can be done in my situation."

And with that parting statement, North Korea's Supreme Leader turned away and walked toward the table laden with an international collection of delicacies.

~

Word of the threat had very carefully been spread amongst the other leaders of the world, yet through some small miracle, word hadn't yet leaked to the general public. Burt had always heard that there was no such thing as a secret in government; people couldn't help but talk about their "secrets." Clearly, that wasn't always the case.

He took a deep breath, filling his lungs with the musty smell that permeated the room. He stood in front of a podium as the last of the nearly one-hundred-and-fifty scientists gathered in a secure auditorium located in Fort Meade. He wasn't sure if his upset stomach was from the greasy breakfast he'd eaten at the hotel, or because he was going to be disclosing to the world's top scientists, his peers, the details of how they would deal with the impending threat.

Burt had steeped himself in academia and the scientific community for nearly three decades, and he knew how things worked. Peer review was required for any serious affirmation of new concepts, and he knew that the idea of telling over one hundred of these people that they'd have to forego the normal procedures for something literally Earth-shaking was lunacy.

A lunacy that was necessary.

As the last of the scientists settled into their seats, Burt leaned forward and tapped on the microphone, panning his gaze across the room.

"Hello everyone," he began, "I'm thrilled to see some old friends in the room, and I'm looking forward to meeting the rest of you for the first time. I just wish the situation wasn't as serious as it is today."

Trying to rid himself of his nerves, Burt took another deep breath and shrugged his stiff shoulders.

"You've all been briefed on what we're facing. You've also been sworn to secrecy, and what is said in this room, stays here. This meeting has two purposes. One, it is for me to explain how we might be dealing with what is already described in the reports that you've received. But it's also a time for us to discuss the ramifications of what is happening, and create a plan on what else might need to be done. Each of your respective countries needs your guidance, and I'm charged with helping coordinate this discussion and summarize the conclusions."

Having given many speeches over his lifetime, Burt's nerves had melted away, only to be replaced with a steely determination to do what needed to be done. When word of Indigo eventually went public, he knew that it was these people who'd have to explain it to their constituents, and if they couldn't, the result would almost certainly be panic. Too much was at stake for him to screw this up.

"First of all, what I'm about to describe has been designed by Doctor David Holmes, who, if you don't know him in person, you certainly know who he is. I wish he could be here, but he's out there." Burt motioned toward the outside world. "He's trying to address the concerns we're about to talk about, so I'm here in his place."

One of the scientists in the front row, an older gentleman with a shock of white hair, stood and asked in a loud voice, "Doctor Radcliffe, I object to the idea that we'd stake the fate of the world on new beliefs or understandings. That's not how things work, and you know it."

Having expected pushback from the audience, Burt shook his head. "Your objection is noted, but I'd assert that you're forgetting our history. Advances in science often come in spurts. Things that are long understood to be fact are suddenly blown asunder by contradicting empirical data.

"Until the late nineteenth century, the scientific world believed in a substance called luminiferous aether, a substance that was purported to be the medium by which light traveled. And then one day in 1905, a man named Albert Einstein tossed aside all that the scientific community believed with his theory of Special Relativity.

"It was only fifty years ago that most thought that the world's oceans came from the Earth's early bombardment by comets and other water-carrying objects. However, only with the passage of Halley's Comet and the spectroscopic analysis of other comets did we determine that those icy objects couldn't have been the basis of our oceans. They had ratios of deuterium-based heavy water to normal water that were twice that of our own oceans.

"Instead, we learned that a large portion of our Earth's own upper mantle is composed of rock known as ringwoodite, that if brought to the surface, could easily bring forth many times the amount of water that we currently see in our oceans. Oh, and one fact to note ... the water trapped within our mantle has exactly the same composition as the water in our oceans. We now know that through many millions of years of volcanic activity, the Earth populated its own oceans, effectively setting aside our old understanding.

"What modern scientists believed for centuries was overturned quickly due to these findings.

"What Doctor Holmes has demonstrated as possible is, in my estimation, no less than what Albert Einstein did with the theory of Special and then General Relativity. Doctor Holmes has turned what we thought we knew on its head."

Knowing that what he was about to say would be controversial, Burt took a deep breath and tried to keep a grimace off his face.

"What I'm about to describe is ridiculously complicated. Some of the things we're going to talk about are going to challenge everything we hold to be true. Trust me, I know how we all are. I'm one of you, and in that, I mean that we're all, by nature of our academic backgrounds, the type who ask lots of questions, debate, and believe in peer review of all things. I'm sorry, we don't have that luxury anymore. Not for this."

A murmur rose from the audience, and a woman stood in the back. "That's crazy," she yelled. "Nothing is so complicated that it can't be debated. If it's so convoluted to explain, then I'd assert it's probably not something we can depend on."

The murmur grew louder as some scientists shifted restlessly and others grumbled in Burt's direction.

Burt pursed his lips at the bold challenge and leaned closer to the microphone.

"I never said I couldn't explain it. I said that for some of you, it would be a challenge to accept." With a surge of indignation, he changed tone, trying to head off what he feared might become a pissing contest. "You can question what I say all you like, but if you believe that science and the way we communicate concepts hasn't been convoluted, you're delusional. Even the simplest thing can be complicated beyond reason. And I'll give you an example.

"I know that some of you may not specialize in physics, but I'm fairly certain you all know that power is not the same as energy, right?

"Power, being a measure of the amount of work being done at any given time, is expressed in watts. However, energy is the amount of work done over a span of time. That's measured in watt-hours.

"So you might say that, 'One watt of power, maintained for an hour, is a watt-hour of energy.' Simple, right?"

Many faces in the audience stared blankly, while others showed signs of annoyance.

"You're all silently staring at me thinking, 'This is remedial crap, why is he doing this?'

"I'm doing it to show you how anything simple can be screwed up when too many people debate what is already working instead of just moving on.

"For instance, a battery's energy isn't expressed in watt-hours; it's amp-hours, which of course means you need to multiply it by its voltage to get watt-hours. Simple yet again, I suppose.

"You might think you know what a BTU is, that's of course the British Thermal Unit, which is equivalent to 1,055 joules. Why 1,055 joules? Oh, because that's how much power was needed to raise the temperature of a pound of water by one degree Fahrenheit.

"Obviously, to know that, we're deep into the memorization area, right?

"What if I told you that the British used to have something called a Board of Trade Unit, also known as a BTU? It was a kilowatt-hour, which I might note isn't the same as the British Thermal Unit version of BTU. This form of BTU didn't equal 1055 joules, but instead was 3.6 mega-joules. Confused yet?

"But wait, there's more.

"In India, a kilowatt-hour is simply referred to as a Unit. So a million units is actually a gigawatt-hour, a billion units is a terawatt-hour, and so on.

"Clearly, many of us have found ways to muck up the way we talk to each other or express common concepts, so let's not pretend that we're innocent of such things.

"You've all been charged not with debating the nature of what we're facing, or the solution that is currently being enacted, but with the ramifications of the solution and how each of your countries must prepare. Each of your respective countries need your guidance. If you can't explain what I'm about to talk about, each and every one of you will be responsible for the inevitable chaos in your respective countries."

Burt panned his pointer finger across the crowd.

"Let me assure you, that if you aren't able to convince your people that all will be fine, there *will* be chaos. It will be you who they'll look at, either as the savior of your nation or the one to blame for its internal strife.

"To help all of you, I'll spend the next couple of hours talking about what Doctor Holmes has discovered. I'll go into the physics involved, and I'm going to ask for no debate on the possibility of it working or not. I'll have you know I watched a prototype in action. It works. End of debate."

Before anyone could object, Burt leaned even closer to the microphone, emphasizing his next statement with a somewhat ominous tone.

"If you have a clarifying question, ask it—but I won't accept anyone slowing this process down for the rest. We don't have the time. All of our lives are at stake. If you're unable to control yourself, you'll be ejected with a prepared summary of the proceedings sent to the head of your government. Am I understood?"

A hand was raised in the middle of the third row, and Burt motioned for the man who raised it to speak.

"Excuse me, Doctor Radcliffe," he said. "I'm not a physicist like many of you, so I won't pretend to grasp what you're about to discuss. However, I'm a climatologist and an oceanographic research fellow. After the mechanics of the solution are discussed, will we then cover the preparations? That's hopefully where I might have thoughts on some things that could be worthy of discussion."

Letting out a breath that Burt didn't realize he was holding, he felt the tension leak out of him. He gave the man a smile. "Yes, of course. We'll most certainly get into the practical matters afterwards. I'll be here as long as it takes for us to discuss things. I simply want all of you to at least have a glimmer of understanding of the solution whenever things do go public."

Burt glanced at the clock on the wall. A warm feeling of accomplishment flushed through him. He'd secretly anticipated a much longer time spent arguing.

"I started this talk by saying that science can occasionally be turned on its head. Well, that's exactly what Doctor Holmes has done.

"Think about this, the concept of negative mass, gravity isolation, and movement beyond the speed of light. Folks, what had been the world of science fiction has shifted hard into scientific fact. Just like the concept of aether, or the origins of our oceans, so much of what we'd assumed has been flipped on its head. It's an exciting, yet terrifying time to study humanity's place in the universe."

Burt attached a portable microphone to his shirt and rolled up his sleeves. Turning to the front of the auditorium, he grabbed a dry-erase marker from a tray running along the bottom of a tremendous whiteboard and began drawing what would end up being the image of the Earth, along with a network of space elevators surrounding its equator.

"Let's begin with the details of what we'll experience when the Warp Ring is activated, and then move on to the theories that led to the solution."

Sitting on the sofa in the Oval Office, Margaret studied the security report as a device in the ceiling projected the holographic image of the Secretary of Defense's face hovering in the middle of the room. His gravelly voice reverberated through hidden speakers.

"Madam President, we believe that the terrorist cells have almost no communication with each other and are receiving signals from a central authority."

"I got that from this report, Walter. What's this about very-low-frequency signals and a terrorist communications network?"

Margaret watched the hologram of Walter as he flipped a page on his copy of the report and cleared his throat. *"Our lab folks out of USACIL managed to extract an implant from one of the dead terrorists. They've determined that the implant was a fairly sophisticated form of wide-frequency receiver."* The Secretary of Defense picked up another set of papers and began reading from them. *"The receiver is no larger than a grain of rice, yet was coded to use the body's electrical pathways as both an antenna and a power source. The receiver is capable of detecting spread spectrum signals, and by virtue of being embedded against the subject's tympanic membrane, it's able to translate the signals into auditory stimulus. The receiver is designed to support both broadcast as well as targeted signaling."*

Margaret stared at the ghost-like image of the former General, hovering four feet off the ground, and pressed her lips together in thought. "So in other words, we've got terrorists with implants sitting on their ear drums that can receive what is in effect global terrorist chatter as well as messages directed to them?"

"Yes, ma'am, that seems to be the case. Pretty advanced technology, if you ask me."

"You're not suggesting a nation-state is backing these assholes, are you?"

"No, ma'am, I have no evidence of that as of yet. But the CIA might have different thoughts on the matter."

"Okay, what else have you got on the terrorists?"

"In all of the captured suspects, we've found a common identifying mark somewhere on their body. A tattoo of an hourglass. We don't yet know its significance, and in interrogations, none of these people were willing to say anything. We're running the image through our systems to see if there's anything we can make out of it."

Flipping to the last page of the report, Margaret came upon a computer sketch of a suspect that she immediately recognized. "Okay, what about our albino friend? What's the story?"

"At the home of one of the terrorist suspects, one of our teams

managed to extract a DNA sample from a handwritten letter that had originated in a small town in southern Romania. With our latest DNA analysis computers, we were able to reconstruct the facial structure. Obviously age, hairstyle, and any acquired scars aren't represented, but the image was immediately earmarked for further analysis by our intelligence folks."

Margaret leaned forward on the sofa and studied the image. The hologram showed a rotating headshot of the suspect, his white skin, fine eyebrows, and white hair with a slightly receding hairline. It sent a shiver down her spine. "He certainly looks like our guy from those intercepted video transmissions. Do we know anything about him? Is he the ringleader or just a mouthpiece? Can the DNA computers give us fingerprints?"

"I asked the same questions. We don't yet know who this guy is, or what his role is with the terrorists. As to the fingerprints, I was told that DNA won't dictate a person's exact fingerprints, so that's a dead end."

Setting the report on the sofa cushion, Margaret rubbed her eyes and gazed at the hovering image of her Secretary of Defense.

"Anything else?"

"No, ma'am. All five branches of the military have teams supporting local police forces in each and every one of our territories. We're managing to keep a cap on these terrorists domestically, and per your orders, we have special operations troops seeking the source. For now, that's about it on that front."

"Walter, just be aware, we're going to have to continue drawing on the military to maintain order, especially on the coasts."

"Understood."

"Thanks, Walter. Dismissed."

The video feed cut off and Margaret sank back onto the sofa, her mind racing.

Raking her hands through her blonde hair, the president turned toward her Chief of Staff who'd been sitting in the corner of the room, listening.

"Doug, get the DOJ on the line. I need to figure a way to legally start jamming all aerial communications that these terrorists might be using. That means radio stations and such might end up getting cut off, and I don't need the ACLU or Congress up my ass over this. We're going to have to start using drastic measures to take control over this situation."

The old man pushed his glasses higher up on the bridge of his nose and nodded. "I'll make some calls and try to set something up for later this afternoon."

Margaret rubbed her fingers on her temples, fighting the nausea that threatened to make her lose her breakfast.

With worry gnawing at her gut, she murmured to herself, "Is what I'm about to do going to save us or destroy us?"

CHAPTER NINETEEN

At the first-ever closed joint session of Congress, there were absolutely no spectators or non-essential personnel in the public galleries or the chambers themselves. All that was said was done so under the confidentiality accorded to matters of national security. Burt had just finished talking nonstop for nearly an hour, and his nerves were frayed.

He waited as a few of the 535 of the nation's elected leaders awkwardly shuffled out of what looked like wooden pews in an old church: not the kind of seats he'd have expected in one of the grandest of the capitol's buildings.

As some senators and congressmen organized themselves into lines behind the microphones that had been placed there for the question and answer session, Burt pulled in a deep breath and knew he was going to get some oddball questions. After all, none of these people were scientists.

When he'd disclosed the threat of the black hole, the crowd had immediately reacted, and Burt realized that many of them hadn't been briefed on Indigo. During Burt's speech, the Speaker of the House had used that damned gavel of his at least a half-dozen times to restore order to the chambers.

Suddenly, the chambers quieted, and the attendees turned as the president made her entrance. Unlike in public forums, or when she gave the State of the Union, she strode briskly past the rows of pews and the politicians lined up at the microphones. She hustled quickly to the front of the chambers and took a seat not more than ten feet from Burt.

There was no glad-handing or sucking up by the politicians, no formal announcements of her presence by the Speaker or Sergeant at Arms. It all left Burt feeling a bit uneasy. This was definitely not how things had run when he'd watched State of the Union speeches on TV in the past.

Margaret gave him a reassuring wink, and the Speaker of the House leaned forward from the row directly behind him. "Are you ready for questions, Doctor Radcliffe?"

Burt nodded. The Speaker banged his gavel three times and spoke loudly into his microphone. "Members of Congress, I expect decorum to be maintained, and with that, Doctor Burt Radcliffe, the President's Chief Science Advisor and Director of NASA's Near Earth Object program, is ready for your questions. The Speaker recognizes Representative Young from the great state of Vermont."

"Doctor Radcliffe," a female voice broadcast through the chamber, and Burt's gaze fell on the elderly black woman standing in front of one of the three microphones. *"If this black hole is so small, how do we know that it will even hit us? Isn't there a chance that it could just pass us by without a problem?"*

"Excellent question," Burt said, acknowledging her with a nod. "It may be hard to imagine that something only a few miles wide could have such a devastating effect, but let me explain it in this way. We are currently ninety-three million miles away from the sun, yet its gravity is strong enough to keep our planet locked in orbit. There are planets much further away, in excess of a billion miles into space, that are similarly influenced by our sun, and locked into orbit due to the effect of the Sun's gravity.

"Imagine that this black hole has nearly three-quarters of the mass of our sun. The same mass as an entire star packed into a very tiny package. So if it helps you imagine it, what would you think would happen if another star wandered through the solar system?"

Burt paused briefly for effect, allowing the visual to sink in. "Chaos would be what happens. Not only does this black hole have the same gravitational influence as any other star, imagine that this thing is rotating like a top. But it's rotating faster than you could ever imagine. What would happen if a star that was spinning like a top came barreling through our solar system?"

Burt jabbed his finger at the audience and said, "I'll tell you. There are two fundamental possibilities. Anything that got too close would get sucked into the black hole and be destroyed. The other option is that anything caught in its wake would almost certainly be flung into interstellar space, where it would quickly freeze, and that includes our planet. I cannot assure you with absolute certainty which we'll encounter, but it will be one or the other.

"So to specifically answer your question, we don't *need* to be hit for this black hole to be a problem. It's already a problem. I didn't cover this in my earlier talk, but we already are dealing with uncomfortable questions coming from astronomers who've not been disclosed on the nature of this disaster. Saturn, which is much closer to the black hole, has already been knocked from its orbit. In fact, we're all already being affected. The trajectory of our orbit around the sun has bulged outward a bit. It's as if a tug of war is taking place between the sun and this primordial threat we call a black hole. Unfortunately, it's a war with no winners if we do nothing about it."

The chamber remained deathly quiet for a few seconds before the Speaker announced, "The Speaker recognizes Senator Hoffman from the great state of Connecticut."

Burt panned his gaze toward a tall, dark-haired man on the far-left side of the chamber. The man's sandpapery voice broadcast throughout the chambers as he spoke, *"Doctor Radcliffe, I'm the chair of the appropriations committee. I've been asking this question repeatedly and have gotten absolutely no responses from the administration. I hope you can shed some light on this. It seems to me that the funding for this grand solution you've talked about has never passed through Congress. Your doom and gloom speech has certainly implied that there's a need for such a thing, yet I know that the funding requests for such emergency measures still need to go through Congress."* The man's voice took a deeper, more aggressive tone. *"Damn it, man, Congress has a responsibility of oversight. Especially with building projects of this scale. Your organization is supposed to advise us and receive consent before going off and doing these things. These things need to be evaluated for merit and prioritization. I demand an explanation, and a promise that such things will not continue without following due process."*

Burt tilted his head at the politician; he couldn't feel anything but a sense of bewilderment. "Excuse me, Mister Hoffman—"

"Senator Hoffman, thank you very much. I'm an elected member of the United States Senate."

"Fine. As to funding requests, you'll need to take that up with the director of NASA, my direct boss, or with the president, my other direct boss. However, considering the situation we're all in, are you seriously asking us to get priorities from your committee? Have you evaluate the merit?" Burt barked out a laugh. "Excuse me, but how many on your committee are experts in astrophysics? How many of you are acknowledged experts in materials science or astronomy? How—"

"Doctor Radcliffe, this is not a joking matter. We will be consulted and fulfill our elected obligations, or we'll cut off funding for your program. And none of us want that to happen."

Immediately a loud murmur rippled through the chamber, as people argued amongst themselves. The Speaker banged his gavel and yelled, "Order! I'll have order!"

Burt blinked at the congressman. The man's words had left him dumbstruck.

Suddenly, Burt felt a tap on his right shoulder, and was surprised to see the President Hager standing next to him, a frown on her face. She covered the microphone with her hand, leaned closer, and whispered,

"I had a feeling this would happen. Other countries have been going through similar issues. It's fine." She motioned for Burt to take the seat she'd just vacated, glanced behind her, and nodded.

The Speaker hammered the gavel with such ferocity that Burt wouldn't have been surprised if the thing had broken in half.

"Members of Congress, I have the high privilege and distinct honor of presenting to you, the President of the United States."

Margaret tapped at the microphone and turned her attention to Senator Hoffman. "Mister Hoffman—"

"Madam President, it's—"

"Shut up, you imbecile." Margaret glanced at the woman next to the podium and whispered, "Turn off their mics."

"When I was privileged to be elected President," she continued, "I knew what I was getting into. Sure, there'd be lots of kissing babies, pardoning turkeys, and signing bills. There'd certainly be a crisis here and there. There would be the occasional natural catastrophe, there would most certainly be fights with Congress over silly things. But let's face it, this job never came with the expectation of having to worry about the annihilation of the human race.

"None of us could have foreseen such an event, and most certainly the Framers of the Constitution wouldn't have written down instructions for dealing with such a cataclysmic scenario in a hidden, for Presidential eyes only envelope.

"However, they *did* anticipate the need for strong leadership in times of rebellion, invasion, or when public safety required it. They knew that the responsibility inevitably would end up having to lie on one person's shoulders. And that would be the President.

"Senator Hoffman's insane desire to mix politics into the survival of the human race is an example of where a leader must just cut through the horseshit and eliminate barriers for those who can truly help, like Doctor Radcliffe.

"Given that, I have absolutely no other choice but to assert, as is my right, article 1 section 9 of the Constitution. I am as of this moment suspending the writ of habeas corpus and declaring martial law."

Burt stared wide-eyed as the doors to the chambers opened and dozens of armed soldiers streamed in and began stationing themselves along the walls. He glanced at the president and noticed her strong, determined expression. She had known something like this would happen, and had planned for it.

"Please take Senator Hoffman into custody." She pointed at the dark-haired senator. Two soldiers jogged forward, grabbed him by his arms, and dragged him kicking and screaming from the chambers.

"By this declaration, I'm suspending all committee operations in Congress. There's no need for them, because soon we'll all be suffering through a curfew and a relocation process. Yes, even me. We'll discuss the details at a later time, but I would like all of you in these chambers to step in line with a new set of assignments. Your priorities will be to help maintain public order.

"In the upcoming months, we will suffer many inconveniences. But we need all of you to communicate with your constituents and to keep things calm. The last thing we need are riots in the streets, but trust me —any public unrest will be treated in the harshest manner imaginable.

"Is there anyone in the chamber who feels that they cannot comply with these expectations? Speak now and I'll contact your state's governor and arrange for you to be replaced so you can go home. However, if I find that any of you are somehow subverting the cause or working against the people's best interests, you will be locked up for an indefinite period of time. Certainly until this crisis is over."

Burt stared at the sea of faces, all of them seeming to have frozen into statues. Evidently, none wanted to give the impression that they were going to argue with this no-nonsense president.

"Good." Margaret nodded. "However, I do want to give you this solemn pledge. Once the danger is over, I will return everything back to the way it was. Trust me, I don't relish what I'm doing."

The president glanced at Burt, and with a barely suppressed smile, she asked, "You ready for more questions? I think things will be more productive now."

Burt nodded, and the president leaned closer to the microphone. "Now that that's over, Doctor Radcliffe, I hope you can overlook some of the unpleasantness of one bad egg. Many of these people are much more reasonable, and I consider many of them to be close, personal friends. They're going to need your help explaining what's going on to their constituents.

"The floor is yours."

CHAPTER TWENTY

Neeta watched as Dave studied one of DefenseNet's space anchors. It was a giant metal box that easily weighed five tons, and it was ready for deployment. However, Dave insisted on inspecting the laser and the rest of the payload. He lifted one of the access panels to look inside and asked, "The laser is rated at six megawatts, right?"

"Yup." Neeta nodded. "The ISF folks finally managed a design that was reliable once it's up in space. All things considered, if we actually needed to shove an incoming asteroid in another direction to avoid us, we'll have nearly 200 megawatts of coordinated laser power to bring to bear."

"That won't be enough," said Bella ominously, who'd been standing next to the wall of the supply room. "While you could destroy some smaller objects, the larger ones are your problem. Even if you fired the lasers today at an incoming asteroid in excess of 20 miles wide, all it would do is ablate parts of the surface, nudging it ever so slightly. Any effect would need to be done with the asteroid further away."

"She's right, Neeta," said Dave. "And besides, even though the lasers on DefenseNet are good on paper and it's how we get the public to understand what we're doing, it doesn't address our immediate needs. We don't have the time necessary for it to be effective against some of what's incoming, and you and I both know that it won't do crap against the black hole."

Having removed the side panel, Dave stared at the text printed on the side of the multi-ton components built into the space anchor. "What about the battery? Can it sustain drops in the power flow coming from the ground without interrupting laser operations?"

"If we encounter a power interruption from the ground, the battery can store enough energy to sustain max output from the laser for probably half a day or so before we see a drop-off. I didn't think we'd need more than that."

Dave gave her the same sidelong glance he used to give when she said something inordinately stupid. "For our immediate purposes, I don't actually give a damn about the laser. The laser is there to justify the rest of this stuff. People can understand the laser, but they don't understand the rest of this. Remember back in the Situation Room when I said that we'd be feeding nearly seventy percent of the world's power output through these so-called elevators? A six mega-watt laser doesn't need anything even resembling that kind of power. Crap, if that's all we needed the lasers for, we'd have stationed them up above with large solar power aggregators to store enough energy for their use. No, in total, we'll be feeding nearly thirty terawatts of power and shunting it across the connected ring at the end of the elevator's spokes."

"Whoa, I didn't think...." Neeta quickly crunched the numbers in her head. "Well, if we have thirty-six of these flying above us, and if you needed to power the ring through the batteries, I don't think you can get all of the power you need out of them fast enough. But even if you could, I'd wager it would drain them in a couple of seconds." Neeta's eyes widened as she envisioned a glowing ring of power encircling the Earth, and only then did things snap visually into place for her. "But there's no way these batteries can handle that kind of power flow. They'll be incinerated."

Dave gave Neeta a knowing smile. "Don't worry, I've asked for some of the goodies I designed to be transported here from the Moon base where I've been hiding for the last couple years. They'll help route and switch the incoming power feeding into what I'm calling the Warp Ring. Just so you know, from my experiments, I got much better results creating a stable bubble by running off the direct current from a battery than I did from what the power grid gives us. That being said, the only reason I designed this with the batteries as the space anchor was to normalize the spikes and drop-offs inherent to the power coming from our electrical substations."

Neeta shuddered. "Um, I don't even want to contemplate what might happen if we're traveling at high speed and that bubble of yours collapses."

"That's why we have the batteries," replied Dave. "A couple seconds should be good enough for any hiccups. Hell, we could even sustain a complete shutdown of one or two spokes at a time, and the power incoming from the rest should be enough to maintain the gravity bubble. I just don't want to take any chances, for some of the reasons you noted." Dave resealed the space anchor's metal enclosure and stood. "This looks good enough. Show me what's been done with the graphene spools. If we can't get this beast up in space and attached to a power source down here, this is all for naught anyway."

As Dave and Bella stood near the doorway, Neeta riffled through a file cabinet in one of the crowded storage offices located within the ISF's headquarters building. It took a few moments, but she finally found the folder that contained the production samples she'd approved just prior to her leaving to work on the West Coast for NASA. She handed to Dave one of the sample sheets of the graphene the ISF had been producing ever since she'd left. "If you look closely at it, it's much thicker than the production methods you'd been using to create your original spools. We discovered a way of creating a thicker fused array of graphene sheets that preserved all of its electrical and thermal conductivity properties while also maintaining the structural integrity."

Waving the nearly transparent sheet in the air, Dave studied it under one of the bright lights on a nearby desk and asked, "How much have we made, and can its production be accelerated?"

Flipping through the sheaf of papers, Neeta skimmed the inventory of the various ISF warehouses across the globe. "I'd say we have nearly 700,000 miles of material, all on gigantic spools, ready to be deployed."

Letting out a deep sigh, Dave grumbled, "That's not enough. We need closer to a million miles if we're going to place an elevator along every ten-degree parallel along the equator."

Neeta frowned, knowing that it had taken almost three years to create what they already had in stock. "Are you sure we need that much? I'll make some calls and see what can be done."

Bella's normally quiet voice carried a worried tone as she blurted, "We must have 828,000 miles of the ribbon for the thirty-six elevators at 23,000 miles each and approximately 170,000 miles to connect all of the space-anchors together."

With a warm smile, Dave reached out to Bella and rubbed the back of her neck. "As Bella affirmed, and if my math is correct, I think 828,000 and 170,000 is just shy of a million miles of material. If we can't get enough material, we can try to space the elevators out further so that we have fewer of them. But I'm not sure if the current flowing through steeper angles are going to change the effectiveness—"

"Enough, we'll get it done one way or another." Neeta groused, as she tapped on her ear bud and said, "Dial Burt Radcliffe."

She waited a moment as her cell phone projected a ringing tone in her ear. One ring ... two rings ... and Burt answered, *What do you want, I'm about to walk into a meeting with more generals than I'd like to ever meet in my life.*

"Burt, we've got issues," she said. "We've only got about seventy percent of the graphene we need for Indigo. I don't think the production facilities we have online can make up the difference in time, and we've only got five months—"

Dave tapped Neeta's shoulder, shook his head, and whispered, "Four months ... we need time for testing of all the power station connections and...."

"Scratch that, Burt, we've only got four months. Can you help?"

"As soon as I get out of this meeting, I'll get right on it. Send me the details in an e-mail, as well as who the manufacturing techs are that we know can do this right now. Whoever needs to get sent to Lord-knows-where to train other facilities, I'll make sure it gets done. You just focus on helping Dave deploy the Indigo solution. Let me worry about getting you what you need. Hey, I have to go; send the details."

The connection dropped, and Neeta turned to Dave with a brief nod. "We'll have what we need."

With a grim expression, Dave wrapped his arm around Bella's waist and gave her a one-armed hug. "While that's being arranged, I'll get the modifications done on the space-based anchors. As we get those deployed, Burt can help get us the supplies we need, and Neeta, can you find out how we're doing on getting power to all of the Earth-based anchor stations? As you know, without power, all of this is pointless."

Neeta sighed, knowing he was right and hating that her life had suddenly gotten so complicated. Working with Dave again reminded her of the pressure she felt when working with someone who seemingly had unlimited intellect and energy.

It made her miss working with Burt and the rest of the crew at JPL.

"I've got a call in to the Secretary of State and the head of the Department of Energy as well. Connections from the national power grid systems to the base stations have been arranged with almost everyone, but I'll check again."

Dave gave her his all-too-familiar expression, the one he got when his mind was churning at a million miles an hour and he was losing patience with everyone around him. "Check right away. I plan on getting my ass up on a shuttle and starting this business as soon as possible. The first station south of us is just outside of Quito, Ecuador, and I want to test the connections as we go along. Those are the failure points. We don't have time for delays."

"Fine, let me go find a secure line somewhere in this building, and I'll get on it now."

As Neeta left the office, with Dave and Bella following close behind, she silently wished for the quiet times she'd experienced when all she had to worry about was monitoring near-Earth objects.

Only a few hours earlier, Neeta, Dave, and Bella had arrived at the Mariscal Sucre Air Base in Quito, Ecuador. Neeta had expected the heat to be overwhelming. Instead, the altitude was what gave her discomfort. At nearly 8,000 feet, the air was cool, but the lower oxygen levels were giving her a terrible headache.

They'd been assigned a multi-bedroom suite in a rather fancy hotel, and as Dave droned on about the upcoming day's plans, Bella had gone to sleep, while Neeta was leaning back in her chair and wishing she could get rid of her headache.

Suddenly, there was a loud knock on the hotel room's door. Neeta hopped out of her chair, and as Dave approached from behind, she peered through the peephole. The familiar voice of one of the Secret Service agents echoed through the door. "Doctor Patel, Doctor Holmes, I've got a courier message for you."

Opening the door, Neeta was met with the steely-eyed gaze of the leader from their security detail. Behind him stood a wide-eyed woman holding a notebook-sized canvas bag to her chest. With Dave hovering behind Neeta, the agent leaned closer and spoke in a very low voice, "I'm sorry to disturb you, but the DCS sent a message." He motioned toward the nervous-looking woman. "She has something coded for your eyes only. I figured it might be urgent."

Neeta asked the courier, "DCS?"

"I work for the Defense Courier Service, ma'am. I carry secure dispatches—"

"I understand," Neeta quipped, and extended her hand. The courier gave her the locked canvas bag, and a three-foot-long metal chain extended from the woman's wrist to the bag.

Neeta glanced at the three-man security detail stationed outside their hotel room and noticed for the first time that a handful of agents stood at each end of the hallway as well. She wondered if they'd always been there, or if something had happened.

"Let's get out of the hallway," Dave suggested.

Turning back toward her room, Neeta motioned for the courier to follow.

Neeta and Dave both took their seats around the dining room table, which they'd covered with a mess of maps and scribbled logistics notes. The courier stood over Neeta, her face expressionless. One of their security agents stood watch only five feet away. Turning the bag over, she saw that the only information written on it was the hotel name and her room number. A heavy-duty metal zipper sealed the bag with a fingerprint lock. Neeta pressed her thumb to the fingerprint scanner, and almost immediately heard a soft click.

The woman nodded. "Doctor Patel, now that the bag's inner seal has been exposed to air, I'm supposed to inform you that the ink will ignite the paper in thirty minutes. I'm to return the remains of the document in the fireproof carrier."

With Dave leaning over her shoulder, Neeta retrieved the envelope from the courier's bag, ignored the "Top Secret—INDIGO" emblazoned across the envelope in glaring red letters, and began reading the contents of the ominous envelope.

Doctors Holmes and Patel,

The president has asked that certain pieces of intelligence be disclosed to both of you.

We have quadrupled your security detail and further work is being done to safeguard your mission.

Unfortunately, we have been made aware of a security breach we believe has come from the maintenance crew working in Andrews. Despite the leak of information, we do not believe that your mission has been compromised.

Our intelligence operatives have intercepted a transmission that indicates Doctor Holmes has become a target.

Rest assured, we'll keep you safe.

Intercepted transmission dated: 13 JUL 2066
Timestamp: 13:51 GMT

"An unscheduled military flight has been booked with presidential authority to the Mariscal Sucre International Airport.

Doctor David Wendell Holmes is currently boarding with several other unidentified civilians. There's a heavy security contingent accompanying them."

Intercepted transmission dated: 13 JUL 2066
Timestamp: 15:23 GMT
Automatically Translated From: Bulgarian

"Praise to God and all his faithful, the time of Armageddon is at hand.

Only through His will can the savior be brought forth, yet we have received confirmation that the Ecuadorian government is cooperating with the U.S. on something that concerns all of the Brotherhood.

An American scientist, David Wendell Holmes, is scheduled to arrive on an American military transport at Mariscal Sucre International Airport. His sudden appearance is unsettling, and we fear that he is working to alter God's plan. He must be stopped at all costs; God's will must be carried out. None can be allowed to interfere.

Spare no expense and have no mercy.
-BR"

Neeta stared at the paper as a chill raced up her spine. If these lunatics knew where they were going, someone inside the government must have leaked the information. She turned to Dave with a worried expression; he sat back in his chair, staring vacantly at nothing whatsoever.

The agent in charge of their security detail pressed his hand to his earpiece and turned to Neeta and Dave. "The hotel has been cordoned off and they're doing a security sweep as we speak. The windows in this room are bulletproof, so you'll be safe staying here until our departure for the anchor site. We'll have a large escort on the way there."

Letting out a deep shuddering breath, Neeta stuffed the papers back into the fireproof bag, handed it to the courier, and whispered, "Tell them, 'Thanks for letting us know.'"

~

Evidently there'd been an attack on the hotel while they slept, but with well over one hundred soldiers safeguarding their location, Neeta would never have known had their security detail not informed them during breakfast.

She wouldn't have thought it possible to get her mind off the anxiety of being a target for some religious nutcases, but the rough trip through the jungle had done the job.

Their escort had managed to find a method of transport that she disliked more than flying—but as the Ecuadorian military vehicle bounced along a dirt road on its one-hundred-mile trek west-northwest of Quito, she felt as if all of her bones were rattling in their sockets. Neeta began to feel a visceral hatred for the personnel carrier she'd been stuffed into the back of.

Sitting opposite from her, Bella and Dave both seemed unaffected by their chaotic surroundings. In fact, Dave had been chattering nonstop since they'd left the hotel located just outside of Ecuador's capitol. As he droned on and on about every last detail of assembling the space elevators on the Moon, Neeta's mind wandered.

Between the acrid smell of the truck's exhaust, the pungent odor of the rotting vegetation from the surrounding jungle, and the bouncing truck, Neeta wasn't sure which was making her more nauseous. The stink permeated the warm, humid air, and it was all Neeta could do to avoid throwing up as she maintained her death grip on the bench seat welded to the bed of the military vehicle. Glancing toward the back of the transport, she saw four men wearing brightly colored Hawaiian shirts, who thankfully looked nearly as miserable as she felt. They were a small part of their government-assigned security detail.

Following behind their transport were a series of identical vehicles, and leading their procession was yet another series of troop transports. In total, the Ecuadorian Army had sent an entire company of heavily-armed soldiers to escort them through the jungle toward their final destination.

Neeta wasn't used to the idea that she needed protection from anyone. Certainly not by well over one-hundred soldiers. But even though the jungles were reputed to be safe, neither the U.S. government nor the Ecuadorian government were taking any chances with the American scientists, Dave especially.

"Doctor Patel, Doctor Holmes," one of the Secret Service agents announced, as he pressed his finger against his ear. "Our escort's commanding officer is riding ahead and says we are only five miles from the location, which should be about ten minutes at our current pace. I also just received a status report from the ISF's monitoring crew out of Quito. They said that the descent of the elevator's guidance system has just broken into the Earth's atmosphere."

Turning her gaze toward Dave, Neeta caught him glancing in Bella's direction and watched with fascination as she lightly touched his arm. They stared wordlessly at each other, and suddenly Dave turned his gaze toward Neeta.

"Perfect timing," Dave remarked. "We'll probably be in visual range of the guidance system in about twenty minutes." He winked at Neeta. "I can tell you're miserable out here in the heat. Truthfully, I'd have figured that you'd be used to the heat with your Indian heritage. I promise that we'll be in and out as quickly as possible."

Neeta's back stiffened and she raised an eyebrow as incredulity flushed through her. "Oh, really? I was born in London, you ass. I happen to be used to air conditioning, cold weather, and fog. You of all people, I'd have thought, wouldn't presume things just because of my complexion."

Dave burst out laughing and shook his head. "Neeta, I love that I can get a rise out of you so easily. You're still as prickly as ever."

Bella wiped a sweaty lock of red hair from the side of her face as she glanced back and forth between Dave and Neeta with a perplexed expression.

Neeta's mind raced with any number of retorts about him being black, and therefore more tolerant of heat from his own African heritage, but she choked them down and controlled herself as she glared at him. The damned bastard was actually looking quite comfortable and wasn't sweating at all. Over the years that she'd known Dave, he'd proved to be one of the few people who'd ever called her out on her sensitivity about stereotypes. As she let her surge of anger subside, she felt slightly embarrassed by her reaction.

She gathered her long, sweat-soaked hair and began to braid it into something more manageable. She tossed Dave a lop-sided grin and groused, "I hate you sometimes."

Dave sat back with a satisfied expression. "Only because I'm always right."

Rolling her eyes, Neeta growled with frustration.

"Daddy, when are you coming home?" Emma asked. Her voice reverberated through the speakerphone in Stryker's small hotel room.

"I'm not sure yet, honey. As soon as I'm done with my work."

"Hey, you know what?" The six-year-old whispered.

"What?" Stryker asked, as he finished shaving at the bathroom sink.

"Mommy says that the Army is a poopy place, but she didn't say poopy, she said the 'c' word."

Stryker wiped his face with a hand towel as he imagined Emma's shocked face when his ex-wife used the word "crap" to describe the Army. When Lainie and he were still married, she'd often used much more colorful language when describing Army life.

"She used the 'c' word, eh?" He smiled and desperately hoped

Emma would keep her six-year-old innocence for as long as possible. "Well, sometimes your mom gets upset."

"She didn't really meant it. I told her that it wasn't a very nice thing to say, and she said she was sorry." Lainie's voice suddenly echoed loudly in the background, and Emma whispered, *"Okay, I have to go. Mom is calling me for school."*

"I love you, Emma."

"Love you too. Bye."

A dial tone blared through the speaker, and the line disconnected, bathing the room in an eerie silence.

Stryker stared at himself in the mirror; the bags under his eyes and the haggard expression reflected the hours he'd been putting in. "Jon," he said to himself, "you're looking like shit."

He glanced at the clock on his nightstand and realized he had a full six hours before meeting with his platoon sergeants.

Enough time to go through the latest intelligence reports the captain had given him.

Suddenly, a loud buzzing echoed from his nightstand. With two quick strides, he grabbed the ringing cellphone and put it to his ear. "Hello?"

"Lieutenant Stryker?"

It was Mia's voice. It had been a couple weeks since he'd last seen her, but her voice was unmistakable.

"You do realize that it's not even 0600, right?"

"Sorry, but I just talked to my brother and he's given me some info I think you might find useful. I'm about to grab breakfast, you interested?"

He pressed the speakerphone button on his cellphone and switched to the map application. "Where at?"

"It's called The Corner Diner. It's here in town at the corner of Leber and Rainier Lane." Stryker's phone buzzed momentarily. *"There, I just sent you the location."*

"Got it. I'll be right there."

Stryker hung up, made sure his firearm was securely seated in its holster, and wondered what the sheriff's brother might have told her.

He grabbed his car keys from the nightstand and felt a smile cross his lips as he considered meeting Mia again.

Having breakfast with an attractive woman was never a bad way to start the day.

～

Stryker walked into the noisy diner, and despite the early hour, the place was packed with people chatting loudly over the sound of an oldies radio station blaring something by Taylor Swift.

The place had a different vibe than the New York City diners he was used to. The smell of bacon hit him like a truck.

Most of the customers looked like construction workers, many of them with their yellow hardhats either occupying a space on their table or under their chair.

Stryker, on the other hand, was fully kitted out in his fatigues, and stood out like a sore thumb.

Panning his gaze across the restaurant, Stryker felt the attention of a dozen or more of the nearby workers shift toward him. The conversations faded as he looked for the town's sheriff.

"Stryker!" Mia's voice cut through the music and murmurs of the diner's patrons.

He glanced to his left and saw her waving from one of the booths on the far side of the restaurant.

As he walked toward her, he barely suppressed a smile. She was wearing civilian clothes and her hair was down, still wet from the shower.

She looked fantastic.

As he settled into the seat opposite from her, a gray-haired waitress came and asked, "What can I get you kids?"

Mia said, "Hi, Debbie, I'll take my usual."

The waitress tapped a few times on her tablet PC's touchscreen. "Three brown-sugar waffles, two slices of bacon, extra crispy, two eggs scrambled, a side of hash browns, and a black coffee."

Stryker stared open-mouthed at Mia. "Good lord, that seems—"

"I'm a breakfast girl." Mia smiled sheepishly and shrugged.

"I guess you are."

The waitress turned to him. "And you, honey? What'd you like."

"Coffee and do you have any Danish?"

"No Danishes, but we have scones with raspberry jelly, if you like."

"I'll take that."

"Any cream, sugar, flavorings?"

"No, black works, and I prefer coffee flavored."

"Anything else?"

"No, I'm good. Thanks."

The waitress tapped a few times on her tablet and walked toward another table.

"A scone?" Mia arched a brow and stared at him. "Lieutenant, didn't anyone tell you breakfast is the most important meal of the day? That's just a snack."

A waitress with a tray full of drinks walked by, wordlessly deposited two mugs of coffee on the table and moved on.

Stryker shrugged. "Well, I guess I'm more a dinner type of guy. And Sheriff, you can call me Jon."

"Will do, and while I'm not in uniform, go ahead and call me Mia." She slid a white envelope across the table. "Billy handed that to me. It's Raven Miller's DD-214."

"So, Raven's former military, eh? How'd your brother get his hands on the man's discharge papers?" Stryker flipped open the envelope and scanned the text.

"I didn't ask." Mia shrugged. "Billy's always had a way of getting into things he's not supposed to. Nothing illegal that I'm aware of, but you know ... sometimes I know better than to ask. As far as this Raven character, I can tell Billy really wants him strung up pretty badly."

Taking a sip of the strong coffee, Stryker shook his head as he read through the suspect's discharge papers. "Raven Blackfeather Miller. Enlisted and Airborne out of Fort Benning, SFAS and Q-Course out of Fort Bragg, and then four years as a Special Forces Weapons Sergeant. This guy was no slouch."

Stryker folded the paper and put it back in the envelope as a wait-ress appeared with their order.

With a heavily-laden plate of food placed in front of her, Mia launched into her breakfast.

Crunching on a strip of bacon, she jabbed the end of a half-eaten piece in his direction and said, "From what Billy told me, Raven was a bomb guy. He spent a lot of time in Eastern Europe back in the 50's when Romania was having those terrorist attacks. You know, when the Muslims and Christians were at each other's throats."

In his mind's eye, he saw the burnt-out hull of the mosque where he'd lost many of his men. It was Bucharest, Romania's capitol: October 3rd, 2055.

Stryker's nose crinkled as he relived the moment from a decade ago. A nearly overwhelming smell of burnt flesh dominated his senses. He swallowed hard against the rising bile. He and his men had been assigned to guard the old mosque near Romexpo, never thinking that the Christian separatists would retaliate against the Muslim place of worship using the same tactics that had been used against them.

Suicide bombers.

"Jon? What's wrong?" Mia asked.

Shaking his head, Stryker grabbed for his mug of coffee and took a deep swallow. The still-steaming liquid burned as it went down his throat and settled warmly in his stomach. He focused back on Mia's brown eyes. "Nothing."

He took a deep breath. "So, this Sergeant Miller was dishonorably discharged. I'll have to look into it. Is there anything else your brother learned about him? Where he went or anything like that?"

"Well, one of the members of Billy's group died of food poisoning." Mia shoveled a large piece of syrup-laden waffle into her mouth. She chewed for a second, swallowed, leaned forward, and whispered, "His name was Cookie, nobody knew his real name, but he made the meals for everyone. It seems that the same day that Raven disappeared, Cookie was making food like he always did when he suddenly fell over and died.

"Cookie was old, could have had a heart attack, but for some reason, Billy decided to feed some of the stew Cookie had been making to one of the dogs, and it ended up dying as well."

"So this Raven guy tried poisoning everyone and took off?" Stryker balled his hands into fists as he remembered his ex-partner's attempt at drugging him.

"Seems to be the case. If you think it'll help, my brother offered to lead you to where he buried the dog. I'd guess the poison might still be detectable."

Stryker pursed his lips as the lyrics of the fifty-year-old Spanish song named Despacito blared through the speakers in the ceiling.

"I might take you up—" the speakers shrieked with high-pitched feedback and went quiet, leaving static playing through the restaurant's sound system.

Mia looked up at the ceiling. "What the hell was that?" She tapped at the phone stud in her ear. "Hi, Meredith, what's up?"

Stryker studied the sheriff's expression as she talked to Meredith. The frown lines at the corners of her mouth deepened.

"No need to dispatch a car, I'm only five minutes away. I'll take a look. Besides, he probably fell asleep."

Mia tapped at the phone stud in her ear, and Stryker asked, "Was that a call from dispatch?"

"Yup, someone called in a complaint about an incident at the radio station."

Hitching his thumb at the speaker in the ceiling broadcasting the hiss of static, Stryker frowned. "You mean the complaint was about that?"

Mia nodded.

He was hit by a wave of apprehension; every hair on the back of his neck stood on end. "Bullshit. No way someone called into dispatch that quick."

Mia's eyes widened and her expression was wary. "Well, the transmission tower is less than a mile from here," she explained as he reached for his phone.

Only two days ago, he and the rest of their battalion had been informed by the head of the 42nd MP Brigade that civilian communications jamming would begin rolling out across the nation.

He hadn't heard anything since then, but maybe that was what had started?

Pressing one of the speed dial buttons, Stryker put the phone to his ear and heard, *"Cohen."*

"Cohen, your team's combing the land just outside the Orting valley, right?"

"Yes, sir. We're following up on a lead we got from the Pierce County PD. What's up?"

"I'm sitting with the Orting chief of police. She and I are going to the transmission tower that's at ..." He glanced at Mia and aimed the receiver in her direction.

"It's where the Trout Spring Hatchery meets with Canyonfalls Creek," she said. "It's a big one-hundred-foot tower with a two-story building at its base and a small parking lot. You can't miss it."

"You get that, Cohen?"

"Got it, sir. We're about ten minutes out. What are we looking for?"

"Meet us at the location, we'll see when we get there."

Mia tilted her heard with a confused expression. "You really think backup is necessary for *this?* The place probably had a generator blow out or something. Do you know something?"

Ignoring her question, he held up a finger and dialed another number.

"What's up, Stryker?"

"Captain, we've got possible activity at a local radio transmission tower. Has the rollout of what Colonel Gibbons had talked about started?"

"I'm not aware of anything being activated in your area yet, but I might not be in the loop. I'll check and let you know. Watch yourself out there, you hear me?"

"Yes, sir. Thank you, sir."

The line disconnected, and Stryker took a quick bite of his scone, dropped a few bills on the table, and stood. "Let's get going." He glanced at Mia's diminutive form. "Are you wearing a vest?"

She wiped her mouth with a napkin and huffed with frustration as she stood. "Don't worry, I've got my vest in the trunk, and my service weapon is always on me." Mia dropped some cash on the table, motioned toward the waitress, and made a beeline for the exit.

～

Stryker tilted his head toward his right shoulder and heard his neck crack as the car weaved through traffic, its navigation system keeping pace with the sheriff's vehicle.

As the cars turned off the main road and proceeded along a packed dirt path winding beside the Puyallup River, the cell phone rang. Stryker leaned forward and tapped the "pickup" button on the old Chevy's touch screen.

"Stryker?" The captain's voice boomed through the car speakers.

"Yes, sir?"

"I just got the G2 on your area. Looks like jamming has begun across all commercial frequencies. A broadcast message to all Washington state residents will be going out through emergency channels about this in the next hour."

A chill raced up Stryker's spine. "Shit! Sorry, sir. But if they're jamming all frequencies, there has to be more than just some localized terrorist thing. What's going on?"

The only noise on the line came from the captain breathing heavily for a full ten seconds. Was he jogging?

"Stryker, I just don't know, and I've got the same questions you do. I'll run them up the chain and see what I can learn. In the meantime, just do what you have to."

"Roger that. Thanks for letting me know."

The connection ended just as his car pulled into a remote parking lot located near the base of a one-hundred-foot tall broadcast tower.

Stryker grabbed the steering wheel, parked next to Mia's police cruiser, and hopped out of the car.

The sheriff stood behind the police cruiser, her hand covering one of her ears as he approached. "Answer, damn it."

She shifted her gaze from the building to another car in the parking lot and back again.

Then, with a loud sigh, she shook her head. "The old coot probably fell asleep again. He isn't answering his phone."

"Old coot?"

"Wendell Litchford. He's a sweet old man who runs the radio station." Mia hitched her thumb toward the old Buick sitting in the parking lot. "That's his. It wouldn't be the first time he fell asleep at the console and the station began broadcasting dead air. I'll go ahead and check things out."

"Hold up a second." Stryker motioned for her to wait as he walked over to his car. Cohen hadn't yet arrived with the CID team and he wasn't supposed to interfere with Mia doing her job.

He also couldn't tell her about the signal jamming. Yet something didn't feel right.

Unlocking the trunk to his car, he opened a large duffle bag and extracted a camera-like device.

"What's that?"

Stryker turned on the FLIR unit and peered through the eyepiece at the building. "It's a thermal imaging camera."

He panned the camera across the building. In the viewfinder, it was almost like the outer walls had vanished as he stared at various shades of blue and one orange-red object inside the building.

"Looks like we've got one person in there on what looks to be the second floor."

"Is he moving?" Mia asked.

After Stryker stared at the color-enhanced thermal image for a few seconds, the figure moved from a sitting position. "Yup, whoever is up there isn't asleep."

Mia huffed. "Well, I seriously doubt I've got much to fear from a seventy-something-year-old grandad."

Putting the camera away and closing his trunk, Stryker hurried after the sheriff, who'd begun walking to the building.

The old guy was probably preoccupied with trying to figure out what was going on with the station's radio signal.

Mia tried the station's front door and it swung open. She walked in and called out, "Mister Litchford?"

Stryker heard a metal clang coming from the stairs and he reached for his sidearm.

Mia moved toward the sound, and he noticed her unfastening the catch to her service weapon. "Mister Litchford?"

A maniacal laugh reverberated through the concrete corridor, followed immediately by the sound of sobbing.

Stryker spied a balding man in his seventies sitting at the base of some metal stairs. He was pressing his hands against the sides of his head and bobbing back and forth, mumbling something.

Moving alongside Mia, he motioned toward the man and whispered, "He's got something in his left hand."

The sheriff moved closer, with Stryker following, his weapon at the ready.

The old man sobbed and kept repeating "I'm sorry" over and over again.

"Mister Litchford," Mia called with a soothing tone. "What's wrong?"

Litchford looked up at Mia and then shifted his bloodshot gaze toward Stryker. "The voices ... I couldn't help myself."

"But now, the voices are gone. I'm not sure what to do anymore."

Stryker couldn't quite make out what was in the man's clenched right hand, but his blood ran cold when he noticed a wire running down his arm.

Mia took a step closer, and Stryker grabbed at her belt and hissed, "Pull back!"

The old man groaned. "I'm sorry, Sheriff. I can't do it anymore."

Without waiting for Mia to respond, Stryker yanked her backward just as the concussive wave blasted them both off their feet.

The world tilted at odd angles as Stryker crashed onto the floor, his breath exploding out of his chest as Mia landed heavily on top of him.

Smoke immediately filled the passage, and the coppery taste of blood coated his lips.

Clambering to his feet, Stryker picked up Mia's limp and bleeding form and struggled toward the building's exit.

Just as he stumbled into the daylight, a half-dozen hands grabbed hold of him, and he barely heard Cohen's voice as the sergeant began yelling orders to his men.

Stryker's knees buckled, and he felt arms lifting him as the men rushed him from the building.

His vision blurred and he closed his eyes. He felt an overwhelming wave of nausea.

In his mind, he could now clearly see the dead man's switch attached to the old man's suicide vest.

He'd seen those before ... in Romania.

As he felt himself being laid on the ground, his mind wandered to the sheriff.

"Mia," he groaned, as someone pressed something against his forehead

Someone pinched his arm, and he heard Cohen yell something about an IV.

Stryker struggled to open his eyes, but the world closed in on him, and everything became silent.

Neeta climbed up to the top of the large concrete building in the middle of the Ecuadorian jungle as Dave stood at the base of a ten-foot metal tower with a flashing red strobe light at its top. He focused on a large tablet PC with a foot-long antenna poking out its side, aiming toward the sky.

Despite being on the roof of a forty-foot building, Neeta felt and heard the hum of the electrical substation that was operating underneath her. She glanced over the edge and noticed that the soldiers had formed a ring around the station, and shook her head. "Well, it looks like we'll be safe in case Bigfoot or the Chupacabra tries to attack."

"They're just doing what they're told." Dave cracked a smile as he tapped on the touch screen. "If you look up, it should be breaking through the clouds in three ... two ... one...."

Shielding her eyes from the sun, Neeta craned her neck and looked up just as a dark object broke through the haze a couple hundred feet above. Her heart leaped as she yelled, "I see it! But it's not quite above us."

"Don't worry," Dave remarked as he stepped away from the center of the roof. "The clouds probably shifted the homing signal a bit, but the rover should auto-center above it. Just watch."

Neeta stared as the dark gray speck grew larger, the sound of its engines growing louder as it approached. She was about to ask if the graphene ribbon had somehow snapped when she finally saw the glint of sunlight reflecting off the nearly-transparent material trailing above the descending transport.

As the object got ever closer, the details of the four-wheeled vehicle under a controlled descent became evident. She glanced at Dave and asked, "You used a lunar rover for the descent?"

Dave covered his ears and nodded as the staccato of the rover's horizontal thrusters altered the course of its fall.

Cringing as the whining sound of the jets grew louder and louder, Neeta watched the four-wheeled vehicle descend slowly and finally touch down on the roof of the building.

Walking toward the rover, Dave touched the end of the 23,000-mile-long ribbon and looked up, a toothy grin spreading wide across his face. "Worked like a charm."

Neeta stared at the clear ribbon as it rose as if by magic into the sky. Her mind had trouble wrapping itself around what she saw. "Amazing."

With a light nudge, Dave pushed the rover forward a few feet, covering the center of the roof where the homing beacon had automatically receded. He tapped on the screen of his tablet, and a slit opened up in the roof. "Time to link the first spoke of DefenseNet to its power source."

"Is there a danger of shock?" Bella's worried voice echoed from the corner of the roof where she'd been watching silently.

Dave shook his head as he fiddled with something on the top of the rover. "No. The current won't be flowing through the connection until we flip a manual switch accessible from within the substation. Even then, the flow of energy is computer controlled, so there's nothing to worry about."

Opening an access panel on the side of the rover, Dave pulled a previously hidden lever, and the metal bar at the end of the ribbon began to flow from the back of the rover.

Hopping to the back of the rover, Dave held up the three-foot-wide ribbon with the heavy metal bar and fed it through the slit built into the roof. "Time to marry the two anchor points together."

Neeta watched as Dave tapped once again on the tablet PC's screen and the slit slowly closed, swallowing the end of the ribbon. With a quick lifting of several latches, and a few more taps on the tablet, the rear top portion of the rover flipped open, leaving the ribbon free of the heavy vehicle.

"Um, Dave, now what?" Neeta asked.

Dave leaned closer to the tablet. "Hey, Byron, you read me?"

"Roger that. I'm still sitting here in the shuttle's cargo bay watching it spill its guts, waiting on you, boss."

"All right, Byron. We're all hooked up here. Launch the anchor into its orbital position and we're all set."

Dave talked back and forth to the shuttle's cargo engineer, who was in charge of putting the business end of the DefenseNet laser and targeting system into place.

As they were talking, the ribbon attached to the roof of the building snapped taut, and the engineer announced, *"The anchor is in position. It has unfurled its communication array, and the business end of the anchor is aiming away from you guys. So I think you did good, boss."*

Dave drummed his fingers on the translucent graphene ribbon, and it was pulled so tightly it sounded as if he were drumming on a wooden surface. Tossing a thumbs-up in Bella's direction he brought the tablet's microphone closer to his face. "Byron, good job. Now get your ass back down here. We've got another run at this in a couple days."

"Roger. Closing the cargo bay doors now. See you back at Canaveral."

With a final tap on the tablet, Dave looked up with a satisfied expression. "Between the time it takes to load the DefenseNet modules onto the shuttle, bring them up there, and drop the ribbons, we're going to need every moment we have to get this done."

Doing the math in her head, Neeta realized that he was right. There would be almost no spare time before testing had to begin. "Dave, other people can also do this and we can run things in parallel."

"No," Dave snapped, suddenly looking flustered. "I don't trust anyone else to—"

"Dave," Bella interjected as she gently placed her hand on his upper arm. "Neeta is right. The thing that takes the most time is for the controlled descent of the ribbon. Why don't you set up two shuttles at once, and then you could stagger the launches? While you're connecting one spoke of DefenseNet, the other spoke is descending."

Thankful that someone was on her side for once, Neeta exclaimed, "That's exactly what I was going to suggest. You can still make sure it's being done right, but parallelize the effort a bit."

With a troubled expression, Dave glanced back and forth between the two women, took a deep breath, and let it out slowly. "Fine, you're probably right."

"We are," Bella remarked matter-of-factly.

Neeta waved away a mosquito she swore was the size of a grapefruit and groused, "Now that the women have had a minor victory, can we get out of here?"

Bella jutted her chin at the rover and asked, "Dave, how are you getting this thing off the roof?"

Dave waved dismissively at what Neeta had thought was an exposed metal beam running along the side of the roof. "Every one of these stations had a crane built into it." He walked closer to the edge and pointed at one of the flat-bed military transports. "It's also why we brought an extra vehicle, to bring the rover back."

Neeta looked at the line of vehicles, and her stomach began acting funny again. "Oh, God, let's get this over with. The sooner we're out of here, the sooner we're done."

Neeta's cell phone rang, broadcasting Burt's caller identification in her ear.

"Burt! We just finished setting the first spoke in the DefenseNet ring. It's amazing to see something just drop out of the sky like that. You should have seen it."

"Neeta, that's fantastic, but not what I called about. I pulled some rabbits out of the hat, and you guys should have about 1.1 million miles of that graphene scaffolding for the elevators in the time you need it. I really need you back in Los Angeles at JPL while I'm here in DC fending off the politicians and ever-widening list of idiots who've been given clearance on Indigo. I can't effectively run the NEO program from here, and you're the only one I can trust who has the clearance for Indigo matters."

Neeta glanced at the receding figures of Dave and Bella, who were walking toward the stairs. "When do you need me to be there?"

"Uh, how about yesterday? I'll send you an email with the details, but there's a whole bunch of things I need to get astronomical surveys on and I need someone local who I trust to run roughshod over some of these people."

Unable to hide the smile growing on her face, Neeta jogged toward the stairs. "I'll be there as soon as I can get out of this disgusting jungle."

"Jungle? Oh yeah, I guess some of those substations are in less than ideal areas. I know you hate getting hot and sticky. You must be in hell."

"Burt, I can't explain how much I love that you said that. I'll be back in L.A. as soon as I can."

"Thanks a lot, I owe you big time."

With a playful tone, Neeta blurted, "And I expect a big payment in return." She froze as what she'd just said registered with her.

"Bye!" She croaked the word out and abruptly hung up, her cheeks suddenly felt like burning embers. "Bloody hell, he probably thinks I was chatting him up! What the hell is wrong with me?"

CHAPTER TWENTY-ONE

It was nearly 11:00 p.m. when Stryker, hefting a large duffle bag over his right shoulder, approached the door to his midtown apartment, praying that he didn't wake the kids. He was going to get enough shit from Lainie as it was for not calling ahead of time.

The last three days had been a whirlwind of activity.

It started with him nearly being blown to pieces by an old man bent on committing suicide and taking anyone he could with him.

Stryker remembered scrambling out of the building, carrying Mia's limp body on his back, but that was about it. The next thing he knew, he'd woken up at the hospital in a really sour mood and with stitches along his hairline from the explosion.

The army docs at Madigan kept him under watch for twenty-four hours and he'd made himself as much of a pain in the ass as possible. After enough grousing and just a little bit of begging, they finally let him out. After all, despite the cuts and bruises he'd received, they didn't really have any other excuse to keep him. He was fine.

In fact, he'd felt a lot better the moment he'd learned that Mia hadn't been killed.

Her death had been weighing heavily on his conscience. Evidently, she'd been struck by several pieces of shrapnel coming off the old man's

211

suicide vest and needed some surgery. Nobody would tell him where she was or any other details, aside from that she'd eventually be okay.

After the doctors at Madigan cleared him for duty, he reported back to his commanding officer, and that's when he was told that he was being redeployed to New York City. He had less than a day to square away any loose ends and catch the first C-130 heading east.

He'd boarded that transport nearly twelve hours ago, and finally he was home.

Stryker put his key in the lock and slowly opened the door.

He was expecting the place to be dark, but almost immediately, he saw Lainie's wide-eyed expression as she stood midway between the living room and the door, staring directly at him.

Shit.

She approached with a stormy expression and whispered, "You—"

"I know, I know. I should have called, but I didn't know I'd be here nor did I have a clue they'd let me bunk at home." He shrugged off the big duffel bag and began rotating his shoulder, trying to work out a kink he'd developed.

Her expression softened as she approached. Lainie reached up and touched his temple. "You're hurt."

Stryker touched the bruised area where the ball bearing from the suicide vest had creased his skull and shrugged. "It's not bad."

Lainie's face clouded up with emotion, and Stryker stiffened, preparing himself for the lecture he knew was coming.

Suddenly, she wrapped her arms around his chest, pressed her head against him and squeezed. "They sent you back because you're hurt worse than you're letting on, I know it."

He sighed and rubbed her back as he felt hot tears against his fatigues.

"Lainie, I'm not lying to you. I'm fine. Hell, I've got three days home and then I'm reporting back in."

She pushed herself back and wiped her face. "You're leaving again?"

"No, at least not that I know of. They actually have me and a team assigned to patrol midtown. Kind of like my NYPD job, just in a different sort of uniform, instead."

"So they're finally bringing the army in?"

Stryker stared at his ex-wife, trying to read the expression of the woman he'd known for more than a decade. She seemed agitated, maybe because he was home and she wasn't expecting it ... but, no. There was something more.

"What's—"

"Daddy?"

Warmth spread through him as he looked up and to his left.

"Daddy!" Emma shrieked as she wiped the sleep from her eyes. She ran down the stairs and jumped into his arms.

"Dad's home?" He heard Isaac's sleepy voice yell from upstairs, and within seconds all four of them were hugging. For a few moments, Stryker forgot everything else in the world, focusing only on what mattered.

Trying to ignore the small army of Secret Service agents and military that always hovered around him, Dave sat back on the beach-side lounge chair, sipped at his piña colada and took a well-deserved break. The pleasant sound of the ocean was something he'd missed when on the Moon. He glanced at Bella, who seemed to be relaxed despite the hectic pace they'd set for installing and checking the connections for all of DefenseNet's spokes. As the salty breeze blew in from the South China Sea, Bella closed her eyes, with only the slightest hint of a smile.

Her head lolled toward him, and she squinted through one open eye. "My body is totally confused. Is it time for breakfast or lunch? Either way, I'm hungry."

Dave smiled. "Well, since we're in Indonesia right now, it's almost 7:30 a.m., so I think we can squeeze in a good breakfast. The rover won't be within range until later this afternoon anyway."

A Secret Service agent approached and handed him a satellite phone. "Doctor Holmes, it's Doctor Radcliffe."

Sitting up, Dave held the phone to his ear. "Hey, Burt, you've got good timing. I was going to call you later tonight. I'm sitting on a beautiful white sand beach on the west coast of Indonesia, just north-west of Lake Maninjau. This'll mark the half-way point."

"That's great progress. In fact, I think you're pushing ahead of schedule, which is awesome. But I'm actually calling to let you know that the president is about to go public with some of the Indigo stuff. I suggest you find a place to watch. She's going live in about thirty minutes."

A surge of excited curiosity washed over him as he motioned for one of the nearby Secret Service agents and whispered, "Can you get us to a TV with access to U.S. channels in thirty minutes?"

After only a second's hesitation, the agent nodded. "Yes, sir. There's a five-star resort only five-minutes away. I just need ten minutes to sweep the area ahead of us, but it's doable."

"Dave, I do want to warn you about something...." Burt's voice rang loudly over the satellite phone. *"Let's just say that what the president says and the reality of Indigo won't exactly match. As scientists, we hate inaccuracy, so I just want you to know that she's not an idiot, and that she'll be purposefully glossing over or understating some things for very obvious reasons. I'm sure you understand, but I wanted to warn you so that you don't get the wrong idea. She's playing a tough game with the public."*

"No worries, Burt. I understand better than you can imagine, and I'll just bite my tongue while I watch. Speaking of which, I'm off to get myself to a TV, so thanks for the heads up." Dave hung up and stood as several of the armored transport vehicles associated with his entourage sped away, off to do their standard security screen ahead of his arrival.

Over the last several weeks, Dave had gotten used to what had initially seemed like paranoid precautions. It was only after he'd read that security briefing that he had much more appreciation for what the agents were doing for him. With that briefing prominent in his mind, he'd stopped getting frustrated with the hassles involved in having all of this security.

As he held Bella's hand and walked toward their heavily armored four-wheel-drive, Dave glanced at her and wondered how much he'd actually care about the world anymore if it weren't for her.

The hotel resembled some of the buildings he'd seen in DC, with white marble columns and acres of carved and polished stone. The opulent surroundings of the hotel were impressive, especially when Dave considered how far this location was from any major cities. As he'd walked through the lobby, he noticed the pink marble pillars in the ballroom and the domed ceiling with beautiful murals of garden scenes. But now, Dave's attention was riveted to the holographic image of the White House projected onto a lonely table in a large ballroom. His security detail had emptied the room and the disembodied sound of a reporter's voice echoed loudly through a hidden speaker. *"And I now pass control to the White House for the briefing that is about to start."*

Uniformed members of the NYPD streamed out of the Midtown South Precinct as the shift changed. A few familiar faces greeted Stryker, and fellow officers patted him on his shoulder as they walked by.

Were it not for a different uniform and the assault rifle draped in front of him, he'd be following them on their patrols.

But things had changed.

He was the platoon leader for just over four dozen members of the Military Police out of Fort Drum, all of whom were standing at attention in front of him.

Taking in a deep breath, Stryker called loudly. "It's nearly 2100 hours and we'll be helping the NYPD enforce the governor's dusk-to-dawn curfew.

"You've all been briefed, but remember, nobody is allowed on the streets unless they're a first responder or being escorted by one. No exceptions.

"NYPD's got the lead on enforcement matters and we're here to back them up.

"Sergeants, make sure you coordinate your squad's movements with your assigned counterpart in the precinct. This should ensure we get maximum coverage of the streets and subways.

"Any questions?"

Stryker paused for a moment and panned his gaze across the platoon, all of them in full battle gear.

"Okay, keep each other's sixes and stay safe. Dismissed!"

The sergeants began barking orders to their respective squads, and the soldiers double-timed it to their assigned locations.

"When you're done with deployment," said a familiar voice, "we need to talk about getting you promoted."

Stryker smiled, turned to his right, and saw the welcome face of Lieutenant Malacaria standing at the entrance to the precinct. "Hey, Lieutenant. Things have definitely gone to hell, haven't they?"

The twenty-plus-year NYPD veteran approached and tilted his head toward Eighth Avenue. "Jon, let's take a walk."

Stryker ambled alongside Malacaria and, despite the warmth of the summer night, a cold shiver raced through him as he stared at the empty thoroughfare. It was eerie with nobody on the streets in midtown.

Tonight was the first night of the curfew, and he'd have guessed there'd be lots of people wandering around claiming they hadn't understood what the curfew really meant, or have some other type of excuse for their having violated the governor's edict. After all, Stryker wasn't sure if there'd ever been such a sweeping proclamation in New York City.

After a few minutes of strolling in silence, taking in their surreal surroundings, they turned on West 42nd Street and approached the shimmering lights of Times Square. "Lieutenant—"

"Call me Matt."

"Matt, did you hear anything about *why* the governor's enacted this curfew? I thought all the attacks here have been during the day."

The lieutenant shook his head. "No idea. We were caught by surprise when the orders came in, and we scrambled to get everyone lined up to enforce them. This is stretching our resources to the limit. I'm actually thankful to have the army help out with this."

Stryker nodded as he passed a huddled group of two street cops chatting with two MPs from his platoon.

The holographic images shimmered brightly overhead as they entered the heart of Times Square.

"Jon, when you got deployed, did you end up dealing with more crazies, like what happened to you with that rookie?"

"You mean religious fanatics?" Stryker glanced at Malacaria and noticed his grim expression.

"You were deployed out West, right? Well, we've been getting lots of those suicidal-type doomsayers locally. Is that what you ended up dealing with over there as well?"

"Yup. For whatever reason, they've not been reporting it in the news, but there's definitely some cult-like thing going on. No idea what's triggering it."

Suddenly, the coruscating shimmer of lights coming from above flickered, and the unchanging glow of the White House's logo appeared on every screen in Times Square.

"What the hell?" Both lieutenants exclaimed simultaneously as they looked up at the images hovering fifty feet above them.

Stryker heard alert beeps coming from both the police and military radios as a message crawled across the bottom of the screen, along with a thirty-second countdown.

"*** *Priority Message – Broadcasting across all channels – Message from the President of the United States* ***"

There were nearly a dozen officers and MPs within sight, all staring up at the holograms as they switched to a live feed coming from the Oval Office.

Holding Bella's hand, Dave sat back and watched the crystal-clear image of Margaret Hager as she sat behind her desk and addressed most of the known world.

"Good evening, my fellow citizens.

"Tonight, I speak not only as the President of the United States, but as a global citizen. To every person within the reach of my voice, I urge you to pause and listen, because what I'm about to say affects us all. In fact, this same message will ripple across the globe as all of the other nations' leaders speak to their citizens, telling them what I'm about to share with you.

"Over humanity's history, there have been times of strife. Times when the people of various nations have not seen eye-to-eye, and instead, have seen fit to wage war against each other.

"Yet in those times of strife, unlikely partners find themselves banding together. Former enemies become allies and even friends.

"Now, we all find ourselves on a precipice, facing an enemy that imperils us all. Not just Americans, but the citizenry of the world.

"I, with the support of the Congress, have signed a binding agreement between the United States and all of the world's nations. Setting aside any of our differences, we array ourselves against a common primordial threat.

"This threat could, if left unattended, be the cause of a catastrophe of unimaginable proportions. Something that could wipe away all life on this planet, from the tiniest of bacteria, to the fish in the sea, and even to us, all of humanity. Gone in an instant.

"What is the threat, you might ask?

"It is the same threat that caused mass extinction on our world in the past, a global terror that none had ever confronted in any way, shape, or form."

"In approximately five months, a series of large asteroids, some larger than the ones that killed the dinosaurs sixty million years ago, is expected to cross close enough to Earth that we stand a good chance of being hit by one or more of them."

The camera followed the president as she slowly backed away from her desk and stood, giving the camera a steely glare.

"As Abraham Lincoln said in a speech given in 1858, 'A house divided against itself cannot stand.' At that moment, President Lincoln was speaking of a division between the states. We have no such division within our country today, yet we've historically not been as close with other nations as we could be.

"I stand before you now. As President of the United States, and as a duly designated representative of the leaders of the United Nations, I promise you that the nations of the world are not divided. We stand together against this common threat."

The president slammed her fist loudly on the desk with a grim expression.

"That threat ends here!

"It ends now!"

She lowered back into her chair and leaned forward, again addressing the world in a firm yet calm manner.

"Through a series of previously classified scientific advances, I am relieved to inform all of you that this global threat is being handled, and we will not meet the same fate as the dinosaurs when a life-ending threat streaked across our skies."

"Thanks to the hard work of many of the world's top scientists, we have a solution.

"Let me repeat that. We have a solution for the incoming threat.

"Most of you are certainly familiar with the International Science Foundation. It is a place where advanced scientific research is conducted. They have made significant advances in a variety of areas, but they are especially known for discovering new treatments for multiple sclerosis and other diseases that had previously been thought to be incurable. I will, for the first time, now unveil something that has been in the works for nearly a decade.

"Our scientists had foreseen the possibility of such an incoming threat and have been working feverishly for nearly ten years on combating it. As I speak to you, we are actively deploying a network of satellites, which will serve as an outward-facing shield against that which threatens our existence.

"It is called DefenseNet.

"Using an array of satellites with unimaginably powerful lasers, DefenseNet will detect and destroy any incoming threat."

Dave leaned closer to the holographic image as he listened to the president's every word. It didn't surprise him that she'd glossed over mentioning him or any of the other people involved. He was one of the anonymous scientists, and at this point in his life, Dave was quite content with that.

President Hager's voice was steady, calm, and well-modulated. She managed to walk the line between being serious and emphatic, and without sounding panicky. He didn't feel sure that many people could have effectively pulled that off.

"DefenseNet will serve as the means by which we'll escape a near-certain death, and for that, we will be ever grateful to our scientific community.

"Nonetheless, I want to emphasize one thing.

"Even though I want to assure you that the citizens of our world are safe, nothing is ever foolproof. There is a very small chance that some object may manage to escape being shoved aside or completely destroyed by DefenseNet.

"When I met just this morning with the governors of our coastal states, we agreed that it is in the best interest of the American people for us to act with an abundance of caution.

"That being said, I've requested the governors of the coastal states to issue evacuation orders for their residents living along the coasts. These evacuations will be completed ahead of the four-month deadline.

"Under the authority entrusted to me by the Constitution, and in conjunction with the UN general security mandate, I have directed that the following take place immediately:

"First: any location within one mile of an ocean and less than twenty feet above sea level will undergo mandatory evacuation to sheltered areas, as designated by each of the states' governors.

"Second: there will also be a suggested evacuation zone if you live within ten miles of the coast and less than fifty feet above sea level.

"Third: I've already informed the Federal Emergency Management Agency to deploy emergency services in all of the coastal states, and they will be building shelters to accommodate each and every person that will be displaced.

"Fourth: I am, as of now activating all branches of our military reservists to assist in this coordinated evacuation of the coastal regions, as well as maintaining the security of those evacuated areas. I've given the orders to recall all of the active-duty members of the military who are stationed abroad to be available as well. Looting and unrest will be dealt with in the harshest manner possible.

"Fifth: Being that our capitol is located in an evacuation zone, I, along with the rest of our government, will be displaced and operating from within a shelter further inland.

"My fellow citizens, let no one doubt that this is a challenging time in the history of our world. I realize that the difficulties of the next several months will be trying for us all.

"No one can foresee precisely what may happen or what the costs will be, but as citizens of the United States, it is in times like these that Americans band together, rising to meet the challenges set before us.

"For those of you who are unaffected by the evacuations, please consider opening your homes, housing others whom you might know, or register with your local authorities if you have spare rooms for those who are affected. This is a time for all Americans to pitch in.

"In this time of crisis, I want to remind you all that the greatest danger we could face is the one in which we do nothing.

"I want to personally thank, yet again, all of those scientists who have been working night and day on DefenseNet. These men and women are the ones to whom we all owe our lives.

"I recall a speech given by President John F. Kennedy, 'We choose to go to the Moon in this decade and do the other things, not because they are easy, but because they are hard.'

"Those words were spoken over one-hundred-years ago, and I'm

sad to say that we've barely stretched ourselves past those, at-the-time, lofty goals.

"When we're on the other side of this crisis and we can all collectively breathe a sigh of relief, I pledge to increase our investments in the sciences to unprecedented levels. This investment will be sufficient to bring about a Renaissance in all fields of science, because it will be through science that the future of humanity will be guided.

"But while our gaze shifts skywards in the next few months as DefenseNet is activated, I pledge that in our lifetimes, we will explore new worlds.

"We will seek out the farthest reaches of our solar system and beyond.

"And in our lifetimes, we will boldly go where nobody has gone before.

"But for now, our goal is a humble one. Now is not a time for panic, but a time for resolute purpose and faith. DefenseNet is our world's shield, and it is that shield which will see us through this crisis.

"Immediately following my broadcast, your state's governor will speak to you with more local details. I just want to repeat once again that I have full confidence in DefenseNet and the resilience of the American people. I will be amongst many of you shortly, sharing the same shelters as all of you, and God willing, we will all soon see the fruits of our current and future scientific investments.

"May God bless the United States of America, and may we all find ourselves changed for the better after this crisis is over.

"Thank you and good night."

With a grim nod, Dave gave Bella's hand a squeeze. Somehow, the president had managed to leave out huge critical details, but at the same time hinted at everything. He muttered, more to himself than anyone else, "Damned right we'll be boldly going where nobody's gone before. And it's going to be sooner rather than later."

CHAPTER TWENTY-TWO

Burt gazed across Carol Chance's ornately carved mahogany desk and studied her expression as she read the report he'd handed her. As the Secretary of Agriculture, the trappings of her job filled the walls of her office in the USDA's headquarters: a motley assemblage of pictures of tractors, cows, and giant fields of wheat, along with a collection of seemingly random certificates and diplomas.

Carol wore her dark hair in a tight bun, and just behind her on a credenza rested a small ceramic pot filled to nearly overflowing with what looked like wooden shavings. Burt sniffed and presumed that was where the strong scent of cinnamon potpourri was coming from.

She suddenly let out a sigh as she lowered Burt's report. "That much? Really? You do realize that by asking for two years' worth of food for every man, woman, and child within our borders, it will completely deplete all of our stockpiles. What then?" The middle-aged woman kneaded her hands together and asked with a tremor in her voice, "Doctor Radcliffe, are we going to survive this?"

Leaning forward in his chair, Burt reached out and placed his hand over hers, giving her hands a reassuring squeeze. "Carol, believe me when I say that we'll be fine." He paused, pursing his lips in thought and leaned back in his chair. "I can give you a little insight as to what will happen, if it will put your mind at ease. However, you must understand that I'm sharing this under the restrictions of the Indigo project, so no further discussion with others, understood?"

"Of course." Carol's voice suddenly sounded confident, but her trembling hands gave away her inner turmoil.

"Carol, there's really nothing to worry about. You were at the briefing when Doctor Holmes described in broad strokes what we'll be doing. Let's just put it in the simplest terms, we'll be traveling for just about nine months. At the end of this admittedly mind-blowing journey, we'll park ourselves just over twelve light years away, around a new star called Tau Ceti."

"Amazing." Carol breathed out the words as her eyes widened, giving her an owl-like expression. It was as if she hadn't truly considered that they'd be leaving the solar system. "B-but Doctor Radcliffe, if it will take us nine months, then why do we need two years' worth of food?"

Burt paused, unsure if he wanted to admit that there was some uncertainty to his estimates. The secretary seemed the fragile type, and he'd seen enough grown people crying with fear when he talked to them privately in their offices. Letting out a deep sigh, Burt admitted, "I'm afraid some of my estimates reflect that I'm a bit uncertain on some things. Yes, we'll be traveling for nine months. The sun's influence on us will be gone very quickly, so we'll not be getting any natural light, per se, during our trip." Burt pointed at the ceiling to emphasize his next point. "When DefenseNet gets activated, it will give off a light. Exactly how bright it will be, and if it will be strong enough to grow crops from, I can't be sure. Also, when we do arrive at our destination and have the light of a new star shining on us again, I can't be sure how long it will take for the crops to adjust and the growing season to restart. So that's why the two years. Just in case. I'm sorry I can't be more precise."

"Oh, thank God." Carol's expression visibly relaxed as she wiped the tears that had welled up and dripped onto her cheek. "I'm sorry, it's just that I'm so worried about screwing things up for everyone. It's not just my kids, and my new baby granddaughter; it's everyone looking to me for things that they'll need to keep them alive. It's having people's lives in my hands that I'm so unused to. And my poor grandbaby, Alicia. She's just now teething and ready for food—"

"Carol, your granddaughter will be fine." Burt spoke the well-rehearsed words he'd used with many people in DC. "Just imagine what new things she'll grow up learning. Imagine how many new opportunities there will be for her. When we begin our lives anew around Tau Ceti, she'll be able to say that she was born around another star. Alicia will have travelled across interstellar space. With the president's and the other world leaders' new investments in the sciences, we'll see a much brighter future, one that holds nothing but wonder and beauty. I just wish I were her age, so I could appreciate what will come in the next fifty years. I look forward to the future; it's going to be incredible."

Carol dabbed her nose with a tissue, stood, and extended her hand. "Doctor Radcliffe, thank you so much for being as thorough as you are. It makes me feel better knowing that you're being conservative about everything. I'll keep you in my prayers. Thank you so much."

Burt shook hands with the woman and left her office, feeling a bit troubled. He'd given many politicians and even some of the military's top generals the same pep talk. Yet so many of them looked forward to the future, not for themselves, but for their children and grandchildren. He'd been an only child, and his parents were now dead. Burt's one regret in life was that he'd never gotten remarried, and had children.

Climbing into his car, Burt immediately typed the address for the White House into the navigation system: 1600 Pennsylvania Ave. His thoughts shifted to his next meeting, which was with the president. The image of her young son toddling around the Oval Office the last time he'd met with her left Burt somehow feeling hollow. While the car zoomed through the traffic, Burt leaned his head back and sighed as he contemplated having kids and again rejected the idea. "It's one thing for someone like Margaret Hager to have kids at her age, she'd been married for fifteen years. If I can't do something great for my kids, at least I can try to do something fantastic for the world. If nothing else, I want to be able to say that I've made a difference. The question is, what will that difference be?"

～

Standing inside the cordoned off area in front of the Port Authority Bus Terminal, Stryker scanned the crowd of evacuees.

The place was swarming with uniformed officers as some in the crowd yelled about their destination vouchers and how members of their family were being separated. Others cried inconsolably and the rest just stared vacantly, as if in shock.

Despite the president's speech, many had expected evacuations to begin in a few months. Most people were hoping that there wouldn't be any need to evacuate.

They were both wrong.

Several members of the NYPD shouted loudly as they corralled the crowd into a semblance of order. In some cases, the officers resorted to physically escorting people into the different lines they belonged in.

It was controlled chaos, and it took all they could do to prevent the panic that was threatening to erupt.

Stryker's men were stationed at the edges of the crowd, and it was on them to keep those who hadn't yet been called for evacuation out of the vicinity.

Seeing a flash of red hair in the crowd, Stryker rushed into the chaos and yelled, "Jessica!"

The redhead didn't respond as an officer guided her to one of the lines. Disappointment washed over Stryker as he realized it wasn't her.

"Jon!"

Stryker turned to his right, and his sister waved at him as two officers led her, his ex-wife, Isaac, and Emma in his direction.

With a surge of relief, he rushed toward them as a uniformed cop smiled and yelled through the chaos. "Stryker, I figured you might want to handle these yourself."

With a huge grin, he waved his thanks at the officer as Emma and Isaac slammed into him, tears streaming down their faces.

Pushing aside his rifle, Stryker knelt in front of the kids and wiped their tears away. "No need to cry. This is going to be an adventure."

"But, Dad," Isaac sniffled, his chin quivering with barely controlled emotion. "Peter at school said we're all going to die just like the dinosaurs did."

Pressing his lips together, Stryker shook his head as his chest tightened with worry. He leaned his head forward and whispered, "Well, Peter is an idiot. Can I tell you two a secret? You have to promise not to tell anyone else, okay?"

Both kids nodded as Lainie and Jessica approached and stood behind them.

"You heard the president talking about something called DefenseNet? Well, I happen to know that some of the best scientists in the whole world have made that to keep us safe. I heard them say it's almost like a magic shield to keep things that might hurt us far, far away. You'll all be safe."

Emma frowned and stuck out her lower lip. "Daddy, there's no such thing as magic. DefenseNet is scientistic."

"You're right." He wrapped his arms around both of them, squeezed them as hard as he dared, and leaned his head against theirs. He inhaled their freshly-scrubbed scent and leaned back to drink in their worried expressions. "I promise that you'll be safe. You have nothing to worry about. It'll almost be like going to overnight camp, and you both love going to camp, right?"

Both kids wiped their faces and nodded, the first hints of smiles blooming on their faces.

"Daddy, are you coming with us?"

He looked up at Lainie and asked, "All four of you are going to the same place, right?"

She wiped at the corner of her eye and said nothing.

Jessica patted the kids' shoulders and said, "We're all assigned to the Poconos Evacuation Center."

He turned to Emma and gave her a kiss on her forehead. "I can't go right now, I still have a job to do. But once I'm done, I'll see about getting over to where you're at. Okay?"

"Promise?" Emma asked with a suspicious expression.

"I promise."

A pang of guilt knotted his stomach as he spoke the words. In fact, he had no idea if he'd be allowed to go to their evacuation site.

One of the uniformed officers came over. "The first round of buses are about to board. They need to go."

Stryker nodded and turned to his family. "Okay, one last set of hugs."

The kids and Jessica gave him their goodbyes, but Lainie couldn't meet his gaze as tears wet her cheeks.

Before he could figure out what the issue was, they were rounded up by the officers who'd begun clearing the front of the bus terminal.

Stryker swallowed hard against the lump that had formed in his throat as he watched his family board the bus.

He took a deep, shuddering breath and prayed that everything was going to be okay.

From within the Oval Office, Burt sat next to the president and watched the controlled chaos coming from the image projected into the center of the room. It was some local news reporter out of South Florida, flying over what looked like a traffic jam.

"This is Jose Luis Ballart reporting from the WSVN weather copter as we hover over the I-95 corridor. The mass exodus of 2066 has now officially begun. As you can see, the north-south corridors are at capacity, yet moving smoothly. As of right now, all of the outlying islands in the Keys and the southern tip of Miami-Dade County have been evacuated. Unlike some of the major delays being experienced by L.A. and some of the other major population centers, we are enjoying a rather smooth evacuation process, thanks to the Florida taxpayers and the recent upgrade of the Automated Vehicle Routing system. If it weren't for that, we might be seeing the half-day stalls that other parts of the country have encountered...."

The president sighed. "So much work to do...." She made a swiping motion with her hand, and the image immediately shifted to one that Burt recognized as coming from one of the cargo shuttles flying high above. An engineer in a spacesuit was busy pulling a long ribbon of graphene from a giant spool and attaching it to a landing rover. The president glanced at Burt and noted, "This is one of the video feeds from above the lunar surface. I know what I've told everyone about us possibly getting hit by a giant rock and the tidal waves and all that crap, but tell me again why the Moon matters so much? Why are we spending so many resources in bringing it along with us?"

Burt tried to keep the frown off his face and swallowed the bile rising in his throat. He hated giving answers he was uncertain about, especially to the president. "Madam President, I—"

"Damn it, Burt!" The president groused as she frowned in his direction. "You're starting to piss me off. I've told you a thousand times, you can just call me Margaret when we're alone."

Burt glanced over his shoulder at the Secret Service agent standing at the doorway and thought better than to argue with her. She was clearly losing her patience and certainly had enough stress without him annoying her. "Well, Margaret, I've told you that the Moon has an effect on our tides. And the best I can tell is that within seconds of us activating the gravity bubble, its influence on us will vanish, causing a sloshing effect as the tides flatten out. Kind of like when you move in a bathtub."

"Right, and that's why we're evacuating everyone so they don't get adversely affected. But if that's inevitable, why bother taking it with us? I just don't get it."

Trying to ignore the former Green Beret's intense stare, Burt hitched his thumb to the video feed still playing from above the lunar surface. "There's two reasons why we're doing that. The first one I don't think is a short-term concern whatsoever. It's believed that the Moon keeps our angle of rotation relatively steady. For instance, right now our winters and summers are what they are because of the steady tilt of the Earth, and it doesn't vary as we rotate around the sun. Without the Moon, the Earth's tilt may end up varying wildly over long periods of time. Meaning that at some point in our future, we could see the Earth tilt much more severely than ever before. Imagine a scenario in which our entire northern hemisphere could face the sun for months on end, while the southern hemisphere goes into an extremely deep winter."

As Margaret frowned, Burt shook his head and remarked, "Truthfully, that's likely something that could happen over hundreds of thousands of years from now or even longer. However, I personally found some of the marine biologists' worries a much more credible and immediate threat. There's a concern that without the tidal activities that the Moon provides us, we'd see a sudden and maybe irreversible falloff of all life in the oceans. Their concern is based on their knowledge that the tides act as a churn for the nutrients from the surface. And in that natural agitation, the nutrients seed much of the food and necessary minerals into the water as part of the biological food chain. You can imagine that if the tide suddenly goes away, the nutrient level in the oceans may drop off and the food chain might be severely altered. It's a credible concern that we can't truly know the effect of, but I'd hate to risk it, considering that Doctor Holmes had already done most of the work up on the lunar surface already."

"That makes sense." The president's deliberate words and pensive expression clearly indicated her mind was preoccupied with what she'd heard and possibly other concerns as well.

Margaret suddenly swiped her hand to the left several times, and the video feed switched repeatedly to different images, many of which Burt didn't recognize.

"Burt, where are we at with Holmes' work?"

The video suddenly switched to what was obviously a military signal coming from somewhere in the ocean. Some of the numbers running along the bottom of the video image were clearly GPS tracking numbers, and before Burt could ask, Margaret volunteered, "That's a video feed coming from one of Doctor Holmes' security details."

Burt quickly swiped the numbers into his phone and the image of the globe flashed onto his handheld PC. "Well, it looks like he's about 2750 miles southeast of Hilo, somewhere near the middle of the Pacific Ocean." Burt tapped on the map to overlay the longitude and latitude values and nodded. "He's on the equator, as I'd expected, approaching 120 degrees West. That means at his current pace, he'll be done in under two weeks. We should be seeing—"

"A giant concrete structure pushing out of the ocean," the president finished, pointing at the image floating five feet in front of them.

Burt recognized the building as one of the electrical substations the IDF had built along the equator. "Yes, ma'am."

Margaret's eyes narrowed as Burt continued rambling.

"That's actually one of the largest water-borne structures ever built, and it's anchored to the ocean floor 14,500 feet below." His attention was immediately drawn to the large flotilla of guided-missile destroyers, military cruisers from a variety of countries, and even one US aircraft carrier. "Why does it look like a war zone?"

"Because it is."

A chill raced through Burt as the president gave him a grim stare. He'd been stunned into silence. He could have sworn that all of the world's countries had formed a treaty of non-aggression. Now he wasn't sure how to respond.

"Put it this way, Burt. We've gotten credible threats on each and every one of these anchor sites. More information about Indigo has leaked. We don't know how much has leaked, but we've had attacks on some of the more remote stations. No harm was done, but we've built small armies around each of these things."

Burt's eyes widened, and Margaret matter-of-factly remarked, "There are some who don't want us to succeed in combatting the threat of Indigo. That's why we're protecting those sites."

Giving the president an incredulous stare, Burt stammered, "I ... I don't understand. Why would someone attack one of the electric substations? There's nothing even valuable there. Is it that Brotherhood group?"

With a grim expression, the president responded with a raspy edge to her voice. "They're fanatics. A death cult. Some intelligence reports assert they might think of Indigo as a sign of the biblical Armageddon and that the Messiah will come as long as we don't interfere with God's plan."

The previous warning he'd received from the British Prime Minister about the death cults rose prominently in Burt's mind as he groaned. "I can't believe they're looking to commit suicide!"

Margaret shrugged; her emotionless gaze was more chilling to Burt than the images floating in his head.

"I thought when I retired from the military, my involvement with other people's deaths would stop. I'm afraid it's only beginning."

CHAPTER TWENTY-THREE

Having gotten used to the heat at the equator, Dave shivered as the chill of the air-conditioned hallway tickled the back of his neck. However, that wasn't what had caught his attention as he walked toward the building housing Mission Control at the Kennedy Space Center. His gaze instead fixed on the photographs hanging on the walls as he strode along the long corridor that connected the buildings of the Space Center's campus.

As he rushed past the clusters of images, Dave caught fragments of the motion-activated narrative spoken through a speaker under the photographs.

"Kennedy Space Center and the adjacent Cape Canaveral Air Force Station have had a major role in human spaceflight during the last century....

"Whether it was the Project Mercury and Gemini flights achieving man's first orbital missions....

"The Apollo program taking astronauts to the Moon....

"The Space Shuttle program was launched and retired in the late twentieth century, only to be resurrected in 2045 to help establish the first permanent settlements on the Moon."

As he walked past a reduced-scale model of the newest in the Space Shuttle series, he trailed his fingertips across its fuselage and smiled. "If it weren't for you, none of this would have even been possible."

Dave glanced at Bella, noticed her shiver, and whispered, "I'll get us both jackets when we get to the control room."

"Are you glad to finally be approaching the end of this?" Neeta's voice startled him as she appeared at the end of the hallway, holding the door open for them.

Dave shrugged. "It wasn't too long of a walk."

"No, I didn't mean the walk from the parking lot...."

Despite Neeta's serious expression, Dave couldn't help but smile at the aggressive woman who'd long ago grown to be a friend.

"You're making fun of me!" Neeta planted her hands on her narrow hips and glared at Dave, all the while struggling to keep a smile off her face. "Oh, you're just an idiot." She glanced at Bella and huffed, "I don't know how you can stand him sometimes."

"Just follow me and I'll show you the control room." Neeta turned on her heel and motioned for Dave and Bella as she disappeared into the darkness of the building that housed Mission Control.

Wrapping the wind breaker around him, Dave's gaze panned across the fifty-foot-wide auditorium-style room. He sat on a large executive-style swivel chair and watched Neeta conduct business in the unrelenting style he'd grown used to.

Neeta pointed at one of the screens, which wasn't reporting a signal. *"Substation 23, where the hell are you? Report in!"* Her voice echoed loudly through the speakers in the auditorium. She tapped on her microphone, muting it, and turned to one of the harried Mission Control engineers. "What's going on with 23?"

"Doctor Patel, I'm in communication with the engineer at the station and they're saying that the substation's experiencing problems with their video feed due to a storm that's blowing sand off the coast of Somalia. They're otherwise ready to go, so I'm patching their data feed onto the screen now."

The one remaining blank spot without any of the reporting information flickered and suddenly showed the amount of power being fed into the substation and the percent of power being routed to the attached satellite flying high overhead.

Neeta glanced back at Dave and nodded. "The alerts have been broadcast. All countries are now running with only critical power usage. All substations are reporting online and ready to go." She pointed at the portable microphone clipped to Dave's shirt. "Just tap that to turn the mic on, and everyone here and in the substations will be able to hear you."

Dave's mind flashed back to those engineers he'd met at the substations. They were all men and women he'd shaken hands and even shared meals with over the last several months. When he thought about DefenseNet, it was their faces he saw: the scared yet serious expressions of the people who knew the importance of what they were tasked with. They'd willingly put their fate in Dave's hands. And it was with those images in his mind that he tapped the microphone and gave his first order.

"This is Dave Holmes with Mission Control. As I call out your substation number, I want you to route ten percent of your available power to your satellite connection.

One...."

Dave paused as he visualized a portion of the flow of electricity entering the substation being routed skyward through the graphene connection. As the power raced upwards, it would in turn be shunted across the long ribbon connecting the ring of satellites that encircled the Earth.

The center screen showed a 180-degree fisheye view of the night's sky above central Florida, as well as the readout from sensors attached to the ring connecting each of the thirty-six satellites encircling the globe.

As the power being reported out of the substation changed, the power flowing through DefenseNet's ring increased.

"Two ... three ... four...."

Dave continued to slowly add power from each of the remote substations, making sure that everything was working as expected. Even though he'd double-checked everything, he knew that any small error could be disastrous.

As the last substation sent a small portion of their potential power zooming up into the DefenseNet ring, Dave breathed a sigh of relief.

There were nearly fifty engineers in the auditorium, all monitoring one variety of signal or another. Not sure who handled monitoring the telemetry and communications, Dave asked, *"T-COM, what's our signal quality on the ring?"*

One of the engineers on the far end of the auditorium leaned forward, and a woman's voice broadcast on the speakers, *"We've got a clean sine wave without any indication of harmonics dirtying the signal. 3.015 terawatts are currently flowing through the DefenseNet ring. All systems are go for power-up."*

Some of Dave's anxiety began to melt away as things fell into place. The adjustments he'd made to the satellites were working as expected, the electrical signal was clean, and his confidence grew with the engineer's confirmation.

With a glance at Bella, who was sitting next to Neeta about twenty feet away, Dave gave her a nod and she returned it with a smile. In his head rattled her unspoken words of reassurance.

"Roger, Mission Control. All substations, commence now with a controlled power-up sequence, maximum power output to stop at eighty percent of capacity and hold."

The numbers on the screens throughout the auditorium began changing rapidly, but Dave's attention focused on the center screen where the sky above central Florida was displayed.

As the midnight sky began to grow brighter, Dave's smile grew wider.

Suddenly, Dave's phone buzzed in his ear, and with a tap on his microphone, muting it, he answered.

"Hello?"

"Hey, Dave, it's Burt. I wanted to congratulate you. I'm standing on the roof of my hotel and you wouldn't believe what I'm seeing. It's the most amazing thing I've ever witnessed. Did you imagine it would be this bright?"

Dave laughed. "Truthfully, I can't tell for sure. I'm stuck in a concrete building and seeing a distorted video image. You're in DC, right? Tell me what you're seeing."

"It's actually beautiful. I'm standing here breathing in the cool midnight breeze with the scent of fresh-cut grass, but instead of the night, it's just bright enough to read one of those old pulpy paperback novels. I see a bluish-white ribbon of light draped across the southern sky. I'm telling you Dave, it's surreal ... hey, do you know what the brightness will be like when we go full-power? I know damned well that after this display gets televised and reported on by everyone, I'm going to have all sorts of folks asking me in the morning."

"Sure, let me ask the telemetry folks here."

Dave tapped his microphone. *"T-COM, what's the brightness we're seeing in our timezone at the equator? Also, do we have accurate readings for the same timezone at other distances from the equator?"*

The same woman's voice spoke only seconds later, *"Mission Director Holmes, we've got a reading of 20,150 lux reporting out of the Ecuador substation. We have 1,450 lux reporting out of Cape Canaveral and 200 lux being reporting out of a weather station in Toronto, Canada."*

Burt clearly had heard the voice, because he responded excitedly in Dave's ear. *"Holy crap, 20K lux? That's practically like the midday sun."*

Dave tapped on his mic once again and responded, "Yup, but that's a pretty quick drop-off of light. I think overall, you'll have to prep folks for most of the world being a bit dimmer than they're used to. Heck, just remember that there won't be a sun-up and sun-down while we're moving. I think everyone's circadian rhythm is going to get shot to hell, but I can't help that."

"Dave, I've got it covered. I'm sure as long as people realize they

won't be starving or dead, they'll be fine. I'm okay telling them to take melatonin pills or some other crap to help them sleep. Anyway, I wanted to give you a call and congratulate you. We're on the precipice of a new era for humanity, and it's because of you."

With a smirk, Dave grumped, "Oh shut up, you know damn well it takes a team. Well, I'm going to get out of here and get some rest while the ring gets some burn-in time. We've got five weeks before we need to leave, so I think we're in pretty good shape."

"Goodnight, but let me warn you ahead of time." The amused tone in Burt's voice was obvious. *"Don't be surprised if you get a congratu-latory call from the president. Try not to bite her head off if she wakes you."*

The phone signal dropped, and he gave Neeta a wave that she correctly interpreted. It was time for her to take over.

As she communicated with the rest of the Mission Control staff about DefenseNet's planned ten-day burn-in period, Dave stood.

Bella joined him as he walked out of the Mission Control building and headed toward the security team that would take him to his hotel for some well-earned rest.

As they passed through the corridor connecting the Mission Control center to the rest of the space complex, Dave paused to look at the pale ribbon of light in the southern sky. He breathed in the sterile air-conditioned air and felt Bella squeeze hard on his arm.

"Something's wrong," Bella announced, and almost immediately Dave noticed the light in the sky flicker and dim.

With his heart and mind racing, he turned back and ran toward the Mission Control building, with Bella chasing after him. Red lights began flashing along the corridor and the sound of a siren echoed through the hall.

Just as he approached the entrance, the double doors slammed open, and Neeta, with an uncharacteristic wide-eyed expression of fear, yelled, "We lost forty percent of the power flowing into the grid!"

"All at once? That's not possible!" Dave lunged into the room and stared at the wall of displays strewn throughout the auditorium.

Pointing at the displays, he turned to Neeta and yelled, "Why are six of the substations reporting zero energy input? What the hell is—"

A team of security personnel burst into the room just as Dave's phone buzzed in his ear.

"Neeta!" Dave yelled over his shoulder, as some of his security detail began escorting him out of the room. "Find out what happened!"

The buzzing in his ear continued. He tapped his ear bud and growled, "Burt, now is not the time!"

"Dave, listen to me. We've got trouble—"

"No shit we've got trouble, we've got multiple power grid failures and I've got to get—"

"Listen to me. It's not your doing or something you're going to fix. We just got a security alert from six of the main electrical grids feeding power into the substations. I'm being dragged away to meet with the president now, and your security detail will be bringing you and Bella here for an emergency meeting. A jet is taxiing onto a runway just miles from your current location."

Dave's mind went numb as he let himself get rushed into an SUV. "Burt, what do you mean a security alert? There's some kind of power failure. We just need to get those fixed and...." It suddenly dawned on Dave that something catastrophic had to have happened. There was no reason for multiple failures to occur at the same time. "What's going on? I don't understand."

Burt fell silent for a moment, and then responded in an ominous tone. *"Dave, I don't know if you've been told, but let's just say that there are those in this world who'd rather see us all die than let DefenseNet do what it's meant to do. The report I just received claims that the grids were attacked by a well-coordinated group of terrorists."*

A chill raced through Dave as the SUV barreled through a manned gate at Cape Canaveral Air Force Station and aimed for a jet on a nearby runway.

"Burt, I thought the Defense Department had the sites completely impervious to attacks, how'd that happen? The grids ... they're repairable, right?"

"Each of the sites had small armies guarding them, so I don't have

any answers, but we'll know more soon enough. However, the images I just received were pretty grim."

Dave rested his head against the back of the leather seat and felt as if a judge had just handed him a death sentence as he whispered, "We're screwed."

CHAPTER TWENTY-FOUR

Margaret listened intently as the Secretary of Defense wrapped up his report on the substation attacks. "In summary," he said, "a total of six of the collector substations were destroyed by what our intelligence sources have determined to be RA-115S Soviet-era suitcase bombs. With a nominal yield of one kiloton each, the sites are beyond repair. A seventh collector substation also was attacked, but unlike the prior six, the detonation did not set off a nuclear reaction and instead destroyed the transmission grid for that area while also contaminating the site with fissile material." Walter Keane's gravelly voice suddenly dropped off as the sixty-something-year-old former general finished reading from the security report and laid it back down on the table.

Margaret scanned the faces of the members of her security council. They all looked haggard and pale-faced, as the grim news settled on them all like a shroud.

Shrugging off the sick feeling of despair blooming within her, the president broke the silence in the Situation Room. "General Keane, are we sure that those substations are completely destroyed? I know those collector substations gathered the power coming in from the surrounding region and fed it to the DefenseNet substations. Couldn't we gather the power lines that were feeding into the destroyed sites and route them to the DefenseNet ones?"

Walter shook his head. "I'm afraid not, Madam President. Each of those bombs destroyed everything within one-third of a mile, which I'll have you know is about the size of the substation itself. What makes matters worse is that the EMP pulse that the blasts generated sent a huge surge through the power lines, destroying the inner workings of the facilities that Doctor Holmes had created."

With a blank expression, Dave interjected, "What about the substations? The ones controlling the flow of power up to the DefenseNet ring. How'd they fare, what about the people in those?"

The general turned to Dave and, with a grim expression, shook his head. "Everyone was lost at the collector stations, I'm sorry to report. Everything within the building was destroyed. In fact, the only thing left untouched was the concrete building itself. I suppose the only good news is that the building is still connected to the DefenseNet ring, whatever good that'll do, and nobody died other than the poor folks at the collector substations."

"Well, that's a relief," Doug Fisher, the president's Chief of Staff, grumbled sarcastically, as he removed his glasses and ran a hand through his thin gray hair. "A load of good that'll do us, general. A couple dozen people in some remote location didn't get killed, but we'll all be dead in a matter of a month or two."

Margaret's stomach turned with nausea as she thought about her son. Despite the anxiety she felt, she turned to Dave and found the strength to keep the worry from her voice. "Doctor Holmes, I want to hear your thoughts. What now?"

Dave leaned back in his seat and ran his hands over his closely cropped hair. He breathed in deeply and Margaret saw a hint of a frown cross his face. "Madam President, I'd always worried that we might have some kind of failure. In fact, I planned for it. We could have dealt with a fifteen percent power hit and still been okay. Maybe twenty percent—I'm not positive. But from General Keane's report, it seems as if we're down over fifty percent, and even if we could spin up the one substation that didn't get destroyed or route whatever sources of power it had directly to our substation, that's still going to leave us down forty percent, well below what we need." Dave shrugged and spoke with an ominous tone. "Even if every country went completely dark and we all lived in caves, it wouldn't be enough. I'm sorry, I don't have any good answers."

Karen Fultondale, the Director of the FBI, suddenly burst into tears and hid her face behind a notebook, the news clearly overwhelming her.

Doctor Holmes glanced at Karen and grimaced, his expression of discomfort matching many of the others in the room. "I hate to say it, but I think we're going to have to make peace with our fate."

The cold hands of dread gripped Margaret around her chest as Doctor Holmes' words sunk in. For the first time in her life, the grim feeling of helplessness threatened to overwhelm her. She took a deep breath as an ominous chill spread throughout the Situation Room, the last hope of humanity fading.

General Keane wiped his face and stared vacantly as his shoulders slumped ever so slightly.

Kevin Baker's eyes narrowed as the Director of the CIA drummed his fingers on the table. He suddenly leaned forward and asked, "Doctor Holmes, is the only issue power? If just one of the substations was able to generate enough power to offset the loss, would your plan still work?"

Margaret frowned as she stared at the thirty-year veteran of the clandestine organization. Not sure what he was getting at, she glanced at Dave as the scientist pursed his lips, seeming to consider the question.

There was a pregnant moment of silence as everyone's attention veered to Dave.

Finally he glanced at Bella and frowned. He turned his gaze back toward Kevin and nodded. "The connection would easily be sufficient to carry the burden, but what are you talking about? There simply isn't enough generating capacity to do what you're suggesting. We're tapping it all as it is."

The CIA Director dropped a coin onto the conference room table. It clattered on the wooden surface and was about to roll away when he slapped his hand onto it and pressed down.

Margaret, along with everyone else in the room, stared at the man, and she silently wondered if he'd finally cracked. She'd only met Kevin Baker six months earlier, and he was like many of the secret squirrel types. Silent, brooding, and usually not prone to joking.

She was about to ask why he asked the question when Kevin suddenly lifted his hand and flicked what looked like molten metal in Dave Holmes' direction.

Margaret launched herself up from her chair when Dave held up his hand, "Wait!"

The president yelled at the CIA Director, "What the hell are you doing?"

"Wait," Dave repeated, as he leaned forward and blew on the drips of metal lying only inches from his seat at the conference room table. Without hesitation, he lifted up the now-solidified metal and turned it over in his hand, a curious look replacing his previously grim expression. "I know this trick." Dave squeezed the metal in his palm for a few seconds and then slowly unclenched his fist as he tilted his hand. The now-molten metal dripped onto the table. Dave glanced at the CIA Director. "It's gallium, right?"

Without the slightest change of expression, Kevin nodded. "Correct, Doctor Holmes. It seems as if you're well-versed in things even beyond your specialty. I'd wager that most people wouldn't have a clue how I did that. That gives me some hope. Maybe you can unravel a century-long mystery we've been hiding."

As Margaret settled back into her chair, she glanced back and forth between the two and growled, "What are you two talking about?"

Dave turned to her as he hitched his thumb toward the Director of the CIA. "I have no idea what *he's* talking about. As to that coin of his, though, it's made of the only metal I know of that is solid at room temperature, but if you warm it even in the slightest it'll melt. Body temperature is enough to do the job."

There was something about what the CIA Director had said that stirred some hope in Margaret. She was ready to grasp at any lifeline, and focused her gaze on Kevin. "Out with it. What are you talking about, and what's this got to do with our situation?"

For a fraction of a second, the CIA Director's face carried a concerned expression that made her rising hope shudder with uncertainty. "Madam President, I'm sure you're not surprised to hear that the CIA has long held some sensitive assets under compartmented restrictions. Only when I was appointed as Director did I become aware of certain assets that have been kept isolated from all access for over eighty years. I've read the old reports on this asset, and all I can say is that it's extremely dangerous. It's been kept locked away deep underground, and despite all the safeguards we've employed, it has a history of spontaneously sending bursts of energy sufficient to knock out the power to nearby towns. In 1981, nearly the entire state of Utah had their power knocked offline when this thing sent a devastating surge that wreaked havoc with the power grid. The Agency, of course, blamed a prison fire for the outage and the entire incident was swept under the rug. After the blackout, all testing ceased. We had no way of safely analyzing this thing without endangering everyone in the surrounding area, so it's been sealed for over eighty years."

"What is it?" General Keane asked. "Where'd we get it from?"

Kevin shrugged. "I'm not exactly sure on either count. We didn't have the technology or the personnel to safely study it, so it's been buried." The longtime CIA agent pointed in Dave's direction. "I was thinking that Doctor Holmes might be able to figure out what it is and somehow harness what might be a tremendous source of power." He turned to the president with a helpless expression. "I'll freely admit that I don't know much more, but given that the situation seems dire, I had to mention what little I do know."

Dave stood and turned toward the president. "To be honest, there's not much I can otherwise do given our current situation, so let me go take a look at this thing. I'll be frank and say that we need some kind of miracle, and maybe Director Baker happens to have one hidden in his back pocket."

Margaret turned to Burt, who'd remained silent throughout the meeting. "Thoughts?"

Burt shook his head and shrugged. "I have no idea what Director Baker's got locked away in his secret hidey-hole, but if I were looking for someone to solve a problem that nobody had solved before, Doctor Holmes would be my first choice. And besides, he won't be much help fixing what's already been broken. While he's off looking at whatever the CIA is hiding, I'll work with others to see if there's anything we can do to eke out some additional power. Maybe we missed something."

Margaret motioned toward the Secretary of Defense. "Walter, can you make arrangements for Doctor Holmes and his wife to go to...." She turned her gaze toward Kevin, and the CIA Director addressed the general with four words. "Homey Airport in Nevada."

The president stood and walked over to Dave, who got up from his chair as she approached. She gave him a hug and whispered in his ear. "Best of luck and Godspeed." She turned to Bella, who cringed as Margaret leaned closer. Sensing the woman's discomfort, the president nodded at her and pointed at Dave. "Keep him out of trouble."

Bella looked up at the president with a stunned expression, which suddenly melted as she smiled and returned Margaret's nod.

With a motion toward the rest of the room, Margaret announced in a firm voice, "I want Kevin and Burt to stay. Walter, you make the arrangements to get Doctor Holmes and his wife on site, then come right back. We've got additional pressing business. The rest of you, thanks for attending, but you're dismissed."

The room cleared out in seconds and Margaret motioned for Kevin to sit closer. "Burt, since you've been disclosed on these matters previously, there's no issue with you hearing this. Let's just wait on Walter to arrive."

Kevin sat next to Margaret as she pressed a button on the table. A hidden speaker suddenly produced the disembodied voice of a White House operator.

"Secure Operator 54391 is online."

"Margaret Laura Hager, 128-45-8934"

"Margaret Laura Hager, confirmed. How may I help you, President Hager?"

"I have an Omega priority request. An immediate audio meeting of the N35 is required. Please patch into this extension when everyone is connected."

"Omega priority audio patch to the N35, confirmed. Once all parties are in attendance, an operator will contact the Situation Room to confirm continued Presidential authorization before attempting to route the call. Disconnecting."

Burt turned to Margaret. "What's N35?"

Walter entered the Situation Room as Margaret replied, "Oh, that's what we call the thirty-five nuclear weapon nations. The same folks that you met earlier." She tossed him a wry grin. "I'm sure you remember them."

Burt's eyes widened. "Oh, those folks. Yup—"

Suddenly a ringing sound alerted everyone in the room to an incoming call, and Margaret remarked, "They can't have gathered everyone so quickly." She tapped the button on the table.

"Secure Operator 54374 is online. We have an Omega priority call from a Head of State."

Margaret's brows knitted together as she asked, "What state?"

"The Democratic People's Republic of Korea. Shall I patch them in?"

Margaret tapped on the table's mute button and glanced at Walter and Kevin. "Either of you expecting a call from North Korea? I've met that little...." She swallowed whatever she was going to say and restarted her sentence. "He's as crazy as they come."

Both of the men shook their heads, but Burt's voice suddenly chimed in. "I met him as well. Remember, I told you he knows Doctor Holmes from school and seemed desperate to talk to him."

With a frown, she motioned toward Kevin. "Can you run out there and bring Doctor Holmes back here really quick? I'm not about to blow this lunatic off, but I don't have anything nice to say to him one on one."

The Director of the CIA bolted from his chair, and moments later, Dave rushed into the room with Bella right behind.

"Doctor Holmes, are you okay with talking with the North Korean leader?"

"You mean Frank?" Dave's eyes widened, and a grin creased his confused expression. "The same Frank from Caltech? You're kidding me."

The president shook her head and pointed at the speaker above the conference room table. "Doctor Holmes, he's on hold and I cannot imagine he's calling to talk to me. We don't exactly get along. Are you okay talking with him?"

"Sure, it's been years, but I'll talk to him."

As Dave sat in one of the chairs, Margaret toggled the mute button and said, "Operator, please patch the call in. We're ready."

"Confirmed, patching call now...."

"Hello?" An accented voice broadcast loudly from the speaker. *"Hello?"* A muffled noise sounding like someone covering a microphone broadcast through the connection, followed by the caller yelling something to someone in Korean.

Dave craned his neck and yelled, "Hey, Frank? Is that you?"

The muffled noise repeated loudly and Frank's voice burst through the speaker. *"Dave! You are there! I tried getting that asshole to get me your number, but he refused. We need to meet now."*

Margaret was about to say something when Dave held his hand up and shook his head. "Frank, I'm swamped right now. Just tell me what you need. Maybe I can help."

"Oh, I'm sorry, I just need ... one second." The sound of the microphone being covered once again was followed by muffled yelling in Korean, leaving everyone in the Situation Room shaking their heads.

Margaret had met the weasel once before, and he was the most annoying ass she'd ever met in her life. If he weren't who he was, she'd have stuffed her fist into that pudgy man's face.

"Remember how we talked about if we could control detonations? The concept of an engine that ran off weaponry to benefit the Earth ... I've got a prototype, but ... I'm not sure how practical it might be. You've got to take a look at this, you're always so good at synthesizing practical applications for things. I know this is a big

advancement, but I'm just not sure what to do with it yet. I need your help."

With both a puzzled and amused expression, Dave winced. "I can't look right this second, but do you have a blueprint or some kind of schematic?"

"Yes! I made all the drawings myself. Nobody helped. All myself." Frank repeated himself as the tone of his voice indicated he was getting more agitated. *"But how can I send it? Do you have e-mail? I can send it right now."*

Dave leaned closer to Margaret and whispered, "I haven't had an e-mail account in four years. Can I—"

Burt scribbled something on a sheet of paper and handed it to Dave.

"Frank," Dave read from the paper, "send it to BR13829@isf.gov and I'll look at it as soon as I get to my computer."

"Okay okay, I'll send it now. We can meet and I can show it to you. We built one. Very very hard to build, but we did it. Yes, we'll meet, right?"

"Frank, give me a little time to look it over. I swear I'll get back to you like I always have in the past. Okay?"

"Oh ... yes, I'm sorry. I was pushing again. I'm sorry." The previously hyper-excited voice had suddenly become much more somber. *"The engine is ready when you are. Okay, I'm sending blueprints for the engine and a schematic for the coherency controller now. Bye."*

A dial tone blurted through the speaker and Margaret slapped the disconnect button, ending the bizarre call.

She grinned at Dave and shook her head. "That's one strange friend of yours."

Dave stood and returned her amused expression. "Oh, he's just excitable. You wouldn't know it, but he's not as crazy as he seems. Some of his ideas are just off-the-charts brilliant, and other times...." He shrugged and laughed. "If that's it, I'm going to go see what Director Baker has got hidden up his sleeves in Nevada."

Margaret waved him away just as a ringing noise echoed through the speaker.

As the president hit the button to pick up the call, Dave hesitated at the door to the Situation Room.

"Secure Operator 54393 is online. We have an Omega priority call that requires presidential authorization."

Margaret tapped the mute button and motioned Dave away. "It's okay. This is the call I was expecting. Thanks again, Doctor Holmes, and I'll pray for your success."

As soon as Dave and Bella left, Margaret tapped at the mute button.

"Margaret Laura Hager, 128-45-8934"

"Margaret Laura Hager, confirmed. We have the conference call established for N35. 34 of the 35 members are on the line. The North Korean representative was unavailable. Shall I patch the call to your location, President Hager?"

"Yes, go ahead."

The sound of a phone ringing replaced the operator's voice, and a series of beeps occurred as voices appeared on the line.

"All right, folks, as some of you already know, we've had another incident with the Brotherhood, this time a major one. Let me just tell you that we're working on contingency plans, but while that's happening, we need to ensure that crap doesn't happen again."

"Margaret," the voice of the British Prime Minister was easy to recognize, *"we have some GPS locations for some of the terrorist cells, but this might require something a bit more drastic, don't you think?"*

"Percy, it's time to rain death on these clowns. Just like they coordinated their attacks, we have to do the same. Let's wipe them all out."

CHAPTER TWENTY-FIVE

Burt watched the Secretary of Defense and the Director of the CIA exit the Situation Room, leaving him sitting alone with the president.

Margaret clacked her fingernails on the conference room table and stared at Burt with a thoughtful expression.

He couldn't tell what she was thinking, but she'd clearly asked him to stay for a reason, and her reasons usually meant something rather significant was going to be asked of him.

"Burt, as you know," she finally said, "we're about to get bloody. The old Soviet KGB assassins used to call it *wet affairs*. It's not something I enjoy, but these assholes are trying to get us all killed and they may very well have accomplished it. I'm not giving them a second chance. I hope you understand why I convened the N35 and we've started that ball rolling."

Burt hated the idea of killing people unnecessarily. It was something that kept him up at night, but he also understood that sometimes there was a greater good in such things. These lunatics were trying to bring about the end of the world as desperately as he was hoping to save it. "Madam ... uh, Margaret, I may never have fought in combat like you have, but I understand perfectly. Even though I can only begin to imagine the bloodshed that's about to occur, and despite knowing that there's always collateral damage that occurs when chaos reigns, I know it has to be done. I'm sad that it has to come to this, but believe me, I understand."

Margaret pursed her lips as she stared intently at him. "I wanted to ask you before I did this. Having done some checking, I know that you've got some family in California. They aren't in an evacuation zone, but if it makes you feel better, I can arrange for them to be taken with us to the Cheyenne Mountain Complex. It's where most of our government will end up going."

Taken aback, Burt imagined the twins along with his brother and sister-in-law. Looking at the expression on Margaret's face, he for a moment didn't see a hard-nosed President or ex-soldier, instead he saw a warm, caring mother and friend. He blinked rapidly as the idea hit him that she'd gone out of her way to look after those he'd cared about.

He took a deep, steadying breath and smiled. "Thank you for even thinking about them. If you don't mind, I'll talk to my brother and let you know. It should be whatever he feels is best for them."

Margaret nodded grimly and her gaze wandered for a moment. "Burt, I'm about to ask you to do something that I know you'll find distasteful." Her gaze locked onto his, and Burt felt the tension emanating from the president; she was deadly serious. "I'm going to initiate an evacuation of all of the Moon bases. I'm sending a company of Special Forces soldiers in full battle gear to sweep all of the miners, maintenance crews, and any living being up there, and ship them back down here. I want you to go up there with them."

Burt's mouth fell open and his heartbeat quickened. His mind raced. "I'm not a soldier, and I've never even been to the Moon. Why in the world would you want me up there?"

"I'm not sending you up there as a soldier, I'm sending you up as one of the preeminent computer scientists we have. I've read your file and have talked with Doctor Patel. It seems as if the Moon is operational and can be maneuvered under the same method as Doctor Holmes planned for the Earth. Burt, we can't risk one of these lunatics gaining access to the Moon's control systems. We can't know they haven't infiltrated the Moon, so that's why I'm sweeping everyone off. In addition, I want you to go up there with two specific objectives."

Margaret jabbed a finger in his direction to emphasize her point. "First, I want you to harden the remote access so that it would be impossible to override the system parameters from down here. I know artificial intelligence was your specialty, but you've written dozens of papers on computer security after that computer incident in LA. Doctor Patel insisted that if you'd stuck to the computer field and not buried it in your past, you'd have revolutionized the way we interact with computers. I tend to believe her."

Burt opened his mouth to object, but Margaret silenced him with a glare and shake of her head.

"No arguments. If by some miracle Doctor Holmes manages to solve our power problem, we cannot risk some lunatic hacker taking remote control of the Moon and crashing it into us.

And if for some reason Doctor Holmes fails and the Earth is doomed, I want the Moon available as an escape pod. This is beyond just my responsibility as the President of the United States; we cannot allow humanity to go extinct. Not if there is any available option. There's enough space up there to house several hundred people and be self-sustained. You will be one of those people."

"Why me? I'd have thought you'd want someone younger, or someone with kids or—"

"No." Margaret shook her head emphatically. "I need you there, because I won't be there. I've already decided that I will not take a place up there while I'm in charge. Not happening. You'll be my designee." The president leaned closer and pointed at the ceiling. "Those people up above ... they'll need a leader, and you have an unflappable quality to you that screams leadership. Doctor Patel may be a fan of your academic accomplishments, but I've watched you over the last few months. There's no doubt, you were born to lead. You don't make enemies, and you're considerate yet emphatic about doing what's right. Burt, if things go to hell, I need you to be up there sailing that ship."

The president's normally serious demeanor softened, and for just a moment, she looked worried. "Please say that you'll do it."

Burt stared at the president, not sure what to say. The idea of being responsible for the last remnants of Earth's population was almost too much to imagine. Yet something about the president's sincere plea stiffened his resolve, and reluctantly, he nodded.

"I'll do it."

~

It was 5:00 a.m. when Stryker stood watch atop the thirty-foot tall concrete barrier surrounding the Indian Point Energy Center.

A cool breeze blew across the Hudson River from the south, bringing with it the scent of the shore.

Turning south, Stryker looked up into the pre-dawn darkness and felt a sense of awe as he spied the shimmering whitish-blue ribbon of light snaking across the southern horizon. A visible sign of DefenseNet.

Sergeant Gutierrez, one of the men standing watch with him remarked, "It's amazing, isn't it? It doesn't seem real."

Stryker nodded as the surreal sight dredged up memories from years ago. "It reminds me of when I was a kid and saw a total eclipse back in the summer of '45. I remember like it was yesterday, staring up at the sky when totality hit.

"The sun went dark and I saw that halo of light surrounding it. It made me wonder what ancient man would have thought seeing that. Their minds must have been blown by it all."

The sergeant snorted in the shadowy dusk of the early morning. "Shit, Lieutenant, I'm looking at that ribbon of light going from horizon to horizon, and even though I know what it is, I still don't get it."

Peering through night-vision binoculars, Stryker panned his gaze across the four-kilometer perimeter, noting the dim glow along the horizon. That, coupled with the absence of the chirping of crickets, was a sure sign that dawn was imminent.

The sergeant standing watch with him shifted nervously as he too peered through binoculars. "Sir, have we finished the evac of everyone from the coast?"

Stryker turned to him and frowned. "Did you catch some movement?"

"I'm not sure. It might have been some deer racing around the edge of the woods on the other side of the river."

"Well, as of yesterday at 1800 hours, the coastal evacuations were completed and all civilians within fifty miles of the coast have been brought inland. There shouldn't be anyone out there, but keep your eyes peeled."

"Roger that."

Stryker's platoon of MPs had been stationed at the nuclear energy facility along with two squads of Army Rangers. Members of the Army Corps of Engineers had been called in to run the plant.

He hadn't been given any intelligence on why this place was bristling with soldiers, aside from it being one of the plants feeding energy into DefenseNet's power grid.

Suddenly, one of the motion sensors activated, and the nearby spotlight on the wall panned slowly across the landscape to the west.

A large buck was bathed in light and bolted back into the woods.

Stryker's radio beeped with an incoming call and he tapped his earpiece.

"Indian Point, this is Major Carl Simpson of the Northeast Quadrant Air Support. Be aware that we've detected mechanized movement approaching your perimeter. Looks like a large group of trucks four klicks southwest of your location. They're heading in your direction. Over."

The hair on the back of his neck stood as he panned his binoculars to the southwest. It was a heavily wooded area with one road cutting through it. "Roger that, air support. Appreciate the heads up."

He switched channels and his voice broadcasted through several key locations throughout the nuclear facility.

"Alert, alert. We've got unknowns approaching from the southwest. Incoming vehicles."

Stryker glanced at Sergeant Gutierrez and even though they'd been manning the West Gate, he motioned toward the gate's control panel. "Turn on all the spotlights. Make sure nothing gets by unnoticed."

Before Gutierrez could even respond, Stryker raced down the stairs and ran across the power plant toward the southwest entrance.

Red lights flashed throughout the facility as soldiers who'd been off-shift rushed to their assigned locations.

Stryker tapped on his radio and yelled, "Southwest Gate, report."

Silence greeted him as he raced across the half mile.

"Southwest Gate, status report!"

Somewhere in the distance shots were fired.

A chill raced through Stryker as he put on a burst of speed.

A voice yelled over the emergency channel, *"God dammit, who's opening the Southwest Gate?"*

Running past one of the reactor buildings, he saw the heavily-reinforced metal gate yawning open.

Something whizzed just past his ear, and Stryker dove for cover behind a nearby dumpster.

A three-round burst of weapons fire chased after him, ringing loudly against the steel container he'd ducked behind.

Stryker charged his weapon and shifted his gaze to the top of the security wall. He peered through the scope on his rifle, and a burning anger bloomed inside him.

It was one of his men.

Lying motionless at the attacker's feet was another MP. Stryker winced as the soldier took aim in another direction and fired a shot.

The security gate clicked into the open position.

With his heart threatening to beat out of his chest, Stryker trained his weapon on his attacker, who stood on top of the thirty-foot wall.

Placing the crosshairs on his target, he focused on his breathing.

With adrenaline racing through his system, he took a deep breath, held it, and squeezed the trigger.

He let the breath out as the man's head jerked backward.

A successful head shot.

Stryker jumped up from his position, raced toward the stairs at the base of the gate and tapped on the radio. "We need MANPATS at the southwest gate, now!"

Panting, he took the stairs two at a time, ran toward the gate control panel, and felt his stomach drop as he saw the carnage of the control circuit for the gate.

Someone had put a bullet in it.

Another soldier clambered up the stairs and asked, "Sir, the gate— oh shit, let me work on this, I think I can jury rig the control."

Stryker stepped away as one of his men tore open the panel, exposing a rat's nest of wires.

Lying only ten feet away were two dead men wearing MP uniforms. One a patriot, the other a traitor.

Stryker knelt by the man he'd been forced to shoot, drew a knife from his belt, and sliced open the man's jacket and undershirt.

He curled his lip up with disgust as he spied an hourglass tattoo on the left side of the man's chest.

Same markings he'd seen back in Washington State.

A cold sense of concern washed over him as he glanced at the soldiers all around him.

Were there any more?

One man on the wall yelled as he peered through binoculars, "Sir, we've got visitors!"

Someone fired a flare toward the southwest that bloomed like a full moon over the field and roadway.

Speakers embedded in the outer perimeter of the power station began repeatedly broadcasting, *"You have entered a restricted military zone. Do not approach or you will be fired upon."*

Two Rangers yelled to clear the way as they raced up the stairs, both carrying long tubes that Stryker recognized as the latest version of the Army's Carl Gustaf portable anti-tank weapon.

Stryker pulled up his rifle, peered through the magnified sight, and watched as a large truck barreled toward them.

One of the Rangers carrying the Gustaf turned to him. "Sir, we've got multiple vehicles incoming."

A large spark burst from the gate's control panel and the MP yelled, "Got it! Sir, I've hotwired the control circuit."

The heavy metal gate creaked as it began to close.

"Excellent, Corporal."

"Sir," the nearest Ranger interjected. "We've got targets painted. Permission to call in an airstrike."

"Granted."

Stryker changed channels on the radio and heard one of the Rangers on the far side of the gate call in to the Direct Air Support Center.

"Any station, any station, this is Indian Five Actual, need assistance. Over."

The radio crackled for a second, then a voice reverberated through his earpiece.

"Indian Five Actual, this is Hawkeye 8, send it. Over."

"Hawkeye 8, request air support, we've got limited MANPAT rounds and multiple incoming. We have targets painted on the field, we'd appreciate an assist."

"Roger Indian, we're scrambling some jets for you. ETA 11 minutes."

Just as the gate shut with a loud metal clang, Stryker switched channels. "Fire at will."

Another flare raced up into the sky, and when Stryker looked through his gun's sight, the details of the truck became clearer.

It was a tractor trailer. There didn't seem to be anyone at the wheel.

Remote controlled?

Nervous energy raced through him as the truck crossed the one-kilometer markers on the sides of the road.

He shifted the sight further away and spied other vehicles in the distance. Stryker gave the Ranger a sideways glance. "Make your shots count on the semi, those other trucks are hanging back for some reason."

"Yes, sir." The Ranger adjusted his mic and yelled, "Hold fire until the first target crosses 500 meters. Quiñones, you take the first shot. If it's a miss, Jenkins, and if there's something left, I'll take my shot."

Almost immediately, a burst of flame belched out of one of the Gustafs on the far side of the gate.

An explosion rocked the dirt just behind the truck.

A miss.

"Firing," someone yelled.

Twenty feet to Stryker's right, another Gustaf fired.

The concussive force thudded in his chest as the projectile launched toward its target.

The truck exploded with a blinding burst of white light.

Despite having squeezed his eyes shut, the light was unbearably bright.

A heartbeat later, a wave of explosive energy nearly knocked him off his feet.

Stryker grunted with surprise as the heat from the fireball singed his eyebrows. For a moment, he wondered if there'd been a nuke in that truck.

After all, the damned thing was a full quarter-mile away.

With his ears ringing and sergeants yelling orders to their squads, Stryker shook his head and peered across the field as debris began raining down across the facility.

One Ranger staggered as he got up from his firing position. "Holy crap! That thing had to have been fully loaded with C4 or something."

He blinked, trying to get the image of the fireball out of his vision. Its light had been so bright, that Stryker wondered if it had done some damage to his eyes.

He trained his weapon toward where the truck had been, peered through the rifle's optics, and his jaw dropped.

There was a twenty-foot deep crater almost fifty-feet wide where the truck had been.

"Sir, one of the trucks just outside the perimeter has peeled away from the rest and is accelerating in our direction. We've only got five more rounds for the Gustafs."

Stryker shifted his gaze, trying to make out the details of the incoming. "Another semi?"

"Yes, sir. And it looks like there's three more."

"Shit, what do they think they're accomplishing?" Stryker muttered under his breath.

He glanced over his shoulder at the nearest reactor building.

If the gate had been open and it had smashed into that building....

He changed channels on his radio. "Hawkeye 8, this is Indian 5, we're under attack. Repeat, the Indian Point *Nuclear* facility is under attack. We need those jets."

Seconds passed as men scrambled into position and the anti-tank weapons were reloaded.

"Roger Indian 5, we've got fast movers en route. They've gone supersonic. They're five minutes from your location. Over."

Pressing his lips together, Stryker breathed heavily through his nose as he focused. Five minutes.

Switching back to the local channel, he barked loudly, "Folks, we have five minutes before air support arrives. Rangers, make whatever ammo you've got count.

"Gutierrez, do we have any RPGs on site?"

"Sir, I'll check."

Stryker peered through the optics on his rifle and watched as the first truck passed the one kilometer marker. Another was moving toward them a good five hundred or more meters behind the first.

"Better hurry, because we're going to need them."

CHAPTER TWENTY-SIX

As the plane descended, Dave's ears popped. He leaned close to Bella and showed her his computer screen. "What do you make of that?"

Pulling her hair back out of the way, she leaned close and stared at the schematic Frank had sent. It looked like a mesh ball with wire-wrapped connections spilling out the top. "It looks like a Faraday cage to me, but why have the wires coming out of it? Is that for grounding?"

"That was my thought, but it doesn't make any sense. A Faraday cage is used to keep something inside protected from the outside. This thing looks like he designed it to hold something in and route the electricity across the top."

Bella pointed at the wires on the top. "Didn't he call it an engine? Maybe it's holding something and venting the energy through the top. Did he say in his e-mail what it's made of?"

"Not in the e-mail, but one second." Dave swiped his finger along the tablet's touchscreen, flipping through several pages of detailed drawings, until he brought up the design prints for the controller, which plugged into the cage-like device. He pointed at some input wires and noted, "This says that the conductive lead is coming from something called a HiMag wrapper. Maybe it's some kind of magnesium alloy? I've got no clue. I remember the conversations Frank and I had about if we could trap the energy from explosives, but that wouldn't do us much good right about now. We'd have a tremendous spike of energy, and then nothing. Maybe if there was a new battery charging capability alongside this...."

The lights flickered in the cabin of the small passenger jet, and the pilot's voice came on the loudspeaker. *"Doctor and Mrs. Holmes, please ready yourselves for landing. We'll be at Homey Airport in five minutes.*

"I'd also like to warn you that since this is a black site, we've got an unusual approach vector and we'll be coming in hot and taxiing directly into a hangar. Agents will be there to escort you as soon as the hangar is sealed."

Dave fastened his seatbelt, gripped the arms of his seat, and warned Bella, "Make sure your seatbelt is on tight. If this guy is saying he's coming in hot, that probably means it's going to be a rough landing."

The engines of the jet whined, and as the angle of the plane shifted downward, Dave grunted. Everything inside him felt like it wanted to come up out of his mouth. The descent grew ever steeper, and he squeezed harder on the arms of the chair. For a moment, Dave felt sure that they'd wreck on some desolate salt bed in the middle of Utah. Yet, at the last second, he felt himself get slammed into his chair as the plane leveled off. Wheels screeched as they contacted the runway. In less than a minute, they pulled into an unmarked gray metal hangar in the middle of nowhere.

Dave breathed a sigh of relief as he clumsily unbuckled his seatbelt. "Holy crap," he glanced at Bella. "Are you okay?"

She nodded as the military pilot exited the cockpit with a smile. "I love those approaches."

"You can keep them," Dave remarked weakly as he stood, his legs feeling weak. As he helped Bella from her seat, the pilot pressed a button on the cabin wall and the nearby door unsealed and yawned open, just as a portable set of stairs were wheeled up against the jet's fuselage.

The pilot waved at the hangar personnel and turned to his passengers. "Looks like your welcoming committee is here."

After being escorted away from the plane by two people who identified themselves as liaisons for the site, Dave found himself in what seemed to be a waiting area, staring at Bella. Evidently someone was supposed to take them to their final destination and what Dave hoped would be the location of the mysterious object.

The cinderblock walls of the waiting room were painted a faded, ugly yellow. The sofa and chairs looked sturdy, but from the previous century. Bella seemed at ease just sitting back on the sofa, waiting, while Dave paced, and grew more and more anxious.

Just when Dave thought he was about to burst, the metal door opened. A harried-looking man in a white lab coat stood in the doorway and blurted, "Doctor Holmes? Mrs. Holmes? I'm sorry to keep y'all waiting, but those morons only just now told me where they stashed you."

"Don't worry about it, and please, call me Dave." Dave shook hands with the dark-haired man with the strong southern accent. "And you are?"

"Chris Wilkinson. I suppose my official title is Technical Operations Officer, but really I'm a signal processing geek. You know, RF and analog signaling and analysis." He smiled warmly. "Oh, and I'm the guy who fixes the bomb tech robots when they've eaten one too many explosive dinners."

"So are you the one who's going to show us this mystery object?"

"Yup, let's go." Chris turned and waved for them to follow. "I only found out about this place just a couple hours ago, and truthfully, I'm thinking the folks at Langley put me on this just because I happened to be on vacation only about one-hundred miles away. I'm not sure how much help I can be on this."

Besides a thick southern accent, Chris also spoke very quickly, so Dave struggled to keep up with what he said.

"I'm telling you guys, it was the strangest thing getting scooped up and raced out here in the middle of nowhere." Chris zigzagged through a series of hallways and kept a count on his fingers for every left and right turn he took. "This place is a maze, so I don't have a clue about what else is here, but I managed to find the entrance to where they're hiding whatever this thing is."

Bella touched Dave's arm as they hurried after the lanky engineer and murmured, "I can feel it."

Chris stopped at an office with a closed door that didn't have any obvious knob. He pressed his finger into a recess next to the door frame and held it there.

Dave turned to Bella and whispered, "What do you feel?"

With a troubled expression, she shrugged. "It's like a vibration, almost like a hum." She pointed to the floor. "Somewhere down there."

The door before them quietly slid open, and as Chris walked in the room, Dave followed, realizing that it was actually an elevator.

As the elevator doors slid shut and they began to descend, Chris turned to Dave and Bella and seemed hardly able to contain himself. "I began reading the notes left behind from the folks who'd studied this thing, and let me tell you," he jabbed his finger in the air, "this is one strange thingamajig. It was built for some kind of skunkworks project located in the old Roswell Army Air Field back in 1947. And that's when the shit hit the fan."

The elevator suddenly stopped and the doors slid open, revealing a long corridor ahead, hewn from the surrounding bedrock. Along the walls were tiny flickering lanterns that looked just like what Dave had seen in museums. "No electricity down here? Batteries?"

"Nope." Chris shook his head. "Ya'll will read all about it, but when that thing acts up, it tends to eat anything electrical for breakfast. Evidently the scientists working on this thing realized that lanterns didn't get knocked out, which is kind of a good thing. I'd hate to be stuck here in total darkness."

Chris stepped out of the elevator, and as Dave followed, he noticed that to his right were a pair of misaligned doors with a large gap above them. Sometime long ago, those doors had opened into an elevator, but now, their rusted remains only partly concealed the darkness of the elevator shaft behind them.

Chris whispered, "Remember when I said that the shit hit the fan regarding this object at Roswell back in 1947?"

It was only when Dave heard what Chris had said and saw the number "51" stenciled in yellow and black on the rusted elevator doors that old memories snapped into place. His heart began racing.

Dave's eyes widened and he gasped, "You're shitting me. That's where we are? This is where the Roswell rumors and all the alien talk comes from?"

"I know, can you eff'in believe it?" Chris shifted his weight from one leg to another, acting as if he would explode from excitement. "I never believed that there even was an Area 51 and that the Roswell stuff was just a bunch of malarkey, but now...." He pointed at the elevator shaft. "There it is, plain as day. It may not be aliens, but there's something going on."

Motioning to the broken elevator, Dave asked, "So, is there another elevator?"

"No, follow me." Chris shook his head and began walking down the long stone corridor. "There's a supply room where I've gathered a bunch of equipment and some of the cleanroom suits we'll need. It's about a half-mile hike, so let me summarize what I've learned so far about this thing.

"Like I said, there was a big incident in 1947. But let me give you some of the background. I'm sure you're familiar with the Manhattan Project. It was as top secret as it gets back in the day, but there were two twenty-three-year-old Alabama boys who most of the Project never knew about: Kyle and Peter Wilkinson. They were instrumental in helping get the equations right for that nuclear bomb.

"You see, back then, they didn't have proper computers. All they had was roomfuls of women on glorified calculators and the beginnings of the first analog punch-card-based computers. Running through the numbers, they had a hell of a time getting the math right for some of those equations. It took forever. Yet, from what I've read, it seems like the Wilkinson boys were some kind of geniuses. Their medical charts showed them as 'psychologically inept, but highly talented.' I'm thinking that might have been some kind of 1940s-speak for high functioning autistics; you know, idiot savants. The kind of folks who can't really do much of anything but one or two things, but those one or two things, they can do better than just about anyone else in the world.

"Well anyway, the government got the bright idea to start using them, and lo and behold, they cranked through those equations like a hot knife through butter.

"After the war, the government gave them their own lab in Roswell and let them tinker, unsupervised. After a couple years, suddenly some kind of electrical explosion happened. That was 1947.

"The boys vanished. Nobody saw hide nor hair of them ever again. I'll have you know, I ain't much for conspiracies and such, but it's not hard to wonder why the Manhattan Project got disbanded right around when those boys disappeared."

Dave's curiosity was piqued. "So what do we know about this thing?"

"Well, their lab was pretty much trashed, and the only thing left in it was a beach-ball-sized metal sphere that sparked like crazy if you did much of anything to it. Unfortunately, those boys weren't much for writing things down. There was almost nothing salvageable from their lab other than what we're about to go look at.

"Anyway, not long after, the object was brought to the Groom Lake facility here for further study. At the time, all they could tell was the ball-shaped metal object was highly reactive to just about any kind of stimuli. It sometimes shot arcs of electricity out the top of it.

"As to its condition, it looked burnt, but other than the heavy discoloration, it seemed to not be heavily damaged.

"The scientists at the time knew they were dealing with something nobody could explain."

Still walking quickly along the stone corridor, Chris looked over his shoulder at Dave and Bella. "Well, anyway, they took all sorts of readings and even measured some of that power that spurted out of the thing. Let me tell you, if that asshole didn't screw the pooch in '81, we probably wouldn't need to be on emergency power just to keep that DefenseNet thing running." He huffed with frustration. "I just hope that NASA's DefenseNet malarkey is worth it all, because whoever's responsible for it is going to have to answer to a lot of people if it doesn't do its job."

Dave smiled as it dawned on him that Chris had no idea who he was, and for some reason, that anonymity pleased him. "So, what happened in '81?"

Chris sighed. "Some crazy and likely underqualified scientist thought he knew what he was doing and managed to piss that strange thing off so badly it ended up freaking out. You'll have to look at the details of what he was trying to do, because it didn't make any sense to me. But that's also when the reports ended. In fact, the entire project got sealed after that."

Bella's hand tightened on Dave's arm and she asked, "What exactly does 'freaking out' mean and what happened to the scientist?"

"Oh, whatever that guy did sent a surge rushing out of that sphere that was so huge, it ended up blowing out the power to darn near all of Utah. The agency ended up covering it up by blaming a fire at the Utah State Prison that had occurred on the same day. As to what happened to the scientist, well ... the report said he died, but it also said they never recovered the body. Just like those brothers, he vanished into nothing. Downright spooky, if you ask me."

Chris suddenly stopped and pointed straight ahead into a darkened corridor. "All right, there's the stairs." He turned to the right and walked into a twenty-foot-long room containing a long table at its center. On it lay a box filled with manila folders stuffed with papers, and lying on the ground near the table were several large unopened boxes. "But before y'all can even think about going down there, you probably want to skim the safety protocols that they used way back then, because I know one of them was that you needed to put on some bunny suits."

"Bunny suits?" Bella asked with a confused tone.

"Sorry." Chris smiled. "One of the safety protocols they wrote down said that anyone studying the thing had to put on a cleanroom getup. You know, booties, mask, the whole surgeon thing, just more of it."

With a healthy dose of caution built into him, Dave walked over to the table and glanced at the file folders. "These are all the files on this thing?"

"Yup." Chris nodded. "Everything from 1947 to '81. Those are all copies, so don't worry about messing them up. They just can't leave this area."

Dave sat on one of the nearby wooden folding chairs and flipped open the first of the folders he extracted from the box.

As Chris began opening one of the other boxes lying on the floor, he mentioned, "Since all the crap down here evidently got fried back in the day, I've brought some analysis equipment that might help you figure out what that beast down below is about."

"Aha, that's why they insisted on treating the sphere with cleanroom procedures." Dave tapped at one of the sheets stuffed into a three-ring binder and read it aloud:

"March 19, 1953. This thing has been venting electricity regularly every forty-five minutes since the day it was found. Frank Burton, may he rest in peace, wasn't paying attention to the time and got caught when this damned thing began to spark. Luckily, nobody else was on site, but it managed to knock out the elevator's motor and there was a report from some tungsten miners about the Northern Lights glowing above Groom Lake. We're pretty sure what they saw was the flash of the electromagnetic charge, which could have excited some of the clouds in the area to fluoresce.

"September 5, 1953. Yesterday Carl Watkins inadvertently left the linen dust cover to the x-ray machine in the chamber when he wheeled it out. He didn't have a chance to retrieve it before the thing was scheduled to blow its top, and boy, did it ever. Let's just say that there's no cover left and the electricity surge still has my hair standing on end—and I was standing up top.

"September 9, 1953. We've confirmed that anything left in the chamber causes a spike in the forty-five-minute surge. Whatever is left

behind, whether it's a human, a screwdriver, or even something as small as an eyelash, is enough to make this thing go nuts.

"September 10, 1953. All further analysis will be done using full sterile garb. Not even a flake of skin will be left behind in that analysis chamber under penalty of dismissal."

"Wow," Chris said. "I must have missed that section." He connected some metal probes to what looked like a very fancy volt-meter, then shuddered and pointed one of the probes in Dave's direc-tion. "I saw the warning about the bunny suit stuff in the front summary, but goddamn that thing sounds just downright ill-tempered."

Dave watched as Chris adjusted the electric field proximity sensor and saw a thick line crawl across the video screen.

"That's weird," Chris commented. "I wouldn't have expected to have any field, but I guess the thing down there is leaking some kind of energy all the time."

"Why's the line so thick?" Dave asked. "Wouldn't you expect a sine wave?"

"Hold on, let me adjust the frequency ... weird, it's still thick."

Bella leaned closer and suggested, "Go as high as you can."

"Yes ma'am." Chris began spinning one of the knobs clockwise, making the line thicken just a bit, but even at the highest frequency, the display couldn't resolve it to anything more than a thick, fuzzy line. "Well, I'll be damned," Chris muttered, with awe in his voice. "What-ever that thing is doing, it's doing it with a frequency past what I can resolve." He glanced at Dave, who was already wearing the cleanroom suit. "Are you sure that the lead foil lining in that getup is enough? For all I know, this thing is spitting out gamma rays at us."

Suddenly the display turned white with a signal overload and then fell back to its previous pattern.

"Looks like our baby just burped," Dave said, as he pulled the hood down over his head and adjusted the collar so he could see clearly. He glanced at Bella, who'd done the same, and then winked at the worried engineer. "Don't worry, that's why we're paid the big bucks."

∽

Dave kept a close eye on the time, turned on his headlamp, and began climbing down the long set of stairs.

As they descended, he suddenly felt that vibration Bella had sensed much earlier.

Even though he felt the vibration, to him it had a sound—almost like nails against a chalkboard. Almost like an engine that had something wrong with it and was about to have a catastrophic seizure.

After five minutes, Dave finally reached the bottom and angled his lantern ahead.

The light poured over a large cavern with twenty-foot-high ceilings. The open area underneath the roof was easily fifty-feet wide. At the center lay a blackened object that looked more like a large, black and silver beach ball than anything else.

Taking a few steps forward, Dave tilted his head, and something struck him as odd about the charred object. A chill suddenly swept through him just as Bella gasped.

"Holy crap, that thing looks almost exactly like Frank's drawings."

CHAPTER TWENTY-SEVEN

"Oh, thank God we reached you! Princess, the authorities are taking your Mum and I out to Corsham. Even though we're nowhere near the coast, they said we're on a special list for safety's sake. They've not given us much choice, but evidently there's a huge underground bunker that the Prime Minister has reactivated and it will keep us safe. Neeta, are you in a safe place, too?"

"I'm safe, don't worry." Neeta got out of her chair and stared blankly at the back of her office door, stunned by what her father had just said.

Burt had mentioned in passing about how the world's governments were scrambling for underground bunkers. He'd also mentioned that the Burlington bunker was being used to evacuate the British government. Neeta knew that Corsham had a huge decommissioned bunker, and suddenly it dawned on her.

There'd be no reason for her parents to get special treatment unless someone had pulled some strings. Tears spilled onto Neeta's cheeks and her throat felt thick with emotion.

"Neeta, it's me," her mother said. *"We've just arrived and they're saying we won't get signal underground. I love you, baby. Stay safe."*

Her mom breathed heavily, and every word came slowly, as if she didn't want to hang up, ever.

"I love you too," Neeta said, and just listened, her heart hammering.

The signal disconnected as Neeta leaned against her office wall and slid to the ground. Wrapping her arms around her knees, she leaned her face into her legs and cried like she hadn't done since she was a child.

With a renewed feeling of determination, Neeta walked into the Jet Propulsion Lab's control room and clapped her hands to get everyone's attention. "Okay folks, let's get our crap straight. We've only got twenty-four days before the first wave of these space rocks reaches us. Our job is to try and buy some time. Who has the latest survey plot of the incoming debris?"

Standing in the middle of a forty-by-twenty-foot room, Neeta scanned the dozen or so tables where a handful of scientists stared into their computer screens. A blonde scientist poked up above a monitor and responded, "Doctor Patel, I've got the completed survey from yesterday. I'll put the data up on screen number three."

Neeta turned to the front of the room where a series of monitors were mounted on the wall. Most screens were filled with the constantly-updated status for the DefenseNet power levels, but screen number three flickered and showed a large white image with a cloud of various-sized dots scattered across it.

Surrounding most of the dots was a dashed red circle. Neeta knew that anything within the circle was aiming directly for Earth.

While Neeta stared at the screen, she asked, "How many targets are in the red zone, and what's the smallest object size in the survey?"

Next to where Neeta was standing, one engineer responded, "There are 13,517 objects in the survey with a minimum resolution of fifty feet. They have an average density of 3,000 kilograms per cubic meter."

Neeta recalled that the density implied stony objects, which are more prone to breaking up in the atmosphere. She smirked at the lunacy of her even caring about the density. It was like asking whether you wanted to be beaten with a wooden bat or a metal one. Either of them was liable to kill you.

She walked closer to the screen and pointed at some of the larger dots. "So, tell me, what's the biggest bloke in the bunch?"

"Doctor Patel, we couldn't resolve all of the individual sizes in the dense cluster of objects at the center, but we've not yet found anything over one-kilometer wide in the first wave."

Neeta took a step back and pondered their problem for a moment. "Show me where the biggest ones are, let's say 500 meters and larger, mask the rest away."

There were only about a dozen or so, mostly clustered in the center. "Good," she whispered to herself, "we might be able to do something useful."

Then she raised her voice. "Someone tell me what the damage profile looks like for a fifty-meter stony asteroid impacting us at a forty-five-degree angle and a thirty-five kilometer per second velocity prior to hitting our atmosphere."

Neeta listened to several of the engineers type, and one asked, "Water impact or land?"

"Let's do both, assume water depth of 4000 meters."

One of the engineers behind her reported, "Doctor Patel, a fifty-meter-wide stony asteroid with that approach angle and velocity will likely begin to break up at about 30,000 feet. I would not anticipate a crater, but there may be a heavy shock wave. Some structural damage to wood-frame houses is likely. In a water impact, I wouldn't expect a tsunami or any major damage to speak of."

Neeta panned her gaze across the room. "Is that confirmed?"

"Yes, ma'am," announced an engineer on the other side of the room announced. "I get roughly the same figures."

"What about a one-hundred-meter stony object with the same parameters?" Neeta asked.

A few seconds passed and another voice reported, "That object will likely shatter high in the atmosphere, approximately 200,000 feet up, but the blast will be gigantic. Nearly 230 megatons in the air, and on ground impact, it will be the equivalent of 32 megatons. The blast will devastate everything in a mile and a half radius. Over water, there's a chance of a minimal tsunami, but no higher than eight feet."

"I get the same figures," another voice confirmed.

With determination flowing through her, Neeta snapped her fingers to get everyone's attention. "Okay, folks, this is what we're doing. Bring the DefenseNet lasers online. We're going to start targeting the biggest rocks, but not for a center of mass hit. This is like billiards. We target the edge of these monsters, it won't do any substantial damage, but the sudden heating and explosion along their inside edge will push these things outward. And just like a properly hit cue ball, it will curve the way we want to.

If we're lucky, we may knock a lot of the smaller debris out of the red zone as well."

Neeta gazed around the room, intentionally making eye contact with each and every person. "You all know what's happened and how our timelines are unexpectedly shifted around. This can buy us the time we need, so each of you is holding the fate of the world in the palm of your hand. Let's not screw this up, folks. Are we clear on the importance of what we're about to do?"

"Yes!" All of the voices rang out.

"Fine, let's get the DefenseNet laser synchronizing computer online. We'll be giving some of these things full-blast doses of what we've got. I doubt any observatories will see the effect of the lasers firing, but just in case anyone sees anything, I'll let the Department of Defense know that some fireworks are about to start."

CHAPTER TWENTY-EIGHT

Gripping the belt strapped across his shoulder, Burt grimaced as the shuttle shuddered with the thrusters firing to slow their descent to the lunar surface. Surprisingly, his nausea settled slightly as the deceleration pressed him against his seat. Never having experienced zero gravity for any length of time, the whole trip to the Moon had unsettled him.

He glanced at the fifty soldiers packed into the passenger compartment with him. None of them seemed to be disturbed by the rattling of the shuttle. In fact, some were still asleep, despite being strapped tightly into their seats.

The comms officer sitting to Burt's left tapped his shoulder and handed him something that looked like a tablet PC with an oversized antenna sticking out its side. "Doctor Radcliffe, we just received a security alert you should probably know about."

Burt studied the rugged tablet and tapped on the alert flashing on the screen.

*** *Security Alert* ***

Intercepted transmission dated: 19 Nov 2066
Timestamp: 13:53 GMT

"Praise to you, my brother. May God bless you and your faith in Him. As has been prophesied, Armageddon is upon us.

It is only through God's design that the savior can be brought forth, and those working in your midst are interfering with His plan.

It is time.

Do what is necessary and you will be marked as one of the righteous in God's eyes.

Praise God and may he guide your hand in His mission.

- BR"

Burt glanced at the time displayed on a nearby bulkhead, and sighed—the message had just been sent. His stomach gurgled and the bile rose up in his throat as he handed the tablet PC back to the comms officer.

The shuttle rocked as the ship made contact with the lunar surface and the lights flickered in the cabin.

With a hard swallow, Burt gathered his resolve, unbuckled from his seat, turned to the captain sitting to his right, and said, "We have to hurry, the shit's about to hit the fan."

∽

"Are you Jeff Hostetler?" Burt asked the gray-haired man who stared worriedly as heavily-armed soldiers streamed through the airlock and began filling the Moon base's transit area.

"Yes, I'm Jeff Hostetler, Chief of Operations for Moon Base Crockett as well as the Director of the Moon-mining operations." The man panned his gaze across the large room filling with soldiers and asked, "What's going on? First thing I know is that I get an alert from the head of security for the ISF that I'm to expect the arrival of soldiers, and I'm not supposed to say anything to anyone."

"Well, I suppose it's on me to explain," said Burt, "and I'll be honest with you. There's reason to believe that the Moon base may have taken on some folks that have an interest in destroying the base, so instead of trying to figure it out and giving them any heads up, the president sent these men to perform a clean sweep of the entire site."

Just as Jeff was about to open his mouth, a soldier approached and addressed Burt, "Doctor Radcliffe, we've got the maps for the base. If you're okay with it, I'll keep some soldiers within the transit area to coordinate off-loading, and I'll begin sending the rest out to sweep from the far ends of the base and then back to this transit area. As we begin gathering the civilians, we'll offload them in the shuttles lined up behind us and continue the sweep through the rest of the site."

Jeff leaned to the side and looked out the loading bay portal. His eyes widened and he pointed to the line of shuttles approaching. "You're evacuating everyone?"

Burt clapped his hand on the captain's shoulder and nodded. "Go ahead, Captain Peron. I'm going to take Mister Hostetler with me to help figure out where some of the things are that I need to mess with."

"Roger that." The Captain nodded curtly, turned, and made a circular motion in the air with his hand. Almost immediately several of the company's lieutenants appeared in front of him. He singled out one of the lieutenants and ordered, "Peters, your platoon goes wherever Doctor Radcliffe goes. I don't care if he goes to the head, you clear the area and make sure there isn't even a roll of toilet paper out of place. It's on all of us that nothing happens to him, and that order comes from the top." He turned to the rest of his lieutenants and said, "The rest of you, gather your soldiers and initiate a clean sweep in all directions. Anyone you find comes back here for evac, no side trips. You got that?"

All of the captain's officers barked, "Sir, yes sir!" and with a quick dismissal, the lieutenants began barking orders. For a few moments, the transit area became a flurry of activity as the troops raced in four separate directions.

The Captain turned to Burt and hitched his thumb toward the lieutenant, who still stood by his side. "Lieutenant Peters will lead your escort. As you heard, General Keane advised that the soldiers sweep the area ahead of you as a precaution. Also, after everyone is evac'd, we'll be taking our pressure suits out and doing a survey of the outside of the Moon base as well as the mining interests. We need to be sure that this place is cleared inside and out."

"Thanks, Captain." Burt picked up a suitcase he'd brought with him and turned to the Moon base's director. "I'll need access to where the signals from the satellite dishes come into the main complex, and also I need to get access to the administrator terminals for the site's primary server."

The Lieutenant pulled out a map and showed it to Jeff. "Sir, can you show me on the map where we're going?"

"The satellite feeds come in through the signal room, right here." The Director pointed at one of the rooms on the map and then traced his finger to another room. "And the main terminal complex where Doctor Radcliffe asked to go is there."

The Lieutenant motioned to two of his sergeants, pointed at the map, and ordered, "Clear those locations and radio back. Go."

The sergeants barked orders to their squad and twenty soldiers raced toward their objective, while the Lieutenant motioned toward the hallway the soldiers had sped through. "Let's take a slow walk toward the objective, and if we're lucky, we'll get an a-okay from them before we get there."

Kneeling in what looked like a rat's nest of network wires, Burt found what he believed to be the communication uplink cables and plugged them into his debugging PC. With a borrowed military-grade satellite phone, he punched in Neeta's number and waited for a connection.

"Hello?" Neeta's voice broadcast through the static-filled connection. Burt could tell by her voice that she was annoyed. *"Who is this and why the hell are you calling at three in the morning?"*

"I'm sorry, Neeta. I wasn't paying attention to the local time." Burt chuckled.

"Oh, Burt, it's you." The tone of her voice softened. *"You're on the Moon now, right? What can I do for you?"*

"Neeta, I'm about to put signal monitors on everything coming into the computer system here, but I need to make sure I've got the right link. Can you do a test ping of the Moon base's computer? Also, can you tell me what the IP address is that you'll be coming in from?"

"Sure, one second."

The muffled sound of a door opening and closing was soon followed by someone in the room greeting Neeta.

Burt activated his packet tracing software and began monitoring the datagrams coming through the satellite connection.

"Burt, I'm logging in now.

"Okay, I've got my workstation's IPv6 address. I sent it via an SMS message to your phone. I'm now sending a ping to Moon Base Crockett's server."

Burt's phone vibrated as he received her message. He glanced at the text and smiled as Neeta's IP address also arrived in one of the Moon base's network routing packets, confirming that he had the right cable.

"I see your ping. I'm about to cut remote access to this site and put up a status portal instead. That way, people can see if things are still okay up here, but they won't be able to send denial-of-service attacks or have any other direct interaction with the onsite control systems." As Burt adjusted a variety of parameters on the network filter driver, saved the changes, and restarted the network filter service, this all began to feel very familiar. "It's like riding a bike, I suppose," he muttered to himself.

"Neeta, if what I did works, the filter driver on this machine shouldn't forward any incoming network packets to the main server. I'll setup a status portal, but can you try a ping first and then see if you can remotely connect to the site's server?"

Burt heard the sound of typing across the static-filled connection. *"Sending a ping now.... Okay, the ping looked good. Now trying to connect to the server. Wow, it's taking longer than I'd expect it to ...*

nope, I just got a timeout error. Whatever you did seems to be working."

A warm feeling of satisfaction flushed through Burt. "I suppose I still know how to twiddle the bits here and there. Thanks, Neeta. How's the debris survey going? Are we going to be able to buy ourselves any time?"

"It's going well, and I'm hoping to buy us some time, but I can't be sure yet. So far, we've sorted through the first cloud of junk heading towards us and we've managed to identify the critical-sized objects. I had the idea to try to use the DefenseNet lasers to nudge some of the big guys sitting in the center of the cloud outwards and try to create an empty pocket in the middle.

"If things go as planned, it could buy us a week or two as stuff flies past us in all directions. We shouldn't get hit by anything substantial. I've been up for thirty-six hours straight, watching and waiting. The center rocks are starting to move, so it's beginning to work, but I'll feel better when I see more. It's really dusty in the center of that cloud."

"That's good to hear. Keep me apprised of anything new. I know how you are, so try not to run yourself too ragged. Get some sleep."

With the sound of a barely stifled yawn, Neeta replied, *"I'll be fine. You just take care of yourself. Okay?"*

"Don't worry, I have a few more things that I need to do here and I'll be heading back. Good night."

Burt hung up and returned the phone to the Lieutenant. As he began packing some of his equipment back into its case, he glanced over his shoulder at the Moon base's director and said, "I'll need access to the primary server's terminal. There are a few things that need to be locked down."

～

Having spent the last four hours in the Moon base's control room, Burt managed to finally locate and download a private copy of the server's boot firmware so he could edit some changes into it. It had been years since he'd rolled his sleeves up and worked on the code responsible for platform initialization, but once he started to trace through the code, it all came back to him.

"Doctor Radcliffe," the lieutenant said softly, and crouched next to Burt. "All the civilians, including Mister Hostetler, are now en route to Cape Canaveral. We haven't found anything suspicious yet." He held up a remote video monitor and noted, "We have six squads now walking outside the base and two near the mining operations looking for anything out of the ordinary. Would you like to get a view from each of the sergeant's helmet cams?"

Burt glanced at the handheld screen, which broadcast eight separate video images, each image hovering above the device. "Sure, is there any audio?"

The soldier had just laid the device on the table next to the open chassis of the base's primary server when another soldier's voice barked through the remote viewer, *"Listen up. Just like back home, do your five and twenty-fives as we walk the area. We don't know what we're dealing with, and remember–this is space. A flesh wound up here can be fatal."*

Burt asked, "What's a five and twenty-five?"

"Sir, that's when a soldier scans the area five and twenty-five meters away. The reason for that is if you're traveling in an armored vehicle, an explosive inside the five-meter radius can take you out, even with armor around you. If you're walking around, then the kill zone is typically anything within twenty-five meters. To be frank, I've never done a training mission in space, so I'm not an expert on how some of the standard procedures change up here." The lieutenant pointed at the laptop that Burt was busily editing code on and asked, "Sir, I don't want to pry, but I'm dying to ask ... are you the same Doctor Radcliffe that received the Turing Award for Fundamental Advancement in Microprocessor Design and Artificial Intelligence in 2055?"

A sense of surprise mixed with amusement filled Burt as he slowly turned to the soldier and stared at the rough-looking man in full battle gear. Burt gave the soldier a lop-sided smile. "How in the world could you possibly know about that, Lieutenant Peters?"

The lieutenant's eyes widened, and he spoke with a reverent tone, "Oh, sir, I'm sorry. It's just that I got my masters in computer science and I was following your work at the time. I just thought it was amazing what you'd done with your AI and CPU designs, and how you integrated the two together." Suddenly the soldier seemed embarrassed and backed away. "I'm sorry, I don't want to distract you."

Burt motioned the man closer. "Don't be silly, I'll walk you through some of what I'm doing here." He pointed at the hardware initialization code he was editing and said, "One of the things I'm doing is modifying the platform's initialization routines so that anyone who wants to access or change the settings of the server needs to go through a biometric scan to confirm identity."

The soldier nodded. "So you're adding physical presence detection. That way only someone who is at the console can make the change, right?"

"Exactly right." Burt nodded, and stared at the soldier, seeing the man in a different light. This was clearly an officer who had his head on straight.

"But sir, why do it in the initialization code? Couldn't you more easily have done it in the operating system?"

Not able to keep the smile off his face, Burt glanced at the curious soldier. "Peters, that's an excellent question. My goal here is to not allow someone to get access to the controls. The reason I'm doing this the way I'm doing it is more for paranoia's sake than anything. I agree that it'd be easier to just make a change to a driver like I did for that network filter I added in the signal room. But let's just say that, if by some miracle, someone managed to come onto the base and wanted to bypass what I've done. They could physically reboot the machine and bypass the control software through several methods. Probably the hardest one to defend against would be if the hacker injected new commands through a dual-ported memory attack.

In this case I'm adding the requirement for both a retinal scan verification and a thumbprint verification into the XIP code."

The lieutenant shook his head. "XIP?"

"It stands for execute in place. It's a small section of the initialization code that is running from a read-only-memory area in the hardware and isn't dependent on the computer's memory. Basically, the most secure portion of the platform's initialization is prior to initializing the machine's memory. With dual-ported memory, hackers have historically been able to inject logic into systems that bypassed some security measures. It's an old technique, but hard to defend against with software. By doing it the way I am, about the only thing anyone can hope to do is to just take a sledgehammer to the server, which still won't give them control of the base."

Suddenly, one of the soldiers' voices coming from the remote video device yelled, "Confirmed sighting!"

"Oh shit," the lieutenant growled. The other soldiers who'd set up a perimeter around the control room were beginning to whisper when the video from all of the cameras flickered and began broadcasting static.

"Hey," Burt exclaimed. A gnawing sense of concern raced through him. "What happened to the video, did something blow up?"

"No, sir," said the lieutenant. "They've initiated a cloaking operation. It's blocking any remote signal that could set off whatever they've found. However, we should still be able to hear what's going on." He raised the volume, and even though Burt couldn't see what was going on, he heard the sharp orders coming from someone in charge of the patrol.

"Clear the area. Give me 250 meters, and I mean now!

"Heller, Smith, and Woods, cordon off the area. Rothfuss, alert the other teams that we've got something and call the EOD guys over."

The lieutenant explained, "The patrol is calling in our bomb disposal unit."

Burt began compiling the computer updates and kept glancing over at the remote video device.

The tension was thick as some of the soldiers filtered in and out of the room, listening to the chatter coming from the patrols.

The lieutenant raised the volume for one of the static-filled images and commented, "This is the EOD team's audio signal."

"Hey, Zimmer, what's going on? What's the Talon reporting back to us?"

Burt glanced sideways at the lieutenant. "Talon?"

"That's what they call the bomb disposal robot."

"Sergeant, it looks like we've got a shitload of IEDs packed in a crate. Spectral analysis suggests that we've got Cyclotol, roughly a seventy-thirty mixture in the containers, but there isn't an activation—no wait, I found them. Sir, there's a bag of piezoelectric igniters, but they're not hooked up to the explosives yet."

Another soldier broke in. *"Zimmer, can the Talon safely extract the crate? If so, there's a crater about two klicks northeast of your position."*

"Roger that. Talon is lifting the crate now; I'll follow half a klick behind."

As the bomb disposal team transported the explosives to a distant location, Burt listened intently. He replaced the firmware on the motherboard of the server, put the machine back together, and applied power.

"Sergeant, the crater wall is too steep to navigate, it's your call."

"Zimmer, just back away to the limit of your remote and dump Talon and its payload in the crater. We'll leave them both behind."

"Roger that, backing away."

It was at that time the video suddenly flickered back to life, and Burt saw a team of soldiers returning from a distant open area on one of the lunar vehicles. He turned to the lieutenant and asked, "Why dump it all in the crater?"

The soldier frowned. "Normally, they'd blow it up from a safe distance back on Earth, but up here, there isn't a good safe distance because any explosion could carry shrapnel for miles. Sticking the bombs far away from anything and having them surrounded by steep crater walls is about as safe as it gets, considering the situation."

Burt nodded, and as the server turned on, it prompted him for identification. He leaned into the visor for the retinal scanner he'd installed and pressed his left thumb on the fingerprint reader. Within a second, his ID was confirmed, and the server's administration console was up and running.

Grabbing the phone once again from the lieutenant, Burt dialed Neeta's number and listened to the crackling sound of the ring originating over two-hundred-thousand miles away.

"Hello?"

"Neeta, I'm about to program in a navigation setting for the Moon. I need your current estimates based on the survey you're doing for when we'll leave and the exact angle of deployment."

"Hold on, give me a second. Some of the debris at the center has started to move outward and we're seeing some of the first collisions. The dominos are starting to fall, so that's good. I'll send the phone you've contacted me with the ICRS coordinates for the multi-hop trip, timings, etc. It'll be like threading a needle, but assuming we can get up to full power, we'll all glide past the first wave of crap and then cut directly toward our final destination. Sending you the navigation plot points now."

Burt felt the phone vibrate as a message came in. Pulling it away from his ear, he looked at it and nodded. "Got it, Neeta. Thanks again, you're a life saver."

"Of course I am." Neeta's voice came across as uncharacteristically jovial. *"I'm expecting you to remember that the next time it comes to my yearly evaluation. At the very least, you can get some decent coffee in this place."*

Burt snorted as he barely controlled a laugh. "Neeta, you're something else. I'll see what I can do. Thanks again, and I'll talk to you later."

The phone connection ended, and with a satisfied feeling of a job nearly completed, Burt typed in the prescheduled launch time, direction, and acceleration rates, locking them all into the system's navigation control system.

The server accepted the input and Burt, with a final set of keystrokes, locked the workstation and ceremoniously wiped his hands. "Well, I've taken care of the unauthorized access issues."

The lieutenant nodded and motioned to the other soldiers, "Okay,

Doctor Radcliffe is done. The sooner we get our asses back to the transit area and off this rock, the sooner you all get some R&R time."

Burt patted the top of the server and whispered a little prayer in its direction.

"I hope I don't need to look at you again for another nine or ten months."

CHAPTER TWENTY-NINE

Bill Jacobs, the Assistant Secretary of East Asian and Pacific Affairs, crouched next to Dave's seat and warned, "We'll be landing soon and I want to make sure you're straight on the protocols for dealing with some of the other nation-states' representatives. You'll be greeted at the airport by Chinese officials and they'll likely be hosting a welcome dinner in your honor. The mood will almost certainly remain cordial, and I wouldn't suggest discussing anything outside of what the president has already publicly divulged.

"However, tomorrow you'll be meeting with North Korean government officials, and I can't stress enough that you can't leak *any* of the details regarding what you've been working on. They're a pariah state for a reason, and even I can't predict what they'll do from one moment to another."

Dave shook his head and smiled politely as the man droned on and on about what he was supposed to do and not do. When the plane banked lightly and the man paused, Dave interjected in a quiet but firm tone, "Listen to me, Bill, and let's get this straight. I know you're trying to do your job, but I won't take my cues on what I will or won't discuss from you. I'm quite capable of handling myself, and I'll be damned if I'll have someone who doesn't even know what's really going on tell me what to do."

Bill opened his mouth and Dave squeezed his fingertips together, motioning the man to shut his mouth. "No, I'm serious. When we're done, I'll say you did a fine job and were very helpful, but don't get in my way or we'll have serious issues. I'll look to you to help me get over any cultural improprieties that I'd otherwise not be aware of with the Chinese officials, but that's the extent of it. Am I understood?"

With a concerned expression, Bill tried to protest, "But—"

"Am I understood?" Dave interrupted, and repeated his question with a louder voice.

The Assistant Secretary's shoulders slumped in defeat. "Yes. I'll do what I can to make this as easy of a meeting as possible."

With a sympathetic expression, Dave clapped his hand on the man's shoulder. "I'm sure you will, but realize that once I meet with the Supreme Leader, not a peep out of you. In fact, I don't even want you in the room. I know this guy, he can be ... skittish at times."

The lights flashed in the airplane as the pilot spoke over the intercom. *"We've just received clearance from the tower at the Shanghai Pudong Airport. The weather is clear and we should be touching down on runway 17L in approximately twelve minutes. Please fasten your seatbelts."*

With a curt nod, Bill stood. "Understood. I'll go take my seat."

As he walked to the back of the large plane, Dave noticed Bella returning from the bathroom and winked. "You have perfect timing, my dear. Looks like we'll soon figure out what Frank has up his sleeves."

Bella sat in the plush leather chair situated directly across from Dave and buckled herself in. "I still don't understand how he could have created something that looks so much like what we saw."

With his elbow resting on the arm of his seat, Dave rested his head on his palm and tapped his cheek. "Trust me, I've been wondering the same thing myself for the last three days." He glanced at Bella and explained, "Frank is an odd one. He's brilliant, or more to the point he's got some ideas that are sheer genius, but he's really sometimes very much like the archetype of a mad scientist. If he were a cave man during the Stone Age, he'd have invented a remote control for a TV, convinced that it was revolutionary, which it would be, but have no idea what to do with it. As for what inspires some of his ideas, and how he manages to get them to work, your guess would be as good as mine. Nonetheless, some of those ideas are almost impossible to ignore, this being one of them."

Bella glanced out the window as the plane banked for its approach. "It's so dark down there, I'd have thought we'd see some of the city lights by now."

"Almost all of Shanghai is barely above sea level. The entire area has probably been evacuated and I'd wager that the power is mostly all shut off, with the exception of the Renaissance hotel where we'll all be staying and the Shanghai Municipal Government Building." Dave scanned the rest of the sparsely occupied commercial jet and he found it somewhat bizarre that there were nearly one-hundred heavily-armed men on the plane with him. All of them served as his escort and protection. Many were fluent in Mandarin and Shanghainese.

"Is Frank going to be at the same hotel?" Bella asked.

"I really don't know." Dave stared into the darkness of the night and shrugged as he saw the dim hint of the partially powered DefenseNet ring. "We're not meeting with him until tomorrow morning at the government building. I think they're taking it easy on us and letting us get a night's rest after dinner. I just don't think they realize how little time we have."

Hearing the sound of the jet's wheels being lowered, Dave's queasy stomach protested. He'd never seen such darkness below him, and couldn't tell if they were one thousand feet or five feet off the ground.

The only visible lights nearby were blinking from the plane's wingtips, and suddenly Dave caught the reflection of what had to be the plane's landing lights bouncing off of the ocean.

With the fear of the plane plunging into the water, Dave's heart raced. He gripped his armrests. Holding his breath, he watched as the flickering light revealed the water getting closer and closer. Just when he felt sure the plane was going to dive into the ocean, Dave felt a jolt as the rear wheels made contact with solid ground.

Letting go of a deep breath, he collapsed against the back of his seat as Bella smiled, looking as relaxed as could be.

He didn't need her to say what she was thinking. Dave knew very well that with the president and the rest of the world's leaders looking to him to rescue them from certain annihilation, they weren't about to send him on a flight that they figured would crash.

As the plane taxied to a nearby gate, some of the plain-clothed agents readied for their departure, and Dave silently hoped that Frank, by some miracle, had something that would be the key to fixing their problems.

Despite the presence of at least a dozen dehumidifiers scattered throughout the large conference room, Dave still detected the musty odor of a building that had had its power turned off for an extended period.

The room was easily one-hundred-feet long and thirty-feet wide, and dominating the length of the room stood a massive table with enough chairs to seat eighty people.

Dave reached behind him and patted Bella's leg. He frowned as he recalled the eerie trip from the hotel through the empty downtown streets to the main government building of Shanghai. "It's kind of bizarre being in one of the largest cities in the world, yet it's a ghost town. I suppose we've both been so busy that there was no way for us to see the effect of the evacuations first-hand." The pang of guilt he felt over so many millions of people being displaced grew as the emptiness of the government building illustrated how his advice had affected people.

Bella, who sat next to Dave at the otherwise empty conference table, reached to him and rubbed the back of his neck. "You're doing this for everyone's safety. They'll forever be grateful."

With a slight shake of his head, Dave sighed. "I'm not looking for gratitude. I just hope I'm not blamed for the end of life as we know it."

A door at the end of the conference room swung open, and the voice of someone yelling in Korean echoed loudly through the room.

Dave stood as a short, chubby man entered, walking backward, all the while yelling at a harried set of Asian men wheeling a large wooden crate into the room.

Once the crate reached the conference room table, the men made quick work of disassembling the container, revealing an object encased in thousands of Styrofoam pellets.

The short man approached the object and brushed the pellets away as the workers bowed deeply and backed from the conference room. Only when the doors shut did the chubby man turn, and Dave couldn't help but smile at the sight of North Korea's Supreme Leader.

Frank smiled ear-to-ear. He walked briskly toward Dave. "My friend, it has been so many years!" The two shook hands briskly, and as Dave turned to introduce Bella, Frank stared dumbfounded.

"Frank, this is Bella, my wife." Dave felt odd saying that, since they'd never formally married, but nothing could have been closer to the truth. He couldn't imagine life without her.

Bella kept her distance, which was normal for her, but Frank seemed stunned to see her for some reason. Maybe he'd never seen anyone with red hair? Dave shrugged and quickly changed the subject. "Frank, I studied everything you sent me, and I've got lots of questions. But first, can you show me what you brought? It looks exactly like the designs you sent."

Frank ripped his gaze away from Bella and nodded excitedly. "Yes, yes. Let me show you. It's a very good design."

As they walked to the far end of the table, Frank pointed at the large metal ball and said, "Let me show you what I have."

Dave studied the object as Frank began rapidly describing some of its features.

The object was about three-feet wide and was prevented from rolling by the wooden base of the crate and the Styrofoam ring it sat on. It uncannily resembled the sphere they'd recently seen at Area 51, only larger.

Frank pointed to the control panel on the side of the ball and pressed a button. The sphere snapped open, revealing its inner workings. "As you can see, the panel allows you to open and close the engine." He reached inside the ball and pointed at the finely wrapped flat cables encircling the inner circumference of the sphere. "I have two layers of superconductive ribbon wrapping the interior, one to conduct the power of the engine to the top, and the other to keep the electrical field in control."

"Superconductive ribbon? At room temperature? What's it made of?"

Frank smiled and puffed his chest out a bit. "An improvement over anything anyone's ever done. It's an improved version of stanene, but without the magnetic effects that kill high-current superconductivity. These ribbons should be able to transmit more power than we can ever produce from all of our power plants combined."

Dave stared at Frank with incredulity. He had a lot of questions about how such a thing had been created, but if what Frank said was true, it would be an unheard-of advance in the material sciences.

Leaning forward and peeking into the sphere, Dave couldn't help but realize that with enough power flowing through the inner loop of the ribbon, it could almost certainly create a gravity bubble just like the ones he'd experimented with at the ISF.

"Frank, this is fascinating. I've done a few experiments that look similar to this, but not quite the same. I would say that if you have a strong power source within these loops, the first layer can act as a stabilizing agent, and the second loop could act as a way of draining the power from the first loop."

"Exactly!" Frank smiled and pointed at the top of the engine, which had a dozen finger-like cables coming out of it. "These are the engine's outflow cables. Even though each cable can carry almost unlimited power, I've split them, so if needed, we can send power across a dozen less-efficient transmission lines."

Frank nodded toward the metal shell lining the inside of the sphere.

"You'll notice that I've coated the inside of the engine with a magnetic liner, which keeps the magnetic effects from seeping out of the engine compartment."

Bella had obviously been paying attention the entire time and asked, "But wouldn't those coils also produce a magnetic bottle effect inside the engine?"

Frank stared unblinkingly at Bella, and for a moment it was as if he'd suddenly become an overweight Asian statue. And then, he turned to Dave with a smile and pointed at Bella. "She's very smart!"

Trying not to laugh at Frank's incredulity, Dave nodded. "That's right, with the way you've designed this, if the power source is inside, wouldn't the magnetic bottle effect get stronger as the power increased? If this works, you could literally have fusion containment inside this, couldn't you?"

"Yes!" Frank's cheeks wobbled as he nodded vigorously. "I tested it already. We achieved a near-perfect mass-to-energy conversion once the fusion process started. Admittedly, we had to cheat and feed energy into the engine to initiate the fusion and test this out, but it worked."

Dave sat back and let what Frank had said sink in. If it was true, Frank may have solved what had been plaguing nuclear scientists for a century. Not only was Frank presenting the possibility of room-temperature superconductors, he'd be the first to demonstrate an efficient fusion reaction. Heck, if what he said was true, then.... He turned to Bella and asked, "If we had a perfect conversion of a gram of material, how much energy would that yield?"

Without hesitation, she said, "Approximately 89.876 trillion joules."

Frank raised his eyebrows and nodded. "That sounds about right."

"That's more than the energy released from the Hiroshima blast back in World War II," Dave noted, amazed. "And all from something the weight of a paperclip. But how do you regulate the power release?"

Frank pointed to the control panel on the side of the ball and explained, "The controls I've established are as simple as possible. A digital rheostat lets me adjust the power flow at increments relative to the amount of energy remaining within the ignition chamber. Right now, I have it regulated so that if you set it to ten percent, that means you'll get a ten percent power flow until the energy is exhausted. Just like Einstein said, mass and energy are interchangeable. You can literally contain an unimaginable amount of energy in here. It's an engine and a battery all at once." Frank wagged his finger at Dave. "But don't set the rheostat to one-hundred percent or the entire store of energy in the magnetic containment vessel will flow out instantly."

"So if you set it at its lowest setting, how long did you calibrate the energy flow to last?" Dave asked.

"Oh, that's easily adjustable. Right now, it's set to one hour at the lowest rheostat setting, but the timings can be adjusted. I suppose we could even make it so that the engine dribbles energy out over a very long time, upwards of a maybe even a decade or so."

Dave frowned as he considered how much energy would be needed for a nine-month journey. He knew that even in the unlikely chance he could get access to all of the world's nuclear weapons, there wouldn't be enough energy for the trip.

"Dave," Bella tapped him on his arm. She leaned in close and whispered, "That magnetic container might be useful for—"

"Oh!" The image of the Area 51 sphere flashed into Dave's mind, and he realized at that moment what he might be able to do.

He lurched to his feet, grabbed Frank in a giant bear hug, and whispered, "You might have saved us all."

Frank blinked rapidly as Dave let go and brusquely wiped his eyes.

"Frank, let's talk about how we're going to use this engine."

Three days later–Area 51

The dry underground tunnel smelled faintly of age, like the scent of paper from a hundred-year-old book. As the half dozen agents gathered around him, Dave tilted the side of his head against his shoulder until his neck popped loudly, reducing some of its stiffness. He focused on each face gathered just outside the stairs that led to the charred sphere. "You all have been briefed on the importance of this mission," he said. "Let me just repeat what everyone's task is." He pointed to the four burly men wearing a head-to-toe fine metal mesh suits. "First, let's talk safety. Thanks to the UNLV College of Engineering, we're all wearing Faraday suits. I know it feels like you're staring through metal gauze, but I have absolutely no idea what's going to happen when we try to move that thing. My best guess is that it's unstable and will shoot sparks in every conceivable direction. If any of us gets hit with an arc of electricity, the suits should conduct the electricity around us and into the ground. At no point in time are you to even think about taking these suits off until we are miles away from here. Understood?"

The men, all CIA operations officers, nodded. Dave laid his hand on the carefully packed engine they'd brought back from Shanghai. "When I say go, two of you lift the front of this crate, two of you lift the back. I'll lead you guys down the stairs and light the way. Once we're down there, you'll quickly but carefully rip open the crate and set the contents on the ground where I say. Just listen to my every word and do exactly what I say, nothing more—nothing less—and we'll be fine.

"Once I say we're good down there, gather up the packing material and race upstairs as quickly as possible without killing yourselves. Once back up on this level, we're going to run, not walk, to the elevators, go topside, and then evacuate to the designated safe zone. Does everyone have that straight?"

The men all nodded, and Dave glanced back at Chris and Bella. "How much time do we have before the next burst?"

Chris glanced at his wristwatch and responded with his heavy southern accent, "I reckon about four minutes, Doctor Radcliffe."

Dave nodded and looked at Bella, who was focused on setting up the remote viewing equipment. "Bella, will we be able to see that monitor from up top?"

Bella handed Dave a video camera. "Yes, I tested it already. I've got a video camera set to watch the screen of this electrical field proximity sensor, and I put a signal repeater near the elevators, and another one up top. If you can set up that camera down below, it's transmitting on a frequency that the repeater will pick up. We'll be able to see both items once we're at the evacuation site."

Addressing both Bella and Chris, Dave ordered, "Once we go downstairs, both of you start heading topside. By the time the rest of us come upstairs, we'll be racing like the devil himself is chasing us."

Bella nodded, and Chris raised his hand and snapped his fingers. "Doctor Radcliffe, thirty seconds and counting."

"Everyone, turn on your lights," Dave commanded. He walked to the top of the stairs and turned his lights on as well.

The drone of Chris's voice was clear as he counted the time remaining, "Three ... two ... one ... surge! It's clear, go, go, go!"

Dave raced downstairs, knowing that there was a lot to do before the mysterious object freaked out again, and he didn't want to be anywhere near this place when the time ran out.

In a matter of two minutes, Dave found himself in the dark cavern with the charred sphere. The agents began uncrating Frank's engine. He knew that there had to be splinters flying all over the place as the crate was being taken apart. There was nothing he could do about it other than hope it didn't matter.

Dave stared at the malfunctioning sphere and thought about the loops of exotic material contained inside Frank's engine. On the way back from China, he'd formulated a theory about how this was going to work, but he couldn't be sure.

His guess was that when the engine sparked, it would provide enough energy to almost instantly cause the gravity bubble to come to life. Dave desperately hoped that that the engine worked the way he'd imagined. If the magnetic bottle didn't contain the surge of energy, he'd probably be incinerated before he ever realized anything bad had happened.

There was also a control outside the engine which increased or decreased the energy flow. The only thing that Frank's engine did when you turned that knob was to barely deform the outer ring so the gap between the outer and inner rings became smaller. Dave's best guess was that the outer ring would begin to syphon energy from the inner ring as they approached each other.

The agents finally removed the top and all four walls of the crate, and Dave, who was standing next to the charred sphere, motioned to them. "Leave that engine on its base and just scoot the whole thing closer."

While they did, Dave placed the video camera within a rubber-lined metal mesh and silently hoped that the mesh wouldn't be needed.

The men placed the engine next to the charred sphere and Dave quickly tapped on the control panel. The sphere snapped open, exposing its inner workings.

"All right, guys, this is where it gets worrisome. *Carefully,* and I mean very carefully, lift the charred smaller metal ball and gently place it inside this bright and shiny new one."

Dave moved out of their way and cringed as the four men crouched and extended their hands. He had no idea what would happen, but the reports clearly implied that people had touched and probed this thing in the past. Heck, they'd moved it and gotten it in that room, somehow. He only wondered if it had gotten more damaged since arriving.

Holding his breath, Dave watched the agents' hands all simultaneously approach the ancient sphere. He breathed a sigh of relief when they touched it and nothing catastrophic happened.

Slowly they lifted the charred sphere and inch-by-inch moved it closer to Frank's engine.

As the men placed the sphere inside the engine, Dave warned, "It's a bit too close—"

A brilliant light flared within the room, blinding Dave and sending him sprawling backward as a cacophony of yelling, electrical arcing, and a metallic clang echoed loudly in the cavern.

His heart thundering in his chest, Dave steadied himself and blinked rapidly, trying to get rid of the blobs of light obscuring his vision. "Is everyone okay?"

He heard an immediate chorus of yesses, but Dave's attention focused on the groan coming from one of the metal-shrouded men. He held his right hand in the crook of his left arm. "What's wrong—"

A chill raced through Dave as he spotted the first signs of blood dripping down the side of the mesh. He pointed at the agent. "Show me!"

The man gasped through clenched teeth as he produced his hand, from which his two rightmost fingers had been severed. Dave cringed and glanced at Frank's engine, which had sealed itself around the blackened sphere.

His mind racing, he tapped one of the uninjured men and tilted his head toward the bleeding agent. "Get him to a medic! The rest of you, evacuate. I'll be right behind you."

The men hurried out of the subterranean chamber. Dave walked toward Frank's engine, and muttered, "Damn thing must have automatically snapped shut with that spark." Guilt washed over Dave as he scanned the floor and realized that the man's fingers were likely in Frank's engine.

Quickly double-checking his own suit and seeing nothing wrong, Dave approached the control panel on the engine and pressed the "Open/Close" button.

Nothing happened.

"Damn it, what the hell!"

Pressing repeatedly on the button yielded nothing, and Dave silently cursed himself, knowing that there wasn't much he could do at that point. It made sense that the engine couldn't be opened if the magnetic seals had clamped shut.

Ensuring that the power knob on the control panel was turned to zero, Dave removed the video camera from the mesh bag and set it back up on its tripod. He quickly gathered the packing material and backed away from the chamber.

Knowing that he'd probably spent too much time in the chamber, Dave raced upstairs and felt the bile rising in his throat as he saw drips of blood along the way.

～

With a heavy burden of guilt, Dave watched as a medic stitched up the agent's hand and then placed a cold pack around the stubs of the victim's fingers.

"Doctor Holmes," the injured agent glanced in his direction and tossed him a smile. "Please don't feel bad about this, the doc says I'll be fine."

Bella whispered, "The medic says that the nerve conductivity is still good. Agent Michaels will be able to get artificial finger replacements."

Nausea washed through Dave as he sighed, wishing he could have prevented that injury. "As far as I know, that was the first time anyone has ever gotten hurt doing something under my direct supervision." He turned to Bella and frowned. "You realize that two of the other agents actually had the fingertips of their mesh suits chopped off? They just barely got their hands out of the way."

Bella rubbed Dave's back. "See, it could have been much worse."

Dave took a shuddering breath and crouched near the remote video feed as the other agents waited patiently for an all-clear. They were ten miles from the Area 51 artifact, hiding behind a nearby stony outcropping. All of them stood on rubber mats on the off chance that the reports of huge electrical surges were true, or if something went terribly wrong. Silently, Dave prayed as time ticked away.

Bella jutted her chin toward the image of the electrical field intensity monitor. "Isn't it weird how before we got some kind of electromagnetic hum out of the sphere, but now, I don't hear anything? It's all quiet down there."

"Well, I suppose that's a good sign," Dave agreed. "If things are working the way they're supposed to, we shouldn't be able to sense anything out of it."

Dragging his rubber mat, Chris approached while announcing, "We've got one minute before the fireworks start."

Recalling how the magnetic seal clamped shut from the spark of energy, Dave could only imagine what might happen during the surge. If everything worked perfectly, the surge would be contained, and in fact, the surge would strengthen the magnetic seal. It would, in effect, bottle up the power now contained within Frank's engine, providing an unknown amount of energy on tap.

But would it work?

With visions of all of the energy in that sphere spewing forth at once, he suddenly feared they might still be too close. For all he knew, if that thing blew, there may not be a safe spot anywhere on Earth. Dave shook his head and pointed up at the night sky. "I hope to God that we don't see anything."

Bella reached for Dave. They held hands as they watched the video feed.

With the phantom sensation of electric prickles all along his skin, Dave watched the monitor nervously, knowing that his mind was playing tricks on him. His breathing became shallow as the final moments approached.

He closed his eyes and silently sent a prayer to any higher power that might have been listening. "God, please let this not end up killing us all."

Holding his breath, Dave cringed as Bella counted down the final five seconds. "Five ... four ... three ... two ... one...."

Dave stared at the monitor, glanced up in the direction of Area 51 and then back to the monitor. Nothing.

Bella squeezed Dave's hand and Chris exclaimed, "Looks like we're all good!"

Dave frowned at the lack of any obvious signs of surges. The field monitor showed no readings whatsoever.

Staring at the remote image of Frank's engine, Dave frowned as he stifled his own cautious optimism. "Well, the video feed in the room is intact. Let's wait another forty-five minutes and see what happens. I don't want to risk anything or anyone again."

Dave wiped the sweat from his face, and still he worried. He had no idea what was inside that mysterious sphere, and even if it all worked, he knew it was a longshot that the strange creation would produce any energy, much less enough to make up what they actually needed. "I just hope this will actually work."

CHAPTER THIRTY

The president stared at the handful of people she'd called into the Situation Room. The rest of the White House was in total disarray as evacuation proceedings were taking place. With Burt, General Keane, and Kevin Baker in the room, she knew this might be one of the last times she'd get a briefing within the White House.

"Madam President," General Keane, her Secretary of Defense, said in a calm yet solemn voice, "the Cheyenne Mountain Complex has been prepared. We'll be moving all essential operations into that location along with critical White House and Governmental Staff over the next two days."

Margaret nodded as she sat back against her chair and silently wondered if she'd ever see this room, or DC for that matter, ever again. "Understood, General." She turned to Kevin, her Director of the CIA, and asked, "Where are we on the N35 response to the terrorist attack and have there been any retaliations?"

"It has been more difficult than we anticipated trying to root out those associated with this death cult. As you know, they've infiltrated many of the major religions, but we've gotten cooperation from the Vatican, as well as many prominent imams and rabbis. Even the Dalai Lama has found those amongst his flock who seek the end of the world as we know it. With their help and the intelligence resources of the N35, we've removed over 200,000 of the most virulent of the cult."

"Didn't you guys say that there were millions of them?" Burt asked. "Isn't there still a risk?"

The general nodded. "There is, and we're still on top of it. We've had nearly three dozen different attacks on collector substations, which our armed forces have rebuffed. Hell, we've shot down two rogue shuttles heading toward the Moon. One launched out of the Ukraine and the other originated from Sri Lanka. They're still out there, like cockroaches, waiting for someone to stop looking."

Margaret drummed her fingers on the table and turned to Burt. "You're sure there's no way to transfer the power reserves on the Moon down here so we can use it, regardless of that crap about tides or whatever?"

Burt shook his head. "I'm afraid not. Unlike here, where we're generating the power actively and sending it up into the DefenseNet ring, Dave didn't have that power generating capacity on the Moon. So instead, he'd spent years trapping thermal energy deep inside the Moon itself. Almost like a battery. There's really no way for us to do the same thing. We don't have time for the mining setup to even try to tap the heat within the Earth, and even if we did have a tap through active volcanoes or anything else, we don't have the technology to deal with the intense temperatures of molten rock."

Feeling resigned to a fate no president in the past had ever faced, Margaret nodded and panned her gaze across the three men sitting around the conference-room table. "We have very little time left, folks. The next briefing will be in our new location." She turned to Burt with a grim expression. "Get ready. Unless something changes, you'll be going on a different trip soon."

Margaret glanced at the altimeter reading of 35,000 feet as the last remnants of the nation's administration evacuated the capitol. Flying in Air Force One was unlike anything she'd have imagined prior to experiencing it. It was literally the equivalent of a flying office with all the same communication capabilities.

Not knowing what the future held, Margaret felt the all-too-familiar burning in her stomach and hoped the stress of the job wasn't getting to her. She tapped her fingernails against the tabletop that served as her desk when suddenly a red LED flickered an alert.

She tapped the touch-sensitive panel on the desk, and a voice immediately broadcast in her office.

"Madam President, this is NORAD control, we have another unauthorized launch detection. Proceed with intercept?"

Margaret frowned. To ensure the public's safety, the world leaders had agreed on a complete moratorium on orbital travel unless explicitly authorized.

"NORAD control, we are still on launch lockdown. Do we have an identity on the vehicle and a projected trajectory?"

"We've detected a multi-stage rocket launching out of the Baikonur Cosmodrome in Western Asia. The trajectory indicates no intent for a suborbital flight. The rocket is at 100,000 feet and climbing rapidly."

"NORAD control, go with intercept. Over."

"Targeting lasers activated ... firing sequence authorized ... fire! Target has been destroyed. Over."

"Roger, NORAD control. Any flights over 100,000 feet are to be intercepted unless given explicit clearance ahead of time, is that understood?"

"Roger."

Margaret tapped at the control panel, disconnecting the call, and grumbled to nobody in particular, "I can't believe they're still trying to kill us all."

The president waited patiently as the site-wide announcements broadcast through the speakers in her private office. *"Recent Evacuees to the Cheyenne Mountain Complex, please report to the barracks wing for bunk assignments and duty rosters."*

As soon as the announcements finished, Burt, who was sitting on the opposite side of Margaret's desk, insisted, "Evacuating now I think is premature. I have faith in Dave coming up with something. Heck, his last report was only a few days ago as he was boarding the flight to come back from Shanghai. He said that the meeting with the North Korean leader had given him some hope."

Margaret's head was throbbing from lack of sleep and Burt, even though he was arguing for patience, wasn't helping matters. "Listen to me, Burt: it takes at least a full day to get people organized and over to Cape Canaveral for takeoff. It takes at least another day to get all your butts over to the Moon. We don't have much more than ten days left. We can't afford to wait any longer. Even though I might be under 2000 feet of granite right now, that won't help the rest of the people who are living in barely passable shelters. If we start getting bombarded by space debris, maybe we'll be okay, maybe we won't, but like you've said before, it's just a matter of a few months more and we'll be dead.

We can't risk the Moon getting hit and destroying our last chance of evacuating any remnant of humanity out of harm's way."

Margaret saw the frustrated expression on Burt's face and slammed her open palm on the desk.

"No more arguing, Burt! Two days. If we don't have a solution in two days, I want you to do what you vowed you would. I need you to take responsibility for what will be left of humanity."

Burt pursed his lips and Margaret could feel the tension emanating from her Science Advisor. He hated the idea of giving up on anything and she knew it. She admired that about him, but Margaret also knew that there were times when things simply don't go the way you want them to.

With a sigh, Burt grumbled, "We have two days. In two days, if we haven't made any progress, I'll do what I have to do." He stared into Margaret's eyes and she felt his emotional pain, despite his calm demeanor. "If the time comes, who else is going up with me? And why am I imagining this as a sick version of Noah's ark?"

The vein in her temple began to throb as she considered the horrendous choices that would need to be made. Burt wasn't wrong about it all being very much like Noah's ark.

Seeing the turmoil he was going through, Margaret hesitated to ask anything else of him. With her head pounding, she took a deep breath, focused on his troubled features, and asked, "What about your family? I kind of assumed they didn't want to come here, since you never followed up with me. There's still enough time to bring them to the mountain and they could go up with you if it comes to that. Interested?"

Burt pressed his lips together and shook his head, remaining silent for a long moment. "Thank you for asking, but unfortunately – they wouldn't budge. My brother and his wife want to meet whatever ends up happening in their own home."

Reaching across the table, Margaret clasped hands with Burt, whose eyes shined with unshed tears, and she whispered, "I'm sorry to be putting this on you—" Her voice cracked and she cleared her throat. "If I didn't think it was the best of a bunch of horrible decisions, I wouldn't do it."

"I know. This sucks all around, but we've got two days. Let's hope it doesn't come to that. Are you okay?"

Margaret leaned back in her chair and pressed her fingers against her temples. She cringed through her headache and pushed Burt's question aside for the moment. "Let's talk some more tomorrow morning. We'll decide on who goes up on the ark then. I'll be very open to suggestions then, but for now, I need to get some sleep."

Margaret had somehow managed to get nearly five hours of fitful rest, but the never-ending anxiety she felt spurred her onward. How could she sleep when the fate of her family, Americans ... the world was on the precipice?

It was the next morning, or at least that's what the clocks all said. The concept of morning, evening, day, or night were all somewhat meaningless in the underground world of the Cheyenne Mountain shelter. Sitting in her office, Margaret stared at the roster of evacuees currently housed in the complex. Hundreds of faces stared back at her as she swiped her hand across the touch-sensitive table, flipping from page to page.

"How do you want to choose?" Burt asked, with an expression bordering on disgust. "Breeding age? Younger than that?"

Margaret shook her head and admitted, "I'm afraid the analogy you gave yesterday to Noah's ark is probably a good one. Whomever we choose needs to go through a quick fertility screening. It would otherwise be pointless to send them." The sour taste of bile rose in her throat as her own words echoed off the stone walls of her office.

Burt posited, "Some may not want to go. We can't afford to take any who have criminal records. Probably need to get a psych screen too." He looked Margaret in the eyes and admitted, "I can't believe it could come to this. We'll have to pick more than are needed, and only the first two hundred and fifty get to go."

Margaret sensed a resignation to what might be the inevitable in Burt's voice.

The desk began blinking, signifying an incoming call.

Margaret tapped the receive button, and only an audio signal came through. *"President Hager? Burt?"*

Burt's eyes widened. "Dave? Is that you?"

"Yup, it's me. I'm done testing this monster and I've got good news and bad. Which do you want first?"

Margaret immediately responded, "Give me the bad, the good news can wait."

"Well, I can't exactly get a full measurement of how much power this thing is generating. I've tried with everything I can get my hands on from the site and even pulled resources from the local universities. No good."

"What do you mean you can't get a full measurement?" Burt asked. "Can't you measure the magnetic field around the power cable and get a reading?"

"Nope, tried it. This thing Frank developed as a power interconnect is a room-temperature superconductor, and from what I can tell,

it's just about perfect. I can't read shit off this thing. There's no magnetic field, yet I know lots of juice is flowing through it, because it's blown any other inline attempt to measure the engine's power output. Even at the lowest setting possible, it's well over the multi-megawatt output level."

"Is that enough for what we need?" Margaret asked.

"I have absolutely no idea. That's kind of why I called it the bad news, because I don't know if it's enough. I can't directly measure the power coming out of this thing, it's that strong. So I suppose it's also the good news. The only next step I can think of, considering how little time we have, is for me to take this thing to one of the anchor points and hook it up. At this stage, what's the worst that could happen?"

Margaret watched as Burt crossed his fingers and closed his eyes for a second, evidently praying. He leaned closer to the table. "Dave, that's absolutely fantastic news."

Margaret stood as she felt a surge of hope rush through her. "Doctor Holmes, I'm going to call and arrange for a military jet escort. Where do you want to take this to?"

"The substation located in the jungles of Ecuador, just west of Quito. That's the closest one to my location."

"Fine, I'll call something in right away and will scramble an entire brigade of soldiers to ensure there's no complications. I don't need to tell you that everything is riding on your success. The least I can do is ensure your safety. Give me a couple of hours to get soldiers en route to the site and we'll get you where you need to go."

"Thank you, President Hager. I'll be frank and tell you that I can't wait for this to all be over so I can go to sleep for a couple of years."

Margaret smiled and nodded. "You and me both. Unless there's something else, I'll make all the arrangements right away."

"No, that's it. I'll crate this thing up and get it ready for transport. Thanks again."

The table flashed as the call disconnected and the open list of the evacuee faces showed on the tabletop once again.

Margaret tapped on the phone icon on the table and within seconds had General Keane on the line.

"General," she said, "our Doctor Holmes might be saving all of our asses again, but we need to get him and his gear over to Ecuador ASAP. Walter, let me be clear about this. Everything rides on him getting there in one piece *with* his equipment. Give me a plan."

"Understood. I can get 5,000 special operations soldiers in-country in ten hours to act as escort for Doctor Holmes. We've got ground transport assets already there from other tasks. Give me thirty-six hours and I can get a division of soldiers on top of the 5,000 already there to create an outer ring and cordon off any ground attacks. As to the air, I'll scramble the Air Force Special Operations Wing to run cover for the site itself. They'll cover from just above ground level to the ceiling of operations. Nobody will get through. On your authorization, I'll commence with ... let's call it Operation Iron Shield."

Margaret leaned her hands on the table and barked, "You've got your authorization. Commence with deployment of Operation Iron Shield. Doctor Holmes needs a coordinated transport with payload from Homey airport to the substation located in western Ecuador."

"Roger that, Madam President. I'll get on it right away."

"Thanks and dismissed." Margaret disconnected the call and stared at the faces of the evacuees. Taking a deep breath, she barely managed to control her reaction to the glimmer of good news.

Margaret turned away from the faces on the table and stared at Burt. "We still have to make these lists."

Burt returned her gaze and carried the barest hint of a smile. "That little substation in the middle of nowhere will soon be the safest place on Earth."

Margaret nodded. "Let's just hope that Doctor Holmes' gadget does what we need it to do." She tapped at the faces staring up at the ceiling. "In the meantime, let's figure out who gets to ride on our little Noah's ark."

CHAPTER THIRTY-ONE

Dave inhaled the humid air of the Ecuadoran plain. The musty scent of vegetation still permeated the air, even though much of the nearby land had been cleared. He tapped on the taut sheet of graphene that rose up into the sky and waited impatiently for the arrival of Frank's engine. Standing at the top of the Ecuador anchor station, helicopters hovered nearby, and every minute or so, a fighter jet would zip by–all assigned to keep watch over the highly secure site. Bulldozers were busy clearing the last of the jungle vegetation within a three-mile radius of the substation. Dave glanced at Bella and pointed at the thousands of soldiers who were creating a multi-layer secure perimeter. The soldiers were everywhere, all of them tasked with keeping him and the site safe as far as the eye could see. "Could you have ever imagined such a thing?"

Bella shrugged. "It makes sense. They don't want to take any chances, especially with all hopes hanging in the balance."

"I know, but it seems like overkill." Dave's gaze veered suddenly toward what looked like an incoming caravan of military assault vehicles, many of them with machine guns installed on their roofs. His heart raced as he spied an armored cargo carrier in the midst of the vehicles. He began walking toward the stairs as he pointed to the line of trucks. "That's got to be the engine. Let's go meet them."

With Bella on his heels, Dave raced downstairs, through the shell of the ruined substation and out the front door.

"Doctor Holmes!" One of soldiers barked at him, and moved in his way. "Please wait here for the cargo. We don't want any accidents."

The man held an expression that brooked no argument. Dave's gaze was drawn to the Special Forces tab the soldier wore on his left sleeve, and it suddenly dawned on him that the president must really be concerned if she'd sent the Army's elite troops to watch over the site. Despite the warmth of the day, a chill ran through him as he wondered if there was something he wasn't being told about the threats against them all.

Under Dave's direction, a group of four soldiers carried the crate into the otherwise inoperable substation. This was one of the substations that had had its contents damaged by the electrical surge that resulted from the suitcase bomb at a nearby collector substation.

As the soldiers unpacked the engine, Dave glanced at the ceiling. His gaze followed the three-foot-wide ribbon of graphene that descended from the closed slit in the roof. The end of the graphene ribbon was attached to a wiring harness that was, in turn, linked to a burnt-out transformer.

Extracting a wrench from his tool belt, Dave loosened the connecting bolts on the wiring harness, disconnected it from the transformer, and inspected the harness's connector.

Bella asked, "Is it damaged?"

Dave shook his head and showed her the shiny gold leads on the end of the harness. "No thermal damage whatsoever."

"Doctor Holmes," said a soldier, waving to catch Dave's attention. "We're done unpacking. Do you want to leave this on its base?"

Turning to the engine, Dave backed slightly away and motioned toward the closed slit in the roof five feet above him. "Can you scoot the engine closer, and bring it under this clear ribbon? I'll hook it up."

Four soldiers carefully slid the base of the engine until it sat directly beneath the graphene ribbon, and Dave proceeded to attach the wiring harness to one of the electrical leads coming out of Frank's engine.

A soldier who'd helped unpack the engine approached Dave and asked, "Sir, is there anything else I can help with? I'm one of the men assigned to this station and will be acting as this shift's maintenance engineer."

Dave glanced at the man's name stenciled onto his fatigues and clapped him on the shoulder. "Sergeant Vasquez, I appreciate the offer, but I've got it for now."

"Yes, sir!"

Dave confirmed that Frank's engine was properly connected to the graphene ribbon, then retrieved a satellite phone from his belt and punched in the numbers to the NORAD Mission Control. The phone rang once, twice ... and then the crackling sound of an operator broadcast through the phone. *"Operator 1543, Cheyenne Mountain switchboard. Where may I connect you?"*

"Operator, this is Doctor David Holmes, ID 591-92-2847, patch me into someone at Mission Control."

"Voice print and ID confirmed, patching you in to Mission Specialist Karen Weisskopf."

Almost immediately, a woman's voice broadcast through the connection. *"Mission Specialist Weisskopf. How can I help you, Doctor Holmes?"*

"I'm about to bring the Ecuador substation back online, but I need you to read back to me the current energy flow going through the warp ring."

"Understood, the current flow into the ring is at 39.3 percent of the required rate you'd specified."

Dave pressed mute on the phone and knelt next to Frank's engine. He extracted a small Allen wrench from his belt and began checking the settings on the control panel.

Kneeling next to him, Bella asked, "I thought we set the control panel's rheostat sensitivity to as high as it will go already?"

He leaned over and gave Bella's cheek a kiss. "We did, but I don't want to take any chances that its settings had somehow changed during the engine's transport."

He applied a small amount of counter-clockwise torque on the wrench, verifying that the engine remained on its highest sensitivity setting. Dave took the phone off mute and said, "Weisskopf, I'm about to activate the Ecuador substation. Let me know what happens on your end."

"Roger that. I'll let you know as soon as I see any changes."

Dave's heart thudded heavily in his chest and he wiped sweat off his palms. Out of his peripheral vision, he noticed that a half-dozen soldiers had gathered to watch him as he double and triple checked the connection and the rheostat sensitivity setting.

In his mind, he feared that the charred sphere was simply sitting inside Frank's engine, inert. And when he turned on Frank's engine, it would drain whatever energy was holding the magnetic seal shut and the engine would pop open and this would all be for nothing.

Dave shook his head as he realized the irony of the situation. It would be no worse if the whole engine exploded when he turned it on. Everything hinged on this working perfectly.

Bella rested her hand on his shoulder and whispered, "You're fine. Let's see what happens."

Taking a deep breath, Dave put his fingers on the engine's power control knob and ever-so-slightly twisted it off the "0" position.

He immediately sensed a tickle in the air. Whether it was his imagination or something else, he couldn't be sure, but his skin began to crawl with a prickly sensation just as the voice on the phone called out an alert. *"Ecuador substation, I just received a large spike of energy from your location. The power reading is increasing across the ring ... we are now at 63.5 percent of operating requirements."*

An overwhelming sense of amazement mixed with relief flooded through Dave as Bella squeezed his shoulder and whispered, "Wow."

With a deep, shuddering breath, Dave clicked the power setting up one notch and stared expectantly at the phone.

"Ecuador substation, we have received another spike from your location. The power has increased to 87.7 percent of operating requirements."

Dave brought the phone closer to his face. "Weisskopf, what's the overall status across the DefenseNet grid?"

"Doctor Holmes, the signal is clean. All systems are operating within normal parameters. I hope I'm not out of bounds by saying this, but thank you."

Dave noticed a couple of the soldiers giving each other fist bumps, and smiled. The weight on his shoulders seemed just a bit less than it had been. "Mission Specialist Weisskopf, there's no need to thank me, but nonetheless, you're welcome." Dave waved toward the soldier who'd previously approached him. "I'm now handing comms over to a Sergeant Vasquez, but I think that'll be all for now." He handed his satellite phone to the sergeant and smiled. "The site is all yours. Don't let anything happen to it."

Stryker had just rotated out of the Indian Point facility and landed at McGuire Air Force Base only twenty minutes ago. A few hundred other MPs from several branches of the military had also just arrived from other parts of the northeast.

A chilly evening breeze blew across the tarmac while Stryker stood at ease, listening to General Harold McCallister's briefing.

The general's voice boomed loudly through an array of speakers, but as the older man droned on, Stryker's mind wandered to his family, especially his kids. He felt sick to his stomach at not having been able to talk to them in nearly two months. His last contact with them was as they boarded the bus at the Port Authority. Glancing at the men and women around him, he knew he wasn't the only one longing for their family.

"As you already know, the evacuations are complete. Taking

advantage of the warm summer and mild fall weather, the evacuation sites have largely been tent cities. All the while, the Army Corps of Engineers, along with FEMA, have been busy creating sturdier and more weather-appropriate shelters, which are now ready.

"Before we transfer the evacuees, we need people at the new locations to help coordinate and deal with security issues as they come along.

"You'll all be deployed to one of a few dozen different evacuation sites. The duration of your assignments will likely be in excess of six months."

Stryker's stomach dropped as he imagined himself being away from his kids for a year or more.

He swallowed hard as the general continued.

"I realize how trying this time is for all of you. For those of you with families affected by the evacuation, I've arranged as best as I can to have you stationed near or at the site where your loved ones are located."

A spark of hope bloomed in his chest as the general's words registered.

Several soldiers had been walking amongst the gathered MPs throughout the general's talk. One of them approached Stryker, glanced at his uniform, handed him an envelope, and moved on to the next MP in line.

He glanced at the envelope with "Lieutenant Jonathan Stryker" printed on its front.

"That's pretty much the end of the briefing. You'll all be gathering further details when you get to your locations. I've got people handing out your assignments now. We've arranged for transports on the far end of the tarmac. Go to the designated line for the location on your paperwork.

"I pray that we all see this through without further incident. Just remember, we're all depending on each other to keep things together until this is over.

"Fall out!"

Stryker immediately ripped open the envelope, extracted the paper inside, and scanned his orders.

He barely suppressed a whoop of joy as he spied his assignment location.

Poconos Evacuation Center.

"What the hell," someone yelled.

Stryker turned and the southern sky grew brighter as what had been a dim ribbon of light suddenly began to intensify.

The line arcing from horizon to horizon had suddenly become too bright to gaze at directly.

The general's voice growled through the speakers once again. *"I said, fall out! The transports are waiting on you."*

With a newfound surge of energy, Stryker raced toward the far end of the tarmac.

He had no clue why DefenseNet had suddenly gotten so bright, but it didn't matter.

Stryker smiled as he imagined seeing his kids again.

For the moment, nothing else mattered.

"Form a perimeter. Get them away from the outer walls!"

Dave rocketed out of bed as heavily-armed soldiers swarmed into their secured barracks, just outside of the Mariscal Sucre International Airport. Bella screamed as soldiers lifted her from their bed, and they were both forcefully escorted away from the windows.

Ripping his arm out of the grip of one of the soldiers, Dave grabbed Bella's hand and yelled, "What the hell is going on?" Soldiers flipped up their mattress and placed it against the windows.

One soldier gripped Dave's arm, leaned close to him, and explained, "Doctor Holmes, the Ecuador substation was just attacked. We've been ordered to initiate an emergency evac—"

Suddenly, the air whooshed out of Dave's lungs as a shock wave blasted him from his feet.

The world seemed to move in slow motion as broken glass, concrete, and dust blasted through the room.

Dave found himself staring up at a hole in the ceiling and couldn't move. His ears rang painfully as he lay stunned.

A soldier leaned over Dave, and a bloody gash across the soldier's forehead dripped on him as the man yelled something he couldn't hear over the ringing in his ears.

The soldier squeezed his neck, his shoulders, and his arms, and it dawned on Dave that the soldier was checking him for injuries.

Suddenly, Dave felt a searing pain as his ears popped and his senses were flooded with the chaotic sounds of war. Men screamed for help from all directions, along with the crash of falling rocks and the chop-chop sounds of nearby helicopters.

With a sudden sense of panic, Dave lurched into a sitting position and frantically yelled, "Bella!"

He scanned the dust and rubble that was all around him, and when he spied the splash of bright-red hair, his blood turned into ice.

Ripping himself from the men who were trying to help him, he crawled to Bella and his throat tightened as he saw her bloody face. Her unblinking green eyes stared up at the ceiling, lifeless.

The lower half of her body has been crushed under the concrete slab from the collapse of the floor above.

Dave's vision blurred as tears flowed and dripped onto her. He gently closed her eyes and wiped the blood from her face.

He leaned down, nestled his head in the crook of her neck, and released a primal yell of anguish. Dave shrugged his arm away from whoever was trying to grab him, and pulled in a deep, bitter breath. He leaned over Bella and gave her a kiss on the forehead, shuddering with grief as he thought of all the things he'd wanted to share with her. He had no words to say. Words were meaningless.

He sat back on his heels and wiped the blood off his hands.

A soldier knelt next to him, and before he could say anything, Dave turned to him and said, "I want her brought with us. She's not going to be left behind in this shithole."

The soldier hitched his thumb to a couple of nearby medics.

"They're here to help you, and they'll bring her with us. We're not leaving anyone behind. But sir, we have to leave. We can't risk another mortar strike against this position."

With the soldier's help, Dave stood and stared at the broken body of the only person he'd ever loved. Even though she looked like she was asleep, some tangible thing had left her, and he felt its absence.

A burning ember inside Dave sparked into flame. His body tensed as rage replaced sorrow. A desire for revenge vaporized whatever grief he was experiencing.

Through gritted teeth, Dave swore, "Dead. I'm going to see whoever did this rooted out of whatever hole they're hiding in, and they'll pay." Balling his hands into fists, Dave tasted blood in his mouth. "They'll all die."

CHAPTER THIRTY-TWO

"There were nineteen long-range missiles sent against the Ecuador substation," General Keane reported with a somber expression. "Our Patriot Laser installations repelled those attacks, however, there were twelve deaths and twenty-three injuries due to mortar attacks targeted against both the substation and the barracks adjacent to the airport in Quito. One of those deaths was confirmed to be Bella Holmes, Doctor Holmes' wife. The substation was not touched, and no further incidents have occurred in the last eight hours; however, I'm sending in more troops and defense batteries."

Margaret's jaw dropped, and she sat back against her chair, momentarily stunned. She glanced up at the clock on her office wall and asked, "Where is Doctor Holmes now?"

"He asked to have his wife buried at sea, so I authorized a stop, a deviation on his return route." General Keane glanced at his watch. "They landed in MacDill Air Force Base about thirty minutes ago. It was the closest coastal installation that I could come up with that had the necessary security in place. I'll be notified as soon as the burial is complete and they're back in the air."

Suddenly, the phone icon on her table blinked as an incoming call was routed to Margaret's office. She tapped on the icon and said, "Yes?"

"Madam President, it's Karen Fultondale. We've got a trace on our mole."

Margaret's back stiffened and she balled her hand into a fist. "Karen, please tell me that the FBI's got an ID on that scumbag. I want to see them drawn and quartered."

"We were able to confirm through video records the identity of our mole, and it turns out to be coming out of the CIA. Let me forward you the evidence of the first leak, including the IP address."

Studying the text scrolling across the screen built into her desk, Margaret felt her lip curling into a snarl.

Intercepted transmission dated: 13 JUL 2066
Timestamp: 13:51 GMT

"An unscheduled military flight has been booked with presidential authority to the Mariscal Sucre International Airport.

Doctor David Wendell Holmes is currently boarding with several other unidentified civilians. There's a heavy security contingent accompanying them."

"That was the message we'd intercepted when Doctor Holmes first departed for the Ecuador substation. Below is what we intercepted yesterday."

Intercepted transmission dated: 20 DEC 2066
Timestamp: 07:26 GMT

"Under heavy security, Doctor David Wendell Holmes is en route to the Mariscal Sucre International Airport.

This may be our last chance to stop him. The time of our savior's arrival is imminent. I pray Holmes can be stopped."

From the religious tone of the message, Margaret had no doubt this was the smoking gun for the recent attack. "Karen, you mentioned you have video evidence?"

"Yes, it was only after the second incident that we managed to ID the suspect. The terminals being used were in one of the CIA annexes, but the passwords were verified to have been stolen. I'm forwarding the video stream now."

A 3D image suddenly popped up from Margaret's desk and she watched as someone wearing a hoodie sat at a terminal and began typing. It took only a moment, but as soon as they finished, they wiped the keyboard with what looked like alcohol swabs and rose from the chair. It was only as the person walked out of the building that an external camera caught the image of the person's face and Margaret yelled, "You son of a bitch!"

"Madam President, we have Greg Hildebrand in custody under suspicion of espionage, treason, and multiple breaches of national security."

"How the hell did he still have access to government facilities? I thought we'd let him go after the assault he'd pulled on Doctor Holmes."

"We're still looking into it, President Hager. For some reason, his clearances hadn't been pulled and he'd managed to get himself trans-ferred into the CIA as an analyst."

Margaret trembled with fury and General Keane, who'd been listening to the exchange, suggested, "We could place him in Leaven-worth for safekeeping until things settle down."

Blowing out a deep breath, Margaret tried to calm herself with only minimal success. "Karen, General Keane will arrange a transfer to the military's custody. For now, let's put Hildebrand away. I don't want that cockroach ever being able to communicate with anyone again."

"Understood, President Hager. Is there anything else you need from me?"

Margaret drummed her fingers on the table and pursed her lips as she thought about what had transpired in the last twenty-four hours. Suddenly, she froze as an idea bloomed into existence. "Karen, go work with whoever you need to and get me images of the destruction of the hotel. I hate to seem ghoulish, but if there are images of bodies, that would also be helpful. That's all I have for now, but get me those images as soon as you can."

"Understood."

Margaret tapped on the phone icon, disconnecting the call.

General Keane tilted his head and stared at the president. "What in the world are you going to do with those pictures?"

With a cold, calculating stare, Margaret gazed off into space and said, "I'm going to go public with this. We've spent too much time trying to handle this quietly. It's time to enlist the world's help."

Margaret watched the live video feed of the dimly-lit night sky above the Cheyenne Mountain Evacuation Complex. Even though the video camera didn't have a view far enough south to see the source of the light, it was obvious that Dave Holmes had pulled off a miracle as the nighttime sky was brighter than it ever had been before.

She glanced at Walter. "Has Doctor Holmes arrived yet? I want to offer my condolences as well as thank him for what he's done."

The Secretary of Defense looked up at the clock on the wall and shook his head. "Not yet, he should be landing at the airstrip in fifteen minutes. Should arrive under heavy escort within the hour."

Margaret glanced at the tabletop, which still had open the contingency escape pod plan, and shuddered. "I was minutes away from ordering Burt to initiate Noah's Ark when I was alerted about Doctor Holmes' success. I'll admit this president gig isn't what I ever thought it would be like. I've never been so sick to my stomach in my life."

The former general looked at her and smiled. "Madam President, I doubt that any prior office holder would have done better, and to tell you the truth, I can't imagine a single one who could have faced such gut-wrenching choices."

"I suppose every president has their moments of turmoil, but nonetheless, it's part of the job. Anyway, just before you got here, I sent Burt to talk to all of the contingency candidates we'd selected and let them know that we are probably going to be standing down on Noah's Ark. It gives him an opportunity to share some good news with some folks, and besides, I figured he needed the stress relief more than I did."

The tabletop suddenly flashed, indicating an incoming call, and Margaret slapped the phone icon to answer it. "Yes?"

"Madam President?"

The panic in the woman's voice sent a shiver running through Margaret. "Yes, this is President Hager, who is this?"

"Oh, Madam President, I'm sorry to have to reach out to you directly. I tried Burt, but he doesn't seem to be responding."

"Doctor Patel? Portable phones don't work within the center, what's wrong? What can I do?"

"Madam President, we've got trouble. Everyone here is doing everything we can about it, but I don't think ... I really need to talk with Burt and Dave. It's complicated. I think I can fix it, but I need their help."

"Doctor Patel, I have no earthly idea what you're talking about, but Doctor Holmes will be here in an hour or so, and I can go hunt down Burt. Hold one second."

Hitting the mute button, Margaret glanced at the tabletop and opened up the Noah's Ark plan once again. A wave of nausea flushed through her, accompanied by cold beads of sweat that made her clothes stick to her skin. Taking a deep breath, Margaret flipped to the last page on the list of faces for Noah's Ark and spotted the image of Doctor Neeta Patel. Margaret had added it after she'd settled the list with Burt. Margaret knew that he needed a second in command, preferably someone younger.

She glanced at Walter. "We need a fast mover to bring Doctor Patel here right away."

The former general nodded. "I'll arrange it."

"Doctor Patel, I'm arranging for you and the others to meet here in the Cheyenne command center. Give your second control of your tasks and I'll have somebody pick you up in five minutes. Be ready."

"Uh ... okay. I'll be ready. Thank you."

Walter sighed, leaned over and tapped on the phone icon to call in the orders. As he dialed the numbers, he glanced at Margaret and grumbled, "We're still in the shit, aren't we?"

Barely controlling her gag reflex, Margaret nodded. "I'm afraid so."

With the last bus of the day having just emptied, Stryker motioned for the next person in line.

He was a dark-haired boy, probably nine or ten.

Stryker held his hand out. "Let me see your ID."

The kid handed over the government-issued ID he'd received during the initial evacuation.

Stryker waved a scanner over the plastic card. The device read the embedded chip and flashed green, indicating it was a valid and unaltered ID card.

He approached the kid with the handheld scanner. "I'm going to flash a light in your right eye. It won't hurt."

Even though the boy carried a worried expression, he nodded bravely and stared straight ahead, unblinking.

Stryker pressed a button on the device, it initiated a quick retinal scan, and the LED printout indicated an identity match.

He scrolled through the boy's records and glanced at him. "Jeff, I'm going to ask you a few easy questions. Just give me the best answer you can. Okay?"

"Yes, sir," Jeff responded meekly.

"How many sisters do you have?"

"I don't have any sisters."

Stryker nodded. "What's your mother's name?"

"Michelle."

"Do you know your father's middle name?"

Jeff paused and scrunched his eyebrows. "I think it's Franklin."

"Other than your mom and dad, who else in your family is scheduled to arrive here?"

"My aunt and uncle are, along with my cousins."

"Their names?"

"Tisha and David are my aunt and uncle. Jeremy, Katie, and Brad are my cousins."

Stryker smiled and gave him another nod. "Okay, we're almost done." He turned and motioned toward the pathway leading to a building behind him. "I'll need you to go back into the exam area. A doctor is going to take a look at you and make sure everything is okay."

With his chin quivering, Jeff asked, "When can I see my mom and dad?"

Putting a hand on Jeff's shoulder, Stryker knelt so he was face-to-face with him. "As soon as the doctors finish their exam, your parents will be waiting for you on the other side. I promise."

Jeff nodded and walked along the path to the outer exam room.

Stryker watched the boy until he disappeared through the swinging doors. Few people knew that the doctor's visual exam was a ruse to look for hourglass-shaped tattoos. What the large x-ray and MRI devices were looking for was beyond him.

Turning his attention to the few remaining people from the bus, Stryker motioned for the next in line.

The charred aroma of hamburgers and hot dogs permeated the building as mess hall workers fed the several thousand people assigned to the Poconos Evacuation Center.

There were at least five-hundred people crowding the tables as Stryker sat down with his family.

He sat next to his sister, and Emma, Isaac, and Lainie settled on the bench seats directly across from him.

Without hesitation, both kids attacked their large bowls of macaroni and cheese.

"Do you kids like the food?"

They both nodded as they devoured heaping spoonfuls of their favorite food.

He bumped shoulders with Jessica and asked, "How're you doing, Jess?"

She took a big bite out of her hamburger and chewed for a moment before answering. "As best as any of us can. I met up with a couple of teachers, and we're thinking about starting some classes for the kids. Do you have any idea if we can order some school supplies?"

"I don't know, but I can ask. The quartermaster can probably get just about anything, I suppose. Just tell me exactly what you need and I'll see what can be done." He turned to Lainie and hesitated.

She looked drawn and had a worried frown. Her plate held a few pieces of fruit and some toast.

"Lainie, how are you doing?"

His ex-wife pressed her lips together and barely shook her head.

She didn't want to talk. Something had been up with her ever since he got called up for duty. Was it because he was wearing a military uniform again?

He sighed and was about to ask the kids a question when a beeping alert sounded over the loudspeakers.

Images flickered along the walls, immediately drawing Stryker's attention.

The screens showed the US Homeland Defense Network logo, along with a countdown of 5 ... 4 ... 3 ... 2 ... 1....

Text scrolled across the screen and Stryker read it aloud for the benefit of the kids.

"The following alert is being sent nationwide. Citizens located in evacuation centers can be assured that their safety is of paramount importance. Screenings have already been done upon entry into the evacuee system."

An image popped up on the screen with a network news anchor reading from a script.

"This is a broadcast coming through the US Homeland Defense Network.

"Many people have been calling 911 emergency centers due to the increased brightness of the DefenseNet grid. There is no need to call authorities regarding this matter. This is normal.

"The scientists are reporting that tests are being done on DefenseNet, and that we should expect the same level of brightness until full activation.

The reporter flipped to another page.

"It is now being reported that the federal government has tightened security within our borders due to increased terrorist activity.

"Borders are sealed, all domestic and international flights have been suspended, and dusk-to-dawn curfews are in place throughout all major cities in the US.

"As many of you have seen reported on this station, there've been increased reports of terrorist acts in our towns and cities over the last six months. Many of these incidents have been initiated by what is now confirmed as a doomsday cult called the Brotherhood. We are asking all citizens to be on alert.

"Members of these cults are known to be motivated by sadistic beliefs cloaked in the guise of a false religion. They are seeking to destroy our world.

"If any of you have suspicions or are concerned about this so-called Brotherhood, contact a uniformed officer immediately."

Isaac turned from the broadcast and stared at Stryker. "Dad, are we—"

"We're all perfectly safe." Stryker reached across the table and squeezed both of his kids' hands. "I'm here to keep you and everyone else safe."

Emma frowned. "Are you going to shoot the bad guys?"

"There aren't any bad guys in here," Lainie explained.

"But if someone needs shooting, you'll do it, right?"

Stryker barely suppressed a smile and stared grimly at his daughter. "If someone needs shooting, I'll take care of it."

"Good." Emma nodded approvingly and turned to her mother. "I told you Daddy would shoot the bad guys for us. We don't need to sleep with you anymore to keep you safe."

Lainie's face turned red as Jessica cleared her throat and said, "Does anyone want some dessert? I know I do."

Margaret had expected Dave to be emotionally crippled by what had occurred, but other than a rather grim demeanor, he seemed unchanged.

She watched as the scientists heatedly discussed the situation.

Neeta had just drawn complex diagrams on a whiteboard depicting navigation plots and acceleration curves when she said, "If we take the Moon and launch it down the middle of the cone of debris, it'll smash straight through without really even slowing down." Drawing arcs away from the Moon, she explained, "The gravity effects will attract the nearest objects to crash into it, and the rest of the objects should slingshot outwards. We'll just need to give it a little time for the hole to expand and it'll be like threading a needle. We can sneak the Earth right through the debris."

"With the loss of the Moon," Dave noted.

"Most likely," Neeta confirmed. "We'll have to assume lack of remote control once it gets hit."

Dave nodded, grabbed one of the dry-erase markers, and began writing some equations that made no sense whatsoever to Margaret. He tapped on the whiteboard and grumbled, "Since our orbital angle is taking us in the direction of the debris, I don't think we can counteract the Earth's inertia and get out of the way before encountering the debris."

Neeta nodded vigorously. "That's why I think the Moon's the only shot we have." She glanced at the others in the room. "Any other thoughts anyone can come up with? Am I missing anything?"

Margaret glanced in Burt's direction. He'd remained oddly silent during the discussion. She cleared her throat and asked, "Let me see if I understand the gist of what you're saying in layman's terms.

"We've got what we believe to be what Doctor Holmes is calling a warp ring around both the Earth and the Moon. It allows us to move in any direction we want, but it's like moving a boat. We can't just change direction instantly, and we aren't like a race car that can go from zero to sixty in nothing flat.

"Because the Earth is moving in a particular direction and it would take too much energy to overcome that momentum quickly and go backward, the plan would be to take advantage of what Doctor Patel had done and slip through the middle of the first wave of debris heading toward us. However, that plan got shot to hell when we realized that instead of creating a giant cylinder of debris that the Earth and Moon could fly through, we found a bunch of giant asteroids that had previously been obscured by thick dust at the end of the cylinder. So instead of drifting through a cylinder, we find ourselves drifting into a cone. Am I right?"

Dave nodded at Margaret. "Yes, ma'am, that's right. Even though that engine we have can produce enough power to do just about anything we need, I don't think the ring is made of strong enough stuff to take a full blast from that engine. So changing the Earth's direction quickly isn't in the cards. We're basically able to steer left, right, up and down–but no reverse. The Moon, on the other hand, has a good amount of thermal energy we can tap, and it's big enough that we could accelerate it in the direction we're going and take out the stuff ahead of us.

"I've plotted out what we need to do. It's kind of like shooting pool. If we do it, and hit the objects hard enough with the Moon, the debris will bounce out of our way and the momentum of the Moon will carry it past where we would change direction anyway. Unfortunately, we'll of course have to deal with the consequences of not having a

Moon anymore, but that's why everyone evacuated the coasts anyway, isn't it?"

Margaret turned to Burt. "Well, what do you think?"

"I think they're right," Burt responded, and with a grim expression, turned to Neeta. "I'll need detailed navigation coordinates and acceleration profiles for what you've plotted out."

Neeta put her hands on her hips and cocked an eyebrow. "If you'd have picked up your phone, you'd know that they're already in your e-mail's inbox."

Burt nodded curtly and asked Dave, "Any further concerns about the plan?"

Dave shook his head. "Not with the Moon part. I think as long as we remotely keep the Moon on course and adjust as we get closer, it shouldn't be a problem. However, we'll have to keep a close eye on the wake of the debris expansion after the Moon hits those asteroids. I think Neeta is right, and we can't follow right behind the Moon because it's going to take a day or so for us to get a big enough hole through the debris."

Burt turned to Margaret and said in a low voice, "We need to talk."

As Margaret settled at the head of the command center's conference room table, Neeta asked, "Where's Burt?"

"That's partly what I'm here to talk about," Margaret responded grimly. After Burt had told her his plan, she reluctantly signed off on it, and after he left her office, she'd actually gotten sick for the first time since this whole Indigo thing started. Margaret didn't think she'd have as hard of a time as she did with the consequences of his plan, but she also knew he was right.

The conference room was bigger than they needed. It easily sat thirty, but gathered around the table were only four people: her, Dave, Neeta, and Walter.

"It's almost time, people," Margaret said. "In about thirty-six hours, with the Moon leading the way, I'll be revealing to the public some of the cards that we've been keeping back. We've done well holding everything together, but the last thing we need now is panic. So tomorrow morning, I'll be giving a speech which details what we'll be doing and what people should expect to see. I'm going to need all of your help with filling in the details, especially the ones about what people might experience. The less of a surprise it is, the better.

"As to Doctor Burt Radcliffe...." Margaret paused and took a deep breath. "You all know what we've been fighting with security-wise. Suicide bombings, insane attempts at destroying our way of life, the desire to see the Earth destroyed." Margaret leaned forward, reached across the table, and briefly placed her hand on Dave's outstretched fingers. "Despite the recent tragedies in Ecuador, we've successfully rebuffed many of the attacks against us. I had also asked Burt to secure the Moon base against any possible attacks. There have been thousands of cyber-attacks on the Moon's servers in the last couple weeks. They were bad enough that they managed to knock the lunar satellites offline. We do have a remote video feed indicating that everything is still operational in the control room, so it seems that all of the remote hacking has been thwarted by what Burt had done up there.

"He also added security measures against any physical intrusion of the Moon base. Luckily, those countermeasures were never needed. Thanks to our Air Force, we shot down nearly half-a-dozen attempts at unauthorized travel to the Moon.

"Most of you never knew that we had a contingency plan for the Moon. On the chance that we wouldn't recover from the initial attack that knocked out power at some of our substations, I authorized Burt to employ physical countermeasures to prevent someone from taking over and changing the preprogrammed navigation settings of the Moon base's server.

"That contingency plan was never needed. Yet as you know, a new contingency for the Moon has materialized.

"I hold full responsibility for this, and I'll carry the guilt to my grave. Nonetheless, Burt is currently en route to the Moon. His countermeasures required him and only him to be the one who unlocks the server and steers the Moon to where it needs to go."

Neeta gasped, and tears dripped down her cheeks. She clasped her hands to her mouth.

"B-but..." Dave stammered, pressed his lips firmly together and shook his head. "Another unmitigated tragedy," he said, with a raw tone to his voice. He swallowed hard. "We need to make sure his self-less acts are remembered by everyone."

"Excuse me." Neeta quickly stood and walked toward the far end of the room, her hands covering her face.

Margaret coughed as she struggled to bottle her emotions regarding the situation. She turned to Dave. "Let's talk more about what we'll do when the time comes. For now, I need your help describing to the world what they should expect to see."

Dave's expression became solemn, yet his voice held a firm strength in it. "Of course. I'll help however I can." He glanced at Neeta and pushed his chair back from the table. "Let me go talk to Neeta."

Margaret sat back in her chair and watched as Dave walked toward Neeta and then held her in a tight embrace.

She whispered to nobody in particularly, "I'll always blame myself for all of this. I wouldn't blame Dave or Neeta at all for hating me." She turned to Walter. "General, I know we're going into lockdown soon, so if Neeta wants transport to another evacuation site, and if Doctor Holmes agrees that it doesn't jeopardize our mission, just make it happen."

"Understood, Madam President."

She watched as Neeta and Dave talked animatedly to each other, and even though Margaret couldn't hear what was being said, she watched as Neeta gave Dave a quick embrace and raced from the room.

As Dave walked back toward Margaret and sat on his chair, Margaret pulled a handheld computer from her pocket, brought up the 'notes' application, and turned her attention back to Dave.

Not having the heart to ask if Neeta was okay, she focused on what she needed to do. "Doctor Holmes, tell me what we'll see from Earth in chronological order, starting with the time the Moon begins to move."

CHAPTER THIRTY-THREE

The heavy thud of Burt's rubber-soled magnetic boots echoed loudly as he plodded through the empty halls of Moon Base Crockett. The silence was eerie, as if he were walking within a tomb. Despite the change in gravity, it was the lonely silence coupled with the cool, sterile air that gave Burt the distinct sense he wasn't on Earth anymore. On the day-long trip up to the base, he'd made peace with the task at hand. In fact, Burt was happy at the prospect of doing what needed to be done. Even though he'd been cornered by a quirk of fate into this position, he knew it would lead to something he'd always wanted.

He wanted to make a difference in other people's lives, even if it was at his own expense.

"Well, Burt," he joked with himself. "Knowing how President Hager is, she'll probably end up erecting statues of your ugly mug in every state of the union."

Remembering well the maze-like hallways of the Moon base's north wing, Burt turned into the control room and sat at the administrator's workstation. He glanced at the clock, and for some reason envisioned a scene in a movie where he'd watched a man kick-starting an old Harley Davidson motorcycle. "Well, I have eight hours until I kick-start the engines on this big rock. Maybe, just maybe, they have some old movies archived somewhere."

It was then that he remembered what Margaret had said about the satellite link going down.

Getting off his chair, Burt knew that the server could wait.

As he returned to the room where the satellite feeds came in, Burt began talking to himself again.

"If I can get the satellite link up, then there may be someone down there who can tell me where the rec room is in this place. They have to have some old movies."

It took him a couple hours to track down the issue, but after isolating the problem to a burnt-out network router and some faulty cables, Burt replaced the broken equipment that connected the satellite to the internal network. He smiled as he saw live network traffic flowing again through the satellite.

As his computer wirelessly hooked into the network feed, Burt carried the tablet back with him, walking back to the administrator's console.

Setting the tablet up on a stand, he leaned his face against the retinal scanner he'd installed and placed his thumb on the fingerprint reader. He immediately felt the click of recognition from his thumb, but got a buzzing sound from the visor.

"What the hell?" Burt growled and tried again.

Again the buzzing sound.

His mind racing, he couldn't fathom what was wrong. Knowing that a person's retina remains the same throughout their life, Burt tried a third time and yet again was denied access to the administrator's console.

He pulled open a drawer full of tools and glanced at the clock. "I don't have time for this shit!"

Luckily, he had the downloaded firmware for the machine and

could try to undo the security measures he'd created, but Burt wasn't sure if he'd be able to do it in time.

As he began taking the platform apart, the tablet had automatically launched a browser when it detected the internet connection.

Burt was beginning to pry off the chip that contained the platform's firmware when the tablet began running a video that was counting down. Turning on the volume, the tablet broadcast an alert, *"This is an emergency alert from President Margaret Hager of the United States for all within viewing range."*

Burt nodded, and as he searched in another window for the source code to the firmware, he heard the message repeating itself until suddenly, the scrolling numbers fell away and a live video broadcast flickered to life. He instantly recognized the background: the Cheyenne Mountain Command Center.

The president took her seat at a table, with the presidential logo that Burt didn't remember being there only a day earlier. She projected the same calm, unflappable expression that all great leaders had, and he smiled as her voice rang clearly through the tiny computer's speaker.

"Good morning, my fellow citizens:

"I am speaking to you again not just as the president of the United States, but as a global citizen.

"I had not planned to give another public address until the time had come when I could announce that the threat overhead had passed and all of our lives could return to normal. However, a recent event has forced me to change that plan.

"I also realize that my voice is reaching far beyond the borders of just these United States, and is in fact being automatically translated into over one-hundred languages. Rest assured that I've been in constant contact with all of the other world leaders, and only moments ago, I spoke to them about what I'm about to tell you.

"There is an old saying that goes, 'May you live in interesting times.'

"Some claim that the saying is a curse, others see it as a blessing.

"Friends, let me assure you that once I'm done with what I'm

about to say, we'll all agree that these are interesting times that we live in.

"As I informed you the last time we talked, DefenseNet is acting as a shield against the incoming barrage of space debris heading toward us.

"I would like to give you a brief update on that, so that you can know what has been happening.

"Even though you can't see it, the world's top scientists and engineers have been working around the clock to defend us against the threat that even now looms ahead.

"As of now, DefenseNet has already destroyed or rendered harmless over 13,000 space objects that had previously been aimed directly for us.

"Yes, I know that number must be shocking to many of you, but every one of those 13,000 is a success story. Each a small victory against something that could have caused us great harm.

"Yet DefenseNet has its limitations.

"When we first detected the debris and I alerted the world, the scientific community thought that the asteroids had been sent flying towards us due to a comet colliding into a field of rubble on the outskirts of our solar system.

"We now know that that wasn't the case.

"Heading our way is an unstoppable force. One that's existed since the dawn of time. This primordial threat brooks no argument, and would bypass any shield we could ever hope to wield against it. It is this threat that flung debris ahead of its approach.

"What is this thing, you might rightfully ask, and what can we possibly do?

"Citizens of the world, a black hole has entered our solar system. An object whose pull is so strong that even light itself cannot escape its grasp. Yet that's exactly what we're about to do.

"Yes, you heard me right, we are standing at a juncture in humanity's path."

Despite the blunt and horrible news, Burt was busy making rapid changes to the console's logic and compiling it. He began to sweat as time elapsed and he still hadn't managed to get the console running. All the while, he kept part of his attention on the president's message. He heard the pitch of the president's voice change. It suddenly carried a tone of optimism and hope.

"Our children, and our children's children will be able to point in the history books and note that humanity made a great leap on this day.

"I know that we've all made huge sacrifices to even get to this stage. Many of you have been displaced from your homes.

"Those of you who are still in your homes are experiencing extensive rationing, which is something that hasn't been seen in this country since World War II.

"However, I do want to make note of one scientist in particular. An extraordinary man who I want everyone to know and appreciate, for he's an example of what is good and just in this world. An example of the silent, self-sacrificing person who works tirelessly for the sake of us all.

"Doctor Burt Radcliffe was responsible for first alerting us all to the incoming threat that we now face. Since alerting us of this threat, he has dedicated every waking moment to the cause of seeing us through this time of crisis.

"Ronald Reagan once said that the future does not belong to the faint-hearted, it belongs to the brave. Burt Radcliffe has epitomized what self-sacrifice and bravery are all about.

"Doctor Radcliffe was recently faced with a task that only he could accomplish, yet in doing so, he knew that he'd be sacrificing himself so that the rest of us could live.

"He made that choice without hesitation and without regret.

"As I speak to you now, Doctor Radcliffe is about to clear the way for us all to have a future that he will never actually see.

"Let us put Burt Radcliffe in our prayers and wish him well on his final journey."

Just after replacing the chip on the console, Burt stared wide-eyed at the screen and couldn't believe what he was witnessing. The president closed her eyes and bent her head in prayer for a few seconds, then looked up with a serious expression.

"Margaret, you're something else," said Burt to the computer screen with a sense of awe. The woman continued addressing the public.

"*I'm sure all of you have seen the miraculous ribbon of light in the sky, and most of you have likely noticed how that same ribbon is now glowing even brighter than before.*

"*When DefenseNet was built, it had one public purpose. It was our shield against that which threatens us.*

"*Yet there was another purpose in its design. That bright ribbon we can all see high in the sky indicates that a new capability has been brought online. In DefenseNet's initial design, our scientists knew that there might be a threat which the shield couldn't withstand.*

"*At the time, they couldn't predict what that threat might have been, and the scientists certainly wouldn't have guessed that we'd be approached by a cosmic terror such as a black hole. Nonetheless, they knew that this secondary ability was one that could save us when all else failed.*

"*What is this mysterious capability, you ask?*

"*It is a capability that can provide an escape from the inescapable. Defense against the indefensible. A miracle when all hope is lost.*

"*Through DefenseNet's revolutionary technology, our scientists have just brought online an escape plan. A way for us to avoid not only the space debris heading our way but the black hole that threatens the entirety of our solar system.*

"*I know what you're all thinking, because these are the same thoughts I had when I first heard of this possibility.*

"*Nonsense!*

"*What do you mean, escape?*

"*Escape to where?*

"*Let me assure you that we are in no danger, but I, along with the other leaders of the world, strongly believe that the public should be aware of what is happening. We believe that you should know the truth, and in knowing the truth, have faith that all will be well.*"

Burt felt the warmth of Margaret's confidence as her voice broadcast across the many thousands of miles. He felt a surge of strength that bolstered the rightness of his fate. If nothing else, Burt knew that his life hadn't been wasted. He reassembled the administrator's console, knowing that he would most certainly be making a difference in humanity's future.

"Like I said earlier, we are standing at an amazing time that all future generations will look back on and speak of in reverence."

Burt plugged in the administrator's console just as Margaret's voice began to grow louder and louder. The power of her message grew, and Burt felt the surge of pride rising within him.

"This is the moment when humanity finally understands that we are all one people.

"This is the moment when humanity takes its first step toward our future.

"This is the moment when humanity will fight back against the darkness and win.

"Let this temporary strife serve as a signal to us all.

"As you see the bright ribbon of light in the sky, let it shine as a symbol of our future. The future is most certainly a bright one to behold. Let's all be worthy of it."

Burt whispered, "Let's all be worthy."

He leaned back against his chair and sighed with relief as the administrator console blinked on and awaited instructions.

As the president continued with her speech, outlining what the public was about to go through, Burt smiled and looked up at the clock. It was almost time.

The scent of freshly brewed coffee pulled him from his thoughts, and a woman's voice spoke, "I brought some of the good stuff."

Spinning toward the source, Burt stared at the last person he'd have ever expected to see. His throat tightened, and no words could form in his head.

Neeta smiled and walked toward him. She offered him a steaming mug of coffee and said, "It's about time we start moving this big rock. Besides–everyone knows you suck at driving."

CHAPTER THIRTY-FOUR

It had been less than twenty-four hours since the explosion in Ecuador took Bella's life. Every moment since then, Dave had been surrounded by people watching him. Somehow he'd managed to push all of his emotions aside, just barely managing to keep himself from flying apart at the seams. But now, in the privacy of his own quarters, with nausea overwhelming him, Dave heaved into a bucket as he emptied his stomach.

Chills raced through him as he recalled Bella's lifeless, green-eyed stare.

He tried to take a deep breath, but it felt like a steel band had wrapped around his chest.

"Bella, I loved you from the moment I first laid eyes on you...."

Dave slid off the side of his bed, slumping down on the floor as his body tingled with pent-up emotions. His mind felt sluggish as he finally allowed himself to absorb what had happened.

He'd never again experience Bella's quirky sense of humor. The way she looked at him with those piercing green eyes. Her sheer brilliance and vitality. The warmth of her embrace that he knew was for him and him alone.

All of it snuffed out for no good reason.

Dave couldn't see a way forward for himself. The heavy cloak of his misery suddenly seemed impossible to bear as he envisioned the loneliness of life without her.

The steel band tightened as despair wrapped around Dave like a shroud. He didn't care anymore. Nothing mattered.

He closed his eyes and, for a moment, hoped the darkness would claim him. But suddenly Bella's face appeared in his mind. Not the dead thing half-buried by rubble, but instead the beautiful woman who loved life. *"If it's possible, you have to try and save them."*

The words she'd spoken all those months ago pierced through the depths of Dave's despair, and he felt the warmth of her presence enveloping him.

People needed him. Even if he didn't think he cared anymore, Bella had cared. Maybe she'd cared enough for them both.

Dave breathed in deeply as the metal band around his chest loosened and he placed his head between his knees.

He imagined Bella sitting next to him, running her fingers over his shoulder, when suddenly, a flood of emotions overwhelmed him and he began to sob.

~

Startled awake, Dave groaned as someone pounded on his door and yelled, "Doctor Holmes, we've got incoming alerts from LIGO."

Grabbing the side of the bed, he levered himself up off the floor where he'd fallen asleep. He staggered toward the door and glanced at the wall clock. He'd only gotten two hours of sleep. He ripped open the door to his apartment, one of the few private rooms in the entire Cheyenne evacuation site, and was greeted with the image of a pale-faced engineer with a Mission Control badge. He barely looked old enough to have graduated college, and Dave suppressed his instinct to yell at him for disturbing his sleep. Taking a deep breath, he frowned and calmly asked, "What did you say?"

"Sir, LIGO is still recording the arrival of gravitational waves, and they're seeing an almost constant barrage of them right now!"

With a deep sigh, Dave waved the engineer away and said, "I'll be right there."

~

The buzz of activity was constant in the Cheyenne Mountain Command Center as dozens of engineers monitored hundreds of satellite feeds and signals coming from all over the world. Despite having been built under a mountain, this Command Center was bigger than any Dave had been in before. With an auditorium that was easily one-hundred-and-fifty feet wide and seventy feet from front to back, it housed more video screens and computers than even the Cape Canaveral Mission Control.

Standing in the center of the room, Dave watched as the right-hand-side display showed the incoming LIGO alerts. He turned to the nearest engineer and pointed at the center screen. "Give me a patch into the Hubble2 satellite. I want that thing aimed at wherever those disturbances are coming from. In addition to visual spectrographic range, I want another feed showing me the color-enhanced images for X-ray and beyond."

"Yes, sir." The engineer typed frantically on the keyboard, stood, and yelled across the room, "Can someone authorize my satellite adjustment commands?"

Dave's mouth had gone dry and his heart thudded rapidly in his chest with the hidden anxiety he felt as he stared at the screens, waiting for them to update. Feeling a tap on his left shoulder, he turned and was surprised to see the president.

"What's going on?"

Dave pointed at the screen on the right and said, "We're getting a huge amount of alerts incoming from LIGO, and I'll bet you anything you want that the alerts are coming from our space-based intruder."

"Sir!" The engineer pointed at the main screen. "I've got the Hubble 2 and IXO 2 satellites online, and they're adjusting their focus to an area approximately 375 million miles away. That should be somewhere near Jupiter's current position."

Dave watched as the angle of the images on the large center display turned. The background stars and lights were all blurry as he imagined the space telescopes turning, changing their field of focus.

Margaret pointed at the large white blob that appeared on the left-hand-side of the video feed and asked, "What's that?"

"I'm going to guess that's an out-of-focus Jupiter," Dave responded, as he watched the blob slowly sharpen into a recognizable image. His mouth opened in shock as the image crystalized, and he saw something he'd only ever seen in simulations.

Long gaseous streamers extended from the surface of Jupiter. As the focus of the image became even sharper, Dave saw the distant tendrils of gas seeming to swirl around an invisible threat.

On the right-hand-side of the screen, the X-ray filtered video feed coming from IXO 2 clearly showed the swirling gas around a dark center. The brilliant flares of intense light exploded in a myriad of computer-enhanced colors around the edges of the black hole.

"My god," Margaret exclaimed. "It looks like Jupiter is being pulled like soft taffy."

Dave nodded. "Madam President, Jupiter is being ripped apart by gravitational forces beyond comprehension. The event horizon around the black hole is rotating at almost the speed of light, and as Jupiter's outflow approaches, the matter begins to get torn apart by the gravitational forces. Those flares of X-ray particles are the last gasps of matter as they're ripped to pieces."

A shiver raced up Dave's spine as the images on the screen brought back memories of those nightmares he'd suffered through almost a decade ago.

"That's our future if we don't get out of the black hole's way."

CHAPTER THIRTY-FIVE

Being the Prefect of the Secretariat for Communication, Reverend Monsignor Domingo Adrian Herrera had authority over all communication coming out of the Holy See in the Vatican. However, after watching the broadcast from the President of the United States, he knew that he needed to consult with the Pope before speaking on his behalf over such monumental messages.

As Domingo walked through the long hallways in the Apostolic Palace, he began to feel every one of his eighty-five years, but he couldn't help but wonder about the future. The American President was a powerful speaker, yet her message was replete with the signs of the Apocalypse.

Kneading his hands, Domingo worried about the crowds that would be gathering in Saint Peter's Square. In two days, all of Christendom would attend Christmas Evening Mass, and the city would have over 100,000 worshippers.

Domingo slowly climbed the steps to the Papal Apartments, and as he crossed the entryway, he heard the powerful voice of the Pope being broadcast throughout the grounds. Such things were simulcast worldwide to the faithful.

"Ave Maria, gratia plena; Dominus tecum: benedicta tu in mulieribus, et benedictus fructus ventris tui Iesus."

Domingo paused and knelt as the Pontiff recited the Angelus prayer.

As the traditional 6:00 p.m. prayer ended, the Pope waved at those gathered in the courtyard below, then turned away from the window. His gaze fell on Domingo, who was just getting up off his knees. The Pontiff rushed over to help him stand. "Domingo, my friend, I hope your arthritis is not hampering you too much and that you are in good health."

The warmth of the Pope's genuine affection removed any discomfort that Domingo may have felt, but he knew that the Pontiff never watched television, so it was his duty to inform him of the latest events.

"Your Eminence, the American President has given word of a great change that is about to come. I fear that the signs all scream of an end to all that we know. There will be great fear in the flock that gathers here in two days, for they will have heard what is coming."

The Pope turned and took Domingo's arm, urging him to follow toward the window. "Tell me, what is it that concerns you? What could the American have said that has you so upset?"

"Holy Father, it was just some of the warnings. It matched the nightmares that I've had of late. The American President spoke of rocks flying down from the heavens, setting fire to anything that they touch. She spoke of the sun itself falling into darkness. I fear that the reactions that everyone will have will lead to panic. There are already riots in the streets of Rome, smoke is billowing from the battles throughout Italy ... it is getting worse."

The Pope laid his hand on Domingo's shoulder and gave it a gentle squeeze. "You forget that the Lord has promised us tribulations such as these, and promised that they hail a new and glorious day. This is not a time to fear, but a time to rejoice. Domingo, when you give the messages to all, I refer you to our Lord's words. The pact that we have is unbroken. I'll quote for you in Acts 2:16 the passage that reads:

'And it shall be in the last days,' God declares,

'That I will pour forth of my spirit on all mankind;
and your sons and your daughters shall prophesy,
and your young men shall see visions,
and your old men shall dream dreams.
Even on my servants, both men and women,
I will in those days pour forth of my spirit.
I will show wonders in the heaven above,
and signs on the earth beneath,
blood, and fire, and vapor of smoke.
The sun shall be turned into darkness,
and the Moon into blood.
Before the great and glorious day of the Lord shall come.
And it shall be that whoever calls on the name of the Lord shall be
saved. "'

The Pope turned to Domingo and smiled. "It is this that you must tell the people. For it is this message that they need to hear. Have faith on this beautiful evening, for tomorrow brings us a greater world."

Taking a deep breath, Domingo kissed the Holy Father's ring and promised, "I will do it right away, your Eminence."

Domingo turned and strode as fast as his feet would carry him.

As he set foot outside the Apostolic Palace, the chilled breath of a winter breeze blew across the courtyard, sending a shiver through his frail body. The brightness of the full Moon drew his gaze upwards into the heavens, and he sent the Lord a small prayer.

As he stared at the Moon, the Pope's words rang loudly in Domingo's head: *"The sun shall be turned into darkness and the Moon into blood."*

At that moment, the Moon flared with a white light that, for a few seconds, rivaled the brightness of the sun. As Domingo shielded his eyes and the brightness dimmed, the Moon turned dark red and seemed to shrink before his very eyes.

With a surge of energy, Domingo raced across the courtyard to his offices. The only thought in his panic-stricken mind was that he needed to give the world the Pope's message.

CHAPTER THIRTY-SIX

Sitting in the mission commander's chair, Dave leaned back as the clock ticked down on the large middle screen. The president paced back and forth as the time elapsed. Dave would have sworn that if she had been a cat, her tail would be swishing back and forth in agitation.

Dave knew only a handful of the dozens of engineers manning the computers. Most of the ones he knew were originally part of the ISF and had gone into careers in the Air Force working for NORAD, the North American Aerospace Defense Command.

As the timer counted down below one minute, Dave tensed. An image appeared on the left-hand auditorium screen: a near-perfect visual of the Moon. The warp ring around it had just begun to glow.

Suddenly, an engineer's voice broadcast through the command center's speakers.

"Mission Commander, we have T-minus 30 seconds until activation. The warp ring around the Moon has begun to charge, and we have a visual signal incoming from the Palomar Observatory. They report having the telescope locked on target."

Dave leaned forward in his seat and the room practically crackled with nervous tension as the launch director counted down the final seconds.

"Five ... four ... three ... two ... one ... launch!"

The ring around the Moon grew tremendously bright, it was almost like looking at the filament of an old incandescent bulb.

Speaking into the microphone attached to his lapel, Dave ordered, "T-COM, give me telemetry data on the Moon's motion. What do we have?"

"Mission Commander, we have lateral deviation from the Moon's normal orbit. Detecting an acceleration of 20 meters per second squared ... correction, the acceleration has increased to 40 meters ... 60 meters ... holding at 60 meters per second squared.

"Mission Commander, the Moon is on target and after thirty seconds, has a velocity of 4,000 miles per hour and has travelled 16 miles."

Dave felt euphoric as he witnessed the creation he'd slaved over slowly break the Moon free from its natural orbit. It was all that he could do to keep the excitement from his voice.

"Roger, T-COM, give me a minute-by-minute update or an immediate one if you detect something unexpected."

Dave watched the video and listened to the regularly updated acceleration numbers and the ever-increasing speed of the Moon. Suddenly the warp ring flared so bright that the entire screen grew white, and then the signal went offline.

"What the hell happened?" Dave yelled needlessly into the microphone, because everyone in the entire auditorium could easily have heard him. "T-COM, what's the status from Mount Palomar? Is the video offline? What's the telemetry?"

The telemetry and communications engineer stammered, "S-sir, Palomar is resetting their imaging computer. Some kind of light flare that overloaded their sensors. They need thirty seconds to come back online."

The president walked stiff-legged to Dave with an expression of both anger and fear. "Did the Moon just blow up?"

Dave covered the microphone and whispered, "I have no idea. We're blind here. I can't see shit without instruments."

The communications engineer reported, *"Mission Commander,*

we're getting several messages from various air bases all reporting the same thing. A flash of light and the Moon turning red and then disappearing."

The president turned to Dave as his mind reeled. A red Moon could mean only one of two things.

"T-COM, we need a visual. Track the Moon's path. Do we have any changes to acceleration data before, during, or after the incident?"

The lost video signal from Mount Palomar came back online. The screen flickered and then showed empty space as one of the telemetry engineers spoke through the intercom. *"Sir, Mount Palomar is moving the telescope along the path the Moon should have taken. Unfortunately, the last telemetry data we received was off the scale, so we can't know for certain what happened."*

Margaret turned to Dave and nodded toward the panning video image of empty space: the place where the Moon should have been. "I don't see rubble or dust or anything. Any theories?"

"Mission Director, we've gotten over 100 confirmed reports of a red Moon and one of our engineers has visually verified that the Moon is currently not visible in the night sky."

Dave shook his head with disbelief and spoke into his microphone. "Keep looking, T-COM. Tell Palomar to focus on the debris field that the Moon was aiming for. Also, where have these messages come in from?"

Hitting the mute button on the mic, he turned to the president and shrugged. "I know what can cause someone to see a red Moon, one of them is easy to explain–smoke from a forest fire can cause that. However, I seriously doubt—"

"Mission Director, the messages ... they've come from everywhere. As far north as Joint Base Elmendorf-Richardson out of Alaska, we have reports from the CFB Cold Lake out of Alberta, and we also have several from McChord Field out of Washington state."

"Well," Dave grumbled. "No chance that we have a forest fire in the middle of Alaska, Canada, and Washington all at the same time. No, this looks like—"

"Mission Director, Palomar is now focusing on the debris field."

Dave stared at the left-hand screen as the fuzzy image came into focus. Slowly the dark image began to show a gray background that seemed out of focus, while along the very edges of the image were dark gray objects hanging in suspension. They were clear images of asteroids, but Dave instantly knew something was wrong.

The president pointed and asked, "Is that the debris field?"

"I don't know," Dave responded gruffly as he stood. He felt that same uncomfortable sensation he always got when he didn't have all the information he needed. He growled into the mic, "T-COM, what's the diameter of that opening? Are we focused in too close? Also, the gray out-of-focus background, how far back is that?"

"Mission Director, Palomar reports that the field of view is 120,000 miles and that the gray background is the second wave of debris, 13,000,000 miles behind the first wave."

Dave felt stunned into inaction, and then a crooked smile bloomed across his face as he glanced at the president. "I suppose it's time for us to fasten our seatbelts. I'm not exactly sure how he did it, but Burt blew a hole straight through that debris field big enough for us to weave our way through."

Dave hadn't considered that the Moon could have accelerated as aggressively as it did. It dawned on him that, due to the Moon's lower mass and the overall larger size of the gravity bubble, it was possible.

A rush of adrenaline raced through him. Dave spoke into his microphone, "T-COM, bring the Ecuador substation comms officer online. I need to talk to him. GNC, I need guidance systems online. Bring the navigation computers up and set controls for immediate readiness.

"Launch Director, do all your system checks. I want a launch sequence started now, with a thirty-minute countdown.

"Doctor Radcliffe blew a hole through that debris field for us, let's not waste it.

"We're about to make history, people."

CHAPTER THIRTY-SEVEN

"What do you mean Doctor Patel was on the Moon?" Margaret stared at General Keane in disbelief. "Why the hell did you let...." She bit her tongue with frustration as she remembered how upset the scientist had been and that she'd given Walter free rein on letting Neeta go to another site. Margaret just never in a million years would have thought that Doctor Patel would go up to the Moon.

Dave, who'd been standing nearby, pressed his lips firmly together, shook his head, and turned away as he focused on the countdown that had already commenced.

"I'm sorry, Madam President, but you—"

"I know." Margaret waved his explanation away. "It's not your fault. I just didn't think she'd give up on life like that ... she would have been such an asset to everyone down here." Feeling the heat rising in her face, Margaret dismissed the general and sat in the nearest chair, deeply regretting some of her most recent decisions.

With fatigue weighing heavily on him, Stryker finally left the evacuation center's receiving area. It had been a full week since he'd arrived, reunited with his family, and helped organize the duty details for the MPs in his unit.

The Poconos Evacuation Center was enormous. It housed over 5,000 people and the buildings occupied nearly four square miles, most of it serving as housing.

Walking along the dirt-packed road that formed the evacuation center's main artery, Stryker heard the sound of rapid footsteps.

"Dad!" Isaac's voice rang loudly.

Both kids raced toward him, and he was nearly tackled to the ground when they slammed into him.

Emma yelled in her high-pitched voice, "Mommy said we can say goodnight before we go to bed."

"She did?" Stryker gazed toward Lainie as she walked through the thin crowd in their direction, an amused expression on her pixie-like face.

She'd been pretty cool toward him when they'd all reconnected at the evacuation site, but lately he'd caught glimpses of her sarcastic humor, despite their grim surroundings.

Lainie rubbed her arms and complained, "It's getting chilly out here."

"Oh, that's a good point," Stryker remarked. He walked over to a large pile of quartered logs and grabbed one of the twenty-five-pound bundles. "Here, I'll bring this over to your bunks. This'll help keep things cozy."

The kids began skipping ahead and Stryker smiled. "They seem to be adjusting pretty well."

"They are," Lainie replied. "I'm actually pretty surprised, considering what everyone around here has been through." She blew into her hands and made chattering noises with her teeth. "I hate the cold."

He wrapped his arm around her shoulder. She shuddered, but didn't pull away. "Are you okay?"

"I'm freezing."

"But it's warm where you and the kids are staying, right? I tried making sure you have enough firewood and those warm chemical packs for the bed."

"We're fine. After Emma kept stealing Isaac's blankets, I made the two of them sleep in the same bed so Isaac doesn't freeze in the middle of the night." She laughed. "I think our little blanket thief might actually be a sleepwalker. One time, I watched her get out of bed, yank her brother's covers off him, and then go right back to sleep. She did it while I was sitting up in bed watching."

Stryker sighed, wishing he could have been there to see it. He'd been sleeping in the barracks to keep peace with Lainie. He turned toward her and she looked up, meeting his gaze for a moment, then turned back to the kids.

"How's Jessica's new boyfriend?"

Lainie shook her head. "I'm not getting in the middle of you two. Go talk to your sister if you want the dirt on them."

The two walked in silence for a few moments. Every once in a while, she'd bump into him, and it made him think fondly of when they used to take walks in Central Park.

Before he knew it, the kids veered off the main street and Isaac swiped his finger on the biometrically keyed door.

The door swung open, and Stryker hefted the pile of wood onto his shoulder. "I'll start the fire for you guys."

Moments later, he had the fire roaring in the small cottage that served as his family's home. He kissed the kids goodnight and lingered in the doorway as he watched them snuggle under the warmth of thick blankets.

Lainie wrapped her arm around his and whispered, "Are we going to be okay?"

Stryker nodded. "I have full confidence in whatever those scientists are doing. I mean, have you seen—"

"No, you goof ball." She gently elbowed his ribs and sighed. "I mean you and me. I miss us."

His heart skipped a beat as he gazed down at Lainie, spying tears in her eyes.

What did she mean? She hated what he did. Hell, he was wearing his MP uniform and openly carrying a sidearm.

"Lainie, I thought you couldn't—"

"The kids need both of us."

A warmth spread through him as he felt her leaning against him. "What do *you* need?"

"You to spend more time with us ... with me."

Just as Stryker opened his mouth to ask a question, Lainie put a finger to his lips. She snaked her arm around his neck and pulled him in for the first real kiss he'd had from her in years.

"Madam President?"

Margaret had calmed herself and was watching the final minutes of the countdown as she received her first update from a nervous FEMA representative. "It was low tide on the east coast," said the representative, "and the water there began rising very quickly. We just received a report that there was a small breach of the sand embankments that the Army Corp of Engineers had built along the coast of South Florida. Luckily, it only affected a lightly-developed area one-hundred-and-sixty miles north of Miami. I've not yet received reports from elsewhere along our coast, but there have been reports worldwide from those countries that were at high tide seeing the water rush out to sea."

Even though Dave had been staring at some of the data scrolling on the video screens, he'd clearly overheard the report, as he leaned back in his chair and commented without taking his eyes off the data on the distant wall, "I know they've been told, but warn your peers in those countries again that the tide will slosh back and forth for a bit before it finally settles down. Now that the Moon is gone and we'll be losing any influence from the sun soon enough, the concept of a high or low tide will end up disappearing."

Margaret leaned forward to get a good look at the blonde woman's badge. The FEMA rep nervously glanced back and forth between Dave and the president. "Listen, Jennifer, calm down. Just do as Doctor Holmes said, keep us apprised of what's going on, and have faith." Margaret looked up at the nervous federal worker and attempted her warmest smile. "Now go ahead and remind all of your coworkers about what Doctor Holmes said. That's something that people should keep in mind if they're going to do their jobs well."

"Yes, Madam President." Jennifer nodded rapidly, turned, and raced from the Control Center.

Margaret watched Dave settle into the Mission Director's seat. Despite the death of a loved one and the news of a colleague's unexpected death, he clearly had swallowed whatever he was feeling and remained in control. She nodded approvingly at the man. He was obviously one of the most intelligent people she'd likely ever know, but he was probably as mentally strong as many of the military personnel she'd served with.

Feeling a surge of relief, Margaret relaxed a bit, knowing that it wasn't her that would likely have to make any decisions for the moment. All of the logistics and details were in Doctor Holmes' capable hands. She turned to the screen and watched as the countdown crossed the five-minute mark.

The Launch Director's voice broadcast through the Control Center's auditorium, *"NORAD Mission Control, we are now at T-minus five minutes and counting for Warp Ring activation."*

Dave's voice carried loudly across the chamber as he spoke into his microphone, *"PAO, start the simulcast of the countdown along with the telemetry readings. Let everyone watch what's going on, especially since all of humanity's fates are now undeniably linked."*

The rail-thin Public Affairs Officer raced from one workstation to another and activated the external broadcast so that the world could see and hear what Mission Control was doing. He turned and flashed a thumbs-up to Dave, then raced back to his terminal.

"For all within the reach of my voice, this is David Holmes, acting as Mission Director and broadcasting from the NORAD Command Center located within the Cheyenne Mountain Complex. We are now approaching the four-minute mark before we activate the Warp Ring around the Earth, which is a component of DefenseNet."

Dave tapped on his microphone, muting it, and yelled across the thirty feet separating him from the Public Affairs Officer, "Can they see the contents of screen one?"

The officer nodded and yelled, "Sir, I'm broadcasting everything from all of the screens."

Tossing a thumbs-up in the direction of the PAO, Dave tapped on the microphone and began to explain as the countdown commenced.

"When the countdown hits zero, you will almost immediately see the Warp Ring get brighter as we activate what I like to call a gravity bubble. This is when we'll actually begin moving.

"Just so you know, when we start moving, you won't feel a thing. We're playing tricks with how gravity works, and even though we'll start moving fairly quickly at a constant acceleration, you won't feel a change in the momentum because we're in that gravity-isolated bubble I mentioned.

"You won't see any immediate changes when things start. However, as time goes on, the Earth will begin traveling faster and faster.

"Even though most of you do realize that the Earth is always moving, for simplicity's sake, let's assume we aren't moving right now.

"Ten seconds after we activate the Warp Ring, we'll be travelling at nearly 1,400 miles per hour.

"After ten minutes, we'll be going over 80,000 miles per hour, and after only five days, we'll be travelling nearly one-tenth the speed of light.

"I know for many of you, it's hard to grasp such speeds, so let me give you something more tangible to compare it against.

"When Voyager 1 blasted off in 1977, it took it thirty-five years to leave the solar system and enter interstellar space. We'll be doing it in five days.

"Over the next few days, you'll notice that the sun will begin to grow dimmer. In addition, the color will change from what it is today, and slowly turn more orange and eventually red. By the time we are five days away, the sun will look like a large red dot in the sky and will slowly begin to fade away.

"As Mission Director, I will give daily updates as we travel to our final destination, a star which, when we arrive, should seem very much like our own sun."

Dave glanced at the countdown time as one of the engineers

motioned toward him. *"This is Launch Control. We are at T-minus 1 minute and holding. All positions stand by to give status."*

Margaret had never seen a launch sequence before, and she watched with fascination as Dave probed each of the Mission Control assets to see if they were all ready to go.

"Launch Director?"

"All systems are go."

"Substation Engineering?"

"All substations are operating within normal parameters."

"Navigation?"

"Navigation is go for launch."

"T-COM?"

"All communications are stable. Launch computers are functioning normally. All systems are go."

Dave sent a thumbs-up to the Launch Director and said, *"Roger that, Mission Control, we are go for launch. Launch Director, commence with countdown."*

Margaret sat higher in her chair as she watched the seconds counting down. It looked as if everyone in the room was holding their breaths. Margaret tightened her grip on the armrests while the final seconds counted down.

"T-minus five seconds ... four ... three ... two ... one ... activate!"

Margaret felt nothing, but one of the video screens that had been focused on the sky brightened slightly as the power was throttled up and sent through the Warp Ring.

"This is NORAD mission control, we have all taken our first step into a new age ... we have confirmed forward relative motion!"

Cheers erupted through the auditorium, and a thrilling sense of euphoria washed over Margaret. Everyone stood, faced Dave, and began clapping. She could only imagine what it must have been like for all of those millions, if not billions, of people who were watching in anticipation. The world was likely cheering along with the people in the control center.

All those promises she'd made to the world, the hopes that were hanging on this one last thread—it had worked. She swallowed hard as the thrill of the moment flushed through her, and she wiped away tears that threatened to spill down her cheeks.

Dave smiled and spoke into the microphone, *"T-COM, post on screen number two our speed and distance travelled. I'm sure we'll all want to be looking at that over the next nine months.*

"Mission Control team, job well done. Remember, we still have a long trip ahead of us. I will report regularly to everyone, starting tomorrow at 2:00 p.m. GMT, which is 9:00 a.m. eastern time."

Margaret stood, walked over to Dave, and gave him a bear hug as she whispered, "You know that you'll be forever known as the father of a new space age."

With a sheepish expression, Dave stepped back and shrugged. "I won't let it get to my head."

With a friendly smack on his arm, Margaret smiled. "We still have a lot of work to do, but for now, it's time to celebrate."

Margaret climbed out of her military transport to visit a nearby shelter in Colorado Springs.

She looked up in the sky, and even though she was bundled up in a jacket, she shivered at the bone-chilling cold. It certainly didn't help that they were 6,000 feet above sea level and it was the middle of winter. It was noon, yet the small orange disk of the sun seemed very far away as the Earth sped toward a distant star.

It had been just over four days since they'd begun their journey. Thankfully, the critical part associated with the first day was over. Dave and the rest of the Control Team had managed to avoid the waves of debris that had been heading straight for Earth and angle the planet toward its final destination.

The only unusual sign at the beginning of their journey was the light show from the shooting stars high up in the atmosphere. By some miracle, none of the debris that ended up hitting the Earth's atmosphere actually landed in any populated areas. There were scattered reports of explosions high up in the sky, though, and in some cases, the explosions were strong enough to rattle windows for hundreds of miles.

Now that the Earth was on the outskirts of the solar system, so many things had changed.

The farther they went, the less difference there was between night and day. At this latitude, the land was in a constant twilight due to the distance they were from the blazing ribbon of light shimmering over the equator.

A colonel from her escort approached, saluted, and motioned to a distant building. "Madam President, evacuation site CS-Alpha is ready for you."

Margaret barely held back her instinct to return the salute, and instead smiled at the fatigue-wearing soldier. "Thank you, Colonel Hawkins, lead the way."

As they walked the breadth of the evacuation site, the colonel said, "Madam President, Evac Site CS-Alpha is an overflow site, so we're mostly housing people that the first line of evacuation sites didn't have room for. About half of our 10,000 evacuees are from somewhere along the coast of California and the other half mostly comes from the Gulf coast."

The colonel panned his arm along the dirt road that ran down the middle of the encampment. "This is the main street, where no motorized traffic is allowed other than emergency vehicles. Otherwise it's a pedestrian-only zone. We have all the comforts of home that you might expect; we've got a PX which takes ration cards as payment, so from there you can buy all of your items—like toothpaste, clothes, and other sundries."

Margaret noticed a red cross painted on a multi-story building ahead and to the right. "Hospital?"

"Yes, Madam President. We've got a one-hundred-bed hospital with a state-of-the-art operating theater located within." He waved to the north and said, "On the far side of the main street is our residential area. It may look like a snow-covered field, but we have well over one-thousand homes, each of which can house up to six people, and a barracks area which can house almost eight-thousand people."

"Where do people go to get information about what's happening? Like, if they want to see what's going on with our travel, or if there's a public address they need to see?"

The colonel pulled a box-like device from his belt and showed Margaret that it had a video screen displaying the broadcast coming from NORAD Mission Control. "Each family was assigned a portable video receiver, and we have a repeater antenna which broadcasts the signal to this location for everyone to see."

The colonel put the receiver back on his belt and turned left toward a very large building. He opened the door and invited Margaret to enter.

The smell of freshly baked bread and hamburgers on the grill hit her.

The colonel remarked matter-of-factly, "This is our chow hall."

The building was easily several hundred feet long, and fifty-feet wide, and had a steady flow of people coming in and out.

"We serve food around the clock, and I'll freely admit that I've probably put on a couple of pounds since I've arrived. It's actually pretty good."

Watching the orderly crowds stand in line to fill their plates and the smiling faces of the kids sitting along the hundreds of bench seats, Margaret couldn't help but smile. Some of the people closest to her peered up as they walked by.

A handful of the citizens gasped, their eyes widening with recognition, and one of the women called out, "President Hager, are we going to be okay? I've heard about the terrible riots in San Francisco, something about a cult?"

Margaret turned and walked toward the woman. Having received regular reports about the bloodshed associated with rooting out the Brotherhood, Margaret wasn't sure how many details of the extermination teams she'd sent out had reached the public.

Laying her hands on the frightened woman's shoulders, Margaret spoke loudly enough for others to hear. "I know you've heard what that group called the Brotherhood has done. Their evil won't be tolerated in a civilized society, and I swear to you—they won't bother us again.

You're safe here, and by the time we get to where we're going, nobody will have to worry about those crazy people again."

One of the men standing nearby was holding a young child, no older than George, and he leaned closer and said, "I was telling Xavier, my son, that it was getting darker only because we were going to a new place. A place where we can all be safe. Isn't that right, President Hager?"

Margaret smiled, cupped the young child's face, and addressed him directly. "Xavier, we'll be traveling super speedy to get to our new home. I know your dad's worried, but I think you can help him. Can you promise me that you'll be a big boy and protect your dad while we travel to our new home? He needs to know everything will be okay."

The young boy blinked and, with a determined expression, gave Margaret a nod. Xavier immediately wrapped his arms around his father's neck, kissed him on the cheek and said, "It'll be okay, Daddy, I'll protect you."

Margaret glanced at the colonel and pointed at the line of people. "Let's get a plate of food. I want to sit with these folks and just talk to them, see how things are going for the rest of them. You know, soak the environment in and see if there's anything actionable I can take away from this."

The door behind them opened and a bitterly cold gust of wind blew in, making the hairs on the back of Margaret's neck stand on end.

As the colonel led her toward the line of people who were waiting for food, she silently worried about what it would be like just a few weeks later as the sun's warming influence completely disappeared.

CHAPTER THIRTY-EIGHT

Staring at the video screen in Mission Control, Dave sat at one of the terminals, feeling ill. He closed his eyes and listened to the doomed voices of the mining crew sending goodbyes to their family. He swallowed hard against the lump that had formed in his throat. Having only just been briefed about the stragglers from several of the mining colonies, who for whatever reason hadn't been able to reach Earth before they left, Dave couldn't help but think about Bella and wonder if all of these deaths were somehow preventable.

He turned to one of the engineers, who had tears running down her cheeks, and asked, "How many does that make?"

The woman quickly wiped the tears and responded, "Sir, that's twenty-two from the asteroid mining expedition, and there were another 125 souls left behind as well from other installations."

Pursing his lips, Dave nodded. Somehow he knew that he'd carry the emotional scars of each of those lost lives. All of them sons, daughters, husbands, wives. People who he felt responsible for.

"Sir!" The engineer pointed at the screen. "That's coming from the Asteroid Survey Ship. They're located approximately in the same position as Earth would have been, had we not left."

"Only forty-five days too late, I'm afraid," Dave muttered deject-
edly as he looked up at the screen.

Then he gasped as he saw something that sent a chill through him.

The space station's wide-angle camera feed was broadcasting
across many millions of miles showing the beginning of the end.

Undulating yellow streamers of hot gases snaked out from the sun.

The black hole's influence was now near enough that the sun itself
was being visibly affected.

Billowing clouds of gas reached across the darkness of space
toward the dark sphere, the ends quickly twirling around the rapidly
spinning black hole. Suddenly, two jets of super-heated gas blasted
from the top and bottom of the black hole.

Dave had seen evidence of such things from hundreds of millions
of light-years away.

He knew that searing waves of energy had to be billowing from the
event.

More streamers from the sun's outer surface were being pulled like
threads toward the incoming doom.

Not having been mic'd, Dave hopped up on his feet, pointed at the
comms engineer across the room, and yelled, "T-COM, make sure
that's being broadcast! I want everyone to see how narrowly we
escaped total annihilation."

The camera angle veered wildly as the space station was obviously
being pummeled by unimaginable gravitational forces, yet the camera's
direction shifted and pointed back at the black hole.

"Someone is still alive there," Dave whispered with awe. "They're
sending this to us as their last selfless act."

The black hole was no longer recognizable.

The darkness was gone, replaced by a tiny, pulsing ball of glowing
destruction, with beams of unimaginable energy spearing into space
from both its bottom and top.

Over the next ten minutes, Dave watched the image of destruction
draw closer and closer.

He'd known from the beginning that the space station was doomed,
but now everyone watching would know it as well.

The licks of spinning hellfire drew ever closer as the video became grainy.

"The transmission from the space station is likely being warped. The signal itself is being bent by the tremendous gravity of the black hole."

And suddenly, the transmission ended.

Dave grabbed a mic and spoke into it, "Let's pray for those twenty-two souls and the other 125 that never made it. We've all just witnessed what could have happened to us all if we'd stayed behind."

Dave frowned as he watched the video feed with the president on his left.

"This is Nigel Collins with BBC News reporting on the great purge of 2066. The wave of chaos that has plagued Britain is now officially over as the last of the death cult known as the Brotherhood of the Righteous have been arrested or killed. From as far north as the Shetland Islands and as far south as St. Agnes on the Isles of Scilly, Britons have rooted out this festering evil that had laid waste to so many innocents over the years. Thousands are now dead, but that pales in comparison to the reported millions who have been killed worldwide."

Dave winced as he watched macabre scenes from all over the world. Funeral pyres in India, mass burials in China, and a veritable slaughterhouse of blood where groups of the fanatics had banded together and were destroyed by the world's armies.

"And to put an end to this scourge, I'm happy to report that a Borislav Rakovsky, the charismatic leader of this cult, has finally met his maker in a bloody battle outside the city of Pernik in Western Bulgaria."

Dave was taken aback by the gory image of a bloodied face with paper-white skin. "An albino?"

Margaret nodded. "I should have gone public sooner about the threat of those assholes...."

Taking in a deep breath, Dave watched as more images of gore and death displayed on the screen and shook his head. "I've had enough of anger and violence." He glanced at the president. "Don't get me wrong, I wanted all of them dead. But I have to admit that for a little while after Bella's death, I wanted to flush all of us down the astrological toilet that was the black hole. I didn't care anymore. But I don't think that's what Bella would have wanted, and it's not what I want anymore. I'm on this Earth for a reason, I know that. At least I know that now."

A ringing sound echoed from a speaker hidden in the president's desk. Dave looked down and saw the name "Karen Fultondale" just as Margaret tapped on the phone icon. "Karen, what's up?"

"President Hager, I have some unfortunate news. It seems there's been ongoing incidents throughout all of the prisons ever since we went public with what the Brotherhood cult has done. The factions that normally formed a stalemate in the prison system had turned to the members of the Brotherhood, and it seems like a wide variety of so-called accidents have happened. Thousands of them. Greg Hildebrand was one of those accidents."

Memories of that asshole raced through Dave's mind, and an anger that he thought he'd laid to rest bubbled up within him.

"Madam President, Hildebrand is dead. I strongly suspect that many of the guards have been complicit in these accidents that are happening throughout the prison system. I wanted to let you know about Hildebrand, but I'm wondering what actions you'd like to take."

With a sneer of disgust, Margaret barked, "Nothing. I might even consider commuting some sentences if we wipe every last one of those medieval animals from the face of the Earth."

Dave smiled as the FBI Director stammered her response.

"Y-yes, ma'am, understood. That's all I have to report."

Margaret winked at Dave and shared his smile. "Thanks, Karen, I'll talk to you during our next scheduled briefing." She tapped the phone icon, disconnecting the call.

Despite the news of the rampant death and destruction, Dave's spirits were surprisingly buoyant. "Soon enough, they'll all just be a memory."

"I certainly hope so," said Margaret, and nodded. "I also asked you in here for another reason. I don't know if you've been outside the compound at all, but the world's getting much colder."

Dave hadn't been outside since he'd arrived from Ecuador. He imagined that the warming effect of the Warp Ring wasn't exactly meeting everyone's hopes in fighting off the icy fingers of interstellar travel.

With a slide of her finger on the table, Margaret raised the volume so that they could hear what was being said nearly 1,400 miles away in Cleveland, Ohio.

"Good morning, folks. This is Peter Weston from WKYC, hovering over the Lake Erie waterfront. And I know for some of you, you're wondering if we should just start calling it the Erie ice rink from now on.

"It is currently one degree Fahrenheit in Cleveland, and it looks like today's high is expected to top out at a chilly fifteen degrees. For those of you keeping track, it has now been forty-six days since our departure, and as you all know, this winter has been one for the record books here in the Rock and Roll Capitol of the World. I just now received a report that says for the first time on record, all five of the Great Lakes have actually frozen over. Yes folks, you heard it here first, ice across all of the Great Lakes. All I can tell you is that you should all bundle up, because it looks like it's going to be a long winter.

"Oh, and if any of you ice fisherman are going out on Lake Erie to try your luck today, I'll be out there with you in a couple of hours, looking for some walleye. Save some for me.

"This is Peter Weston with WKYC saying, 'Keep warm and hug your loved ones tight.'"

Dave felt the president's gaze and he knew what she was thinking. She wanted to know if there was anything he could do about the cold.

Margaret tapped a button on the table and the video feed disappeared. "I've gotten reports that the polar ice caps are expanding at an unprecedented rate and sea levels have already dropped several inches worldwide. From what the climatologists are saying, they've estimated that globally, we are about twenty degrees cooler than we would normally be."

Dave turned his gaze toward the president and completely empathized with her concerns. He had the same worries. "I'd heard that food isn't a problem. People are otherwise getting by okay and not hungry, right?"

"Yes," Margaret confirmed. "Food supplies are actually fine. With the round-the-clock light near the equator, they're hitting records on food production, and luckily that excess is offsetting the food deficit we're seeing in the more northern and southern latitudes. Dave, do you think there's anything that can be done about the temperature ahead of getting to our destination? I'm just afraid that we may have some serious issues if it gets too much colder." The president cocked one of her eyebrows and gave him a half smile. "If you don't have any ideas, I understand–but you're usually full of surprises."

Dave turned to the president and said, "I may need to go get some lab equipment to test a few things—"

"Done."

"I'll need climate reports across all the latitudes north and south of the equator, and I suppose I'll need to talk to somebody who has a clue about meteorological models."

"No problem." The amused expression on the president's face grew obvious. "I'll make a few calls. Consider it done."

"After we're all settled, I'm taking a long vacation and hiding in a cave somewhere." Dave groaned as he stood. "Once I have the data, I'll need a couple days to crunch the numbers, but I'll see what I can do."

"I have complete faith that you'll do what you can." Margaret winked.

~

Standing in one of the half-dozen dining halls, Stryker and Lainie stood in front of the screen, waiting for one of the regular communications from NORAD.

Nearly everyone in the evacuation center tended to gather around the many video feeds to get the latest regularly scheduled news. If nothing else, it was soothing to hear from the people steering them to a new place.

Stryker blew a smoke ring with his breath as Lainie leaned against him, shivering.

Ever since they'd left the sun and everything humanity had ever known behind, it had gotten much colder.

The temperature had fallen so dramatically that some of the pine trees had literally exploded from the cold.

He and the rest of the MPs worked constantly to keep as much heat in the homes and gathering places as possible.

It wasn't enough, but everyone was coping as best they could.

Sometimes, Stryker wasn't sure what to make of Lainie. One moment she desperately wanted his company, and the next, he sensed some deep-seated fear within her. If nothing else, he and Lainie were living under the same roof again, though not always in the same bed.

He glanced at his kids who were rolling a ball back and forth with some of the younger kids. Either way, Emma and Isaac seemed excited to have everyone together.

He wrapped his arm around Lainie's waist and pulled her close. "Are you okay?"

"I'm still freezing."

Isaac and Emma broke away from the other kids and rushed toward them. The youngest slammed into his leg and gave him a big hug.

"So," Stryker asked, "are you two excited about the stuff the president said? I mean, when *I* was a kid, I could only dream of going to visit a new star. It's like stuff from my fantasies is becoming real."

With a pensive expression, Isaac nodded. "I think that's all pretty cool."

"Um, Daddy?"

"What, Emma?"

"Are vampires going to become real?"

Stryker laughed and shook his head. "No! What in the world would make you think that?"

"Well, you said sometimes fantasies become real. Aunt Jessica was reading a book about vampires to us and I was just wondering."

"No, vampires aren't real," Stryker reassured her.

"But what if they become real?" Isaac suddenly held a worried expression.

Stryker reached over to one of the strands of braided garlic hanging from the ceiling and broke off two cloves.

"Here," he said, handing Emma and Isaac one clove of garlic each. "Don't worry, but if you see a vampire, just show him this and he'll run away. Trust me, that's how it works."

Emma held the clove tightly in both hands and nodded. "It's true, they said that in one of Aunt Jessica's stories."

Stryker tousled both kids' hair and grinned at Lainie.

She'd been staring at him, and just before she turned away, he thought he'd caught a glimpse of her smiling.

After lots of tedious discussions with climatologists, who he at times felt were pulling answers out of their butts, and with the results from some of his own experiments, Dave had enough information to risk making a few changes.

He clipped a microphone to his lapel and glanced toward the Public Affairs Officer, who gave him a thumbs-up.

"This is NORAD Mission Control reporting in on the fifty-sixth day of our travels. Dave Holmes speaking again." Dave spoke into the microphone as he took his seat in the Mission Director's chair in the middle of the Control Center. "So far, we have travelled nearly 451 billion miles, which is about the same distance as light travels in approximately twenty-eight days.

"T-COM, bring up the video feeds from Mount Palomar and the GALEX2 orbiting telescope and put them on screen three."

Dave glanced at the constantly-updated telemetry data displayed on the screen on the left-hand side of the auditorium. They were at nearly ninety-nine percent of the speed of light, and he knew that in the next five minutes, they were going to make history yet again.

Hearing the door open and close behind him, and with the way that many of the Command Center staff began staring in his direction, Dave didn't have to look to know that President Hager was approaching.

"Doctor Holmes." The president's voice had a tinge of excitement in it. "This is another momentous occasion, isn't it?"

Dave muted his microphone. "It is. We're knocking on the doorstep of light speed."

The president took a seat to the right of Dave and asked, "I know I missed your call earlier, so do you think you'll be able to help with the cold weather?"

Dave nodded. "I did some testing, and it's not a perfect answer, but I think we'll be able to push a little bit more power through the Warp Ring. That'll end up making it a little brighter and should hopefully hold off some of the chill."

"We're now on average about twenty-two degrees lower than our previous average temperatures across the globe. How much do you think it will help?"

"Truthfully, I don't think it'll do much. Talking with some of the climatologists you hooked me up with, the best I think we can do is hold the current temperature. Maybe warm things a degree or two."

"Oh." Margaret sounded disappointed.

Dave turned to her, pointed to the ceiling, and explained, "You have to realize that the light we're getting from the Warp Ring can't compare to the overall power of the sun. Heck, not even close. And besides, it turns out we could probably push a bit more power than I'm planning on putting in with a good safety margin, but that'll end up scorching the areas along the equator. As it is, with the adjustment I'll be making, those folks will end up being about ten degrees warmer than normal. We can't exactly risk going much more than that."

The president nodded. "I understand."

"I should probably tell you the good news," Dave quipped.

Margaret leaned forward and stared quizzically at Dave. "Good news?"

"Yes," said Dave. "With the extra power I'll be putting into the Warp Ring, it'll change our acceleration curve quite a bit. It should shave about two months off our travel time."

"That's fantastic news!" Margaret's eyes widened, and she smiled from ear to ear.

Dave leaned back into his chair. "I figured that might soften the blow when you explain to everyone about the weather and what we can expect."

Margaret peered at the video screen displaying the contents from the telescopes and asked, "I know hitting the speed of light is a huge milestone, but what's with the telescopes? What are you looking for?"

"Well, I actually wanted to confirm something I'd always suspected." Dave raised his hand and pointed toward the video screen on the right side of the auditorium. "The video on the upper half of screen three shows what's behind us. None of the light is actually visible to the naked eye. We've red-shifted everything so far that it's at a longer wavelength than we can see. It's deep into the infrared."

Margaret shook her head and gave Dave a crooked smile. "Doctor Holmes, pretend for a moment I'm not well-versed in science. Red shift?"

"Oh, sorry. The way you see an object is based on the light that's being projected from it or reflected off of it. In the case of stars, they're projecting light." Dave paused and rubbed his chin, trying to think how to best explain the concept. "Let's say that you have a long string that you're waving back and forth. Imagine that the waves in the string is what light really looks like. It's simply a series of energy waves. Those waves all have a certain length to them. If you ran farther away with the end of the string, the waves would get longer. Light does the same thing when you move away from it. The wave still catches up to you, but from your perspective, it seems to be just a little bit longer. The longer the wave, the redder it appears. Eventually, the wave gets long enough that our eyes can't detect it. That would be when the light enters the infrared range, and that's what the upper half of screen three is showing. The stars behind us might not be visible to the naked eye, but for a telescope that can sense infrared, we can see it just fine."

"Is that why the Moon appeared to turn red," Margaret asked, "because it was racing away at such a high speed?"

"Yes, exactly right." Dave felt a moment of sadness as he was reminded of Neeta's ill-conceived choice.

The president pursed her lips in thought. "So is it like a rainbow, and if you're approaching, the waves get shorter, so they get more purple?"

Dave smiled. "We call it blue-shifting, but you're right. As we approach the light, the wavelength gets shorter and shifts further and further into the blue, then violet, and eventually into the ultraviolet range, which we cannot see except with special equipment. The lower half of screen three is showing what a satellite-based telescope can see, and most of what you see ahead in that sky is in the ultraviolet range. I'm actually most interested in seeing what happens to the light we're seeing when we finally reach the speed of light."

Dave glanced at their current speed and took his microphone off mute.

"T-COM, bring the Ecuador substation comms officer online."

"Ecuador substation is now online."

"We are at 99.5 percent of the speed of light and rising. This is Mission Director to Ecuador substation, increase power output by ten percent."

Dave watched as the total power flowing through the Warp Ring slowly rose, and correspondingly their speed began to climb ever faster.

With a smile, Dave turned to Margaret and asked, "Have you ever watched an old TV show called Star Trek?"

"Of course, I always had a thing for that Asian commanding officer," Margaret admitted with an uncharacteristic expression of embarrassment. "It's not a coincidence that my husband is the strong silent Asian type. I just can't remember the character's name."

Dave laughed. "His name was Sulu."

"That's right, Sulu! So you watched that old show too? I'd never met anyone else who ever pulled that out of the archives."

Dave smiled as he watched the speed approach 99.9 percent of the speed of light. "I've always wanted to say this...."

Just as the Earth's speed was about to cross that longstanding barrier of the speed of light, Dave pointed his arm forward and spoke into the microphone, "Mister Sulu, ahead warp factor one!"

At the exact moment that the Earth's speed crossed over the speed of light, the speakers crackled to life.

"Warp factor one, confirmed, sir!"

Dave barely managed to mute his microphone as he burst out laughing. The T-COM officer stood from his station, looked back at Dave, and gave him two smiling thumbs up.

Leaning closer to Margaret, who was also smiling, Dave commented, "I think we have another Star Trek fan."

Margaret glanced up at Dave and said, "We're truly now in a new era."

Dave turned his gaze at screen three and pointed at the upper half, which was completely black. "Just as I suspected, nothing. Even the telescope can't see anything behind us."

"I'd have thought we'd still see something. Shouldn't the wave just be even deeper into the infrared scale?"

Shaking his head, Dave glanced at their speed as it continued increasing past the speed of light. He felt a sense of accomplishment that nearly matched the moment when they'd first begun moving. "You'd think that would be the case, and normally I'd say you're right. However, if you think about it ... we're now travelling faster than light—"

"Oh!" Margaret exclaimed. "The light can't reach us anymore because we're outrunning it, right?"

"Exactly." Dave pointed at the lower part of screen three. "And that's also why we can still see the stars ahead of us. Well, at least we can with a UV detector."

Margaret stood and asked, "So how far out are we from our destination?"

Dave tapped on his microphone. "GNC, as planned, switch to our

ICRS2 coordinates using Tau Ceti as the origin and project based on our location and our current acceleration what our new arrival time is."

A few seconds elapsed before a response came back.

"Based on current data, we are approximately 154.75 days from orbital entry around Tau Ceti."

"Roger, GNC.

"To all that are listening, we are now travelling faster than the speed of light. Hang in there, and if all goes as planned, we'll get to where we're going about 63 days ahead of the previous schedule.

"I will report again from NORAD Mission Control at my normal hours. This is Dave Holmes, signing off."

Removing his microphone, Dave felt surprisingly calm as he stood, turned to Margaret, and said, "The next real milestone will be as we slow down and glide into position around our new star."

CHAPTER THIRTY-NINE

It had been almost two months since Stryker and his family had left the evacuation center. Lainie had spent a full week airing out the apartment, trying to rid it of the musty smells that inevitably developed when no air circulated in an enclosed place.

For Stryker, he couldn't have predicted how all of this would have ended. Yet here he was, standing in the back of an exhibit located in the Bronx chapter of the Burt Radcliffe Science Campus, holding hands with his ex-wife as the kids watched a short film on space exploration.

Lainie leaned her head against his shoulder and Stryker remarked, "Who'd have thought you'd have all these kids mesmerized by a movie all about science? The kids are really enjoying this place ... and I'm really liking our time together as well."

"Me too." Lainie squeezed his hand. "I don't want it to change."

"Even though I'm now back on the force?"

She sighed and hugged his arm. "It's who you are, it's just taken me a long time to learn how to accept it."

With butterflies in his stomach and his palms getting sweaty, he leaned his head against hers and whispered, "Will you marry me ... again?"

Lainie stiffened and Stryker turned her around to face him. Tears dripped onto her cheeks and he wiped them away with his thumbs. "What's wrong?"

She glanced down and held both of his hands in hers. "I have to confess something."

Stryker's eyes widened and his heart thudded loudly in his chest. "What?"

"I've been keeping a secret for a while, and I didn't know how to tell you...."

"What secret?" His mind raced into any number of dark alleys, and concern flushed through his very being.

She looked into his eyes as the movie ended and the kids began cheering. "What do you think about having another baby?"

"Well, I hadn't really—" He gasped. "No! Really?" A smile bloomed on his face as he leaned closer and whispered, "Are you pregnant?"

She nodded with a bashful smile.

Shock and happiness flooded through him as unbidden tears blurred his vision. "I love you, Mrs. Stryker. Please say you'll marry me, again."

"Yes, I'll marry you."

Stryker wrapped his arms around Lainie and gently lifted her off her feet just as Emma and Isaac found them.

Isaac yelled excitedly, "I really want to be an astronaut," while Emma proclaimed, "I'm going to be a 'physics-shun.'"

Dave walked into the Oval Office, peered at the room, and couldn't help but feel amazed at how bright everything was. After having lived inside a mountain for seven months, the brightness of the world and their new star was something he had to get used to again.

The president jumped from her chair and greeted Dave with open arms. "How are you doing?"

"I'm doing well," Dave replied. He in fact did feel better than he had in ages. He sorely missed Bella's companionship, but having immersed himself in the details of travel, and communicating regularly to the world about what to expect, it had all left him too busy to focus on his own troubles.

"Please, sit–let's talk a bit." Margaret guided him to a nearby sofa.

Dave glanced out the window at the bright sunshine and smiled. "It's so much nicer here than being in that shelter. I'd almost forgotten what it was like to be aboveground."

"I couldn't agree more, yet there's so much to do." The president nodded as she took a seat across from him. "The weather has changed quicker than I could have imagined. They're actually predicting that we'll hit eighty degrees today in DC. I read a report this morning saying that the ice caps had finally stopped growing and the climatologists think that globally, we'll get back to a pre-incident normal within two years. I don't think anyone could have guessed how quickly the planet's weather would change during our trip."

"Oh, definitely not," Dave harrumphed. "Those climatologists hadn't ever modeled such a thing, so I'm pretty sure they were just fabricating their numbers to help everyone feel better. The data those people had given me was all over the map. I'm beginning to wonder how many of their overall predictions are educated guesses versus scientific modeling."

Margaret smiled at Dave. "The weather isn't the only thing that's changing. Would you believe that crazy friend of yours in North Korea actually lowered his border? For the first time in generations, the people of North and South Korea are freely mixing. Rumor has it that many of the Supreme Leader's generals were executed to make that happen, yet it still happened." She turned to her desk and pointed at a stack of papers. "You see that? That's a few hundred requests from universities across the country applying for federal grants to expand their science programs.

"It shouldn't be a surprise that science is the new 'in' thing." The president leaned forward and looked in Dave's eyes. "There's a thirst for exploring our new environment. I find it ironic that it took the near-annihilation of our world to change peoples' attitudes, but our society wants to be a part of this new era. I think it has sunk in, and the public realizes for the first time that it wasn't talk, we really *are* in a new era. They want to explore our new solar system, study physics, learn about medicine, you name it–science is sexy. I'd never have guessed, but governments worldwide are setting aside their past aggressions and they want to look toward the future. I just got off the phone with the Israeli Prime Minister, and you know what he said?"

Dave shook his head.

"He told me that instead of the religious graffiti that used to fill some of the slums in poorer parts of Israel, they are now seeing images of rocket ships, comets, and pictures of astronauts. Dave, what you've inadvertently managed to do is inspire the entire world. I need your help with this."

Dave opened his mouth to say something, but before he could utter a word, Margaret continued to excitedly talk about recent events. "I just yesterday came back from the UN General Assembly," she said, "and there's a move afoot to construct a long-term plan for ceding more control not to the politicians, but to a yet-to-be-constructed scientific body. To head such a body, your name was obviously the first on the list."

"Not a chance in hell do I want to deal with governing anything." Dave shook his head vehemently.

Margaret smiled warmly. "I'm not asking that of you. I just want you to be involved. You have no idea how much people are talking about you. You're the voice that kept them comforted and sane through this journey. It certainly wasn't me. By reputation alone, you're almost a god-like figure to a vast majority of the world. You can do so much good with that...."

"I won't commit myself to anything for now. Besides, I want to take some time off and just think about what I'll do next."

"Oh, there's no immediate rush." Margaret smiled warmly. "The way these things work, it almost certainly will take quite a bit of time. I was just hoping to seed that thought in your head so that you might consider getting involved."

Dave rolled his eyes and returned Margaret's smile. "I'll think about it." Quickly changing the subject, he asked, "So did you guys ever settle on what you're going to do now that we're in a shorter orbit than we used to have?"

"Actually, yes." Margaret had a mischievous expression. "I put forward UN Resolution 12219 and it was approved without any real arguments."

"So?" Dave asked. "Are we going from January and ending at October now?"

"I think you'll get a kick out of this, because nobody else even blinked an eye when I suggested it. For the first time ever, we're going to have a universal calendar, and since we're orbiting a new star and the length of the year has shrunk to 300 days, we all agreed to reset the calendar to a new beginning. The first day in orbit is now officially known as Stardate 1.0. The first number is the year and second number is a day, from 0 to 299."

"Stardate 1.0 ... I love it." Dave chuckled. "It'll take a while for people to get used to, but I'm sure soon enough, people will look back at the old month-day-year format and think it was ludicrous."

Margaret pulled an envelope from her stylish dress jacket and handed it to Dave. "This is for you. You don't even need to open it now; I can tell you it's a receipt. While I was in the UN, there was another resolution that got an almost unheard of unanimous approval from the UN General Assembly. It does two things; one was depositing into an account all of the back pay you should have received throughout those four ridiculous years you were in hiding, and the other thing it does is restore your position as the head of the ISF. The job is yours whenever you want to take it back."

Dave stared at the envelope, at a loss for words. He'd assumed that he'd end up in a think tank in DC or something else, but hadn't considered the idea of going back and being involved with the ISF again. A thrill of unexpected excitement rushed through Dave as he looked up at the president and beamed. "I c-can't thank you enough for putting yourself out on my behalf."

Shocked at the level of emotion he suddenly felt bubbling up inside him, he swallowed hard and repeated once again, "Thank you."

About an hour before sunrise, Dave sat on the beach and stared as the waves broke on the sand. The warm breeze blew from the east, carrying the scent of the ocean, and he recalled how much Bella enjoyed the smell of the saltwater. He missed her desperately, but Dave also found himself yearning for the often-grumpy visage of Neeta wagging her finger at him, and he regretted not ever having a chance to know Burt more than he did.

"I'm lonely," Dave admitted it to himself. He knew that the only cure he had for loneliness was diving headlong into his work.

It had been just over two months since the world had settled around its new orbit. In those two months, so much had happened. As part of an agreement with the ISF, Dave had its headquarters facilities moved to central Florida, making it an official part of Cape Canaveral. It was his idea that the ISF should be closely associated with the space industry.

He'd finally bought a nice house, and even though he had nothing to do with government, the U.S. still had a detail of Secret Service agents assigned to him day and night.

Dave pulled the tripod of the telescope he'd brought closer and aimed it at planet Epsilon, the fifth planet circling Tau Ceti. Earth was now the sixth.

He glanced over his shoulder and noticed Tony, one of the agents assigned to him. Dave knew him well enough to know that the man was an amateur astronomy buff. As Dave peered into the telescope and aimed it at planet Epsilon, he said, "It's amazing how big Epsilon is. I know it's only about 23 million miles away, but it's huge. Over four times the Earth's mass. One day, we'll be visiting that place."

"Doctor Holmes, why is that star shimmering like that?" Tony asked. "If I didn't know better, I'd say it looks like it's getting bigger."

Dave looked up at where Tony was pointing and made a humming noise. "That's strange." He turned the telescope, and aimed it toward the gleaming white dot.

He peered into the eyepiece and, with a twist of the focusing ring, suddenly burst out, "What the hell? It can't be...."

"What? What is it?"

"Holy shit, Tony, it's the Moon! Our Moon!"

Dave's mind raced as he thought of the possibilities. He grabbed the telescope and began trudging through the sand, marching toward the car, all the while babbling in a manner that he was sure seemed incoherent. "If they really accelerated that quickly ... yes, that's why they seemed to disappear and everyone reported a red Moon. They actually did red-shift away and ... holy crap, they might actually still be alive! How's that possible?"

Tony yelled, "Slow down, you're not making any sense!"

His security detail clambered after him as Dave continued talking, even though he knew that Tony had no clue what he was talking about. Sometimes, when Dave's mind raced, he needed to verbalize his thoughts to help him sort through things. "Neeta probably programmed in the navigation on the Moon, and for all we know, the Moon might be coming into this area on autopilot. They probably didn't make it, but maybe they did."

Dave climbed out of the sand and ran toward his car. "We're only five minutes from the base. Let's find out!"

Showing his badge, Dave walked into the Mission Control Center, where only a handful of people worked at that early hour. He snapped his fingers to gain the attention of one of the engineers and yelled, "We have an incoming satellite! I need you to hail it!"

"Incoming satellite? What satellite?"

With a smile, Dave made a big circular motion with his hands. "It's a big, round rocky one. We used to call it the Moon. You're probably familiar with it."

The engineer blinked for a moment, unsure what to say, and then immediately dove for the nearest terminal. "Sir, I'm scanning the frequencies and I don't see ... oh wait! I've got a weak signal that matches Moon Base Crockett's frequency. I'm hailing it."

"Moon Base Crockett, this is Mission Control, can you read me?"

Dave paced back and forth as he waited anxiously for a response.

"Moon Base Crockett, this is Mission Control, can you read me?"

Dave turned to the engineer and said, "Isn't there a video feed that we used to get? See if it's active and patch into that as well."

"Yes, sir." The engineer's fingers became a blur on his keyboard, and he then pointed to the main screen. "Got it. Displayed on screen one."

Dave's heart raced as he saw what looked like the control center for the Moon base. It was still active.

Suddenly there was motion on the video feed. Burt walked into the room and began typing on a computer terminal. He glanced up into the camera and smiled. *"I read you loud and clear, Mission Control. It's good to be back in touch."*

Dave yelled, "I need a mic!" An engineer raced up to Dave and handed him a portable mic. He spoke into it. "Holy crap, you're alive!"

"How're you doing, Doctor Holmes? It's good to hear your voice. Unfortunately, I don't have a video feed on my end, but you sound great. We're still about six hours away, but if you don't mind, I'm going to get Neeta to put the Moon back into its normal spot orbiting the Earth."

Dave felt weak with relief as he stared at the screen. His throat suddenly felt thick, and he swallowed hard.

"So Neeta's okay?" Dave asked. "Where is she?"

Burt nodded. *"She's fine. She's just—oh, here she is—and I suppose I'll let her do the introductions."*

Dave watched Burt step out of the way, and Neeta's face appeared prominently on the screen. To Dave's amazement, a newborn infant rested quietly on her shoulder.

"Hi, Dave. I'd like you to meet Denise Radcliffe. She's two weeks old now."

Dave stood and spoke in a reverent tone. "She's beautiful. But ... how? Neeta, how did you all survive?"

Neeta smiled, her eyes glistening, and a tear rolled down her face. *"As I took the shuttle to the Moon, I came up with the plan. The warp ring around the Moon is much larger than Earth's, yet the Moon's mass was also significantly smaller than the Earth's. The acceleration profile we could initiate was much greater than we could do with the Earth. And because the warp ring was so large, I could hit the accelerator and pull all of the debris that was inside the ring away with me. The only thing that was tricky was whether or not I could thread the needle without us getting hit by anything.*

"We lucked out."

Dave blinked, and his cheeks began to hurt from smiling. "That's sheer genius ... oh shit!"

"What?" Neeta asked, as she turned back to face the camera.

"In just a couple of hours, nearly the entire world is about to have a ceremony that commemorates what you guys did ... dying to save our world. They've got statues and parks and all sorts of crap strewn throughout the globe." Dave began to laugh. "Well, you two are definitely leaving your mark on this world one way or another. I'm just glad you're alive."

Burt nudged his way in front of the camera and winked. *"To tell you the truth, the world can keep any of their ugly statues of me."* He leaned down to kiss the top of the baby's head, and Neeta grabbed Burt's hand and kissed it. *"These two girls are the only mark on this world that I care about making."*

EPILOGUE

Dave settled into the Mission Director's chair and clipped his microphone onto his lapel.

"T-COM, where are we with Explorer 1?"

"Explorer 1 has broken through planet Epsilon's troposphere and is at 90,000 feet. It is 348 miles from its landing target and descending at 4,000 feet per minute. Its current horizontal speed is 950 miles per hour. We should have touch down in approximately forty-five minutes."

Dave nodded. Everything seemed to be going as planned. "Roger that. T-COM, what are the temperature readings currently, and is there something wrong with the live video feed? Didn't I ask for it to be activated?"

"Mission Director, the video feed activation request was sent three minutes and fifteen seconds ago. Currently, the temperature at 85,000 feet is 17 degrees Fahrenheit, and infrared readings suggest that the surface temperature at the landing zone is approximately 153 degrees."

Neeta walked over from one of the terminals and chided Dave. "You do in fact realize that the two planets are 23,000,000 miles apart, don't you? It's going to take no less than four minutes for a command to be sent, responded to, and then received back here." She gave him that you-should-know-better expression that she usually reserved for people who said something inordinately stupid. "Those signals we're sending and receiving are still limited by that inconvenient speed-of-light thing."

"Remind me to talk to Frank again sometime about that." Dave crossed his legs and huffed with impatience. "For all we know, he might have come up with some crazy idea that breaks more of the rules and solves that problem."

Neeta pointed at the screen, which began displaying video images of the explorer module gliding through clouds and automatically adjusting its approach angle due to sudden cross-winds. "Well, until you and Frank pull a rabbit out of some hat, I suppose it's lucky that Burt's new AI and CPU designs are in the updated Explorer 1 module. Looks like the autopilot is working pretty well."

"Amen to that, my friend." Dave agreed.

It had been nearly twelve hours since Explorer 1 landed on planet Epsilon and deployed its rover. Dave watched as the rover raced over the dry, rocky path.

Neeta pointed at the screen and the camera veered wildly as the rover automatically turned to avoid a crevasse and continued toward what looked like a distant pile of rubble on the horizon. "Isn't it strange how straight that path is? I hate to speculate, but it almost looks like a road ... an old cracked and unmaintained one, but a road nonetheless."

Dave tried to remain skeptical, but something inside him felt she might be right—and that's what kept him awake at two in the morning, watching. "Maybe it's an old, dry riverbed."

Neeta gently smacked him on the arm and aimed a laser pointer at the edge of the so-called riverbed. "Dave, give me a break. If it were a riverbed, you wouldn't see the edges fall off like they do. This straight path is elevated above the rest of the ground by almost six inches. I don't understand how it could be natural, not with those straight lines going for as long as they have."

"GNC," Dave spoke into his microphone. "How far ahead is that outcropping on the horizon?"

"The rover's telemetry readings say it is 14.3 miles away."

Leaning back in his chair, Dave waited and silently wondered if there was any logical explanation for a straight elevated path that went on for miles and miles.

It was 3:00 a.m. and the rover slowly navigated through the rubble at the end of the long, rocky path. Dave had lost any hint of exhaustion.

"I don't believe it," he said, staring in awe at the unmistakable signs of what looked like demolished buildings amidst the rust-colored sand that made up the majority of this planet's surface.

Neeta pointed at some of the gray rubble. "Look at all those straight edges. Wait, that's a partially-collapsed wall with what looks like a window in it. Holy crap Dave—there is, or was, something on Epsilon that built this. There can't be another explanation!"

A flash appeared on the video screen and the speakers in the auditorium activated. *"Mission Director, the rover has detected movement."*

The camera angle turned quickly, and in the distance Dave saw a grayish blur zip across the reddish-brown background.

"Rover 1 has taken evasive maneuvers."

With his heart racing, Dave stood and watched helplessly as the rover tried to race away from the rubble. Any commands he sent now would take relatively forever to get there; the rover's artificial intelligence chip was in charge.

As the rover stumbled and climbed over rocks to get back to the outskirts of the demolished city, the camera angle suddenly veered upward and a warning printed on the video feed said, "Ground Traction: 0%."

The camera veered back and forth in a wild and unpredictable manner. It suddenly showed a metallic skull-like face, with lights where the eyes should have been, peering into the camera.

Neeta gasped. "Is that a ... robot?"

As all variety of warnings scrolled across the corner of the video broadcast by the rover, the metallic creature tilted its head quizzically in view of the rover's camera. Suddenly, a metal finger jabbed at the camera and the image went blank.

Dave fell back into his chair and weakly asked, "T-COM? What've you got?"

"I-I'm sorry, sir. We've lost contact with the rover."

AUTHOR'S NOTE

Well, that's the end of *Primordial Threat*, and I sincerely hope you enjoyed it.

I'll freely admit that when I began writing this story, I felt like I'd turned a page in my writing "career." For a long time, I'd written things geared for my kids to enjoy, mostly epic fantasy. However, it was never anything I took too seriously. I did it because it made my sons happy.

Along the way, I'd made friends with some rather well-known authors, and when I talked about maybe getting more serious about this writing thing, several of them gave me the same advice, "Write what you know."

Write what I know? I began to think about Michael Crichton. He was a non-practicing MD, and started off with a medical thriller. John Grisham was an attorney for a decade before writing a series of legal thrillers. Maybe there's something to that advice.

I began to ponder, "What do I know?" And then it hit me.

I know science. It's what I do for a living and what I enjoy. In fact, one of my hobbies is reading formal papers spanning many scientific disciplines. My interests range from particle physics, computers, the military sciences (you know, the science behind what makes stuff go boom), and medicine. I'm admittedly a bit of a nerd in that way. I've also traveled extensively during my life, and am an informal student of foreign languages and cultures.

With the advice of some New York Times bestselling authors, I started my foray into writing novels. With Primordial Threat, it's easy to imagine that I might focus solely on science fiction, but I'd note that I've always been a sucker for mainstream thrillers, especially those with international settings. Elements of that may have leaked into this novel, and I hope it was a welcome aspect to the story. I'd always been given the advice to not mix genres, ever, but I sometimes don't listen.

As I wrote that line, my wife was looking over my shoulder and claimed I never listen. *Thanks, dear.*

Truthfully, I hadn't intended to self-publish this novel. My intent was to send this to mainstream publishers. After all, I got lots of rave reviews from the traditionally published authors who'd read the manuscript. They were all very kind and a great source of encouragement.

I eventually did submit the story to acquiring editors at major publishers, and even though I'd received some interest from them, they all in the end felt it wasn't right for their particular audiences at that time. In hindsight, it's very difficult for an unknown author to "break into" traditional publishing, and for the acquiring editors, it's a big risk taking a chance on an unknown author. These are things I can fully appreciate.

Given that, I was faced with a choice of leaving the stories in a desk drawer and moving on with my life, or taking a chance and seeing if I could find the audience for my stories.

Obviously, I'm stubborn and chose the latter.

I'll assume that if you've just read these last few paragraphs, you've only done so because you've read this novel in its entirety, and I've hopefully kept you entertained. If so, that means I've found you! You're that elusive "audience" that the publishers had said they didn't know how to reach.

Yay!

If I could ask anything from you, dear reader, it would be to please share your thoughts/reviews about the story on Amazon and with your friends. It's through reviews and word-of-mouth that this story will find other readers, and I do hope *Primordial Threat* finds as wide an audience as possible.

Again, thank you for taking the chance on a relatively-unknown author and reading his debut science fiction novel. I should warn you, it's only the beginning.

It's my intent to release at least two books a year, one in the science fiction/technothriller category, similar in style to this book. The other book would be best categorized as a mainstream thriller with international influence.

You'll also find that at the end of each of my books, I talk about what's real and not real regarding the science. If you're curious about the scientific elements in this book, please check out the addendum.

That being said, I have released another story at roughly the same time as this novel. A mainstream thriller titled, *Perimeter*.

If you'll indulge me, below is a brief description of *Perimeter*:

Levi is a "fixer" in a fix.

The CIA needs his help. The Russian mob wants him dead.

With enemies closing in and nowhere to turn, he learns that the one person who may hold all the answers ... is his dead wife.

PREVIEW OF DARWIN'S CIPHER

Jon LaForce scrambled down the steep path leading into Tikaboo Valley and took a swig from the cheap red wine he'd bought from a nearby gas station. Almost immediately a flush crept up his neck and warmed his cheeks.

He'd just been fired for the second time this month.

He wasn't sure what had brought him out into the middle of nowhere in southeastern Nevada. When he was a kid, his friends used to talk about coming out here to spy on the military planes as they took off and landed. They used to whisper about secret experiments, mysterious clouds in the sky, and of course, UFOs. After all, this was supposed to be where they kept those aliens. Area 51.

Jon didn't believe any of that crap, and he doubted any of his friends had ever had the guts to actually sneak onto the grounds or even come out this way. And as he looked around, he had to admit they weren't missing much. Just acres of thick desert sagebrush.

Taking another swig from his bottle, Jon felt the buzz from the alcohol as he scrambled down the slope. Suddenly, something broke through the thick sagebrush at the bottom of the hill. Jon drew his Glock from its holster and took a shooter's stance. Bobcats sometimes prowled this area.

But it was just a stray dog. Dark brown coat, long tail, floppy ears —might be a chocolate lab.

Jon holstered his gun and whistled. "Hey, boy, what are you doing out here?"

The dog wagged its tail furiously and bounded toward him.

He screwed the top back on the wine bottle and held his hand out for the dog to sniff. As the animal huffed at his hand and ran its nose up and down the legs of his trousers, Jon noticed a bloody wound on its front right leg.

"Did something take a bite out of you, old boy?"

The dog whined and glanced back toward the scrub.

Jon scratched the dog's head. "Your coat's nice and shiny, and you look well fed." He shook his head and patted the dog on its back. "What are you doing out here? Someone's probably looking for you. Maybe I should get you to a shelter and see if they can find your owner. I sure as hell can't take care of you. I can barely take care of myself nowadays."

A rustle of movement sounded in the sagebrush about fifty yards away. The dog whined, took a few steps up the slope, and turned to Jon as if to say, "Are you coming?"

Jon drew the Glock once more and took a step toward the sound.

The lab darted in front of him and gave a low growl.

"Shh..." Jon stepped around the dog.

The dog whined, nipped at his pant leg and pulled hard on his jeans, trying to drag him up the slope, away from the sound.

"What the hell are you doing, mutt?" Jon yanked his leg away and gave the dog a sideways kick, which it easily dodged.

The dog backed away, whining, then yipped once and raced up the hill.

At the base of the slope, two dark animals burst through the sage-brush. Two more dogs, both nearly identical in appearance to the chocolate lab.

But very different in demeanor.

These dogs had neither wagging tails nor lolling tongues. They eyed Jon menacingly, lowered their heads, and stalked closer.

M.A. ROTHMAN

Jon aimed his gun and called out in a friendly tone, "Hey, boys, are you missing a friend of yours?"

As soon as he trained the Glock on the animals, they split, one going to his left, the other to his right.

His heart thudding, Jon aimed at the dog on his right. The animal immediately darted behind a boulder.

It was almost as if the animal knew the gun was dangerous.

Hearing the other dog's nails scraping on the gravel, Jon wheeled around and fired a warning shot.

The animal continued to advance, but it used a jerky zigzag pattern, making it difficult to aim.

A chill raced up Jon's spine.

His gun arm shaking, Jon focused on the approaching dog. For a split second his mind flashed back to his time as an artilleryman in Afghanistan. Back then, he'd shot at enemies he could barely see. Now, for the first time in his life, he was within spitting distance of his target as he squeezed the trigger.

The animal had just begun to leap when the bullet slammed into its shoulder. It fell to the ground with a whimper.

At almost the same moment, Jon felt over one hundred pounds of canine smash against his back. The second dog knocked him off his feet and clamped its vise-like jaws on the wrist of his shooting hand.

Jon struggled with the growling animal. He started to yell when his voice was suddenly trapped in his throat. The dog he'd shot had clamped down tightly on his throat.

He fell back onto the dirt, his windpipe closing under the crushing force of the animal's impossibly strong jaws. His vision wavered as he strained for breath.

His heart pounding with terror, he prayed. *My God, there's so much I could have...*

The world faded to black.

～

Hans Reinhardt stood at the top of the rocky slope and breathed in the

392

acrid smoke of burning sagebrush. A half dozen men in fatigues spewed hellfire from their flamethrowers, and all across the burning landscape, stones cracked in the fierce heat.

The operation had been going well—until now. Now everything had turned to shit. A complete disaster. Despite the assurances from his bosses in the German Federal Intelligence Service, not to mention the US handlers in Langley, Hans knew it was time to reset. He needed to move the operation to a more remote location. One with less chance of… "incidents."

The base commander, an Air Force colonel, walked up and stood beside him. "His name was Jonathan LaForce, Marine artilleryman, ten years out of Afghanistan with an honorable discharge."

"What the hell was he doing here? I thought this base was secure."

The base commander shifted his weight nervously. "The base *is* secure. However, we'd underestimated the containment measures needed in the kennel. I reviewed the security tape myself, it seems one of the experiments figured out how to open the latch to its stall. Once it escaped, the others managed to copy its actions. And before anyone could stop them, the animals had dug a hole under the perimeter fence."

Hans kicked a stone off the rocky escarpment and ground his teeth with frustration. "A dead Marine is the last thing we need. How big of a problem is this going to be?"

The colonel's discomfort increased. "The good news is, he was one of those disaffected types. No family, and it looks like he was out of a job. A wanderer who probably won't have anyone searching for him, at least not for a while. We'll deal with his remains."

"And the experiments? Have they all been tracked down and decommissioned?"

"We tracked five of the animals through the signal coming off their PIT tags. We captured and disposed of them." The colonel blew out a deep breath. "Unfortunately, we have not yet been able to locate the sixth. I've sent out the drones. They're programmed to run grids across the terrain, looking for the animal's signal. We'll find it."

Hans silently wondered how such an incompetent ass had come to be the base commander at a supposedly high-security location. "We don't have time for a lengthy search, Colonel. We cannot have one of our experiments encountering civilians."

"We'll track the dog down—"

"That's not a fucking *dog*, you moron!" Hans snapped. "It's a specially bred nightmare with enough strength and intelligence to escape your so-called 'secure' kennel and take out an armed ex-Marine who got in its way."

The colonel's eyes narrowed and his jaw tightened.

"Listen to me," Hans continued. "Both my neck *and* yours are on the line if any of this gets out. We can't risk our arrangement being exposed. And let's face it, your government has already proven itself incapable of keeping things out of Wikileaks."

"Mr. Reinhardt," said the colonel, "believe me, I know exactly what's at stake. You do *not* need to remind me. This is a black operation, and it's staying that way. I'm overseeing the cleanup personally." The colonel pointed toward the nearby slope. "We found some blood that we believe is from the missing animal. It's wounded, which will limit its ability to elude us. Between the contractors on foot and the drones in the air, we'll find it."

Hans glared. "You damn well better."

~

Frank O'Reilly poured a few inches of pea gravel into the fence-post hole he'd just dug. He glanced over his shoulder at Johnny, one of the ranch hands he'd recently hired.

"Make sure you get at least three inches of these rocks into the hole and tamp it down good, like this." he said, tamping the rocks down with a large wooden pole. "We need a solid footing for the fence posts. Them cattle will rub up against just about anything, so these here posts need to be sturdy, you understand?"

"Yessir, Mr. O'Reilly. And you need them posts eight feet apart so them sixteen-foot planks can span two openings, right?"

"That's right. Make sure them posts are square with the ground and space them evenly."

Frank handed Johnny the post-hole digger and smiled. The ranch hand had just turned eighteen, and Frank couldn't help but remember when his Kathy was that age. Johnny had that same lively spirit and energy that reminded him of Frank's baby girl when she graduated high school and took off for the world.

He patted Johnny on the shoulder. "You got this?"

"Yessir, but if'n you don't mind my asking, why all of a sudden you taking on help? You fixing to retire?"

Frank laughed and shook his head. "Johnny, I might be fifty-three, but I've still got quite a bit of life left in me. Just get the job done, and you best be minding what I said about doing a quality job. I'm going to check all your work, so don't take no shortcuts, you hear?"

"Yessir. Don't have to worry about that." Johnny hefted the post-hole digger and walked to the next flagged spot.

As Frank turned away, he nearly tripped on a dog that was sitting on its haunches right behind him.

"Damn it, where the heck did you come from?"

The chocolate lab just sat there with its tongue lolling. A beautiful animal. Shiny coat, heavily muscled body, and obviously well-fed. Not a stray.

Frank held out his hand. "Are you friendly?"

The dog stood, and its tail became a blur. It sniffed at Frank's hand, then lowered its nose and sniffed at his boot and up along his jeans. Finally, it sat back on its haunches, licked its lips, and whined. Its bright brown eyes stared up at him, glanced at his trousers, and then back up at his face. It whined again.

Frank tilted his head, unsure what the dog was trying to say. Then it hit him, and he laughed. "Ah! I know why you're so interested in me." He pulled a folded-up piece of homemade beef jerky from his pocket and tossed it gently to the dog.

The animal snatched it in midair and chewed contentedly.

"Well, I best be off, pup. I'll get a tongue-lashing if I'm not home in time for supper."

Frank walked the roughly half a mile to the modest white ranch-style home he'd built almost thirty years ago. As he drew near, he heard paws padding along behind him. *Figures. I know better than to feed a strange dog.* He purposefully ignored the animal and started up the steps to the front porch.

The aroma of roasting beef was in the air.

Megan stepped out onto the porch. "Oh good, you're back. Dinner is almost ready. Go get washed up."

He gave her a peck on the lips. "Smells good."

She looked past him with a puzzled expression. "You made a friend?"

The lab now sat at the bottom of the porch steps, looking hopeful.

Frank shook his head. "I made the mistake of giving him some of the beef jerky."

Megan pushed her shoulder-length auburn hair behind her ears, knelt, and patted the wooden deck of the porch. "Here, boy, did you like the jerky?"

The dog bounded up the stairs and lay down in front of her, its belly up and its long tail sweeping back and forth over the wooden planks.

Megan giggled as she rubbed the dog's belly. "You're such a good boy." She looked up at Frank with that sheepish smile he knew so well. "Do you think anyone owns him?"

"No idea. He just wandered up. He's obviously been cared for, but he's not wearing a collar or anything." He hesitated. "I thought after Daisy died, you swore—"

"Oh, you poor thing!" Megan exclaimed. She was examining the dog's front right leg. "It looks like he got into a fight or something."

The dog whimpered as she fussed over his injury.

"I'm sure he'll be fine," Frank said.

"No." Megan stood and wiped her hands on her apron. "We're going to take him to the vet and get him looked at."

Frank wondered how much the vet would try to gouge him for. "He's not even our dog."

Megan turned and gave him that look that said her mind was set.

"Then we can have the vet check him for one of them chips they put in dogs nowadays."

Megan was five feet tall and built like a pixie, but once she set her mind to something, she was immovable. If thirty years of marriage had taught Frank anything, it was that.

He raised his hands in defeat. "What about dinner?"

"Dinner will keep." Megan walked into the house and motioned for the dog to follow, which it did. "I think we still have Daisy's old bowls. I'll see if this boy is thirsty while you go call the vet and tell him we're on our way."

The examination room doors opened and a blue-smocked veterinary assistant with a long black ponytail stepped out. "O'Reilly?" she called.

Frank waved. "Right here."

Her gaze shifted to the chocolate lab lying between Frank's and Megan's feet. "And what's your name, gorgeous?"

"He doesn't—"

"Jasper," Megan announced, as if that had always been his name.

Frank groaned inwardly. He hoped she wasn't getting attached. This animal belonged to someone. No way would a stray look as healthy as he did.

"Well, let's get Jasper weighed and see how he's doing."

"Jasper" stood the moment Megan did, and he obediently trotted after her into the examination room. Frank, shaking his head, followed.

The veterinary assistant—the name "Sherri" was stenciled on her scrubs—stopped beside a large metal scale. "Let's see if we can coax Jasper on here."

Before Megan could even nudge the dog in the right direction, Jasper walked over and stepped on the scale.

"Hah, what a good boy," Sherri said. "Wow, 125.8 pounds. I'd never have guessed it." She scribbled the weight on a sheet of paper and slid it into Jasper's chart.

"Do you have one of those chip scanners?" Frank asked. He ignored Megan's severe look. "Jasper just wandered onto our property today, and he has no collar or tags. We don't know anyone who's missing a lab in our area. But we wanted to do the right thing and see if he'd been chipped or not."

"Oh, of course. Be right back." Sherri disappeared through another door while Megan began fervently petting the top of Jasper's head. Moments later, Sherri returned with what looked like a thick stick with a small loop on its end.

Megan grabbed Frank's hand as the veterinary assistant approached Jasper.

Sherri passed the wand back and forth over Jasper's back. "Hmm. Most vets inject the chip between the animal's shoulders, and I'm not seeing anything there."

Megan squeezed Frank's hand tighter.

"Let's just make sure there isn't one anywhere else." Sherri slowly moved the wand over Jasper's hindquarters and then back toward the front again. As she neared the right front leg, the dog whined.

"It's okay, Jasper," Megan said soothingly. "She's not going to hurt you."

The veterinary assistant paused over the dirt-encrusted wound. "Poor baby, you've got an ouchie. Dr. Dew will make it all better." She finished dragging the wand over Jasper and shook her head. "No chips that I can find."

Frank sensed Megan's smile without even having to look. He sighed wistfully with the realization they had just adopted a dog. "Okay," he said. "In that case, in addition to tending to that wound, let's get Jasper a full workup."

"Okay. Dr. Dew will be in to look at Jasper in a bit. And since it looks like Jasper is favoring his right front leg, we may need to take x-rays and sedate him to treat the wound. It'll be at least four hundred dollars." She raised a questioning eyebrow.

"Just fix him up," Megan said quickly. "We'll pay whatever is necessary."

Frank kissed the top of Megan's head. There was no arguing with Mrs. O'Reilly over such things.

～

Frank spent nearly an hour in the waiting room, with Megan fidgeting the whole time. And when at last the vet appeared—without Jasper—Megan grabbed Frank's arm and held it tightly.

The vet was a huge man with a bodybuilder's physique, yet his voice was soft, almost effeminate. He gave Frank and Megan a wide smile. "Jasper will be coming out of sedation in about twenty minutes, but he'll be fine. It looks like he must have gotten into a fight, and the wound got infected. Luckily, the x-rays showed no breaks. However, it's fortunate that we did that x-ray, because I probably wouldn't have seen this otherwise."

He pulled a clear plastic baggie from his lab coat and handed it to Frank. It contained a four-inch-long metal wire.

Dr. Dew showed his arm and pointed at a four-inch length above his wrist. "That wire managed to lodge itself between the skin and muscle just above the wound. I have no idea how it could have gotten in there, but it came out without any problems."

"So... he's okay?" Megan asked.

Another broad smile. "Jasper's still a little loopy at the moment, but he's just fine. All stitched up. He's on antibiotics, which he'll need to take twice a day, and I'm also going to give you guys some ointment that needs to go on the wound on a daily basis."

Barking sounded from the back, and the exam room doors burst open. Jasper came bounding into the waiting room, his gait a bit awkward, one foot wrapped up like a mummy. He raced straight to Megan and spun rapidly with excitement as if he'd expected to never see her again.

Sherri came in right behind him. "I'm sorry Dr. Dew, but Jasper woke up way early and began frantically pawing at the door. I didn't want him to pull any of his stitches. It looks like he really wanted to see his mommy."

Megan scratched Jasper's head. Clearly the two had already formed a bond.

"Well, we can't have this big guy breaking down any doors," said Dr. Dew, laughing. "I'm quite sure he's the heaviest *healthy* lab I've ever encountered, and it's not even close. It's odd, because he doesn't look like he'd be any heavier than seventy-five pounds or so, which is still heavy for a lab, but this boy has got some incredibly dense musculature. And judging by his teeth, he's still young. He might grow a bit more yet."

Frank groaned. "I'm already tired just thinking about how much work it'll be just keeping him fed."

Jasper walked away from them, grabbed a doggie blanket that was tucked under one of the waiting room chairs, brought it back, and laid it on Frank's lap.

Megan smiled. "Aww, he heard you're tired and he brought you a blanket."

Dr. Dew patted Jasper on his head. "You're one smart dog."

Jasper sat up a bit straighter and woofed in agreement.

Frank couldn't shake the feeling that something wasn't right about this animal. But as he watched Megan fawning over Jasper, he knew that what he thought no longer mattered.

ADDENDUM

As a child, I always had an active imagination and would continuously drive my parents crazy with a myriad of "what if" questions. After a while, they shoved me at the local public library, and that's when I was finally introduced to the world of books, and more specifically, science fiction and fantasy novels. My earliest influences were J.R.R. Tolkien's classics, as well as those of Isaac Asimov. Titles such as these tickled my imagination both as a child and into adulthood.

My formal background has kept me fully immersed in the world of science for decades. Given my science background and my access to some folks in academia who are theoretical physicists, it shouldn't be a surprise that I've found ways to draw from both my background and theirs to produce stories that involve technology in some way or another. Many might consider this novel as a hard science fiction tale, and I suppose they'd be correct.

One might ask, "What is hard science fiction, and is it something that I can read?"

To me, the key thing that differentiates hard science fiction from "soft" is that in the former, science is not just an ingredient of the story, but a key part of it.

However, in my honest opinion, that shouldn't mean you need

advanced degrees to understand what is happening. All you should need is a love of good stories that contain science and technology. It is up to the author to make the science portion accessible to all that would read it.

In this tale, I've strived to maintain some level of scientific accuracy to the things that a reader is exposed to. Certainly, there will be elements in any tale of fiction that are impossibilities today. However, built upon a solid foundation of science, I attempt to venture forward with some predictions of what could be, and from that, construct a tale that should hopefully be entertaining and maybe somewhat enlightening.

In this addendum, I wanted to note some things that I've used in this story, and give you, the reader, an insight into how some elements of hard science might relate to them or serve as inspiration. For example, I've created in this story what in essence comes down to a warp engine of sorts. Sure, there are absolutely no such things in today's science that exhibit such properties, guilty as charged. However, such a thing isn't in the realm of complete and utter fantasy; there's actually reasonable physics behind it! I've introduced strange concepts associated with magnetic confinement of fusion, and having that serve as an engine of sorts. Would it surprise you to learn that such things are in fact aspects of today's fusion research? I also speak a lot about something called DefenseNet; could such a thing actually be made? Or maybe the concept of a space elevator seems crazy to you, but would you believe that such things are hypothetically almost within our grasp today?

All these things have a basis in academic research. Let me hopefully tantalize you with the possibilities, as I point out things that might have initially seemed like works of fantasy, but have real science behind them.

As I give very brief explanations of what may be very complex concepts, my intent is to only leave you with sufficient information to give a remedial understanding of the subject. However, for those who want to know more, it is also my intent to leave you with enough keywords that would allow you to initiate your own research and gain a more complete background understanding of any of these topics.

This should also give you a peek into some of the things that have influenced my writing of this story, and maybe have you start asking what all authors inevitably ask themselves, "What if?"

DefenseNet:

In this story, I introduced the concept of DefenseNet, a futuristic solution that serves as a means of fending off incoming asteroids that might be aimed for Earth. As you ultimately learn, DefenseNet is a complicated solution containing multiple parts, including the concept that Dave Holmes calls a Warp Ring. I'll go into that piece later in this addendum.

Let me simply focus on the concept of fending off incoming asteroids.

In this story, DefenseNet employs a series of high-powered lasers to act as a shield against incoming threats. In some popular stories, people might choose to blow things up or somehow attach rockets to an asteroid to move it out of the way, both of those approaches are hugely impractical for any number of reasons. Certainly one of the biggest issues is the time it takes to respond to a threat and actually reach the object.

The statistics I gave for an incoming asteroid threat within the book are actually accurate.

If we had a stony meteorite that was 100 meters wide entering the atmosphere at a normal (45 degree) angle and at an average speed (35 km/s), the impact would be the equivalent of a 32 megaton nuclear explosion. It would hurt, and hurt pretty badly.

I'd note that those impacts don't happen every day, but something 100 meters or so hits the Earth every 6 or 7,000 years. We're due.

That being said, the concept of DefenseNet is actually practical inasmuch as we would depend on two things:

1. Knowing about the incoming threat soon enough to make a difference.
2. Having a sufficiently powerful laser(s) to aim against the object.

We today have the technology to launch space-based lasers, and with enough time and investment, we can stand a reasonable chance of detecting incoming threats. There are many ongoing projects associated with Near Earth Object collision avoidance. Some proposed projects have intended to use lasers (e.g. Strategic Defense Initiative, DE-STAR, etc.)

The concept is actually quite simple. A highly focused energy beam (e.g. LASER) would be used to raise the surface temperature of a portion of an asteroid to ~3,000 degrees Kelvin, causing a violent reaction at that spot which would eject material from the surface of the asteroid, thus shifting the asteroid's trajectory ever-so-slightly. In other words, you'd have a big rock which you really have no chance of destroying, but by heating the edge of one, you can cause a violent reaction on its surface. The small explosion that would occur from such superheating would nudge the incoming threat just a bit. The further away, the more effective this approach is.

I'd further note that with a laser, you won't find a faster means of delivering an impactful solution to a discovered target. Speed of light is still pretty fast.

Magnetic Confinement Fusion:

One of the key items that was introduced in this story was a mysterious engine created by Frank, and it introduced a wide variety of new concepts. One of them was a room-temperature superconductor called stanene. Although this is one of the holy grail items of science, it is actually something people are experimenting with.

However, in Frank's engine, a concept was introduced that seemed completely fanciful, but is actually based in reality. That is the concept of containing a fusion reaction in a magnetic field. Some keywords that readers can use if they want to further research such topics would be magnetic bottle, magnetic mirror, or tokamak.

The difficulty with controlled fusion is in creating the conditions in which two atoms can effectively be squeezed together such that the force of squeezing overwhelms the inherent repulsion of the nuclei. One of these squeezing methods employs extreme temperature increases of the material in excess of 10,000,000 degrees. Under such conditions, the substance turns into a plasma, and further pressure needs to be applied so that fusion would actually occur.

Under such conditions, the atoms can be manipulated within the confines of magnetic fields.

Granted, that I've taken the concept and gone beyond known technology. However, the extension isn't necessarily within the realm of fantasy. What I stipulated in Frank's engine was that fusion could occur, energy is released, and the store of energy could strengthen the field even more—producing an even higher efficiency matter-to-energy conversion and thus confining what is essentially a very hot and volatile system within an unimaginably strong magnetic confinement.

Fusion today is not an efficient process, but most scientists believe that via some method of magnetic confinement, it will eventually become efficient.

Einstein's equations describe the relationship of mass to energy and energy to mass, and they make clear that vast stores of energy are contained in the smallest amount of matter. Therefore, one could imagine a future where power is never at a premium.

Hopefully, that time is not that far away.

Warp Ring:

In this book I describe what Doctor Holmes called a Warp Ring, and oftentimes I refer to the phenomenon it creates as a gravity bubble.

The concept is simple to imagine, inasmuch as you wrap something (e.g. a ship, Earth, etc.) in a bubble, and it is the bubble that travels at tremendous speeds while everything within the bubble doesn't have any relative sense of motion whatsoever.

Definitely sounds like something out of pure space fantasy, but would it shock anyone to know that there are scholarly papers discussing the topic? I used one of these papers in particular to form some of my model of what this warp ring could do.

I refer you to a paper produced by Miguel Alcubierre called, "The Warp Drive: Hyper-fast travel within general relativity."

For purposes of research on practical experiments to some of Doctor Alcubierre's work, I would also refer you to Doctor Harold "Sonny" White, working out of the NASA Johnson Space Center. He had an excellent paper titled "Warp Field Mechanics 101".

I'll admit that for many folks, this is where the explanation should probably stop, but I'll just briefly touch on more advanced topics.

One should note that Doctor Alcubierre mentions general relativity in the title, and he does so for very specific reasons. There's a difference between general relativity and special relativity.

For special relativity, observers from different reference points will measure mass and speed differently, because space and time will expand and contract so that the speed of light in a vacuum is constant to all observers.

Sometimes these things are best explained with an example. For instance, I may turn on a flashlight and the light pouring forth will be traveling at 300,000 kilometers per second, usually denoted as the symbol "c". If I'm on a spaceship traveling at .5c and I turned on that same flashlight, the light pouring forth is also traveling at c.

I know for some of you, you're scratching your head and asking the following question. If you were standing on Earth and could see the light from the spaceship rushing by, wouldn't the light be going 1.5c, and if it isn't, why not?

For the person in the space ship, all seems to be going normally, when in fact, time and space have warped around them. Time is moving slower for them, and distances are contracted. That's what allows the person in the spaceship and the person watching the spaceship to both observe things comply with special relativity.

I'll leave the reader to stew on that for a moment, and I offer a good-natured apology if it is confusing, it *is* a complicated topic.

However, special relativity is actually a subset of general relativity. General relativity is describing spacetime itself. Spacetime is actually a model in which space and time are woven together to simplify talking about the four dimensions that would normally involve space and time. Here, Einstein determined that large objects cause a distortion in spacetime, and that distortion is known as gravity.

Anything that proposes traveling at arbitrarily high speeds would need to take advantage of this warping of spacetime.

The Warp Ring leverages this fact in the same way that Doctor Alcubierre's paper does. It harnesses the expansion and contraction of space itself and in so doing, envelopes the object in a bubble of sorts. The object (e.g. ship, Earth, etc.) isn't moving, but space itself is moving around it.

In the case of this story, the Earth is riding on this distortion, kind of like a surfer rides a wave.

I'd also suggest reading up on inflation theory. It does provide some good background reading if you're inclined to learn more about faster-than-light movement.

As an aside, I will note that things like time dilation have been experimentally verified. I'll refer you to the U.S. Naval Observatory experiments by Hafele and Keating, which documented what happened when four incredibly accurate atomic clocks were synchronized and two of them were flown around the world while the other two remained stationary. When the clocks were brought back together, the time had shifted ever-so-slightly for the clocks which had been traveling at jet-like speeds. For them, time had slowed ever-so-slightly.

The explanations I give in the book are actually congruent with the concept of the Warp Drive that Doctor Alcubierre mentioned.

The only things we're missing are a substantial (ridiculous amount) of energy and the still theoretical concept of negative mass.

In attaining some of these things, you could imagine our ability to wrap an object (e.g. ship, Earth, etc.) into a bubble of sorts. This bubble is gravitationally isolated and when the bubble itself moves, the contents within it don't even sense the movement.

Kind of cool, don't you think? I'm waiting for Doctor Holmes to be born, so he can fiddle with things and we can make it so.

Space Elevator:

Space elevators have been written about for quite a while in the science fiction realm, but there isn't that much fictional about them.

First of all, what is a space elevator?

Simply put, imagine if you could put an object high enough up in space that it would maintain geosynchronous orbit. We do that all the time when we launch satellites. Such an object could act as an anchor for an elevator of sorts.

Imagine if you could drop a rope down from such a height and tie it down wherever it lands on Earth. You could conceivably build something that climbs up and down that rope and easily bring objects into space.

Why bother?

Well, with today's technology, it is very resource expensive to bring things into space. You could easily imagine that if the Earth had a myriad of space elevators, it would be much easier to assemble large objects (e.g. spaceships?) in space.

So what's the issue, let's get started!

The issue has always been, and still largely is, the material that you'd make this hypothetical rope from.

I like to use examples when explaining things, so let's do that.

You need to be roughly 22,000 miles above the Earth to maintain geosynchronous orbit. That's the height where the gravity pulling you down and the centrifugal force that makes you want to fly away are effectively even.

That means we need rope that is 22,000 miles long at a minimum. So how much does such a thing weigh?

I'll take for an example the lightest climbing rope I could find. This rope weighs 48 grams per meter and has a rather impressive 1660 pounds of carrying capacity.

Well, how much does 22,000 miles of that rope weigh?

With my handy calculator in hand, it turns out that it comes to about 1,699,467 kilograms, or about 3,746,683 pounds just for the rope. That basically means that the rope isn't strong enough to even hold itself up nor any payload.

That illustrates the biggest problem space elevators have faced: what to make them out of.

In this story, I talk rather extensively about graphene. I'll leave it to the reader who is interested to read up more about graphene and its capabilities, but let's just say that if the mass manufacturing of graphene can be achieved (which is not an impossibility), then that would make something like a space elevator extremely practical.

I'll further note that graphene has rather amazing physical properties such as electrical and thermal conductivity that surpasses those of many of the known "best of" types of conductors.

ABOUT THE AUTHOR

I am an Army brat, a polyglot, and the first person in my family born in the United States. This heavily influenced my youth by instilling a love of reading and a burning curiosity about the world and all of the things within it. As an adult, my love of travel and adventure has allowed me to explore many unimaginable locations, and these places sometimes creep into the stories I write.

I hope you've found this story entertaining.

- Mike Rothman

You can find my blog at: www.michaelarothman.com
I'm also on Facebook at: www.facebook.com/MichaelARothman
And on Twitter: @MichaelARothman

Printed in the USA
CPSIA information can be obtained
at www.ICGtesting.com
CBHW022038210624
10453CB00010B/92